THE ONE WHO STOOD BEFORE US

EYEWITNESSES TO THE RESURRECTION

KENNETH A. WINTER

rnessLessons

JOIN MY READERS' GROUP FOR UPDATES AND FUTURE RELEASES

Please join my Readers' Group so i can send you a free book, as well as updates and information about future releases, etc.

See the back of the book for details on how to sign up.

∼

The One Who Stood Before Us

... Eyewitnesses to the Resurrection

The Eyewitnesses Collection – Book 3

Published by:

Kenneth A. Winter

WildernessLessons, LLC

Richmond, Virginia

United States of America

kenwinter.org

wildernesslessons.com

Edited by Sheryl Martin Hash

Cover design by Dennis Waterman

Cover photo by Lightstock

ISBN 978-1-7349345-2-6 (soft cover)

ISBN 978-1-7349345-3-3 (e-book)

ISBN 978-1-7349345-4-0 (large print)

Library of Congress Control Number: 2021900668

DEDICATION

This book is dedicated to you, the reader,
in the hope that you will have a fresh encounter
with the One who stands before you.

∾

These are written so that you may believe that Jesus is the Christ, the Son of God,
and that by believing you may have life in His name.

John 20:31 (ESV)

∾

CONTENTS

FROM THE AUTHOR

A word of explanation for those of you who are new to my writing.

You will notice that whenever i use the pronoun "I" referring to myself, i have chosen to use a lowercase "i." This only applies to me personally (in the Preface). i do not impose my personal conviction on any of the characters in this book. It is not a typographical error. i know this is contrary to proper English grammar and accepted editorial style guides. i drive editors (and "spell check") crazy by doing this. But years ago, the Lord convicted me – personally – that in all things i must decrease and He must increase.

And as a way of continuing personal reminder, from that day forward, i have chosen to use a lowercase "i" whenever referring to myself. Because of the same conviction, i use a capital letter for any pronoun referring to God throughout the entire book. The style guide for the New Living Translation (NLT) does not share that conviction. However, you will see that i have intentionally made that slight revision and capitalized any pronoun referring to God in my quotations of Scripture from the NLT. If i have violated any style guides as a result, please accept my apology, but i must honor this conviction.

Lastly, regarding this matter – this is a <u>personal</u> conviction – and i share it only so you will understand why i have chosen to deviate from normal editorial practice. i am in no way suggesting or endeavoring to have anyone else subscribe to my conviction. Thanks for your understanding.

～

PREFACE

~

Over two thousand years ago the Father sent His Son. As the Son of God, He has no beginning and no end. Before the beginning, He was. Throughout time, He always has been. Throughout eternity, He always will be. The Son always has been the Father's plan to redeem a lost and dying world back to its Creator. The plan, just like the Son, was never an afterthought. The plan has always been in the heart of the Father. And the Son has always been the heart of the plan.

For the plan to accomplish all that the Father intended, He could not send His Son solely as the Son of God. The Son of God would be able to perform the miracles of healing and the restoration of life. He would be able to heal the blind, still the storms, and raise the dead to life. He was with the Father, when together they created all things, so all things are under His authority – including life and death.

The Son of God would be able to teach the Word of God. As the apostle John writes, Jesus is the Word from before the beginning. The Word became flesh and dwelt among us. Jesus could teach as the Son of God without peer and without error.[1]

But the Son of God could not fully accomplish the Father's plan. In order to do that, He needed to come to this earth also as the Son of Man.[2] He needed to take on flesh. He needed to become a part of creation itself. He needed to be Creator AND Creation. He needed to live among us, as one of us. He needed to live out the truth as the Son of Man that He was teaching as the Son of God. He needed to model as Creation the life that the Creator intended. Otherwise that life would be beyond our grasp. His teaching would have had no relevance. His truth would be meaningless. The only way for His teaching to become meaningful and relevant was for Him to show us how to live as the Son of Man.

And He could only pay the price for our sin as the Son of Man. Only as the Son of Man could He be the unblemished Lamb of God.[3] Only as the Son of Man could He be tempted as we are … and yet remain sinless.[4] Only as the Son of Man could He defeat sin by taking on our sin.[5] Only as the Son of Man could He defeat death.[6]

As, no doubt, you have heard before, Jesus was as much God as if He were not man at all, and as much man as if He were not God at all.[7] As the Son of Man, the Son of God came to dwell among His creation as His Creation.

As the Son of Man, He had an earthly mother and an earthly father. He had half brothers and sisters. He had uncles and aunts, and cousins. He laughed. He cried. He worked. He played. He had compassion. He had a sense of humor. He had family. He had friends. He had followers. And, as we well know, He had foes.

God inspired the writing of His Word through men that we might know Him and, in so doing, know the truth.[8] Every word is inspired by God for doctrine, reproof, correction, and instruction.[9]

Throughout the Bible we see stories of men, women and children who came in contact with their Creator. In the case of the Gospels, they were family, friends, followers, or foes of Jesus. In the majority of instances, we do not know many of the details surrounding their lives. God determined that those details were not important in order for us to understand the truth of His Word.

The purpose of this book is for you to see and experience the Living Lord Jesus – the Son of Man and the Son of God – through the first-person eyewitness accounts of forty "people" before whom He stood. Some are family. Some are friends. Some are followers. Some are foes. Some are real people pulled from the pages of Scripture. Some are fictional, created to represent those who were unnamed.

In many instances, fictional details have been added to each of their lives where Scripture is silent. The intent is that you understand these were real people, whose lives were full of all the many details that fill our own lives. They had a history before they met Jesus ... and they had a future after they met Him.

i have included a listing of characters in the back of the book. Its purpose is to note whether a fictional background and/or name has been added, or if the character is entirely fictional. You will also see those for whom, to the best of my knowledge, i have not changed any details. Most notably, i have endeavored not to change any details concerning Jesus except for the interactions i have written between Him and the fictional characters in these stories.

As the author, my desire is that you witness the Savior through their eyes in a way that He comes alive to you – perhaps in a new way – through their stories. Let me be clear – this is a fictional work set in the midst of true events. At its core, it is a story of the latter years of Jesus during His earthly ministry through His death and resurrection. It is not just one story; it is a collection of forty individual short stories. Each story stands alone; but, each story also builds on a previous story. In several instances, you will see the same event described by multiple eyewitnesses because not everyone responded or reacted the same way.

Hopefully, you will see that i have taken great care in the writing of this work to guard the sanctity and truth of the Gospel message. My goal is that this book prompts you to consider the truth as recorded in Scripture. My additions are purely for your reading entertainment as you consider those truths.

Just like my Advent books, i have also written a set of stories for children. They have been published in a companion book to go along with this one. **The Little Ones Who Came** is an illustrated "chapter" book designed for children ages 8 and up. It contains ten short stories that are first-person accounts of a child or young teen who also was an eyewitness to the events surrounding the ministry, crucifixion and resurrection of Jesus.

All of the children are fictional characters, but there is an explanation at the end of each story describing what is fiction and what is fact. Each of the ten children is introduced in this book. So, you will see how the first-person accounts of the two books complement one another.

For example, we start with Sarah's account of the day her father, Simon Peter, and others left their homes to follow Jesus. We see the impact on her life and the events that unfold thereafter, as her life is changed by Jesus. Then we turn to nine other children who came to know the truth about Jesus, including Yamin (the son of a tanner), Rachel (the daughter of the high priest), Aquila (the son of the Roman prefect), and Naomi (the granddaughter of a pharisee).

The Little Ones Who Came stands alone as a chronicle of the events leading up to and following Easter for children, but it can also be used in conjunction with this book to help further family conversations about those events. More information about this children's version is available at the back of this book.

Similar to my novels and other short stories, you will encounter fictional twists and turns i have interjected regarding certain day-to-day events. Again, my prayer is that nothing in the story detracts from scriptural truth, but rather, while remaining true to the biblical story, tells it in a way that creates an interesting and enjoyable reading experience.

Throughout the stories, many instances of the dialogue are direct quotes from Scripture. Whenever i am quoting Scripture, you will find that it has been italicized. The Scripture references are included in the back of this book. Those remaining instances of dialogue that are not italicized are a part of the fictional stories in order to help advance the storyline. However, i have endeavored to use Scripture as the basis in forming any added dialogue spoken by a historical character, with the intent that i do not do anything that detracts from the overall message of God's Word.

The stories and the truths shared in this collection are relevant to every day of our lives throughout the year. But i intentionally chose to write forty stories so that one could be read each day for forty days leading up to Easter Sunday – whether or not you observe the season of Lent.

As with my other books, i pray that this book stimulates conversation. So, like my other fictional works, i have established a discussion group inside of Facebook for that purpose. If you are on Facebook, i invite you to join **The One Who Stood Before Us** group and i look forward to hearing from you there.

In the meantime, i pray that the grace of the Lord Jesus Christ – the One who stood – and stands – before us, be with you.

JOHN – THE BELOVED

*M*y name is John. I was the youngest disciple of Jesus of Nazareth, having been born in Bethsaida of Galilee in 6 A.D. Many of you have read my account of the ministry, death, and resurrection of Jesus, known as the Gospel according to John. You may be aware that Matthew, Mark, and Luke all wrote their accounts before I did. Matthew relied on his own firsthand knowledge together with stories he heard from other witnesses. Mark's account was greatly influenced by the recollections of my good friend Simon Peter. Luke, however, gathered his research through the testimonies of a multitude of people.

God led me to write an account of what I personally witnessed. As a result, there are details you will hear from the others that you won't hear from me – because I wasn't there. But conversely, you will read details in my account that you will not find in the others, because I was uniquely allowed to witness those events.

This book of stories has been compiled with much the same intent as I wrote my Gospel account. I want you to hear from firsthand witnesses about the ministry, death, and resurrection of Jesus. The time period of these stories spans the last three and one-half years of His earthly life and ministry.

I am fully aware that God uniquely ordered my steps and my life so I could walk alongside Jesus as He interacted with a diverse group of people. I was at the Jordan River when Jesus was baptized. I was in the room when Jesus had a private conversation with Nicodemus. I was with Jesus on the mount of transfiguration. I was allowed to enter the high priest's home on the night Jesus was arrested. Some have asked how a Galilean fisherman such as myself could have such access. So, allow me to begin my story by sharing exactly how the Father enabled me to accompany His Son.

My great-great-grandfather on my mother's side was a Benjamite who was born in Babylon. The southern kingdom of Judah had been conquered many years earlier by the Babylonian King Nebuchadnezzar, and our ancestors had been taken as captives to Babylon. Later, under Persian rule, many of our people began to return to Jerusalem. But my ancestors remained in Babylon for several hundred years until my great-great-grandfather's three sons chose to return to the land of Israel.

The eldest son, Hillel, and the youngest son, Camydus, chose to return to Jerusalem. Many of you are familiar with Hillel. He became a revered sage, scholar, and leader of our people. Because he was one hundred twenty years old when he died, many of our people still to this day compare him to Moses. Most of you are also familiar with Hillel's grandson, Gamaliel, who in turn became a respected scholar and teacher in his own right, as well as a respected elder within our Great Sanhedrin during the years surrounding the time of Jesus's trial.

Most of you also know the grandson of the youngest son, Camydus. His name was Annas and he became high priest at a young age. He and his son-in-law, Caiaphas, were behind the plot that led to the crucifixion of Jesus.

.   .   .

The lesser known of the three brothers who departed from Babylon was the middle son, Shebna. Unlike his scholarly brothers, Shebna was a merchant who chose to make his home in Capernaum. His granddaughter, Salome, became the wife of Zebedee the fisherman, who was my father. That means that Gamaliel, Annas, and I are all second cousins once removed. My ancestral pedigree as the great-grandnephew of Hillel has opened doors for me within Jewish society on more than one occasion.

I am the youngest son of Zebedee and Salome. My brother, James, was born ten years before me. Of the two of us, he was the one most like our father. James was a born fisherman. If Jesus had not called him to be one of His disciples, James would have been content to live out his days on the sea harvesting fish.

I, on the other hand, sensed that God had created me for a different purpose. Though I, too, enjoyed the sea and life in our village of Bethsaida, I was drawn to more scholarly pursuits. My mother said I inherited that desire from her side of the family.

When I was still a boy, my mother frequently took me to visit her family in Capernaum. There, I would frequent the synagogue and sit at the feet of a teacher by the name of Nicodemus. This was before he became part of the Great Sanhedrin in Jerusalem. Rabbi Nicodemus helped nurture a greater thirst within me for the truths of Scripture.

On two occasions after my bar mitzvah, when our family was in Jerusalem to celebrate a holy feast, Nicodemus arranged for me to visit the Hillel school of instruction so I could sit under the teaching of my distant older cousin Gamaliel. It was there I first met the high priest, Caiaphas. The more I sat at the feet of Gamaliel, the more I wanted to learn. But my desire was not to gain intellectual understanding; I desired to have a relationship with God – a relationship like that of the prophets and the patriarchs.

.   .   .

When I was sixteen, I heard about a prophet whose name was also John. He was said to be a voice crying in the wilderness. Many said he had been sent by God. My friend Andrew also had a desire to learn more about this man. So, the two of us approached my father and Andrew's older brother, Simon. He and my father were partners in our fishing enterprise. We asked permission to leave Bethsaida to seek out John the baptizer. Gratefully – and I might add, graciously – they permitted us to abandon our responsibilities within the family business and follow the leading of our hearts.

For two years we were disciples of John. He spoke like no one we had ever heard. For four hundred years there had been no prophet in Israel. But God had very clearly now raised up John to be His messenger. He told us how an angel had appeared to his father in the sanctuary of the temple and foretold of his birth. The angel said that John would *precede the coming of the Lord, preparing the people for His arrival.*[1]

On several occasions, scribes and Pharisees were sent by the Sanhedrin to investigate John's teaching. Some came as seekers, but more came as accusers. John was not a respecter of persons or position. He spoke plainly, and he spoke truth. He never compromised truth to placate the religious leaders. Since many of the leaders were more concerned with their personal positions than with truth, John never hesitated to rebuke their hypocrisy. The more he rebuked them, the more they took offense and sought ways to discredit him.

Since many of them knew me from my time in Jerusalem, they would seek me out once they knew I was one of his disciples. I'm not sure if they wanted me to help silence John's antagonism toward them or if they wanted to turn me against him. But in either case, they were unsuccessful.

Toward the end of my second year with John, a Man approached him at the Jordan River and asked to be baptized. A short while later, when Jesus was passing by, John turned to Andrew and me and said, *"Look! There is the Lamb of God who takes away the sin of the world!"*[2] Immediately, we turned and began to follow Jesus.

. . .

I will never forget the first thing Jesus said to us. He turned around, saw us following, and asked, *"What do you want?"*[(3)]

The question startled us. If this Man truly was the Lamb of God, wouldn't He know what we wanted? Wasn't it obvious? But, instead of answering His question, I asked, *"Teacher, where are You staying?"*[(4)] Of all the questions we could have asked, where He was staying was the least of our concerns. We wanted to know for certain who He was and where He had come from. We wanted to know why He had come and what He planned to do.

I will never forget the way He looked at us that first time as we struggled to answer His question. Then after we spoke, He smiled – one of those smiles when even His eyes lit up. And He said, *"Come and see."*[(5)]

I didn't know it at the time, but I would soon come to realize that He already knew everything about us. He not only knew who we were and all that we had ever done, He knew all we would ever do. He knew us better than we knew ourselves. And as we spent the remainder of that day and evening with Him, He astounded us with His knowledge – of the Scriptures, of us, and of the Father. Before the evening was over, I knew He was the One I had been seeking all of my life. I knew I would follow Him for the rest of my days.

A few days later, Andrew and I both introduced our brothers to Jesus. We wanted everyone to know Him. Our lives had already been changed in our short time with Him, and we wanted everyone else to experience that transformation.

We had no idea what to expect on the journey before us, but it didn't take long for us to get an idea. Andrew and I, together with a few others, traveled with Jesus to Cana. He had been invited to attend a wedding celebration.

. . .

When we arrived, He introduced us to His mother, Mary. She greeted us warmly and assured us that we were welcome guests at the celebration. As it turned out, the bride was Mary's goddaughter – the daughter of her dearest friend. Jesus explained that this friend, whose name was Salome, just like my mother's name, had befriended Mary before Jesus was born. When many people questioned the circumstances surrounding Mary's pregnancy and turned away from her, spreading false rumors and accusations, Salome had stood by her. It was important to Mary that Jesus be here for this wedding, and Jesus clearly wanted to honor His mother by doing so.

A few hours into the celebration, Mary quietly approached Jesus to tell Him that the hosts had run out of wine. Apparently, other guests had also brought uninvited friends with them, so there were many more guests than the hosts had expected! Running out of food or drink would be a social disgrace that would cause great embarrassment to Salome and her husband. Mary wanted them to avoid that humiliation.

I thought it curious that she told Jesus in a way that indicated she expected Him to do something about it. What could He possibly do? Jesus's reply to His mother was even more curious: *"Dear woman, that's not our problem. My time has not yet come."*[6] But Mary appeared to ignore His response and brought several servants to Him. She told them to do whatever He told them. Obviously, she believed Jesus could solve the problem.

As those of us who had come with Him watched, Jesus told the servants to fill all six of the nearby stone jars with water. I couldn't help but think, "They don't need more water, they need more wine."

But it was what Jesus told the servants to do next that surprised me even more. He told them to dip out some of the water from one of the jars and take it to the master of ceremonies. I continued to watch in amazement.

What will the master of ceremonies do when he tastes the water the servant brought him?

I grimaced as I watched him taste from the cup, until I heard him exclaim to the bride's father, *"A host always serves the best wine at the first ... but you have kept the best until now!"*[7]

I looked across the room at Mary as she looked across the room at her Son. It wasn't solely the look of a grateful mother; it was gratitude for faith that had been rewarded. No one else at the celebration knew what Jesus had done. We alone had witnessed Jesus perform the miraculous. Everyone else enjoyed the benefit of the astonishing feat, but we had witnessed God's glory in the miracle.

Though it was only the beginning of what we would see, I knew at that moment that I believed in the One who stood before me. All my life I had desired a relationship with God, but now I was just beginning to understand what that meant. It wasn't about the breadth of knowledge I could gain; it was about the depth of my belief. And I believed I would always be a disciple whom Jesus loved.

That is why I have written my story – so that you, too, may believe that the One who stood before me *is the Messiah, the Son of God, and that by believing in Him you will have life.*[8]

~

JOHN – THE BAPTIZER

I am John, and I have the distinction of having met Jesus before I was born. Jesus's mother and my mother, Elizabeth, were cousins. Mary, who was pregnant with Jesus at the time, came to visit my mother when I was in her womb. She later told me that when Mary approached, I jumped for joy the moment I heard her voice. That's how my mother first knew that Mary was pregnant. Even in the womb, I was announcing the arrival of the Promised One!

Jesus and I have something else in common. An angel named Gabriel was sent by God to our respective parents, before either of our mothers was pregnant, to announce our forthcoming arrival. In my case, Gabriel told my parents that my mother would conceive a child who would prepare the people for the arrival of Jesus. Mary and Joseph were told by Gabriel that the Spirit of God would come upon Mary and she would conceive the Son of God. I was born six months before Jesus.

Jesus and I first saw each other when we were little boys. Though we lived in different towns – me in Hebron and Jesus in Nazareth – our families would travel to the temple in Jerusalem for the annual observance of Passover. On two of those occasions, I can recall seeing Jesus. Our parents introduced us to each other as cousins. From the moment I met Jesus, I knew there was something different about Him. He, his younger brother, and I played together while our parents caught up on family news. But both occasions were brief, and I don't remember much else about our time together.

My parents told me that I would one day prepare the way for the coming Messiah, but it was not until I saw Jesus the second time that they told me He was the One. I didn't see Him again until just a little over a year ago.

It was soon after that second occasion that my father became sick. His illness prevented us from traveling and, several years later, led to his death. Both of my parents were elderly. My mother was already advanced in years when she gave birth to me. Caring for my ill father took its toll on my mother's health as well, and she died soon after my father.

My parents had made arrangements that upon their death I was to go live with my older cousin, Adriel, and his wife, Joanna. They live among the Essenes in Qumran and adopted many of their practices and beliefs. They live very simply, requiring very little. Their diet consists of locusts and wild honey – both of which are plentiful in that region, and their clothing is woven from coarse camel hair.

The Essenes have separated themselves from other Jews. They do not believe the teachings of the Talmud like the Pharisees do. And they resent the compromises of truth made by the Sadducees for political gain. Thus, they avoid the temple and focus solely on the teachings of the Torah.

They express their piety and devotion to God through a purification ritual of baptism by immersion. They believe the act of baptism cleanses them of their sins before God. I, however, already knew that baptism apart from a heart of repentance before God is merely a pious ritual. Baptism is meant to be an outward testimony of a repentant heart turning from sin and turning to God. It is to bear witness of our expectant anticipation of the coming Messiah.

. . .

As I approached my late twenties, God showed me it was time for me to leave Qumran and travel far and wide preaching the message of repentance in preparation for His coming Son. The presence of the Spirit of God became obvious as growing numbers responded by repenting of their sins. I began to do most of my preaching along the Jordan River so I could baptize these new believers. As the Spirit drew more and more people to come to the river, I came to be known as John the baptizer.

It didn't take long for the Pharisees and Sadducees to hear about the crowds gathering to hear my preaching. They wanted to place my ministry under their authority. They apparently thought I would be flattered by their interest and succumb to their offer of increased power and prestige.

But God had also given me the spirit of Elijah. I rebuked them for their advances and their selfish ambition. I told them that my preaching had nothing to do with "my" ministry. I was a servant and messenger of Jehovah God. I feared Him and not any man. The only authority He had placed me under was His, and I would continue to obey Him and not the leading of men. As you can imagine, the Pharisees and Sadducees did not like my response.

There were some among them who came with true hearts of repentance. Those I willingly baptized and rejoiced in their transformed hearts. But there were others who wanted to be baptized as a pious ritual to elevate their standing before men.

I denounced them, saying: *"You brood of snakes! Who warned you to flee the coming wrath? Prove by the way you live that you have repented of your sins and turned to God. Don't just say to each other, 'We're safe, for we are descendants of Abraham.' That means nothing, for I tell you, God can create children of Abraham from these very stones.... I baptize with water those who repent of their sins and turn to God. But someone is coming soon who is greater than I am.... He is ready to separate the chaff from the wheat with His winnowing fork. Then He will clean up the threshing area, gathering the wheat into His barn but burning the chaff with never-ending fire."*[1]

· · ·

As you can imagine, I did not garner popularity with the Sanhedrin – but that was never my concern. Confronting their hypocrisy did, however, seem to draw others who were seeking truth. In response to the message of repentance, they asked, *"What should we do?"*

I replied, *"If you have two shirts, give one to the poor. If you have food, share it with those who are hungry."* Tax collectors came to be baptized and asked, *"Teacher, what should we do?"* I replied, *"Collect no more taxes than the government requires."* Even some of the soldiers asked, *"What should we do?"* To them I replied, *"Don't extort money or make false accusations. And be content with your pay."*[(2)]

No one was beyond being saved, but some like the religious leaders thought it did not apply to them. The people soon began to ask if I were the Messiah. I told them, *"I baptize you with water; but someone is coming soon who is greater than I am – so much greater that I'm not even worthy to be His slave and untie the straps of His sandals. He will baptize you with the Holy Spirit and with fire."*[(3)]

One day, I received word the Herodian ruler, Antipas, wanted me to come see him in his palace in Tiberias. He, too, had apparently heard of my growing popularity and wanted me to come pay him homage. He believed that my appearance before him would garner greater respect for him among the people.

But I knew all too well that Antipas was not repentant. He had married his brother's wife, Herodias. They had both divorced their spouses in order to be married to one another. It was an adulterous affair. I would not bow before this wicked ruler.

Instead, I continued to preach as God had called me to do. "Repent and be saved!" I declared. "The Messiah is coming! He will judge all people. And those who are not His will be cast away. *Even now the ax of God's judgment is poised, ready to sever the roots of the trees. Yes, every tree that does not produce good fruit will be chopped down and thrown into the fire."*[(4)] Each day I kept watch for the coming Messiah. I knew it was only a matter of time.

A growing number of those who were baptized asked if they could become my disciples. I quickly sensed that some wanted to follow me because of the notoriety they thought it would bring them instead of being led by God. Most soon turned away, but a few became faithful helpers and followers. There were twenty men who now surrounded me as disciples.

It was a diverse group including the fishermen (Andrew and John), the former zealot (Simon), the shepherd (Shimon), as well as those who had previously been religious scholars, tax collectors, carpenters, and tradesmen. God was enabling the ministry to multiply through these added servants – and we shared a common hunger to know more of God, to walk before Him uprightly, and to see His promised Messiah. We all looked forward to that day!

One day, as the crowds were being baptized, a Man came walking toward me. He was dressed as a humble carpenter. Many years had passed since I last saw Him, but the Spirit of God revealed that the One coming toward me was the Lamb of God, who would take away the sins of the world.

Jesus said to me, "I have come to be baptized." But who was I that I should baptize Him!

"I am the one who needs to be baptized by You," I replied. *"Why are You coming to me?"*

Jesus said, *"It should be done, for we must carry out all that God requires."*[(5)]

. . .

So, the two of us entered the river together, and I baptized Jesus. As I brought Him up out of the water, the heavens opened, and the Holy Spirit descended upon Him like a dove. And I heard a voice from heaven say, *"You are My dearly loved Son, and You bring Me great joy."*[6]

Jesus departed shortly thereafter just as inconspicuously as He had arrived. I saw Him walk off in the direction of the wilderness. I turned to my disciples standing nearby and said, *"He is the Lamb of God. I have been baptizing with water so that He might be revealed to Israel."*[7]

For six weeks I continued to look toward the wilderness awaiting His return as I preached, baptized, and prepared the way for Him. I had no idea where He had gone or what He was doing. I later learned that the Father had directed Him to go out into the wilderness to be tempted by Satan. For forty days and forty nights Jesus ate nothing, and for forty days and forty nights Satan tempted Him. Satan couldn't touch Him as the Son of God, but perhaps as the Son of Man Jesus would be unable to resist him. But at every turn, Jesus defeated the tempter.

After those weeks passed, I again saw Jesus approaching. But this time He didn't stop, He simply continued on His way. I turned to those disciples who were standing with me and said, *"Look! There is the Lamb of God!"*[8]

God had called me to minister here by the river, calling people to repentance and preparing the way for Jesus. He didn't release me to follow Jesus that day. I was to remain here. But my disciples immediately knew that God was calling them to follow His Son, so off they went.

I would not see Jesus again after that day – at least on this side of heaven. As the weeks passed, I continued to hear more and more about Him – the truth He was teaching, and the miracles He was performing. I even sent messages to Him on two occasions, and He was faithful to send back replies.

. . .

I don't know what the weeks and months ahead will look like, but I sense that my time on this earth is drawing to a close. I have done what God called me to do. I have been a voice in the wilderness preparing the way for the Promised One – the One who stood before me!

~

ANDREW – THE INTRODUCER

I am Jonah's youngest son, Andrew. I never knew my mother since she died in childbirth. My father had no idea what to do with a newborn baby. He was a fisherman who had spent most of his life fishing the Sea of Galilee. My mother's sister stepped in to help him raise me, and I stayed with her and her family for the first few years of my life. My aunt's family lived in our village of Bethsaida on the northern shore of the sea, so I still got to see my father from time to time.

When I was six years old, my father decided it was time for me to come home and live with him and my brother, Simon. My brother is fifteen years older than I am, so in some respects it was like having two fathers. They both kept a very protective eye over me. From the very start, I looked up to my big brother. He didn't seem to be fearful of anyone or anything. And he never hesitated to speak up and give his opinion.

When talking about our respective dispositions, our relatives would often say that Simon takes after my father and I take after my mother. I am more soft-spoken and much less animated. My father once joked that people run from Simon's high-spirited nature right into my approachable and welcoming arms. I'm not completely sure how he meant that, but I took it as a compliment.

. . .

There was never any question that my father and brother loved God with their whole hearts. I remember many an hour singing songs of praise to Jehovah God as we worked the nets in the boat. It wasn't the most melodious music you ever heard, but it was definitely the most heartfelt!

I loved my father and my brother, and I remember our times together with great affection. They both taught me how to be a successful fisherman, though I don't think I ever quite developed their same enthusiasm for it. But it is honest work – and it put food on our table, a roof over our heads, and provided food for many in our surrounding communities. We were grateful to Jehovah God for His provision and the strength He gave us to provide food for others.

My father was in partnership with another fisherman named Zebedee. The two men had been friends for most of their lives, and they each had two sons. Zebedee's sons were James and John. Our father and Zebedee had decided years ago that they could accomplish more together than they could apart. I don't know that I understood or fully appreciated that decision until I was fourteen years old.

That was when my father died. We were pulling in the nets one early morning on what appeared to be a bountiful catch when suddenly my father dropped his rope and clutched his chest. He collapsed in the boat and let out his last breath. Simon called out to Zebedee to come help us. But there wasn't anything that any of us could do.

In some respects, Zebedee became our surrogate father that day. Simon was in his late twenties and was already married to Gabriella, but it was still good to know that we had someone older and wiser to whom we could turn.

As the years passed, I became discontent. I was grateful to God for His provision to our family through the fishing business, and I wanted to support my brother in the effort. Simon was now the patriarch of our family and as such had stepped into the role as Zebedee's partner. I owed both of these men so much and didn't want to disappoint or abandon either of them.

But I could not deny a longing in my heart. I believed Jehovah God had created me for a different purpose. In recent days I had been hearing about a prophet by the name of John the baptizer. He was preaching a message of repentance and telling our people to prepare for the coming arrival of the Messiah. All my life, I had heard that the Messiah could come at any time, but this prophet was speaking of His coming with an urgency and an authority that exceeded anything any of us had ever heard.

I am just a few months older than Zebedee's youngest son, John. We have been close friends since childhood. We had recently begun talking about what it would be like to seek out the baptizer and learn from him about the coming Messiah. John is actually better schooled in the Scriptures than I am. He had on occasion sat under the teaching of some of the most prominent rabbis in Jerusalem. As we discussed the Messianic prophecies and the reports we continued to hear about the baptizer, our hearts began yearning to learn more.

We decided we must tell Simon and Zebedee. We believed Jehovah God was leading us to travel to the Jordan River to listen to the baptizer and sit under his teaching. To their credit, Simon and Zebedee listened to us with open hearts and open minds. The two of them, together with John's brother James and Simon's brother-in-law Thomas, would not be able to carry the added workload created by our absence. They would need to hire two fishermen to replace us, which would be an added expense. Graciously they agreed to pray and consider our request.

A few days later they told us we could go. They, too, wanted to learn more about the message of the baptizer. We would be their eyes and ears to report back on all that we learned. Within a matter of days, they hired our work replacements and released us to go. One of those hired was my friend Philip. We had grown up together playing along the sea.

. . .

Simon and Philip even volunteered to sail us across the Sea of Galilee to its southern shore. From there it would be a three-day journey on foot to the place where we had last heard the baptizer was preaching.

When John and I spotted him, he was standing on the west bank of the river. A large crowd had gathered, and he was standing in the middle of them. He was quite a sight! His clothes were woven from camel hair. His hair was disheveled. He spoke with a booming voice and his movements were even more animated than Simon's. But as we looked at the people in the crowd, not one person was speaking or moving. He had their undivided attention as he shouted:

"Prepare the way for the Lord's coming!
Clear the road for Him!
I baptize with water those who repent of their sins and turn to God. But Someone
is coming soon who is greater than I am – so much greater that I'm not worthy
even to be His slave and carry His sandals. He will baptize you with the Holy
Spirit and with fire."[1]

After he had finished preaching, many in the crowd made their way to the water's edge and were baptized. As a matter of fact, before the day was over, John and I were baptized, too!

We saw a handful of men who were John's disciples. He was teaching them from Scripture, and they were helping him with ministry to the ever-growing crowds. John and I quickly decided that if we wanted to learn more about the Messiah we needed to become a part of that inner circle.

When we approached the baptizer about becoming two of his disciples, he stared at us silently with a gaze that seemed to penetrate our souls. Then he said, "Our food is locusts and wild honey. Our bed is the ground we walk on, and our roof is the sky above us. If you have come out of idle curiosity, go home! But if Jehovah God has led you here, you are welcome to join us."

We became his newest disciples that day and continued to follow him for two years. We saw the ever-increasing number of religious leaders who came to satisfy their curiosity and suspicions about the baptizer. On many occasions, the religious leaders recognized my friend John from his time with them in Jerusalem. Seeing he was one of the baptizer's disciples, they would often come to him with questions about the prophet. John told me that most of the time, they were not seeking truth; rather, they were seeking to find fault.

I, too, had many opportunities to speak with those who came. Two were friends who had come together. One was a shepherd named Shimon, and the other was a zealot named Simon (not to be confused with my brother). I could see that these men were sincerely seeking truth. They had many questions that I could not answer, so I introduced them to the baptizer. Soon, they were also baptized and remained to become two more of his disciples.

As the months passed, the baptizer continued to preach, the crowds came, people repented, and many were baptized. Periodically, we would send messages back to our families in Bethsaida about all that we were witnessing.

One day, John and I were standing with the baptizer when someone came walking in our direction from the wilderness. Each day we would see people arriving in large numbers, but they would always be traveling along the riverbank – either from the north or south. It was rare to see someone coming from the wilderness. So, this solitary figure caught our attention.

As the Man drew closer, it became apparent He did not intend to join the crowd that had gathered. Rather, He continued to walk on by. As He did, the baptizer looked at Him and declared, *"Look! There is the Lamb of God!"*[2]

John and I knew immediately that we were supposed to follow this Man. It was as if He had walked in this direction just so we would follow Him. And the baptizer's reaction to our hasty farewell confirmed that he also knew we were to follow this Man. We looked over our shoulders and saw that Shimon was following with us, as well.

We had walked only a few steps when the One we were following turned around and looked at each one of us intently. It was as if He were looking into our souls.

He asked us, "What do you want?" Almost in unison we replied, *"Rabbi, where are You staying?"*[3] With an inviting smile He answered, *"Come and see."*[4]

It was four o'clock in the afternoon when we arrived at the place He was staying in Bethany. We remained with Him for the rest of the day.

We learned that His name was Jesus of Nazareth, and He began to teach us by saying, "You search the Scriptures because you think they give you eternal life. But the Scriptures point to Me! If you truly believe Moses, you will believe Me, because he wrote about Me."[5] Moses wrote:

> *"The Lord your God will raise up for you a prophet like me from among your fellow Israelites. You must listen to Him. For this is what you yourselves requested of the Lord your God when you were assembled at Mount Sinai. You said, 'Don't let us hear the voice of the Lord our God anymore or see this blazing fire, for we will die.' Then the Lord said to me, 'What they have said is right. I will raise up a prophet like you from among their fellow Israelites. I will put My words in His mouth, and He will tell the people everything I command Him.'"*[6]

Jesus went on to teach us out of the writings of the prophets explaining what the Scriptures said. He spoke with an authority like we had never heard. The hours passed quickly as He explained one truth after another. Our hearts felt strangely warm, and we knew that He was the One about whom the prophets had written.

As the hour drew late, we knew it was time for us to leave so He could rest. John and I decided to travel to Bethsaida to tell our families all that we had heard from Jesus. We wanted them to know the Messiah had come! Jesus told us that He would be traveling to Bethsaida and we would see Him again in a few days. So, we departed in haste knowing we would see Him soon.

It took us three days to reach Bethsaida. Simon, Zebedee, James, Thomas, and my friend Philip were cleaning their nets when we arrived. It had been over two years since we had seen them, but John and I were both too excited to engage in small talk.

"We have met the Messiah!" we exclaimed. "The baptizer declared Him to be the Lamb of God who takes away the sins of the world! We have sat with Him and the Spirit of God has confirmed to us that He is the Promised One!"

We didn't have long to wait for Jesus to arrive. It was the very next day when I saw Him approaching along the shore. I could see that Shimon was still traveling with Him. I called to Simon and Philip, and John called to his father and brother, and we all made our way to see Jesus.

As we drew nearer, I saw Jesus looking intently at Simon. I had already realized that Jesus looks intently at everyone. It was as if He could see into your very soul and know everything you had ever done … and everything you would ever do. He seemed to look at you as if He were seeing you for who and what you would become.

. . .

He apparently saw Simon that way – because when I introduced my brother to Jesus, He said, *"I will no longer call you Simon for you will be called Peter, which means 'a rock.'"*[7] He saw my brother Simon – or rather, Peter – in a way that even Peter could not see himself. And for the first time in his life, Peter was struck speechless. He quietly stood there looking at Jesus while John introduced his father and brother to the Master.

Next, I introduced my friend Philip to Jesus. Philip looked at Him with that disarming smile of his, which broadened even more when Jesus said to him, *"Come and follow Me."*[8] It appeared that Zebedee would need to hire another fisherman, because Philip never looked back when he began to follow Jesus.

As a matter of fact, he and I left to go into the village to find our friend Bartholomew, who was also called Nathanael. He, too, was a fisherman. He was originally from the village of Cana, but he was now living in Bethsaida. He was known to be a jester and often found humor in even the most unusual situations. Philip told him, "Andrew and I *have found the very person Moses and the prophets wrote about! His name is Jesus, the son of Joseph from Nazareth."* Bartholomew immediately exclaimed, *"Can anything good come from Nazareth?"* To which Philip replied, "Don't believe us, *come and see for yourself!"*[9]

As we approached, Jesus looked intently at Bartholomew and called out to him, *"Now here is a genuine son of Israel –* a man who says what he thinks." Bartholomew replied, *"How do you know about me?"* Jesus explained that He had seen him standing under a fig tree before Philip and I had gone to find him. But Jesus had been nowhere near. And we had not told Jesus we were going to get Bartholomew. But somehow Jesus knew.

Immediately, Bartholomew exclaimed, *"Teacher, You are the Son of God – the King of Israel!"* To which Jesus replied, *"Do you believe this simply because I told you I had seen you under the fig tree? You will all see much more than this! Come, follow Me."*[10]

· · ·

Jesus told us He needed to go to Cana to attend a family wedding. He invited us to follow Him. Peter, Zebedee, and James said they needed to stay in Bethsaida to attend to business, but the rest of us – John, Philip, Bartholomew, Shimon, and I – traveled with Him to Cana. Along the way, He continued to answer our many questions and taught us from the Scriptures. We marveled with every step we took.

It didn't take long for me to discover that I would always be marveling at Jesus. There was no question that the One who stood before me had been sent by God. He is the Messiah! He is the One who was promised. And I want to introduce everyone to Him that I possibly can.

SALOME – THE MOTHER OF THE BRIDE

My name is Salome and my husband, Joachim, and I are the proud parents of the bride. We are hosting a wedding feast today in celebration of the union of our daughter, Mary, and her husband, Jacob! She is marrying a good man from a respectable family here in Cana. Family and friends have come from all over to join us in the celebration of this special day.

My parents traveled from the nearby village of Nazareth – the town where I grew up. And a lot of my aunts, uncles, and cousins made the long journey north from my ancestral home of Hebron. It is always a delight to gather with family – particularly for something as joyous as a wedding celebration.

Our special guest for the wedding is my childhood friend, Mary. She is both the namesake for our daughter and her *"kvaterin"* – though you may be more familiar with the term "godmother." Mary is five years older than I am and we both grew up in Nazareth. When I was a young child, she often helped my mother take care of me. I always looked up to her and in many ways, she was the older sister I never had.

. . .

When I was ten years old, Mary became betrothed to a carpenter named Joseph in our village. He was an older man who had been a widower for a number of years. Our entire village celebrated their engagement knowing that happiness had been restored to Joseph's life. Mary was well-liked by everyone in our town. Her radiant joy confirmed her exuberance over their match, so the entire village looked forward to their union.

But suddenly everything changed. A few days after Mary returned from a three-month visit with her cousin, Joseph and Mary's father announced that the betrothal period was being cut short. Without the benefit of a wedding feast to celebrate the culmination of their union, Mary immediately moved into Joseph's home and became his wife. That decision prompted idle tongues to wag. But the din soon turned into full-scale gossip when people found out that Mary was three months pregnant.

She and Joseph tried to explain to everyone how an angel had appeared to both of them separately, announcing that the child she was expecting was the Son of God. The Spirit of God had come upon Mary while she was still a virgin and God's Son had been conceived. Mary was the virgin whom the prophets had foretold would conceive a child. And the child was the Promised One who would save us from our sins! This was good news over which we should all be rejoicing!

But sadly, most of the townspeople did not believe Mary and Joseph. The town turned its back on them and treated them like outcasts – including my parents, at first. But I always knew that Mary was telling the truth! And I stood by her side when very few did. I helped her with her chores – but mostly I was a friend she could count on. And the feeling was mutual!

Six months later we all traveled to our respective ancestral homes for a census ordered by the Roman emperor. My family and I went to Hebron; Mary and Joseph traveled to Bethlehem. Her son, Jesus, was already two years old when she and Joseph returned to our village. By then, the townspeople had found new things to gossip about, and their ill treatment of Mary and Joseph seemed to subside. The couple still received the occasional disparaging look; but, for the most part, things seemed to return to normal.

I was happy to have my best friend back home and I helped her around her house as much as I could. Over the next few years, she bore four more sons and two daughters. She even named her youngest daughter after me. I became a babysitter for them all! But I will tell you – provided you can keep a secret – Jesus was my favorite!

He was always mature for His age. As a toddler, He had a calm and caring disposition. Whenever He was around you, He would look at you as if He knew your inner thoughts and genuinely cared about you. As He grew, He never spoke a mean or disrespectful word. He was always obedient to His parents. He was a caring elder brother. And, even as a young boy, His understanding of Scripture far exceeded mine – and that of the rest of the people in our town – including the rabbis!

Joachim is from Cana, so when we married I moved here. Gratefully, Nazareth wasn't too far away, and Mary and I were still able to see one another often. She came to help me when my daughter Mary was born, and each of my children thereafter.

Her husband, Joseph, died about eight years ago. I admire the way Jesus has taken care of His mother and His family ever since. He has been a good Son! But Mary tells me that Jesus has now left their home to do what His Heavenly Father has put before Him to do. Her second oldest son, James, has now stepped into the role of caring for his mother and younger siblings. I would expect, however, they all will soon marry and settle into their own homes. In anticipation of that day, Mary recently moved to Capernaum where she has other family.

I am grateful that all of her children have come with her to join us for this special celebration – even Jesus! Mary told me He might not be here. It had been two months since she had last seen Him. Though she was confident that He remembered the day, she was concerned that He may have been detained by other matters.

But soon after she expressed her concern, Jesus arrived! Mary's face glowed as her oldest Son entered the courtyard. He smiled broadly and affectionately embraced His mother before warmly greeting the rest of us. He had the ability to brighten a room with His very presence, and He lifted our hearts just by being here. My youngest daughter, Ruth, was especially glad to see Him. She had always looked up to Jesus as if He were an older brother. He had always paid attention to her from the time she was a toddler, no matter what else He was doing.

He introduced us to a number of His friends and followers whom He had brought with Him. Most of them appeared to be fishermen – John, Andrew, Philip, and Bartholomew were all about my daughter's age. His friend, Shimon, who told us he was a shepherd, was closer to my husband's and my age. They all seemed to be somewhat in awe of Jesus and grateful to be in His presence.

Jesus said He hoped it was all right that He had brought them along. I assured Him we were honored that His friends could join us for the celebration. I told them to make themselves at home. I must confess, however, that I was a little nervous since other friends had also brought uninvited guests. I hoped the food and wine would hold out to satisfy the additional appetites and palates!

My husband and I were committed to spending quality time with each and every one of our honored guests. Gratefully, Mary had told me not to worry about any of the other details. Our friend, Samuel, who was acting as our master of ceremonies, would make sure that everything took place in its proper time. Mary would keep a watchful eye on everything else to make sure all went as planned. Joachim told the servants to take their directions from her.

. . .

As the afternoon grew late, I noticed out of the corner of my eye that Mary had gathered several of the servants together with Jesus, and He was giving them instructions. They were standing near the large jars of water used by our guests to cleanse their hands and feet when they arrived. Apparently, the water had run dry and the servants were refilling the jars.

But then I noticed something very unusual. One of the servants withdrew some of the water with a ladle and proceeded to bring the ladle to Samuel. To my horror, Samuel lifted the ladle to his lips. He was getting ready to drink water intended for washing hands and feet!

After taking the drink, Samuel promptly walked straight toward my husband. I was now fully distracted by all that was going on. I was concerned that Samuel was about to complain that the servants had offered him a ladle of unclean water. But then my fears were put to rest when I heard him tell Joachim, *"A host always serves the best wine first. Then, when everyone has had a lot to drink, he brings out the less expensive wine. But you have kept the best until now!"*[1]

Joachim had no idea what Samuel was talking about, but he received the comment graciously. I, however, looked at Mary. She was looking at Jesus, as were the servants and His friends. They were all marveling at what had just occurred.

The wedding feast ran well into the evening – and we never ran out of wine or food. And many guests commented we had saved the best for last. I knew that wasn't the case. At the time, I didn't totally understand what had happened – but I knew that Jesus was at the center of it. And I knew that whatever He was at the center of would always be good.

As the evening concluded, Mary and her family were the last to leave. Jesus said He was going to travel with them to Capernaum and spend some time with them. I knew His mother's heart was glad. I wondered how much more family time Mary would enjoy with her Son. I embraced my friend and her family and thanked them all for coming.

As I looked at the One who stood before me – now a grown Man – I couldn't help but think back to that gentle little boy with the calm and caring disposition! And I realized that part of Him would never change!

ZEBEDEE – THE FISHERMAN

My name is Zebedee, and I grew up here in Bethsaida along the Sea of Galilee. I believe that even a bad day on my fishing boat is better than any day on dry land – but don't tell my wife! Though, truth be told, she knows me better than I know myself. Salome (not to be confused with Mary's childhood friend who has the same name) and I have now been married for thirty-three years. Though she grew up as a merchant's daughter, she quickly learned what it was like to be a fisherman's wife, and she never complained. I am a truly blessed man because of her.

We have two sons – the eldest is James and he is ten years older than his brother, John. James takes after me – he is a fisherman through and through. Though John is a hard worker here on our boat, I know that he longs to be elsewhere. The rabbi from Capernaum has twice arranged for him to attend the school of Hillel in Jerusalem. All his life he has sought out opportunities to study the Torah.

Slightly more than two years ago, I released him to travel down to Perea along the Jordan River with my business partner's younger brother, Andrew. The two young men had their hearts set on being taught by the prophet in the wilderness known as John the baptizer. My partner,

Simon, and I knew we needed to release them to pursue their calling from Jehovah God.

We were amazed when they returned two months ago to tell us they had met the promised Messiah. The One who God promised to our people almost two thousand years ago has finally arrived! Generations have come and gone with the hope they would see Him – and now we have that privilege! Simon, James, and I listened with excitement as John and Andrew shared their good news.

But then the good news got even better! The next day Jesus arrived in our village. We met Him face to face! And when He spoke to us, it was as if He had known us all of our lives. From the moment we met Him, we knew that Jesus of Nazareth was the Promised One. John and Andrew had known that day in Perea that they must follow Him. Now, two of my paid workers – Philip and Bartholomew – knew they, too, must leave and follow Him.

Simon, James, and I looked at one another and resigned ourselves to the fact that we needed to stay here in Bethsaida and continue to earn a living so these young men could follow Jesus. Even though that is what we knew we needed to do, each of us thought seriously about following Him, as well!

John, Andrew, Philip, and Bartholomew returned home a week later. But we knew they were only back temporarily. They told us an extraordinary tale of how Jesus had turned water into wine at a wedding celebration. He was now spending time with His family in Capernaum, so our young men had returned home for a short stay.

Over the next few weeks they continued to amaze us as they recounted Jesus's teaching. The promised Messiah had come! Soon we would be delivered from the bondage of Roman rule and God would establish His kingdom here in our midst. We knew the time had arrived!

· · ·

After several weeks, Jesus arrived back on our shore. It was early one morning, and we had been fishing all night. We had nothing to show for it except our tired bodies. We were finishing our night's work by mending and cleaning our nets and preparing to go home. But Jesus's arrival reinvigorated us.

There were several others who were now traveling with Him. Two of the men were His cousins – James and Thaddeus. Jesus had invited them to leave Capernaum and follow Him as His disciples. Also joining Him was their mother, His aunt Mary. She explained to us that she is married to Jesus's uncle, Clopas. She confided that she had felt led by God to come along and provide a woman's helping hand to her nephew and her sons.

Along the way, they had encountered a man named Simon. He explained that he was seeking Jesus. At one time, he was part of the zealot movement endeavoring to overthrow Roman rule. But he had abandoned their revolutionary ways and had become a disciple of the baptizer. Andrew and my son John were delighted to see their friend and were overjoyed that he, too, had chosen to follow Jesus as one of His disciples. We immediately started to call him Simon the zealot to prevent any confusion between him and my partner Simon – whom Jesus had renamed Simon Peter. We had a good time catching up with old friends and making new ones.

Jesus was already becoming well-known in Galilee, so it didn't take long for word to spread through our village that Jesus was on the shore. As people gathered, Jesus began to teach. But soon the crowd was pressing in on Him. Jesus turned to Simon Peter and asked him to push one of the boats away from shore so He could sit in it and teach the crowd from there.

We lost track of time as we listened to Jesus. No one wanted Him to stop, but eventually He needed to rest. When He finished speaking, He turned to Simon Peter who was there in the boat with Him and said, *"Now go out where it is deeper, and let down your nets to catch some fish."*[1]

.   .   .

The sun was high in the sky, and we all knew this was the worst time to try and catch fish. *"Master,"* Simon replied, *"we worked hard all last night and didn't catch a thing. But if you say so, I'll let the nets down again."*[2]

Jesus nodded with a glimmer in His eye, so Peter released the nets. At first nothing happened, and Peter looked at Jesus as if to say, "See, Master, I have done what You said with little to show for it." But suddenly his attention turned back to the nets. They were filling with fish! He and his brother-in-law, Thomas, earnestly called out to the rest of us to bring out the other boat and come help them.

I am fifty-four years old. I have fished on these waters all of my life, but I had never seen a catch of fish like that one! The nets were so full they began to tear. As we hauled in the harvest of fish, our boats were on the verge of sinking. Fortunately, we weren't that far from shore or we wouldn't have made it.

When we got to shore, Peter fell to his knees as he turned and looked at Jesus. Then he said what all of us were thinking: *"Oh, Lord, please leave me – I'm such a sinful man."*[3] To which Jesus replied, *"Don't be afraid! From now on you'll be fishing for people!*[4] Come, follow Me!"

Peter looked at me and then at his wife, Gabriella, standing onshore. She and Salome were standing with Jesus's aunt watching all that had happened. Gabriella smiled and nodded at her husband. My son James also turned to look at me with an expression that told me what was in his heart. Both of the men knew they needed to go.

Then our last remaining worker, Thomas, also looked at me. All of the fishermen who worked with me were about to leave and follow Jesus. And I knew they needed to go. They didn't need, nor were they seeking, my approval. They were acting in obedience to the Messiah and that doesn't require anyone else's approval. Their looks were simply to bid me farewell.

.   .   .

But then Salome approached me and said, "Zebedee, I believe that I, too, am supposed to follow the Master. I am to offer my help alongside of Mary." What could I say? My wife was also responding to the invitation of the Master. Of course, she needed to go! I wasn't only saying farewell to all of my partners and workers, I was releasing all of my family! I could hire other workers to help with the business, but I couldn't replace the members of my family who wouldn't be sitting around our dinner table each night.

Then I realized that Jesus's calling on my family was also a calling on my life. There was a part of me that wanted to push my boats up onto the shore and follow Jesus with my family. But I knew that wasn't what Jesus was calling me to do. He was calling me to stay – and that would be the harder of the two choices.

Jesus was calling me to carry on with my business to help provide the financial support He, my family, and the rest of His followers would need in order to carry out the work. I wasn't being left behind; I was being asked to be faithful to a different calling.

Suddenly I realized Jesus had turned His attention toward me. As our eyes met, I could almost hear Him say, "I know it's hard. *But truly, I say to you, there is no one who has left house or wife or brothers or parents or* children – or has let them go – *for the sake of the kingdom of God, who will not receive many times more in this time, and in the age to come eternal life.*"(5)

Soon I was standing there watching Jesus walk away. Right behind Him were my wife, my sons, my partners, and my friends. I would be less than honest if I didn't confess that at that moment I felt very alone. I knew it was the right thing to do, but that didn't keep me from feeling that deep ache of loneliness.

But then I heard a still small voice say to me, "*Be strong and courageous. Do not fear or be in dread, for it is the Lord your God who goes* – and stays – *with you. He will not leave you or forsake you.*"(6)

. . .

At that moment, I entrusted my wife and my sons to the One who had stood before me. And I entrusted my life to Him, as well. I knew He would order all of our steps and give us the grace and strength to accomplish all that He set before us. I knew we were just beginning to understand who He is and what He is calling us to do. Every journey begins with a single step, and the One who had stood before me had just led all of us to take that first step.

~

NICODEMUS – THE INQUIRER

$\mathcal{M}$y name is Nicodemus, and I grew up in Capernaum along the Sea of Galilee as the eldest son of a respected family in our village. My great-great-grandfather led the group of settlers sent by our Hasmonean king, John Hyrcanus I, to establish this fishing village. This was a part of the expansion led by the Hasmoneans to populate more of the wilderness lands north of Judea. My great-great-grandfather had been chosen to lead the effort because our village was to be named in honor of his father, Nahum.

Nahum, my great-great-great-grandfather, was a priest who fought bravely alongside Judas Maccabeus in the successful revolt against the Seleucid Empire. Nahum died in battle. To honor his heroism and his memory, our new settlement was called Capernaum, meaning "Nahum's village." The Hasmoneans also awarded a financial tribute to his surviving family. Those riches funded the settlement of the village and also provided the seed money for our family's wealth, which in turn multiplied with each succeeding generation.

In 65 B.C., my grandfather partnered with a merchant named Shebna who had recently migrated to our village from Babylon. The two men were both visionaries and saw the financial opportunities created by Herod the Great's economic expansion. Our region – and our families – prospered as a result of that foresight. Shebna was also the younger brother of Hillel the Elder. That family connection would later enable me to sit under his teaching.

As a son of means, I enjoyed a life of position and privilege. I am a Pharisee, as were the many generations of my family that went before me. I attended the School of Hillel in Jerusalem and sat under the elder's teaching for eight years along with other privileged students who were being groomed as the next generation of leaders. I had the proper pedigree, wealth, and training. The only blemish on my record in the eyes of some is that I was born a Galilean. In some circles of Judean society, particularly among the Sadducees, I am therefore seen as a second-class Jew.

My schoolmate Annas never saw me as his equal because of my place of birth, although our teachers viewed us as two of their top students. Annas went on to become our high priest and continues to have significant authority over our Sanhedrin to this day.

After completing my studies, I returned to Capernaum where I could mentor and train the next generation without being marginalized by Judean bigotry. I was a respected rabbi within my home synagogue and very soon became the leading elder.

Over the years, Jehovah God has permitted me to teach many promising young men. One of those who stands out is John, the son of Zebedee. Though John did not live in Capernaum, his mother's family does. She is the granddaughter of Shebna, my grandfather's business partner, so I have taken every opportunity to nurture John's thirst for truth and understanding. I even made arrangements for him to study under his distant cousin, Gamaliel.

· · ·

Soon after my return from my studies in Jerusalem, I was chosen to be one of the twenty-three judges who make up our local Sanhedrin in Capernaum. I hope it was my excellent understanding of the law and my wisdom that prompted my selection. But I am certain my wealth was a factor, as well. Regardless, I served our people and the position to the best of my ability.

For those of you who may not be aware, every significant village, town, and city throughout our provinces has a local Sanhedrin charged with adjudicating religious, civil, and criminal matters. Under our current Roman rule, we may not invoke capital punishment or judge matters having to do with political rebellion. Otherwise, the Romans permit us to handle all other matters in accordance with our laws and beliefs.

Matters that cannot be resolved by the local Sanhedrin are referred to the Great Sanhedrin in Jerusalem, which is comprised of seventy-one judges from throughout the land. This council is the final court of appeal for matters regarding Jewish law and religion. Four years ago, I was chosen to serve as a part of this council. High Priest Caiaphas currently presides over us. He is the son-in-law of our former high priest Annas. His view that Galileans are "second-class" citizens has not changed – which means he and some of his cronies still look down on me, despite my personal achievements.

Gratefully, there are others on the council, such as Gamaliel (Hillel's grandson) and Joseph of Arimathea, who were also fellow schoolmates and who do not share Annas's low opinion of me. Jehovah God continues to place Annas in my path to teach me humility!

The Great Sanhedrin meets in the Hall of Hewn Stones. The hall was built into the north wall of the temple – half inside the temple and half outside, with doors on both sides. Even the positioning of our meeting place reflects the power we have been given over all aspects of Jewish life. It is a power that can be used to honor God and serve our people, or to foster selfish ambition, personal gain, and coveted power.

.   .   .

The presence of both motives is clearly seen among the members. My friends Gamaliel and Joseph represent the former; Annas and Caiaphas clearly represent the latter. My prayer is that I might be an influence for good, bringing honor to Jehovah God – and ours might be the majority opinion within the council. I fear, however, that is not the case.

An example of using position for personal gain is evident in our council's rulings over how we worship God. When King Solomon had the First Temple built, there were birds, sheep, and cattle available for purchase outside the temple. This allowed traveling pilgrims, who could not bring their own offering, to purchase one of these animals to follow the requirements of the sacrificial laws. Solomon had established an area outside of the temple called the stoa, which was the place where these animals were housed and purchased.

When the Second Temple was established, that same practice was followed. But when Annas became high priest, stalls and tables were set up inside the temple walls in the outer court. Some say it was done out of necessity; I fear it was Annas's desire for financial gain. The practice has continued ever since. And the volume of trade inside the temple has multiplied. Increasingly, priests have deemed animals brought to the temple to be blemished and therefore unsuitable for sacrifice. That makes the purchase of an animal or bird from within the court necessary.

Also, rulings were made that Roman coinage could not be used for offerings in the temple; only temple coinage could be used. So, money-changers were set up in the court to exchange coinage – at a significant profit. The profits went to those who were in positions of power within the Sanhedrin, and the rest of us seemed powerless to do anything about it. Regrettably, over time the practice became so common that no one gave it a second thought.

In recent days, all of my Sanhedrin brothers and I have become aware of a rabbi by the name of Jesus. Some have already discredited Him because He is from Nazareth in Galilee. But most of us have been intrigued by the miracles He has reportedly performed and His teachings. He teaches in a way that is unlike any other, and His command of the Scriptures is unmatched.

Last week at the beginning of the Passover celebration, Jesus came to town. I am certain He has been in the temple on previous occasions, but this was the first that I – and many others – were aware of His presence. He created quite a stir!

When Jesus entered the outer court of the temple, He looked at the merchants selling their cattle, sheep, and doves, as well as the dealers exchanging money. I am told He reached down and gathered some ropes by one of the stalls and made them into a whip. Then He did something no one anticipated – He turned to the merchants and shouted, *"Get these things out of here! Stop turning My Father's house into a marketplace!"*[1]

He then proceeded to drive out the animals and chase the merchants out of the temple. He turned over the money-changers' tables. They quickly gathered the coins, stuffed them into the pockets of their cloaks, and scurried out.

Our council was meeting at the time, but the commotion outside quickly drew our attention. When we walked out into the court, most of the animals and merchants had already fled. No one had even thought about stopping Jesus! No one had questioned His authority to clear out the temple!

Annas and Caiaphas, along with a few others, looked agitated as they huddled together. But, even in their anger, they made no attempt to stop Jesus. They knew ... I knew ... we all knew that if Jesus were confronted, He would rightfully rebuke us all from the Scriptures for letting this abomination take place. We knew it was wrong. The people knew it was wrong. But Jesus was the only One to confront us in our sin!

· · ·

Annas and Caiaphas knew better than to publicly challenge Jesus. They didn't want their evil deeds to be revealed or their authority weakened. So, they chose to do nothing … at least for now. But I knew their silence was only temporary.

As I stood there watching Jesus, I was ashamed. How many times had I walked through that court and done nothing? How many times had I ignored the sin in God's temple?

After the scene quieted down, Caiaphas and Annas approached Jesus and asked, "*What have You done? If God gave You authority to do this, show us a miraculous sign to prove it.*"[2]

"*All right,*" Jesus replied. "*Destroy this temple, and in three days I will raise it up.*"[3]

"*What!*" they exclaimed. "*It has taken forty-six years to build this Temple, and You can rebuild it in three days?*"[4]

They had no idea what Jesus meant. None of us did. But they knew they could not confront Him any further, so they turned and walked away.

Over the next few days, I watched as Jesus healed many who were brought to Him. People began to gather around Him in great numbers as He taught in the temple. I knew I needed to know more. Also, as a member of the Sanhedrin, I needed to be certain that this Man was not leading our people astray.

Jesus had several men with Him who were obviously His disciples. One of them was John, my student from the synagogue in Capernaum. I approached him and asked if he would arrange a time for Jesus and me to meet. "I have many questions for your Rabbi," I said. "I see that you have come to follow Him. Would you permit your former teacher the opportunity to do the same?" John agreed and arranged for us to meet two nights later.

Jesus and I were to meet away from the temple so we could have a quiet, uninterrupted conversation about spiritual matters. I was preoccupied each day with my responsibilities within the Sanhedrin, and Jesus was actively teaching from sunrise to sunset. Now we could both relax and talk through the night without interruption. The only other person in the room was John. I trusted him, and I knew this would be a safe place for us to talk.

"*Rabbi,*" I began, "*we all know that God has sent You to teach us. Your miraculous signs are evidence that God is with You.*"[(5)]

Jesus wasted no time with shallow compliments. Instead He moved right to the heart of the matter as He replied, "*I tell you the truth, unless you are born again, you cannot see the Kingdom of God.*"[(6)]

"*What do You mean?*" I exclaimed. "*How can an old man go back into his mother's womb and be born again?*"[(7)]

Jesus replied, "*I assure you, no one can enter the Kingdom of God without being born of water and the Spirit. Humans can reproduce only human life, but the Holy Spirit gives birth to spiritual life.*"[(8)]

"*How are these things possible?*" I asked.[(9)]

Jesus replied, "*You are a respected Jewish teacher, and yet you don't understand these things? I tell you what I know and have seen, and yet you won't believe My testimony. But if you don't believe Me when I tell you about earthly things, how can you possibly believe if I tell you about heavenly things? No one has ever gone to heaven and returned. But the Son of Man has come down from heaven. And as Moses lifted up the bronze snake on a pole in the wilderness, so the Son of Man must be lifted up, so that everyone who believes in Him will have eternal life.*

"For this is how God loved the world: He gave His one and only Son, so that everyone who believes in Him will not perish but have eternal life. God sent His Son to save the world through Him.

"There is no judgment against anyone who believes in Him. But anyone who does not believe in Him has already been judged for not believing in God's one and only Son. And the judgment is based on this fact: God's light came into the world, but people loved the darkness more than the light, for their actions were evil. All who do evil hate the light and refuse to go near it for fear their sins will be exposed. But those who do what is right come to the light so others can see that they are doing what God wants."[(10)]

At that moment, I knew that everything Jesus was telling me was true! Sitting before me was the Son of God. He was the Promised One. He was the One God said He would send to deliver His people from our sins. But there would be people who loved darkness more than light – like Caiaphas and Annas. When Jesus cleansed the temple the other day, He was shining God's light on their evil. He was exposing their sins ... and my sins.

But those who want to do right come to the light. I wanted to do right. That's why I had come tonight. I want to do what God wants. And I know there are others who want to do the same.

Over the next few days, I wrestled with a decision. Do I leave the Sanhedrin to follow Jesus like John has done? Or do I follow Jesus from within the Sanhedrin? Does God want me to be light from within the council? I came to the decision that He wants me to stay. I don't know for how long, but perhaps I can be of greater help to Jesus from within the council than from outside of it.

· · ·

All I know for certain is that the One who stands before me is truly the Son of God. I have been born again and I am His follower.

~

ENDORA – THE WOMAN AT THE WELL

*M*y name is Endora and I am neither Roman nor Jew; I am a Samaritan, living in the village of Sychar. You might think you have never heard of our village before, but you would be wrong. We actually have quite a history – much of which you already know!

Our village and this entire region were cursed from the start. One night after the floodwaters had subsided, our patriarch, Noah, became drunk and was lying naked in his tent. His youngest son, Ham, walked in on his father. But instead of respectfully covering up his father, he left him uncovered and went to tell his brothers about their father's indiscretion. Ham's older brother Shem immediately went into the tent and covered his father.

When Noah awoke from his drunken stupor, he learned what Ham had done. Because of the disrespect of his youngest son, Noah cursed the descendants of Ham's youngest son, Canaan. This entire region became inhabited by the descendants of Canaan – and this village, which was known as Shechem at the time, was born ... under that curse.

. . .

The same day Noah cursed his youngest son, he blessed his oldest son, Shem, asking God to prosper and bless his descendants. Part of that blessing was that Canaan's descendants would always be inferior and lowly before those of Shem.

About 350 years later, one of Shem's descendants, the patriarch Abraham, set up camp by an oak tree just outside of this village. That night God entered into a covenant with Abraham, promising to give his descendants all of the land of Canaan. Even the land the Canaanites possessed would be taken from them because of the curse.

It was 160 years later that Abraham's grandson, Jacob (who would later become known as Israel), also made camp in this very place. He bought this piece of land where I am standing right now. He built an altar of sacrifice to Jehovah God and dug a well to water his herds and flocks, intending to peaceably settle here. But a prince of the village defiled Jacob's daughter and her brothers sought retribution by slaughtering all of the men and seizing the women and children as slaves. But some of the villagers survived and escaped punishment. Jacob's family moved on, and this village slowly rebuilt from the ashes of destruction.

The Israelites returned to inhabit this land 300 years later. They built an altar in this valley between Mount Gerizim and Mount Ebal. They called it the place of blessings and curses. Gerizim represented blessings and Ebal represented curses. Fittingly, they brought the body of Jacob's favored son, Joseph, to this very place for burial. It was a reminder to the Israelites of the faithfulness of God in fulfilling His promise and His blessing. But in many ways, it also was a reminder of the curse to the descendants of Canaan. In the years that followed, our Canaanite blood intermixed with Israelite blood and we became worshipers of Jehovah God.

This region and our village became part of the kingdom of Israel and remained as such for more than 500 years until the nation split into two kingdoms. Two hundred years later, our people were taken captive by the

Assyrians. Most of our people were taken to Babylon, but some of them escaped captivity and remained here to live and intermarry with their conquerors.

When the Israelites were released from captivity and slowly began to return to this land, they again saw our people – now known as Samaritans – as lowly and inferior. The curse of Ham continued to cast its shadow over us.

We no longer saw the temple in Jerusalem as our place of worship. We were not welcome there. So, we built our own temple at Gerizim – on the mount of blessing – in order to worship Jehovah God.

The hostility between us and the Jews of Judea and Galilee continues to run deep. It has been fostered for thousands of years, and in many respects, it began with a curse. This hatred has passed from generation to generation. Jews will have nothing to do with us, and we will have nothing to do with them. We both take great strides to avoid one another. Interestingly enough, we are both now subjects of the Roman empire. Rome views us as being the same, but nothing could be further from the truth! So, as I said at the start, I am neither Roman nor Jew; I am a Samaritan – and I am proud of that!

I was the eldest daughter of a poor family, and my parents struggled to keep us fed. My parents made an arrangement for me to be married when I was thirteen years old. My prospective husband was a wealthy widower who was fifty years my senior. He wanted a young wife and was willing to provide my father with a few shekels to finalize the agreement. My parents saw the marriage as an opportunity for me to have all that they could not provide, and a means to help them provide for my younger siblings. My husband was kind to me as long as I met his needs.

But four years after we married, he died. I was a seventeen-year-old widow with no children to care for me. My parents were unable to take me back in. So, when my dead husband's oldest son (from a previous marriage) offered to marry me, I readily accepted. He had inherited his father's wealth and now earnestly wanted an heir. After two years of marriage, he divorced me because I had not borne him a child.

I was a few months short of my twentieth birthday and I was now a divorced woman without a child and no means of support. Though my prospects were limited, I still had one thing going for me – I was a desirable young woman. It wasn't long before another older widower by the name of Ibrahim came along and proposed marriage.

Ibrahim was a kind and gentle man. Though he was not as wealthy as my first husband, he truly cared for me. The twelve years of our marriage were the best years of my life. I felt safe and loved. But I did not bear Ibrahim a child. As a result, when he died, I was again left a penniless widow without anyone to care for me.

I married twice more after that. My fourth husband divorced me after five years of marriage so he could marry a younger woman. My fifth husband, as it turned out, was prone to violence. If his heart had not stopped suddenly one night, I fear my years would have been cut short.

So, at age forty-five, after being married five times, I am a barren widow. I am also the subject of gossip in our village and an object of derision. I am currently living with a man named Murjan who cares little about what people think of him … or me. I feel safe with him, but I have no interest in becoming anyone's wife ever again! Our living arrangement has given the women of our village another reason to gossip about me.

The water source for our village is the well Jacob dug many years ago. Fortunately, it has remained intact as a part of the blessing of Shem and never fell to the curse of Ham. For hundreds of years our ancestors have been coming to this well for water at dawn and at dusk.

. . .

Several years ago, however, I decided I could no longer follow that tradition. I was tired of the looks from the other women and their hurtful words, which were said just loud enough for me to hear. So, I started going to the well at noon each day.

Recently, I saw a stranger seated beside the well. I decided He must be a traveler passing through our village. I also noticed that He had a couple of companions with Him, but they were standing at a distance.

I decided to ignore the Man and do what I came to do. Just as I began to draw from the well, He said, *"Please give Me a drink."*[1] It was obvious He was a Jew. His appearance and His manner of speech left no doubt. I was surprised that a Jew would dare speak to me! *"You are a Jew,"* I said, *"and I am a Samaritan woman. Why are You asking me for a drink?"*[2]

The Man answered, *"If you only knew the gift God has for you and who you are speaking to, you would ask Me, and I would give you living water."*[3]

Living water? What was this Man talking about? So, I replied, *"But Sir, You don't have a rope or a bucket, and this well is very deep. Where would you get this living water? And besides, do You think You are greater than our ancestor Jacob, who gave us this well? How can You offer better water than he and his sons and his animals enjoyed?"*[4]

The Man again replied, *"Anyone who drinks this water will soon become thirsty again. But those who drink the water I give will never be thirsty again. It becomes a fresh, bubbling spring within them, giving them eternal life."*[5]

I had no idea what this Man was talking about! I was starting to think He might be crazed, but nothing in His demeanor indicated that. I decided to pursue His statement further.

. . .

"Please Sir," I said, *"give me this water! Then I'll never be thirsty again, and I won't have to come to this well anymore."*[(6)] I honestly would have welcomed any remedy that saved me from making this journey to the well each day!

But He surprised me by changing the subject, saying, *"Go get your husband."*[(7)] I promptly told Him I didn't have a husband. But then He said, *"You're right! You don't have a husband – for you have had five husbands, and you aren't even married to the man you are living with now."*[(8)]

How could this stranger possibly know that? How could He know anything about me? I studied Him a little more closely. Had He somehow heard the gossip about me? But He wasn't saying those things in a condemning way. He was saying them as if He were a friend who knew all the details of my life. Who was this Man?

As I stared at Him, I realized He was not looking at me with desire as some men did. Neither was His look judgmental nor condemning. Rather, He looked at me as if He knew all I had ever been. And I began to realize He could see all I would ever be.

He knew I had come to the well at the noon hour to avoid the other women of the village. He knew of the scorn and belittling I endured. He knew my heart had been hurt so many times that it had become callous and hardened. He knew I would no longer permit anyone to hurt me again.

"Sir, You must be a prophet,"[(9)] I said. *"Why is it that you Jews insist that Jerusalem is the only place to worship, while we Samaritans claim it is here at Mount Gerizim, where our ancestors worshiped?"*[(10)]

He replied, *"Woman, the time is coming when it will no longer matter whether you worship the Father on this mountain or in Jerusalem. Indeed, the time is here now – when true worshipers will worship the Father in spirit and in truth."*[(11)]

. . .

Each time He spoke, I could feel the hardened shell around my heart softening just a little more. I felt strangely safe talking to Him – even safer than I had with Ibrahim. Could this Man possibly be the One whose coming had been foretold? I looked at Him and said, *"I know the Messiah is coming – the One who is called Christ. When He comes, He will explain everything to us."*[12] My heart stopped beating as I waited for Him to respond. Then He said, *"I am He!"*[13]

My heart leapt as I heard the truth. I knew this was the Promised One! I felt a flood of emotions. I felt forgiven. I felt cleansed. I felt safe. For the first time in my life, I felt free! And immediately, without any thought about why I had come to the well, I ran back to the village as quickly as I could to tell everyone about the Man who *"told me everything I ever did!"*[14] Here I was – the woman who had made it a practice of avoiding everyone – and now I was seeking out everyone to tell them about this Man.

On my way back to the village, I passed some men who apparently were traveling with Him. They were returning with food they had purchased in the village. They looked shocked that Jesus had been talking to me. Ironically, I had seen them earlier in the day on my way to the well. They had turned their heads as we passed, clearly showing their contempt and disapproval. But the One they were following had not turned His head away from me! And as a result, I would never turn away from Him!

I ran straightaway to tell Murjan about the Man at the well. Then I went out into the streets and began to tell everyone who would listen. At first, they were astounded that I dared to speak to them. Some just ignored me. But soon a crowd gathered and began to listen intently. I told them, "Don't just take my word, go and see this Man for yourselves."

Murjan and I followed them as they went to find the Man. Soon they were begging Him to stay in our village. I learned His name was Jesus. He agreed to stay, and over the next two days many more in our village heard His teaching and His message of Living Water. And many, like me – including Murjan – believed. Soon people throughout the village were proclaiming, *"We believe, not just because of what the woman told us, but because we have heard Him ourselves. Now we know that He is indeed the Savior of the world.*"(15)

I had no idea what was going to happen that day at the well. I had no idea that my life was about to change forever. But now I know that the One who stood before me has filled me with Living Water – and I will never thirst again!

~

CHUZA – THE STEWARD

$\mathcal{M}$y name is Chuza. I am the son of Shachna, and I serve as the royal chamberlain (a senior official) to Herod Antipas, the tetrarch of Galilee and Perea. My father grew up in Capernaum. As an adult, he became the business manager for the senior Roman centurion stationed in that city. He was greatly admired for his capabilities and recognized in ways he didn't even realize. That is, until one day, he was told to appear before the king, Herod the Great.

My father had no idea why he was being summoned. He was relieved and honored when Herod explained he was being appointed to manage the construction of a new city along the coast of the Mediterranean Sea. The city was to be called Caesarea Maritima, in honor of the Roman emperor, Augustus. It was to be the showplace of the province, boasting a deep-water harbor, an ornate palace, and sporting arenas rivaling those of Rome itself.

Herod had a grand vision to bring economic prosperity to the region and Caesarea Maritima was central to those plans. He gave my father great latitude in selecting the most gifted architects and designers, the most skillful craftsmen, and the finest materials. I was nine years old when construction began, and the work concluded just prior to my twenty-first birthday.

As a young boy, I shadowed my father and watched him with great pride. He led this massive undertaking with wisdom and grace. His workers honored and respected him. During the latter years, I served alongside him as his apprentice and assistant. I never once heard King Herod voice anything but satisfaction with my father's work and the progress of the project.

When everything was completed, Herod honored my father by naming him the royal chamberlain – which meant he directed the royal household and was answerable only to the king. Herod was known for his impatience and fits of rage, but he never showed my father anything but the utmost respect.

I learned much from my father and continued to serve alongside him in the palace until the day Herod died. Afterward, the Roman emperor divided the kingdom with Judea, Samaria, and Idumea being ruled by his son Herod Archelaus and his son Herod Antipas ruling over Galilee and Perea. Respecting my father's abilities, Archelaus retained him as his royal chamberlain.

But Archelaus's rule was cut short when he was removed by Caesar Augustus, and the Roman prefect Coponius was installed in his place. My father decided it was time to step down as chamberlain and advised the incoming prefect to choose me to assume his role. Coponius was facing enormous challenges resulting from Archelaus's poor leadership, so he was only too happy to have someone step into the role with little disruption.

I quickly learned that being the chamberlain was very different from being the assistant to the chamberlain! The responsibility now fell squarely on my shoulders. I was grateful that my father was still available to provide wise counsel whenever I needed it. Over time, I grew more comfortable and confident in the role – and the prefect frequently praised me for the way I handled his household.

I had been in the role for three years when Coponius was reassigned to another post; his replacement had already been selected by the emperor. Before he left, Coponius told me that Herod Antipas wanted to offer me a position in his court. Coponius gave me permission to consider the opportunity. Apparently, the incoming prefect was bringing his own chamberlain, which meant I was no longer needed in Caesarea.

That turn of events actually worked in my favor. My new master and king, Antipas, told me of his plans to construct a new capital city for the provinces under his rule along the shores of the Sea of Galilee. The city would be called Tiberias in honor of the current Roman emperor. Antipas explained that the city would rival his father's city of Caesarea Maritima in its majesty. He knew my father had supervised the construction of that city, and he knew I had assisted my father.

I am just a few years older than Antipas, so we grew up in the palace in Caesarea at the same time – though obviously in very different stations. Still, we were well-acquainted with one another. He told me he knew I had the ability to oversee the construction of his new city – and even more importantly, he knew he could trust me.

As I mentioned earlier, my father grew up in Capernaum in Galilee and he was now planning to move back there. So, the opportunity for me to also relocate to Galilee to oversee the development of Tiberias was an added bonus. I accepted Antipas's commission. I would report only to him and would have his complete authority backing my every decision.

While visiting Capernaum, I met a young woman named Joanna, and it wasn't long before her parents and mine thought we should be married. And truth be told, Joanna and I both thought so as well! Arrangements were made, and six months later we married. I couldn't imagine life being any better. Jehovah God had blessed me with a loving wife and had granted me the opportunity to serve our ruler – and our people – by building a new thriving city that would bring added benefits to our region.

It took ten years for the city of Tiberias to be completed. The city is surrounded by seventeen natural mineral hot springs to its north, west, and south, and the inviting waters of the Sea of Galilee to its east. All of this makes it a pleasant place to live.

My only disappointment was that our most religiously orthodox Jews decried the building of cities such as Tiberias. They believed that our region was becoming Hellenized in appearance, in culture, in language, and in religion. They refused to settle in Tiberias and influenced many others to do the same. As a result, we were forced to resettle segments of the non-Jewish population from other parts of Antipas's domain in order to populate the city.

When construction of the city was completed, Antipas honored me by making me his chamberlain. He gave me responsibility over not only the management of his household but also the administration of his efforts to appease the anxiety of the orthodox Jews. That responsibility would eventually afford me the opportunity to financially support the ministry of Jesus. But I am getting ahead of myself!

Joanna, our four-year old son Samuel, and I moved into our new accommodations inside the palace, which were exceeded only by those of the royal family – and life for us was good. That is until Samuel fell ill at age ten. He developed a high fever that the court physicians were unable to treat. Each day our son became weaker, and each day we had less and less hope.

Someone in the palace told us about a miracle worker named Jesus of Nazareth. He was creating quite a stir throughout Galilee. Witnesses said He could make the blind see, the deaf hear, and the lame walk. Joanna and

I did not know whether He could heal our son, but we knew the physicians could not.

Joanna learned that Jesus's mother had recently moved to Capernaum, so we made arrangements to take Samuel there. Antipas graciously permitted us to take whatever time we needed to see if this Man could heal our son. We set sail from Tiberias and within a few hours made the journey to the north shore of the sea. When we arrived in Capernaum, we learned that Jesus was not there but was expected to arrive soon. He had been delayed in His travels through Samaria, of all places, but was expected home within a few days. He would be traveling back through Cana.

Joanna and I knew our son wouldn't survive another trip. But we also knew he did not have many days to live. So, Joanna and Samuel stayed with her parents in their home in Capernaum, and I set out on a day's journey walking to Cana – in the hopes that I would come upon Jesus along the way.

It was early afternoon when I arrived in Cana. I asked if anyone knew the whereabouts of Jesus of Nazareth. He was obviously well-known and well-liked in the village because I was immediately directed to Him.

When I approached Jesus, I explained my son's condition and begged Him to go to Capernaum to heal my son. I was desperate. Jesus could see it in my eyes and hear it in my voice. But surprisingly, He did not reply with compassion as I expected. Instead, He turned His face in the direction of the crowd gathering around Him and asked, *"Will you never believe in Me unless you see miraculous signs and wonders?"*[1]

Thinking that Jesus did not understand the urgency of my situation, I said to Him, *"Lord, please come now before my little boy dies."*[2]

. . .

I did not know it at the time, but my statement to Jesus revealed my ignorance about who He was and what He was capable of doing. But I was certainly not alone in my misunderstanding. I would venture that most everyone within the sound of His voice still had no idea who He was.

First, I mistakenly believed that Jesus had to be in the physical presence of my son in order to heal him. Second, I believed that Jesus's miracle-working power was limited to healing and not to restoring life. I was looking at Jesus through the lens of my own understanding, not through the realization of who He is.

But graciously, Jesus showed me compassion and said, "*Go back to your son. He will live!*"[3]

I now had three options. I could continue to beg Jesus to return with me. I could attempt to use my position as Antipas's royal chamberlain to command Him to come with me. Or, I could take Him at His word and trust that He had the power to heal my son just by speaking those words.

I am one with royal authority. I enjoy the trust of Herod and direct many as the manager of Herod's household. I am accustomed to giving a command and having it obeyed. But today, I am in no position to command. I am a beggar before this King, and He has given a command. I will trust Him in His mercy. I will trust Him by faith. If I can't trust Him in what He has said, then I can't trust Him at all!

So I turned, without any further hesitation, and began my journey back to Capernaum. As I walked away, I heard Jesus commend me for my faith to those standing around Him. At that moment, I knew my son had been healed.

. . .

I wanted to get back to Capernaum to see with my own eyes, so I traveled for several hours until nightfall. I stopped to rest overnight and then continued on my journey.

As I neared Capernaum, I saw some of my servants running toward me. As they drew closer, I could see how happy they were. They were overjoyed to tell me my son was well. He had been healed!

What I had believed came true! But did it become true when I believed it, or did it become true to me when I heard about it from my servants? I now know that it is the former, not the latter. Truth becomes reality when I believe it – not when I see it!

I rejoiced in the news and praised God for His faithfulness. Then I asked the servants when my son had begun to get better. "*Yesterday afternoon at one o'clock, his fever suddenly disappeared,*"[4] they replied. I knew the answer before they even responded. My son had been healed the very moment Jesus said, "*Your son will live.*"[5]

On that day, I believed in Jesus – not only for what He had done – but for who He is. When I arrived in Capernaum, I told Joanna, and she, too, believed in Jesus. We told her parents and my father – and they believed. When we returned to Tiberias, we told our entire household, and they also believed.

Even Herod Antipas asked me what had occurred. He listened with interest as I explained what happened. But I could see that He did not believe. He rejoiced in our good news, but he never accepted it for himself.

God continues to allow me to provide financial resources from the royal treasury to help support Jesus in His travels and ministry. Joanna is now traveling with the other women and men who are following Him. While she assists Jesus in His work close by, I do so from afar. But we both follow Him.

I enjoy the favor of my king in his palace, but more importantly, I enjoy the favor of the One who stood before me. I will serve Him, the true King, with my life … for now and forevermore.

≈

LAZARUS – THE FRIEND

*M*ost of you know me as Lazarus, but some of you may know me as Simon. My sisters and I live in Bethany. Our father died a few years ago. As his only son, I inherited his property and became the patriarch of our family. Neither of my sisters is married. My oldest sister, Martha, keeps our lives functioning in perfect order. She has the gift of organization and is the model of a hard worker. Our home is immaculate and the picture of efficiency. Our younger sister, Miriam, whom many of you call Mary, has a sweet spirit and a tender heart. She is as compassionate as Martha is industrious. My father once said that if a man could marry both of his daughters, that man would have found the perfect wife!

Our father was a successful vintner. He inherited his land from my grandfather about the time Herod the Great became the tetrarch (governor) over the region. The economy flourished under Herod's reign through the expanded trade, which was a result of his new port city of Caesarea. Our father capitalized on the new trade opportunities by quadrupling our harvest. He achieved this by planting land that had previously remained idle under his father's oversight and by employing improved irrigation and pruning techniques.

. . .

I did not inherit my father's ambition to increase the output of our land, but I did learn from him how to manage what we have. So, the land continues to provide handsomely for me and my family. I employ an overseer named Amari to direct the day-to-day operations. My father employed Amari's father in the same capacity, so Amari and I grew up together. I trust him as if he were my brother – because in many respects, he is.

Our vineyards are located in the fertile Jordanian valley. My father built our residence away from the vineyards in the heart of Bethany. As a matter of fact, my father's success enabled him to become one of the more prominent men in Bethany with one of the largest homes. Our family continued to enjoy that elevated social status even after his death.

That is, until something totally unforeseen occurred. One day I noticed skin lesions on my arms and legs. They weren't visible to others because they were covered by clothing. At first, I didn't think anything about them. I thought they may just be some form of rash. But as the weeks passed, they didn't go away; in fact, more began to appear. Then I developed a numbness – at first in my hands, but then in my feet, as well.

Initially I kept my condition hidden from everyone, including my sisters. But I realized that for their protection, I needed to get a diagnosis for my ailment. One of our leading local priests, Phinehas, is also a good friend of mine. He and I grew up together, and he is a frequent dinner guest. One night when he was dining with us, I drew him aside and showed him some of the lesions and described my symptoms. Immediately he affirmed my suspicions. I had leprosy!

Our laws are very clear regarding what I needed to do. Without any further hesitation, I assembled Martha, Mary, and Amari, and from a safe distance told them of my condition. As you can imagine, they were devastated by the news. Our charmed life had just been irreparably shattered. After delegating my responsibilities to them, I set out from our home that very evening and made my way out of town.

. . .

I traveled north and eventually came to an area outside of one of the villages in Galilee. Leprosy is known as the "living death" among our people. Many believe that lepers are being punished by God for our sins, which makes us feel ashamed. That shame made me get as far away from Bethany as I possibly could.

Those of us with the disease are considered unclean and we are not permitted to come within six feet of another person. As a matter of fact, on a windy day we aren't permitted to be any closer than one hundred fifty feet. I wanted to put an even greater distance between me and my friends and family because I didn't want to see their look of pity mixed with fear.

Our disfigurement causes our appearance to be a warning to others to stay away. We are cast out of our homes and our villages to live solitary lives until we die – or until somehow, by the grace of God, we are miraculously healed. I was not holding out for a miracle.

It is a hopeless existence. Since lepers are unable to work, we have no way to provide for our needs. We depend on the gifts of family members or those who show us compassion. As a result, more lepers die of starvation than they do the disease. And leprosy is no respecter of persons or position. It afflicts the affluent and the poor equally.

I was in a better position than most. My family was affluent, so my sisters made sure that I lacked for nothing. Bear in mind, my needs were simple – food, clothing, and bedding. But still, my desperation consumed me.

My sisters came to visit me on more occasions than I would have liked – for their sakes. One of the things lepers long for is the simple act of physical touch. And as grateful as I was for my sisters' visits, each one acutely reminded me that I would never again feel their touch. As the months passed, my condition continued to deteriorate. I knew the signs, and I knew my death was near.

. . .

One morning, I was staring blankly off into the distance. My eyesight had worsened to the point I could no longer distinguish features, just shapes. I saw what appeared to be a Man walking in my direction. As best I could tell He was surrounded by a large group of followers. Those walking with Him were asking Him questions, and He was answering them. He obviously was a teacher of some sort. As they got closer, I heard someone address Him by name – Jesus!

Even here in the middle of nowhere, I had heard of a Man named Jesus. People said He was possibly the promised Messiah, and that He had the power to heal. At that moment, I knew what I had to do. I didn't think about it. I didn't hesitate. I just started running toward Jesus! I don't know where my strength came from. For weeks now I had barely been able to move. But suddenly I was running!

Imagine how strange – and frightening – the sight of a leper running toward them must have been to the crowd with Jesus. As I think back, I wonder if any of them picked up sticks or stones to throw at me to keep me away.

As I approached Him, I stopped and bowed my head. I am sure everyone was astonished that I dared to come near Him. But I didn't even see them. I knew there was only One in their midst who could possibly heal me. I could barely speak, but somehow I was able to whisper, *"Lord, if you are willing, You can heal me and make me clean."*[1]

Then Jesus did the unthinkable! He walked right up to me, not keeping the six-foot distance, and He reached out ... and touched me! I could not remember the last time anyone had touched me. I heard an audible gasp from the crowd. What had Jesus done? He had now made Himself unclean by touching a leper! Why would He do that? He could have simply spoken, but instead He touched me!

Then Jesus said, in a voice loud enough for everyone to hear, *"I am willing. Be healed!"*[2]

. . .

You're not going to believe this, but instantly I knew I had been healed. Strength that had been gone for years entered into my body. My eyesight became clear. My numbness was gone, and feeling had returned. My skin was clear. Every blemish was gone! All within the blink of an eye! When the sun rose that morning, I had thought it was the day I was going to die. But instead, it was the day Jesus gave me new life! I was healed!

Everyone around us stood in silence. I fell to my knees. The strength had returned to my voice and I wanted to thank Him. But the words that came out of my mouth did not carry the weight of the gratitude I wanted to express. As I knelt before Him, Jesus looked down at me and told me not to tell anyone what had happened. He said, *"Go to the priest and let him examine you. Take the offering that is required in the law of Moses for those who have been healed of leprosy. And allow the priest to publicly declare that you have been cleansed."*[3]

As I rose to my feet, I instinctively reached out and embraced Him. The crowd gasped for a second time – but their gasps turned to silence when Jesus smiled and returned my embrace.

As I stood there with His arms wrapped around me, He said, "After you have seen the priest, go and be restored to your sisters. They have prayed to the Father on your behalf. Tell them that the Father has heard and answered their prayers. You and I will be together again soon, and you will see Me accomplish even greater things to the glory of the Father. Go and be declared clean, for what I have made clean can never again become unclean!"

Then He let go of me and stood directly in front of me smiling. It had been a long time since anyone had smiled at me. My sisters had stopped smiling at me long ago. Strangers looked at me with fear. Fellow lepers looked at me with despair. But Jesus smiled at me! So, I basked in His smile, just like I had basked in His embrace.

. . .

Soon He turned and continued on His way northward. I turned south and began my journey to Bethany. I had left my home downhearted and in despair. I never anticipated I would be able to return home. But now, here I was – and I could not wait to get there and see my sisters. My pace was brisk, and my heart was full to overflowing.

When I arrived on the outskirts of Bethany, I went to the outer boundary of our family's vineyards and sent word for Amari to come to me. As he drew near, I could see his apprehension. I was still wearing the clothes of a leper. But as he grew closer, I could see his hesitance melt away. I told him to stop and remain six feet away from me. Though I had been healed, I still needed to present the offering required by law just as Jesus had told me. No one would be allowed to come closer to me until that had been completed.

I proceeded to tell Amari all that Jesus had done. You can imagine his questions! After I had answered him to the best of my ability, I asked him to get me everything that would be needed for the healing ceremony. I instructed him to carry a message to Phinehas the priest, as well as my sisters, to let them know what had happened. I told him to tell my sisters to stay away from me until the cleansing ceremony took place.

I bathed and shaved my entire body as required by the law. Phinehas then examined me and sprinkled me, using a hyssop branch, with the blood of a bird that had been sacrificed. My sisters sent a new garment for me to wear. I continued to stay away from our home for eight more days as the law required. On the eighth day, I presented two rams and a female yearling to Phineas as an offering of cleansing. As my sisters watched, the priest declared that I was clean.

Immediately, my sisters ran and embraced me. I told them what Jesus had done and all He had said. I told them that God had heard and answered their prayers. It was as if Jesus knew every word they had prayed. I told them that Jesus had said He would see us soon. We would need to be ready for His visit.

. . .

I owe Him my life. It wasn't a bird, two rams, and a yearling that made me clean. I was made clean by Jesus – by His word, by His act … and by His touch. And as He said, whatever and whomever He has made clean can never again become unclean!

My journey with Jesus did not end that day; my journey had only just begun. He has promised that I will see Him accomplish even greater things to the glory of the Father. I don't know what that is or all that lies ahead in my journey, but I will continue to follow the One who stood before me.

~

YANIS – THE PARALYTIC

*M*y name is Yanis. I grew up in the hills overlooking the Sea of Galilee not far from the road that now leads from Tiberias to Nazareth. The men of my family have been shepherds as long as anyone can remember. I never had to wonder what I would do when I grew up. Because I am my father's oldest son, there was never any question that I, too, would be a shepherd – and one day my father's flock would become mine.

My father began teaching me how to care for our sheep and goats when I was still very young. We kept the animals in the fold during the months of January and February to protect them from harsh weather. Our fold was a walled enclosure behind our home with a roof overhead to help shield the animals from the elements. Though we never experienced the snow and cold weather that others did farther north, our winters were still very rainy and cool.

I'll never forget the first time my father told me to feed the animals in the fold. I was eight years old. When they heard me enter, every one of them, young and old, stopped what they were doing and turned their heads to look at me. My father told me to talk to them so they would begin to know my voice.

. . .

The older members of the flock walked toward me to get a closer look. They knew I didn't look or sound like my father. They began to look at me so critically from beneath those shaggy eyebrows that I started to get nervous. They were trying to decide if they could trust me. I worked to control the nervousness in my voice.

I could tell they were anxious as they looked at the food I set before them. They smelled it and then they tasted it. When they decided it was the same food my father gave them each day, they seemed to calm down. As they began to eat, I continued to talk to them. Eventually, they began to know my voice and decided they could trust me. That began a lifelong relationship.

Each year I looked forward to spring. Come spring, the sheep – and the shepherds – are both ready to get out of the fold and step out onto the fresh, green grass pushing out of the ground. The sheep's winter fleece is sheared and the sounds of new life echo as lambs are born. As a boy, I began to name each new lamb and kid. It always amazed me how quickly they learned to respond to their names.

There is nothing like spring in the hills of Galilee! As you look toward the eastern horizon, you'll see the morning star fading into daylight, as if it were welcoming the rising sun. It's calling out to the birds to awaken and serenade the hills with their songs of joy. The flowers are just beginning to paint the hillside with the colors of spring. Yes, there is nothing like spring in the hills of Galilee!

When summer heat set in, we would move our flock to cooler pastures on even higher ground. For days on end, we would work and sleep outdoors, allowing the flock to graze on the steep green slopes. We would construct a temporary sheepfold to shelter the flock and protect them from jackals and hyenas. We took turns with the other shepherds standing guard over the sheepfold gate. If the howl of a hyena or jackal panicked the flock during the night, our reassuring voices would calm them down.

· · ·

Often, one of the animals would wander off. That's why we named each one and kept a close count – if one went missing we were able to call it by name. Sheep can find some of the most dangerous places to become stranded. They will step onto a precarious ledge just to get a taste of a small clump of grass.

Fortunately, my father had taught me to carry a staff among other things. He taught me how to gently wrap the crook of my staff around a stranded sheep and lift it safely into my arms. He showed me how to place a rope around a sheep's midsection to lower it to safety. My father also taught me how to use a rod and a sling to fend off the advances of any attacker. Once I found and rescued a lost sheep, I would lift it and carry it on my shoulders as we returned to the flock. It helped reassure the animal that though it had been lost, now it was found and safe.

Last year, I was off looking for one of our lost sheep. It was early spring. It had been raining for almost a week and the hillside was muddy. I spotted the lost lamb on a ledge sticking out from a steep crag. I had long ago stopped trying to figure out how sheep could ever put themselves in such danger. I knew I needed to climb to the top of the crag and reach down with my staff. The rocks were slippery, so I carefully made my way to the top.

I was able to hook the sheep on my first try. As I began to lift him toward me, he shifted in the crook of the staff and I lost my balance. Suddenly I was sliding down the steep face of the crag. While still cradling the sheep, I reached out with my free hand to grasp something to stop my fall. My hand kept grabbing air until I landed on my back on a rocky ledge. Snap! Suddenly, I realized I couldn't move. The sheep fell right on top of me, so I clutched him to my chest.

I didn't have any feeling in my legs. One was limply hanging over the ledge, and the other was somehow folded underneath me. I knew I was too far away from the other shepherds for them to hear me shout. But I trusted that my father would eventually come looking for me.

I don't know how long I laid there on that ledge. My pain eventually overtook me and graciously I became unconscious. It was my father who found me, and who, with the assistance of several other shepherds, successfully lowered me to the ground. They contrived a pallet so my father and four of my friends could carry me home.

It was the next day before I regained consciousness. The last thing I remembered was lying there on the ledge with the sheep on my chest as I called out to God to rescue me … and like a Good Shepherd, He had.

One of our neighbors traveled to Tiberias to find a physician who could attend to me. After setting my leg, which was broken in two places, the doctor turned to me and my parents and said, "The rock you fell on, young man, injured your spine. I'm sorry, but it is doubtful that you will ever walk again." That is difficult for anyone to hear – but especially a seventeen-year-old with his whole life ahead of him. I tried to be brave for my family as we absorbed the news – but inside I was still calling out to God to rescue me.

As the months passed, my broken leg healed – for all the good it did me. I still wasn't able to get out of bed. I was grateful for my four friends. Whenever they weren't in the hills watching over their sheep, they were there by my side. They did everything they could to encourage me and cheer me up. But still the days passed slowly – and I continued to call out to God to rescue me.

Eventually spring returned, and my friends insisted I was not going to miss the sights and sounds of new life. They took me on my pallet to the top of the hill to look down on the sea. They set me down on the ground so I could feel the fresh grass, smell the new flowers, and hear the birds as they delivered their spring songs. I longed to run free and climb the hill with the flock – so I continued to call out to God to rescue me.

.   .   .

One day, my friends came to me with stories about a Miracle Worker by the name of Jesus. He had lived in nearby Nazareth, but now He was traveling throughout Galilee. My friends told me they had heard how He could make the blind see, the lame walk, and the leper clean. Perhaps He could make me walk! It was the first time I permitted myself to have a glimmer of hope.

"We hear He is in Capernaum," one of my friends announced.

"But that's a day's journey away," I said. "And that's if you have two good legs and are able to walk!"

"Yes, but the four of us have eight good legs and we are able to carry you!" my friend replied with a smile. There was no talking them out of it. And I began to have hope that the Good Shepherd had heard my cry.

It took us two days to make the journey. When we arrived in Capernaum, we learned that Jesus was teaching in the synagogue.

It seemed as if every man from every village in all of Judea and Galilee was gathered in that place! The crowd had spilled out into the street and courtyard surrounding the synagogue. There was no way we could enter. My friends had carried me all this way, but now we weren't going to be able to get to the Miracle Worker. My heart sank – and again I quietly called out to the Good Shepherd to rescue me.

One of my friends suddenly looked up and pointed to the roof of the building. "All of our lives we have been rescuing stranded and injured sheep by lowering them to safety," he said. "This isn't any different! We have not traveled this far to turn away!"

They carried me up on the roof. There was a man there observing the commotion below. I could tell from the way he was dressed that he, too, was a shepherd. He didn't try to stop my friends; he just watched to see what they were going to do. In a matter of moments, my friends were removing roof tiles near where Jesus was speaking. Initially no one seemed to notice, which gave my friends the confidence to keep going.

Once they made the opening large enough, they attached ropes to the four corners of the pallet. By this time everyone inside the synagogue was looking up at us – including Jesus. My friends were not going to stop because of a few stares! They began to gently lower me through the opening. The crowd parted as my friends lowered me onto the ground right in front of Jesus.

As I lay there on the pallet gazing up at Him, He looked at me and smiled. Somehow, I felt like I had seen His face before. Then I realized I had – on the day of my accident. As I had lain unconscious on the ledge, I saw Him looking at me just as He was right now – and He had told me He would rescue me. Standing over me was the Good Shepherd! He had heard my cry then and He heard it now. He was going to rescue me! He would free me so I could walk again. He would raise me up!

Jesus looked at me, looked up at my friends, and then turned back toward me and said, "*Young man, your sins are forgiven.*"[1] Immediately the religious leaders in the room began to cackle like hens. "*Who does He think He is?*" they exclaimed. "*That's blasphemy! Only God can forgive sins!*"[2]

Having heard them, Jesus replied, "*Why do you question? Is it easier for Me to say, 'Your sins are forgiven,' or 'Stand up and walk'? So that you will know that I have authority to forgive sins, I now say to this man, stand up, pick up your mat, and go home!*"[3]

The Good Shepherd had just told me to get up. I heard His voice. I knew His voice. I knew I was His sheep. And I knew there was only one thing to do. Get up! The crowd gasped as I jumped to my feet. My friends cheered. And I stood there not quite knowing what to do next. I bowed before Him, then looked into His eyes and thanked Him. I reached down, picked up my pallet, and walked out of the room. The people parted and marveled as they watched me go by.

By the time I got outside, my friends were already there to greet me. As we embraced, I realized that Jesus had not only touched my life that day, He had forever changed my friends' lives, too. As we stood there together praising God, the man who had been on the roof approached us.

I asked him who he was. "Me? My name is Shimon, and I'm just another shepherd," he said. "A shepherd who now follows the Good Shepherd." His eyes brightened even more as he looked into mine and said, "And He just rescued another sheep! You're why He came here today. He knew you would come. He came to forgive you of your sins – yours and those of each of your friends. As you return to your homes, tell your families and friends what He has done. Tell them that today you have all been rescued by the Good Shepherd." With that, he turned and walked away.

My thoughts turned back to Jesus. The Good Shepherd had stood before me! He had told me to get up, and I had obeyed. I knew I was His sheep. And I knew there was only one thing I needed to do – and that was to stand up. Now I knew there was one more thing I needed to do. I needed to tell everyone I encountered about the One who had stood before me and rescued me!

~

SUSANNA – THE GRIEVING MOTHER

I am Susanna, and I grew up here in the small village of Nain in southern Galilee, which is about ten miles southeast of Nazareth. The majority of the people here are farmers. We live off of the land that God provided us. Wheat and barley are our seasonal crops, along with our summer crops of fresh vegetables. But olive oil and honey are our two primary cash crops, so our village presses are active year-round. We enjoy a bountiful harvest each year from the numerous olive tree groves surrounding our village.

The first settlers in Nain also discovered many natural beehives located in the caves and rock cavities surrounding the village. They soon realized they could increase honey production by adding hives made of straw and unbaked clay. Increased honey production led to the export of two derivative products from our village – beeswax and honey wine.

My husband's family owned and operated the largest olive oil press in the village. Kadan inherited the business when his father died soon after we were married. Most of the olive producers in our village used my husband's press to grind their olives into oil. Each year harvests were plentiful, demand for olive oil was high, and Kadan's business prospered.

. . .

One other thing you should know about our village is that Mount Tabor, the highest peak in this region, is only two miles north of us. Over the years, it has become customary to light beacons at the top of Mount Tabor to inform the northern villages of our Jewish holy feast days and the beginning of each new month. The beacons can be seen for miles when the fires are lit.

Lighting the beacons for the feast days reminds us of God's faithfulness in our past, and the monthly beacons remind us of His continuing faithfulness in the days ahead. And they remind me that darkness cannot overcome the light. As a matter of fact, the light shines brightest in the midst of darkness.

I was abruptly and painfully reminded of that fact several years ago when Kadan died in a tragic accident. Our son, Zohar, was eight years old when his father was crushed by a large millstone while making repairs to the press. It was the second darkest day of my life. Kadan was not only a good husband, father, and provider – he was my best friend. He and I had been friends from childhood, and our marriage had been arranged when we were children. We both were our parents' only child, so in many respects, we had grown up like brother and sister.

Our lives were so intertwined that when Kadan died, a piece of me died with him. Zohar became the only light left in my darkness. Kadan and I had named our son Zohar because his name means "light." We knew God was placing a light in our family the day he was born, but I never realized just how much I would one day need that light!

Gratefully, the press mill passed to Zohar as my husband's heir; otherwise, a distant male relative would have inherited it and we would have had no source of income. I was able to employ some of the men who had worked for my husband to run the mill until my son was old enough to take his rightful place.

·   ·   ·

Kadan had already introduced Zohar to the work at the mill, but now that my husband was gone, my son became even more intent on learning how to manage the business. Gratefully, my husband's workers were good teachers and patiently trained Zohar. Each day I saw him become more like his father – hardworking, fair in his dealings, wise in his decisions, and liked by all. I knew Kadan would have been proud of the man his son was becoming.

I never really recovered from the loss of my husband, but Zohar brightened my days, and I was hopeful about his future. And I knew he would take care of his widowed mother.

Six months ago, on my son's eighteenth birthday, he told me he was ready to take over the family business. The men who had been teaching him confirmed that they, too, believed he was ready.

Zohar also had his eye on Zahara, a young woman in our village. He had decided to wait until he was managing the mill and could adequately provide for her before he asked her father's permission to marry her. His desire to marry Zahara had been further incentive for him to learn the trade well – and the incentive had worked!

A few days later, Zohar and I met with Zahara's parents and we reached a marriage agreement. They became betrothed and the marriage feast was planned for six months from that date – which is today. As I looked at my son and his betrothed, I saw the same happiness Kadan and I had felt. I forgot my own grief as my heart overflowed with joy thinking about the wonderful life ahead for this couple.

Remember when I said Kadan's death was the second darkest day of my life? Well, exactly one month ago, we were all making preparations for the wedding feast. Zahara and I were discussing some of the details that still needed to be finalized. All of a sudden, one of the workers from the mill burst into my home. He had urgent news. There had been an accident! Zohar had been making repairs to the oil press. While he was in the crushing basin, the pillar holding the crushing stones gave way. The entire structure had collapsed on him. The other men were working to free Zohar, but this man had been sent to alert me.

Zahara and I ran the short distance from my home to the mill. When we arrived, I saw my son lying on the floor beside the press. They had apparently been able to free him from the rubble, but no one was attending to him. There he lay, bloodied and bruised, but no one was treating him. I immediately cried out asking if they had sent someone for a physician. They hesitated – and then told me they had not. "Zohar is dead," one of the men said. "He was already dead when we removed the stones from on top of him. Susanna, we are so sorry!"

I don't remember anything after that. I knelt down and cradled my dead son's head in my lap. Zahara knelt beside me, and we both wept uncontrollably. The darkness in my life had returned – and this time it had snuffed out all of the light.

After a short while, others began to enter the mill. I saw Zahara's parents come in and embrace her. Soon they turned their attention to me. The midwife of the village arrived. She immediately looked over Zohar's dead body and confirmed that there was no life in him. The priest followed right behind her and soon the two of them, together with Zahara's parents, were making burial arrangements. My son would need to be buried before sundown and it was already approaching the middle of the afternoon.

I couldn't even think about the details. I was grateful that others were handling the arrangements. The one person who understood my agony was Zahara – and I was the one who most understood her pain. So, the two of us just held onto each other. I cradled my son's head in my lap for at least an hour, until the priest gently told me I needed to let him go so his body could be prepared for burial.

. . .

Several of the women walked Zahara and me back to my home until it was time for the burial procession. As the minutes passed, even with Zahara sitting beside me, I felt completely alone. My husband was gone and now my son was gone. I was a widow with no one to care for me. My son's business would pass to one of my husband's distant relatives whom I didn't even know. I felt like my life was over. The wave of grief that had already overtaken me was now joined by the wave of despair.

Our burial ground was just outside of the village. At this time of day, that ground stood in the shadow of Mount Tabor. As we began to make the journey, I remember thinking that the signal lights of the mount would shine over my son's grave. It's strange the things that come to mind when you're numb with grief.

The priest walked at the head of the procession. He was loudly proclaiming all of my son's good works. I walked immediately behind the priest with Zahara right beside me. A group of mourning women, including Zahara's mother, surrounded us. Zohar's body was being carried behind us on an open bier made of wicker wood. I had requested that his face not be covered. His hands had been folded and carefully placed on his chest.

There were holes in the bier through which poles were inserted. The poles were being carried by four of his friends – some of the very men who just a few hours earlier had feverishly attempted to rescue him. The men were walking barefoot to ensure they would be sure-footed, and the bier would not be jostled in any way. The sounds of the loud lamentations pierced the air. It was a tragic and hopeless scene.

As we made our way, I saw a Man walking toward us. He, too, had a large group surrounding Him – but theirs appeared to be a much happier occasion. He looked like He may be a Teacher and they may be His disciples. He and His entourage were headed into the village while we were headed out.

· · ·

Through tear-filled eyes, I could see His compassion toward me. I had no idea who He was, but I found a slight degree of solace in His expression. As our two groups passed one another, He looked at me and said, *"Don't cry!"*[1]

Though I was grateful for His sentiment, I couldn't help but wonder to myself, "What do you expect me to do?" He continued on past me, but I could tell He was walking toward the wooden bier on which Zohar's body had been carefully placed. Next He did something completely unimaginable – He laid hold of the bier to stop the procession.

Everyone in our procession gasped … as did His followers! What He had just done was a violation of Jewish law. Except for those preparing the body for burial, no one is permitted to touch a dead body or the coffin. To do so amounted to the worst kind of defilement. What's more, He had just disrupted me in the midst of my grief!

But as taken aback as we all were, it was nothing compared to what He did next. He stood there looking at my son's body for a brief moment and then said, *"Young man, I tell you, get up!"*[2]

I couldn't believe my ears! Then immediately, Zohar sat up! Now I couldn't believe my eyes! My son who had been dead sat up! And he began to talk to his friends who were carrying the bier. I couldn't hear what he was saying, but I saw the look of amazement on his friends' faces. Gently they set the wooden bier on the ground, and this Man took my son's hand to help him stand up. Then He helped Zohar walk to me. Was this real? Was I dreaming it?

Zohar wrapped his arms around me, and then I knew this was real. My son was alive! Then Zohar embraced Zahara. Tears were streaming down all of our faces. Tears of sorrow had been replaced by tears of sheer joy! Everyone else stood in absolute silence as the three of us embraced. Where moments earlier there had been death and hopelessness, this Man had restored life and hope!

. . .

After our moment of celebration, we all began to tremble with fear. I fell to my knees before Him and asked Him who He was. Before He could answer, some of those with Him said, "This is Jesus, the Promised One!"

He gently reached down and lifted me to my feet. As I stood there looking into His eyes, I was reminded of the woman from Shunem whose son had died, and yet God had raised him from the dead through the prophet Elisha.

I had always heard that story growing up. You see, our village of Nain is located on the same hill where the ancient village of Shunem was located. I thought it was an amazing story. But now I knew it was true! God in His goodness had now chosen to restore life on this hill of a second son – my son!

Word quickly spread across the region – *"A mighty prophet has risen among us! Surely God has visited His people today!"*[3] But I knew as I watched Jesus walk away that day He was more than a prophet. He did not raise my son from the dead because He had been granted temporary authority; rather, He is the One who has authority over death!

We celebrated the wedding feast of Zohar and Zahara today! It was a great day of rejoicing. It was a day of new life – life given, life returned by God, and a new life as husband and wife. But it wasn't only Zohar who was given new life that day – so was I. And I knew that I would follow Jesus. Tomorrow I would leave to join the other women and men who were following Him.

I would no longer live in the light cast from the fire on top of Mount Tabor. Now I would walk in the light that radiates from the One who had stood before me.

～

JAMES – THE SON OF THUNDER

I'm James and you've already met my younger brother, John, and my father, Zebedee. I grew up in Bethsaida, and I am one of the fishermen Jesus called to be fishers of men.

I am one of the older disciples, though I am six years younger than my lifelong friend, Simon Peter. He, his brother Andrew, my brother John, and I enjoy a unique relationship that sets us apart from the other eight apostles. The four of us grew up together. Simon Peter is the oldest, followed by me, then Andrew, and the youngest is John. Simon and I are the eldest sons in our families, so we understand the responsibilities that order of birth brings. That, combined with the proximity of our ages, has caused us to be close friends. The same can be said of Andrew and John.

The four of us have spent more time together in the close confines of a fishing boat than we could ever count. We've worked together, we've slept together, we've cried together, and we've battled the sea together. We know we can count on each other no matter what happens.

For all of our similarities, there are also some very clear differences. Simon Peter is the natural leader among us – partly because he's the most impetuous. He never hesitates to step out boldly ... even when he is wrong. And you rarely have to wonder what he is thinking because he is not one to keep it to himself. Though I, too, hold pretty strong opinions about most things and am outspoken, I usually wait to see how Simon Peter reacts before I make a move.

Andrew is the diplomat among us. He never met a stranger. He is the least intimidating of the four of us. Though we all care deeply about one another – and others – Andrew does a better job of showing it.

John is the smartest. He not only has more formal education and knowledge than the rest of us, he also has the wisdom to apply it. Though I am his older brother, I rely greatly on his wisdom – then once the plan is made, I make sure it's accomplished.

All of our gifts complement one another, and we learned long ago that we could accomplish more working together than apart. That's why Simon Peter and I, together with my father, knew we needed to allow Andrew and John to leave and seek out John the baptizer. We knew their journey would enable all of us to discover the truth as well. And that decision ultimately led to our meeting Jesus.

The day Jesus caused fish to fill our nets after we had fished all night with little to show for it, I knew – just like the others did – that I had to leave my home and follow Him. My heart compelled me. My head compelled me. My very soul compelled me. I didn't need to rely on John's wisdom or Peter's impetuousness that day. I knew beyond any shadow of a doubt that I needed to follow Him. And I will forever be grateful to my father that he never tried to talk me out of it or remind me of my responsibilities as his eldest son. Rather, he released me – he released us all – to seek after God's will for our lives with a generous spirit and an encouraging word.

It wasn't long after when Jesus looked at John and me with a smile and announced that He was giving us a new nickname – "Boanerges" which means "the sons of thunder." It was just like that first day when Jesus told Simon His name was now going to be Peter. Jesus was looking at Simon through eyes that could see what he would one day become – the rock through whom Jesus would ignite the building of His church.

And He was looking at us through those same eyes. He saw that one day we would boldly proclaim His truth – just like thunder. I always thought it was interesting that we were the only three disciples Jesus gave special names – and we were the ones He permitted to join Him on a few special occasions.

But if I had to choose one of the most amazing moments we had following Jesus, it was when He taught us that just because we were following Him, that didn't mean we wouldn't pass through any storms.

Jesus had spent the day teaching a large crowd along the shore of the Sea of Galilee. There were so many people pressing in on Him that we had arranged to borrow a boat so He could be seated while He addressed the crowd. We anchored the boat just offshore. It never ceased to amaze me the way Jesus was able to teach for hours on end without a break. And unlike the rabbis who often recited the law in ways that were difficult for most people to understand, Jesus spoke using stories and parables that enabled all of us to better grasp the truth. We had now been following Him for over a year and I had rarely, if ever, heard Him tell the same story twice. He appeared to have an endless supply of parables with which to explain the truths of God.

He started soon after daybreak that day and continued nonstop until the sun was preparing to set. Finally, He told the crowd to make their way to their homes and He told the twelve of us to get into the boat. The boat was the type and size that our family had grown up on – about eight meters in length and two and a half meters wide – so it could accommodate our number. He told the women and the remainder of those who were traveling with us to remain there in Capernaum and await our return. Then He told the twelve of us, *"Let's cross to the other side of the lake.*"[1] He directed us to cross to the village of Gergesa on the eastern shore.

Jesus headed to the back of the boat and laid down for a well-deserved rest. We could tell from His breathing that He had fallen into a deep sleep even before we had set sail. The trip would take us about two hours.

An hour into our journey, a storm blew in without warning. Sudden squalls were not unusual on the lake, particularly this time of year. Our autumn winds tend to blow from the west, funneling between the hills and whipping the lake into a fury of waves. But that night, the winds and the waves were more severe than any we had ever seen. The high waves were breaking over the boat, and we began to take on water. By then we were all bailing water, but we could not keep pace with the sea.

John looked at me as we were attempting to secure the sail and said, "This storm could sink us!"

Peter yelled to Thomas, "Go wake up Jesus and tell Him that we're about to sink in this storm. We need Him to help bail water!" Thomas made his way to where Jesus was still soundly sleeping despite the howl of the wind and the violent rocking of the boat. He reached down and shook Jesus awake saying, *"Teacher, don't You care that we're going to drown?"*[2]

As Jesus opened His eyes, He looked at Thomas and then at the rest of us; He saw the fear written all over our faces. As He stood up, He looked at the waves crashing over the sides of the boat. Thomas was preparing to hand Jesus a bucket to help bail when suddenly Jesus did the unexpected. With a booming voice of authority, He said, *"Silence! Be still!"*[3]

At first, I thought He was speaking to us! I think everyone did. It never occurred to us He was speaking to the wind and the waves. But the wind heard him and immediately stopped, and the waves settled into a peaceful calm. We had never seen anything like it! We had seen Jesus heal the blind and the lame. We had seen Him raise a young man from the dead. We had seen him fill our fishing nets to the point they would burst. But in our wildest imaginations we never thought He could command the elements of nature and they would obey His voice!

Awe and fear immediately overtook us. We looked at the sea and the horizon. We looked at the water rapidly escaping the boat deck through the side drains. Then we turned and looked at Jesus – with our mouths gaping in awe and disbelief. Jesus looked at us and said, *"Why are you afraid? Have you been with Me all of this time, but still have no faith?"*[4]

I heard Bartholomew softly say to no one in particular what all of us were thinking: *"Who is this Man that even the wind and waves obey Him!"*[5]

Jesus laid back down and slept the rest of the way. I don't think any of us spoke a word until we arrived at the shore. We just continued to marvel at what we had just witnessed ... and who Jesus is!

I can't speak for anyone else, but I learned three valuable truths that day. First, Jesus says what He means, and He means what He says. When we first got into the boat, He told us we were going to the other side. He knew we were going to encounter the storm. He always knows! And He knew that after He stilled the storm, we would arrive on the other side. He would always be true to His word, no matter what we might encounter!

Second, He was right there with us the whole time – sleeping peacefully, I might add. He was never anxious. He was always in control. And that would be true no matter what storm we encountered. He would always be with us and He would always be in ultimate control. We could trust Him and place our faith in Him.

Third, He has power over all things – illness, storms, even death – and we will never truly understand any situation until He has spoken, and we have heard from Him. Whether He said, "Man the buckets and bail the water!" or "Silence! Be still!" – it didn't matter. I would trust Him whatever He said!

It wasn't long after that we learned King Herod Antipas had imprisoned John the baptizer. He had silenced John's prophetic voice by placing him in chains and hiding him away in prison. We all knew that God had called John to be a prophet – a voice in the wilderness. But as his days in prison turned into weeks, he was unable to do the very thing for which he had been created, called, and placed on this earth. That was John's storm. And instead of being fearful he was going to drown, he became depressed and discouraged. Why had God permitted him to be imprisoned and his voice silenced?

One day we were in the wilderness just outside of Nain, and Jesus was teaching a large crowd that had gathered. Two of John's disciples brought Jesus a message from John in prison.

They said, *"John sent us to ask, 'Are You the Messiah we've been expecting, or should we keep looking for someone else?'"*[6] Jesus replied to them, *"Go back to John and tell him what you have seen and heard – the blind see, the lame walk, those with leprosy are cured, the deaf hear, the dead are raised to life, and the Good News is being preached to the poor."*[7] And then He added, "Tell him that I said, *'God blesses those who do not fall away because of Me.'"*[8]

After the men left, Jesus explained to us that John would know He was referring to the prophecy of Isaiah: *"And when He comes, He will open the eyes of the blind and unplug the ears of the deaf. The lame will leap like a deer, and those who cannot speak will sing for joy. Sorrow and mourning will disappear, and they will be filled with joy and gladness."*[9]

Others, like me, were asking Jesus why God had permitted John to be imprisoned and his ministry to be abruptly halted. John had been faithful. Why had God not allowed him to continue in the ministry through which so many lives were being transformed? There were still so many who had not heard!

Jesus explained that John's ministry had not been brought to a halt; rather, it soon would be greatly multiplied. Though John – and others who would follow – could be physically imprisoned, or worse, the message could never be imprisoned! Walls may imprison us. Our physical lives may be taken. But God's truth and His glory will endure – and the eyes, ears, and mouths of the blind, deaf, and dumb will continue to be opened. The lame will continue to be healed. And those who are spiritually dead will be raised to life. All for the glory of God!

A few weeks later, another message arrived for Jesus while He was teaching a large crowd. On this occasion, the message had been sent by Chuza in King Herod's palace. The messenger told us that he needed to immediately deliver the message and return to the palace. We assured him he could tell us, and we would convey the message to Jesus.

He informed us that the baptizer had been beheaded on Herod's order. We all gasped. It felt like someone had hit us in the stomach with all of their might. My brother John and Andrew both fell to their knees. None of us could believe our ears!

As we were grieving, I looked over at Jesus and our eyes met. The sadness I saw told me He already knew. He had already known the day He sent the message back to John – "Tell him that I said, '*God blesses those who do not fall away because of Me.*'"[10] John was now experiencing those blessings to their fullest. He had not fallen away. He had remained faithful to the end, and the experience of those blessings would now last for eternity.

The storm had now passed. The baptizer was in the Father's presence. His storm had ended much differently from ours on the sea. But both storms would ultimately lead to the glory of God. John was at peace. He had accomplished all God had given him to do.

.   .   .

When Jesus was done speaking to the crowd, the One who stood before us left in a boat to get away from the crowd. He went to a remote area to be alone and talk to His Father about their servant John. And those of us who remained knew we could trust Jesus at His word. We could trust that He was with us through every storm. And we could trust His power over all things.

~

ENOS – THE DEMONIAC

*M*y name is Enos and I was born in Gerasa, the largest of the ten cities commonly known as the Decapolis situated to the east of the Jordan River. The Decapolis is not a province like Judea or Galilee. Rather, the ten cities are the main population centers scattered across the eastern frontier of the Roman Empire, and they are tied together by a network of trade roads. Each city functions as an autonomous city-state with no Herodian ruler and no Roman prefect.

Since the beginning of their occupation, the Romans built temples throughout our cities to foster the worship of the Roman emperor. Now, fifty years later, many folks view him as more of a god than a political ruler.

You won't find many Jews in our cities. We are primarily inhabited by Gentiles who do not adhere to Jewish dietary laws. That means you will see things in our region that you would never see on the western side of the Jordan – such as a herd of pigs.

My father was Jewish, and my mother was Gentile. My father was a servant in the palace of Herod the Great in Caesarea Maritima. One day he stole a jeweled cup thinking no one would ever miss it. But someone did, and soon it was discovered that my father was the thief. He knew his offense was punishable by death, so he fled the palace and eventually made his way to Gerasa – outside of Herod's reach.

Here, he met my mother. They married, and eventually had a son – me. Though my father earned an honest living once he arrived in Gerasa, I seemingly inherited his penchant for stealing. My transgressions were minor at first, but as I grew into adulthood my crimes became more daring, and I began to treat my victims more brutally. As a matter of fact, not long ago I traveled to Judea to explore the opportunities there. I met up with a man named Barabbas, and together we found the road between Jerusalem and Jericho to be quite lucrative as we relieved merchants, tax collectors, and priests of their possessions.

After a while, the Roman soldiers got close to catching us, so Barabbas and I split up. He went north to Galilee, and I returned here to Gerasa where I met a group of thieves who told me they worshiped Orcus – the Roman god of the underworld. I told them I did not worship any god. Growing up, I would listen to my father tell stories about the God of the Jews, Jehovah God – but he did not follow Him; they were simply stories. But the more these men talked about Orcus and his blessings on their undertakings, the more I listened. I soon became intrigued by how passionate my new friends were about worshiping their god.

Eventually, I was completely fascinated, beyond even what my friends believed, as I spent more time at the temple to Orcus in Gerasa. That fascination developed into a blind adherence to the satanic worship practices taught by the temple priests. That is what led me to that fateful day!

The priests told me that the demons of Orcus were seeking a human host through whom they could express their power. If I were willing to be that host as an ultimate expression of worship of Orcus, I would enjoy wealth and power beyond imagination. I would be invincible. But while I was expecting wealth and power, what I got was torment and bondage that I could not escape.

The priests were correct about one thing. Once I was filled with demons, I was stronger and had more physical power than anything I ever imagined. However, my thoughts and my actions were no longer under my control. I became violent and crazed. Even the priests sought to subdue me without success. They bound me with heavy chains that I was able to break and cast off with little effort.

What I remember most is the torment. I had no peace – every moment was filled with suffering and accusation. The demons accused me, and very soon the entire city was accusing me of every possible evil deed, thought, or action.

The officials of Gerasa quickly decided I needed to be taken far away to protect the people of the city. They took me north to the wilderness outside the village of Gergesa on the eastern shore of the Sea of Galilee. They bound me with heavy ropes and chains that somehow restrained me during the journey. Once there, they left me to live among the tombs.

Days became weeks. Weeks became months. Months became years. I could not escape my torment. I would throw myself off of a cliff, but I would survive the fall. I constantly beat myself and slashed my body with stones – but nothing brought relief. I couldn't sleep. I was exhausted but unable to rest. I screamed at the top of my lungs, but all I received in return was an echo. Nothing could console me. I lived among the dead as one who could not die. I feared my torment would last forever … until one morning everything changed.

A fishing boat was being pulled ashore by what appeared to be a number of able-bodied fishermen. Fishing boats never came here. No one ever came ashore here! Everyone knew I was here – and they knew to avoid this place.

. . .

I saw a Man on the boat who appeared to be the leader. Suddenly, my demons rose up with a fury. For the first time, I could tell they were fearful – and their fear seemed to be directed toward that Man in the boat.

They compelled me to run toward Him – and it was the first time they made me do something I truly wanted to do. When I arrived at the boat, the demons forced me to bow before the Man. As I did, He said, *"Come out of the man, you evil spirit."*[1] Without my saying a word, this Man knew demons were living within me.

In reply, the demons screamed, *"Why are You interfering with me, Jesus, Son of the Most High God? In the name of God, I beg You, don't torture me!"*[2] They knew this Man's name – Jesus – and they were obviously afraid of Him.

Then Jesus demanded, *"What is your name?"*[3]

The demons replied, *"My name is Legion, because there are many of us inside this man."*[4] Then they begged Jesus not to send them out of me. I had given up hope years ago that I would ever be freed of these demons – but now I dared to hope.

The demons begged Him over and over not to send them to some distant place. Did my ears deceive me? It appeared that they were about to depart from me. The question was no longer if they would go – my relief was imminent! The only question was where would they go? And I, and they, knew Jesus was not going to permit them to enter someone else!

Not far away was a herd of two thousand pigs feeding on the hillside. *"Send us into those pigs,"* the demons begged. *"Let us enter them."*[5]

"Go!"[6] Jesus replied.

. . .

As I reflect back on that moment, I realize the demons knew who Jesus was. They knew He was the Son of the Most High God. They knew His power. They knew His mission. They knew the prophecies in Scripture that they would one day be judged by Him, and He would cast them into eternal damnation. They also knew the day of judgment had not yet come. So, when they asked to enter the pigs they thought they were entering into a safe place.

But demons can no more see into the future than you or I. They only knew what God had said through His prophets. Beyond that, they had no foreknowledge. So, when Jesus gave them permission to enter the pigs, they had no idea what was coming next! But Jesus did!

And that entire herd of pigs plunged into the lake and drowned!

Now, before you get too choked up over those pigs, think about how much Jesus must value me. He valued me over the lives of those pigs. That's how much He treasures all of us. Some time later, I learned that He loves me so much that He laid down His own life for me. That's how much He loves all of us and wants us to be free! Jesus not only freed me of the demons, and they were many, He forgave me of my sins – and they were many more.

Apparently, the herdsmen ran into Gergesa and told everyone what had just happened to their herd of pigs. The people came running to see for themselves, and soon a crowd had gathered.

They saw me sitting with Jesus. They knew I was the crazed man who was possessed by demons. Yet, here I was sitting fully clothed and perfectly calm! They couldn't understand what had happened and they became afraid. Soon they were pleading with Jesus to go away and leave them alone.

. . .

As Jesus began to make His way to the boat, I begged to go with Him. But He looked at me and said, *"No, go home to your family, and tell them everything the Lord has done for you and how merciful He has been."*[7]

So, I did what Jesus said. First, I went home to tell my parents. Then, over the months and years that followed, I visited all of the cities of the Decapolis and proclaimed the great things Jesus had done for me. Many, particularly those who had known me before, came to believe in Him.

The last time I saw Jesus was that day He departed on the boat. As I stood there watching Him sail away, I suddenly realized that He had traveled across the lake for the sole purpose of saving me. I realized that the One who had stood before me loved me so much that He had come for me – not only across a lake – but from heaven to earth. And He had given me a purpose – to tell everyone about Him!

~

DEBORAH – THE SUFFERING WOMAN

*M*y name is Deborah, and I am my parents' eldest daughter — their most favored daughter. They named me after the prophetess who served as the fourth judge of our nation over a thousand years ago, before kings reigned in Israel. She was a strong woman and a formidable leader who brought peace to the land by defeating the mighty Canaanite army led by their feared general, Sisera. My parents were hopeful I would emulate her strength, courage, and wisdom.

I grew up in the village of Magdala. Until Herod Antipas built the city of Tiberias, Magdala was the most important city on the western shore of the Sea of Galilee. My father was sent from Jerusalem to serve as the chief rabbi of our local synagogue by the high priest himself. It was a high honor and our family was well-respected in the community.

As a result, I enjoyed many privileges growing up. I never wanted for anything, including friends and companionship. Other girls sought me out and were honored to be my friends. My parents began to plan who my husband would be while I was still a child. It was difficult for them to identify a family they believed held the same social standing within our community. But eventually they chose Matthias, the son of a member of our local Sanhedrin.

. . .

Matthias's parents were equally concerned about their social standing and agreed that our betrothal would strengthen the position of both families. The announcement of our betrothal while Matthias and I were still teenagers was met with approval and celebration throughout the city. He and I were the most envied and considered to be without peer. We were to be married when I turned eighteen.

My mother planned every part of our wedding celebration with painstaking detail. It would be the major social event of our city for years to come. In many respects it was like a marvelous dream filled with the happiest of endings.

A few weeks before our planned wedding feast, I woke up to discover I was experiencing an unusual flow of blood. I screamed and called out to my mother. She assured me there was no reason to be alarmed, and it would pass in a few days. Her assurance gave me confidence. We decided that I just needed to rest. My mother cleaned my bed linens, my clothing, and helped me take added measures to contain my bleeding.

However, one week later, I continued to hemorrhage. My mother decided to call one of the village's trusted midwives to get her opinion on what we should do. The midwife prescribed an elaborate herbal remedy and promised me the bleeding would stop in a few days. However, those days passed but the bleeding did not!

My mother told my father what was happening, and he immediately sent word for the local physician to come. After the doctor learned how much blood I was passing and how long it had been taking place, he prescribed a different regimen of treatment.

In accordance with the law of Moses, I was considered unclean. Initially, I experienced the normal separation from others that was expected of a young woman during her cycle. But as my condition continued, my separation from others became more pronounced. I had not seen Matthias in over a month. My father kept his distance because he could not be deemed unclean by association. As a soon-to-be-married young woman, my days should have been filled with celebrations and joyful gatherings with friends. But instead, they had become days of isolation.

As my wedding day approached, our two families decided to postpone the ceremony. The physician's treatments were unsuccessful, and my condition had not improved. I began to hear whispers, when others thought I couldn't hear, that this must be a judgment from God for unconfessed sin.

My parents decided to send me to Jerusalem to see a respected and prominent physician. Surely, he would know how to treat me and put an end to my suffering. My father arranged for a cart and donkey to carry me there. My mother, the midwife who was helping to treat me, and several servants accompanied me. The seventy-mile journey was slow and arduous, and took us five days. I was terribly weak by the time we arrived.

The physician in Jerusalem initially gave me cause to hope. He was very knowledgeable and assured me he would diagnose my ailment and find a treatment that worked. But days turned into weeks and weeks became months. I was no better than when I first arrived in Jerusalem. The only thing that was beginning to lessen was the bag of money my father sent with my mother for my treatment.

While we were in the city, my mother went to the temple on multiple occasions to consult with the priests. We attempted to follow their spiritual remedies just as faithfully as we did the physicians' medical remedies – but again, with no success. Finally, my mother told me we had no more money, and we needed to return home.

As difficult as the journey had been to Jerusalem, at least then I was hopeful for a cure. Now as we returned to Magdala, I had no hope whatsoever. All my life I had been bubbly and vivacious, but now I was sullen and depressed. Six months had passed since my originally planned wedding date.

The day we arrived back in Magdala, Matthias's father and mother came to visit my parents. After hearing that my condition was unchanged, they decided the betrothal contract between Matthias and me needed to be canceled. My uncleanness prevented me from being an acceptable wife for their son. Though my parents attempted to dissuade them by asking for more time to find a cure, Matthias's parents were resolute. Though I had feared this outcome, hearing the decision was final shattered what remaining hope and spirit I had left. I had not seen Matthias since all of this began, and now I knew I would never see him again!

There was nothing more that could be done for me. We had attempted all of the possible remedies prescribed – both medical and spiritual. We had even tried all of the home remedies that were suggested. I can assure you that the effects of many of the remedies were worse than the illness itself.

As the months continued to pass, my condition took a toll on my family, as well. My parents and my siblings were losing their positions of stature in the community. There was talk that my father needed to step down as chief rabbi. Surely, my "uncleanness" was causing him to be unclean by association – and how could anyone abide the teaching and counsel of an unclean rabbi?

My parents never told me how they were being treated, but occasionally I would hear a whisper or witness a look. I realized that if I remained in their home, my entire family would suffer the effects. I knew I needed to be brave like the prophetess Deborah and take steps to protect my family. I announced that I was going to move to another town so they would no longer be saddled with the shame of my condition. At first my mother and father stringently objected, but eventually they saw the wisdom of my decision.

. . .

I decided to move to the village of Capernaum. It wasn't that far away, but it was far enough that I would be out of sight, and my family would no longer be weighed down by the constant reminder of my condition. Joy could return to their household, and I would live in a place where I was no longer under the critical eye of those who were certain I had committed some unforgivable sin.

My parents helped me find a small home in Capernaum and provided me with an ongoing stipend to help me afford my meager expenses. As required by our laws, I went to the chief rabbi in Capernaum – a man by the name of Nicodemus – and told him of my plight. He listened with a sympathetic ear. He told me that he had a daughter, and he would be just as brokenhearted as my parents if she suffered my condition.

But he went on to tell me what I already knew – that regrettably, no one in the village would be permitted to have direct contact with me. I would live as an outcast – but he would pray that Jehovah God would heal me and deliver me from my pain. I thanked him for his kindness but had little contact with him after that day.

He did send me word twice that he had heard of new remedies that were successful in other cases. He directed me to the village physician, but in both instances the remedies had no effect on me other than draining my already limited resources.

Rabbi Nicodemus moved away four years ago to take a position in Jerusalem, and Rabbi Jairus took his place as chief rabbi. Prior to this week, I have seen him on two occasions – but his response to me was the same as that of his predecessor.

Last week was my thirtieth birthday, but there was no celebration. The past twelve years have not been kind to me. My condition has not improved since the first day I fell ill. I have not experienced one day of relief; neither have I experienced one day of joy. I look like I am at least fifty years old.

. . .

I am alone. I have no friends. I have very limited contact with the people who live around me. Most of the people in the village don't even know I exist, with the exception of one young girl by the name of Ilana. She is the chief rabbi's daughter, and on more than one occasion she has extended kindness by leaving wildflowers at my door in an effort to cheer me up.

My parents continue to send money to provide for my needs, and on rare occasions my mother visits me. She would come more often, but I have discouraged it. I see myself as a burden to my parents and want to free them of their burden … and I want to free myself of the bondage of my continuing hopelessness.

I have decided to take my own life – tomorrow. I am making my final preparations. I know it will disgrace my family, but it will not be any greater than the disgrace I have already caused them. I pray they will forgive me and understand my choice.

As I was going over my plan, I heard excited voices outside my home. "Jesus is arriving!" they exclaimed. "Let's go see Him as He arrives!"

Jesus is quite the celebrity in our village. His mother lives here, as do other members of His family, though I have never met them. Even though I am sheltered from most of the outside world, I still have heard about Jesus. I have heard that He made the blind to see, the lame to walk, and even raised those who were dead to life. There have even been rumors that once, at His spoken word, a storm and the sea were stilled.

Suddenly, I wondered if I should follow the rest of those going to see Him on the shore. Could He possibly heal me? I had tried everything else, why not try Him? For the first time in many years, the faint flame of hope unexpectedly ignited in my heart. I covered myself so I would blend into the crowd. I did not want anyone to recognize me and point to me as unclean.

. . .

When I arrived at the shore, I saw that Rabbi Jairus was kneeling before Jesus. As I watched, the rabbi got up from his knees, and he and Jesus started walking toward the village. Jesus was obviously on important synagogue business. I wouldn't even be able to get close to Him. The crowd surrounding Jesus seemed impenetrable. How could I possibly get close enough to speak to Him? And besides, I am a nobody. I am just one of the many nameless, faceless, desperate people in the crowd.

But a voice in my head said, "What would the prophetess Deborah do? Would she resign herself to defeat, or would she step out in courage?" I suddenly knew I had to try. So, I mustered the little strength I had left, and began to press my way through the crowd. I was approaching Him from behind so I would be as inconspicuous as possible. Fortunately, the crowd was also pressing in front of Him and slowing down His progress. It was just enough that I was able to get near Him.

I decided He didn't even need to speak to me. I was convinced that all I needed to do was touch His garment. I was certain that would be enough to make me well. Jesus was my last hope! And I would not be deterred!

I continued to push forward until I was within inches of Jesus. I reached out my hand ... and gently touched His robe. Immediately, I knew I was healed! After twelve years of bondage to this illness, I knew I had been set free.

I stood still as the crowd moved around me and continued to press forward. I knew my quest was over. I had experienced the healing I had come to believe was no longer possible.

Then all of a sudden, Jesus stopped and turned around. His eyes met mine, and I heard Him say, "*Who touched My robe?*"[1] I saw one of His followers lean toward Him and say, "Master, *look at the crowd pressing in on You. How can You ask, 'Who touched My robe?'*"[2]

. . .

But I knew that He knew! With fear and trembling, I fell down before Him. As I looked up into His eyes, I saw a kindness, a gentleness, and compassion unlike anything I had ever witnessed. And I told Jesus what I had done and why.

But as I spoke, I had an overwhelming peace that Jesus already knew the answer. He had known before the day began that He would encounter me, and I would touch His garment. It was almost as if He had been waiting for my arrival. I may have thought I was just a face in the crowd, but I was now convinced that I had, in fact, been one of the reasons Jesus returned to Capernaum. He had prompted me to come see Him. He had ignited that ember of hope in my heart.

And when Jesus said to me, *"Daughter, your faith has made you well – go in peace – your suffering is over,"*[3] I walked away with more than just a physical healing. I walked away with my sins forgiven and my hope restored. In fact, I realized I had never truly been alone. He had seen me – and known me – and planned for this day right along!

Later that day, I traveled to my parents' home in Magdala and told them what Jesus had done. All they needed to do was take one look at me to know I had been healed. Joy and laughter had returned to my life ... and now my life would never be the same.

My parents wanted me to move back home and begin to rebuild my life. I thanked them for their kindness and their support, but I told them that Jesus had already rebuilt my life. I knew what I must do. I would go and follow the One who had stood before me and taken away my suffering by the mere touch of His robe.

∾

JAIRUS – THE FAITH-FILLED FATHER

J am Jairus, the chief rabbi of the synagogue here in Capernaum. I grew up right here on the shore of the Sea of Galilee. Many of the families in our village make their living from the sea, and though I am not one of them, I can't imagine living anywhere else!

I grew up under the teaching of Rabbi Nicodemus. He taught me to understand not only the letter of the law of Moses, but also the spirit. I learned that the heart of who we are as God's chosen people is clearly recited in the first two lines of the Shema prayer:

"Hear, O Israel: The Lord our God, the Lord is One. You shall love the Lord your God with all your heart and with all your soul and with all your might."

First and foremost, we are to love God … because He first loved us. Yes, He gave us the law, but He gave it to us because He loves us. We do not obey the law to earn His love; we obey His law because He loves us, and we love Him. Rabbi Nicodemus taught me that many of our people have lost sight that God's love is the foundation of His law. Therefore, many have turned the law from the blessing God intended into a burden and have taken the freedom He intended us to enjoy into enslavement.

.   .   .

Many of our people have lost their joy under a weight that God never intended, but that too many of our teachers have placed on us. I fear that too many of our religious leaders, particularly in Jerusalem, have chosen to corrupt the law into something that brings them greater power and greater profit. It is becoming difficult to see God in the midst of the burdens being placed upon His people.

I am, however, grateful that there are still men whom God has elevated to positions of authority and who hopefully will help us turn our eyes and hearts back to God. Rabbi Nicodemus is one of those men. I was honored to sit under his teaching, and I was honored that he recommended me to follow him as chief rabbi four years ago when he left to serve as a member of the Great Sanhedrin in Jerusalem. I pray that Jehovah God will enable me to lead as well as Rabbi Nicodemus.

Two years ago, a Man came to our synagogue for the first time. His mother, Mary, the widow of a carpenter named Joseph, had recently come to live in our village from the town of Nazareth. This Man, whose name I soon learned was Jesus, is Mary's eldest son. I'll never forget that first sabbath day when He arose to teach.

I handed Him the scroll containing the messages of the prophet Isaiah. He unrolled the scroll and found the place where this was written:

> "The Spirit of the Lord is upon Me,
> for He has anointed Me to bring Good News to the poor.
> He has sent Me to proclaim that captives will be released,
> that the blind will see,
> that the oppressed will be set free,
> and that the time of the Lord's favor has come."[1]

He rolled up the scroll, handed it back to me, and sat down. Every eye in the synagogue was fixed on Him, waiting for what He would say next. After a moment, He spoke these words: *"The Scripture you've just heard has been fulfilled this very day!"*[2]

. . .

He then proceeded to teach us many things about the One whose coming was prophesied by Isaiah. All who heard Him – including me – were amazed by His teaching and the authority with which He spoke. He had an understanding and recollection of the Scriptures that surpassed any teacher I had ever heard. And the words He spoke were words of life, quite unlike those of many of our teachers of religious law. None of us wanted Him to stop! We wanted to hear more. He told us we would ... another time.

Suddenly, a man possessed by a demon cried out, shouting, *"Go away! Why are You interfering with us, Jesus of Nazareth? Have You come to destroy us? I know who You are – the Holy One of God!"*[3]

But Jesus reprimanded him. *"Be quiet! Come out of the man!"*[4] He commanded. Immediately, the demon threw the man to the floor as those of us gathered in the synagogue watched; then it came out of him without hurting him any further.

Everyone was amazed, and many exclaimed, *"What authority and power this Man's words possess! Even evil spirits obey Him, and they flee at His command!"*[5] As you can imagine, the news about what Jesus had done quickly spread through our village and the surrounding villages. I knew I wanted to know more about this Man. His words and His actions were alive, and my spirit bore witness – they were truth!

A man named Simon was with Jesus that day, and apparently Jesus had renamed him Peter. I already knew Peter. His wife, Gabriella, had grown up here in Capernaum, and she and her daughters had recently come to live here with her mother now that Peter was traveling with Jesus. After Jesus left the synagogue that day, He went to the home of Peter's mother-in-law, whose name is Milcah. He invited me to walk with Him.

Peter's daughter, Sarah, had brought word to the synagogue that Milcah was very sick with a high fever. When Jesus arrived at the home, Gabriella begged, *"Please heal her."*[6] Jesus made His way to Milcah's bedside and looked down on her with compassion. But then He spoke sternly – not to her – but to the fever! He rebuked the fever … and immediately it was gone! Within moments her temperature returned to normal. Milcah arose from her bed as if she had not been sick and began to prepare a meal for her guests.

I stood there staring with my mouth open! In a matter of a few short hours, I had witnessed Jesus teaching in a way I had never known. I had seen Him cast out a demon in a way I had never seen. And now I had seen Him heal a woman with a mere word in a way I had never witnessed. Who *was* this Man? I needed to know!

About eight months later, a royal procession arrived in our village. It was King Herod's chamberlain, Chuza, and his wife, Joanna. His father and her parents lived in our village. At first, I thought they had simply come for a family visit. But soon I learned their ten-year-old son, Samuel, was ill with a high fever. They had come seeking Jesus.

They learned from Mary that He was expected any day, but He had not yet arrived. The last she had heard He and His followers were in Samaria near Sychar. They would be returning by way of Cana. Chuza decided to leave his wife and son here in the village and go out alone to meet up with Jesus. As I looked at young Samuel lying there on the bed, flushed with fever, I was reminded of how Jesus had merely spoken a word and Gabriella's mother had been healed! I knew that if Chuza was able to get Jesus back here in time, his son would also be healed!

But soon after noon the next day, there was still no sign of Chuza – or more importantly, Jesus. Samuel was about the same age as my own daughter, and I feared he would soon die. Jesus was going to be too late to save this young boy. I couldn't imagine the grief these parents would experience. I heard the boy gasp for what I was afraid was his last breath.

But suddenly, the boy began to stir. He sat up in bed as if nothing was wrong. The midwife, who had been there with his mother taking care of the child, checked and confirmed the boy's fever was gone! I looked around the room to see if Jesus had entered without notice – but He was not there. It was about one o'clock in the afternoon. Moments before, the boy had been at the threshold of death, but now he was acting as if he had never been sick! It was just like that day with Milcah! But, Jesus had not been here this time. What had happened?

It was the next day before we would learn from Chuza that Jesus had simply spoken the words there in Cana, *"Go back to your son. He will live!"*[7] He had spoken those words at the exact moment I heard Samuel gasp. Jesus had spoken, and a boy who was miles away had been healed!

Another day, not long after the incident with Samuel, Jesus was teaching and healing in the synagogue. I had never seen that many people gathered. There was no room to move in the synagogue, and people were standing outside straining to hear and get a glimpse of Jesus.

Several religious leaders had traveled from Jerusalem with Rabbi Nicodemus to witness the miracles and teachings of Jesus firsthand. The night before, Nicodemus had told me about a conversation he had with Jesus in Jerusalem several months earlier. He said he truly believed Jesus was the Messiah! My spirit bore witness to that same truth!

But the rest of the Pharisees and Sadducees who were traveling with Nicodemus did not share that belief. They had come to prove that He was a fraud, or perhaps one of Satan's demons. It was obvious these men feared Jesus – the same way the demon had feared Jesus that day in the synagogue.

As Jesus was speaking in the synagogue, I heard a noise overhead. Someone was removing some of the roof tiles. The hole grew larger and eventually we saw a man being lowered on a pallet by four other men. As it turned out, the man was paralyzed … that is, until Jesus said to him, *"Stand up, pick up your mat, and go home!"*[8]

·   ·   ·

The man did just as he was told. But Jesus didn't only heal the man's paralyzed legs, He told him his sins were forgiven. The religious leaders from Jerusalem sounded like a bunch of plucked roosters. They were the only ones standing in our crowded synagogue who did not believe Jesus was who He said He was! And I mean they were the *only* ones – because I, too, came to believe that He was the Messiah that day!

I am grateful that I have had many conversations with Jesus since then. I have been able to teach the Scriptures here in the synagogue in a way I previously did not understand. My eyes have been opened ... and so has my heart.

That brings me to today. Last evening my twelve-year-old daughter, Ilana, fell ill with a high fever. It was the same fever my wife and I had witnessed in others. Most of those people had died – except Milcah and Samuel. Jesus had healed them!

Jesus had been here before my daughter became ill, but then He and his disciples had departed by boat and crossed over the sea. Many of His followers had remained here in Capernaum, though, so I knew He would be returning soon. I continued to keep watch for Him. I knew He could heal my daughter!

Soon I began hearing an excited commotion in the street. I heard some of the people shouting, "Jesus is back! They are about to arrive on the shore!" I ran as fast as I could and got there just as He was stepping out of the boat. I fell at His feet and pleaded with Him – *"My little daughter is dying. Please come, lay Your hands on her and heal her so she can live."*[9]

Without saying a word, Jesus reached down, helped me to my feet, and the two of us began to make our way toward the village. Our progress, however, was slowed by the crowd pressing in on Jesus from all sides. We had not made it very far when Jesus abruptly stopped and asked, *"Who touched My robe?"*[10] I heard one of His disciples lean toward Him and say,

"Master, *look at the crowd pressing in on You. How can You ask, 'Who touched My robe?'*"[11]

As He and I both turned around, I saw a woman timidly kneel before him. As she looked up at Jesus, I saw it was Deborah. She had been afflicted with an issue of blood for many years. There had been nothing that anyone could do to help her. Even I had known her desperation and felt sorry for her when she came to me for help. I had none to give. But Jesus did! I could see that she had just been healed. My heart truly wanted to rejoice with her. But my mind was focused on my daughter. I wanted Jesus to turn and make haste with me, but He was ministering to this broken woman before Him.

While Jesus was still speaking to Deborah, messengers arrived from my home. Taking me aside, they told me, *"Your daughter is dead. There's no use troubling the Teacher now."*[12] It was too late for Jesus to do anything! I knew He could have saved her, but now it was too late.

But Jesus overheard the messengers, took me by the arm, and said, *"Don't be afraid. Just have faith."*[13] Then He stopped the crowd and told them to remain on the shore. He invited only a few of His disciples to come with us.

When we arrived at my home, Jesus saw the weeping and wailing of the people who had gathered to mourn. As we walked inside, Jesus asked, *"Why all this commotion and weeping? The child isn't dead; she's only asleep."*[14]

The people in my home looked at one another and then laughed at Jesus. I knew many in the crowd had not seen Him perform the miracles I had seen. But they had heard!

As Jesus looked at them, their laughter stopped and turned into an uncomfortable silence. Because of their faithlessness, He told them all to leave my home. Afterward, Jesus walked with my wife and me, together with the disciples who had accompanied Him, into the room where my daughter was lying. Then He took her hand in His, and said to her, *"Little girl, get up!"*[15]

Immediately, she sat up! Just like Milcah had and just like Samuel had! It was as if nothing had ever happened. Ilana stood and began to walk around! She walked to her mother and me and gave us both hugs. Then she hugged Jesus. I cannot begin to describe my feelings or those of my wife.

Jesus could not only heal those who were sick, and enable the lame to walk, He could restore life to those who were dead. Some would later say that my daughter wasn't really dead, she was only asleep. I suggest they talk to us or any of those who mistakenly laughed at Jesus that day.

My wife and I were filled with inexpressible gratitude when Jesus told us to give Ilana something to eat. The crowd that laughed earlier was so dumbfounded to see our daughter walking about they just stood in silence.

It wasn't until later that I recalled the fact that Deborah had been ill for twelve years. And my daughter had been struck dead of fever at the age of twelve. The Father had permitted both so that He might be glorified through the Son. It was a reminder that neither time nor distance can ever limit Jesus from bringing glory to the Father.

Though Jesus gave us "strict orders" not to tell anyone what had happened, there was no way it would remain a secret. Everyone in our village knew that day that the One who stood before me is the only One who has the last word over death.

∾

JONATHAN – THE BOY WHO GAVE WHAT HE HAD

*M*y name is Jonathan and I am ten years old. My parents and I live in the village of Chorazin in northern Galilee. It is a smaller village than most, with about one hundred families calling it home. I have lived here all of my life. Most of the buildings in our village were built using a black volcanic rock that is found nearby. It gives Chorazin a very different appearance. Everything is a beautiful color of ebony!

The village is surrounded by groves of olive trees. My dad once told me that some of the trees date back to the days when our patriarch Abraham was a boy my age. Those trees produce the finest-tasting olives you have ever eaten! Many of the families in our village make their living from those olives. The olives of Chorazin and the olive oil they produce are traded far and wide throughout the region.

Our family is one of the few families that doesn't earn its living from the olives. My dad is a shepherd. He raises sheep and goats. Just recently, he began to let me help him shepherd the flock. But that wasn't always the case!

. . .

You see, I am actually my parents' third child. Both of my older brothers were stillborn. My parents named my oldest brother Samuel, and our middle brother David. Though they never lived outside of my mother's womb, we remember them always. Each year we recognize their birthdays and I think about what they would be doing at this age. I would have liked to have known my older brothers. I would have liked to play with them, confide in them, and learn from them. My parents and I talk about the day when we will all be together in heaven. I so look forward to that day!

My mother tells me that she and my father named me Jonathan because it means "God has given," and they knew I was His gift to them. They tell me I brought joy back into their home and their hearts.

I was just a few months old when they discovered that I was deaf. Some of our well-meaning neighbors asked if God was punishing them for unconfessed sin in their lives. I don't think they meant to hurt my parents, but I know they did.

Despite being sad over my deafness, my parents never looked at me without a smile on their faces and joy in their eyes. I have never known a day without love – and I am so grateful to Jehovah God for His goodness to me!

While I was still very young, my mother began to teach me signs I could make with my hands so we could communicate. The first words she taught me were "I love you!" As time passed, my vocabulary of signs became pretty extensive. Sometimes it was fun knowing that no one else understood what my parents and I were saying to each other … but other times it was hard. The other boys in our village never wanted to play with me. Often when we were with other people, I would see them talking together and so wish I knew what they were saying. I did learn some words by reading lips, but I wasn't very good at it. And since I couldn't hear, I couldn't speak, so it made it difficult when I was around other people.

. . .

I spent all of my time growing up in the company of my parents. One or both of them was always with me. On a few occasions, my dad took me with him as he watched over the sheep, but he was always afraid that something might happen to me while his attention was directed elsewhere. Since I couldn't call out to him, and he couldn't call out to me, he thought it would be safer if I stayed home with my mom.

Not too long ago, two strangers came to our village. They told everyone they were followers of a Man named Jesus. My parents told me that one of the men stood up in our synagogue and talked about this Jesus. Many of our people had heard of Him. Some said He had made the deaf to hear, the blind to see, and the lame to walk. It was even said that He had restored life to the dead. My mom told me that the prophet Isaiah had long ago written about a Man who would come and do these things. The man who spoke in the synagogue said that Jesus was that Man!

My parents talked all that day and night about whether Jesus could restore my hearing. My dad wasn't sure. He didn't want me, or them, to be disappointed again. But my mom decided they needed to find out! So, the next morning, after my dad had taken the sheep and goats into the hills to pasture, she took me to our neighbor's home.

The two followers of Jesus, whom I later learned were Shimon and Simon, were staying with our neighbor. My mother asked them if Jesus could heal me so I could hear. She explained that I had never heard a bird sing, or the sound of the wind when it blows, or even the sound of her voice. She asked, "What do I need to do so that my son can hear?"

Shimon began to talk to her. I had no idea what he was saying, but I later learned he was explaining that Jesus had sent the two of them to our village. He apparently had sent other men out in pairs to other villages, too. He told them to preach the Good News and heal in His name. Shimon told my mother he would pray and ask God to bring hearing to my ears.

· · ·

I saw a tear trickle down my mother's cheek as she gently placed her hand on my shoulder and directed me to walk toward the man. I didn't know what he was going to do, but I trusted my mother – so I trusted this man. He placed his hands over my ears. I looked up and could see that he was speaking. At first it was just silence, but then something happened!

All of a sudden there was something different taking place. I couldn't describe it at the time, but I was actually hearing sounds – and those sounds I now know were words. Though I couldn't understand him then, the man was saying, "... Father, we ask You to unblock his ears and enable him to hear so that he and his parents, and others in this village might believe on Your Son, Jesus Christ of Nazareth."

As he took his hands away, I immediately raised my hands to my ears. I was experiencing a new sensation! For the first time in my life I could hear! I didn't fully realize it yet, but God had given me hearing ... for His glory and the glory of His Son! I looked at my mother with excitement. I didn't know any words to speak, so I told her with signs, "I can hear!" Then she spoke to me. She spoke my name, "Jonathan!" I had never heard anyone speak my name. I had never heard my mother's voice ... until that moment!

Tears flowed down my mother's cheeks as she and I embraced for a long time. Meanwhile, the two men and our neighbors were shouting and giving glory to God! And quickly the news spread throughout the village! My mother and I left to find my father. As we ran toward him on the hill, my mother shouted to him, "He can hear! Jonathan can hear! God has given him hearing!" My dad looked at me in disbelief, but when he saw the smile on my face, he wrapped his arms around me, drew me close, and shouted heavenward, "Thank You, God!"

Later that day I went to find the man who had prayed for me. I wanted to know more about the Jesus who had enabled me to hear. Even though I could now hear sounds, I didn't understand what most of them were. That would take some time for me to learn – but my parents and others would teach me.

. . .

The two men remained in the village for two more days. I now understood that the man who had prayed for me was named Shimon. I learned to say his name – after I first learned to say "Mama" and "Papa!" And then I learned to say "Jesus!" I remained close to Shimon for his remaining time in our village. Though I did not understand most of his words, my heart told me that he was speaking truth.

Before they left Chorazin, Shimon again prayed for me. This time he asked God to make me into one of His mighty men – one God would use to lead others to salvation and to bring great glory to His name. If I had understood what Shimon was praying, I would have told him that Jehovah God had already begun to do that! As they left, Shimon told me he would see me again!

A few days later, I was on the hill watching our flock with my dad. He was teaching me how to be a shepherd, and we were learning how to talk to each other using words. Off in the distance, my dad and I spotted a large crowd gathering in the valley. Just a little way up the hill from the crowd was a Man who appeared to be speaking to them. Everyone in the crowd was paying close attention. My dad said we were going to lead the flock closer to Him so we could hear what He was saying, too.

As we got closer, I noticed a group of men standing near the Teacher. Suddenly, I realized that one of the men was Shimon! I began to wave to get his attention. I knew he saw me when he waved back! I asked my father for permission to go see him. My dad said, "Yes, but stay in a place that I can see you and you can see me. And take your sack of food with you!" With that, I was off as quickly as I could run. When I arrived by his side, Shimon waved at my dad to let him know I was there and he would keep an eye on me.

As we sat in the grass, I asked him if the Man speaking was Jesus. He smiled and nodded. I didn't truly understand most of what Jesus was saying. Shimon was able to explain a little bit to me. But I was just happy to be sitting with Shimon and listening to Jesus's voice.

As the afternoon continued, a few of Jesus's followers approached Him and said, "*Send the crowd away to the nearby villages and farms, so they can find food and lodging for the night. There is nothing to eat here in this remote place.*"[(1)]

But His followers were surprised when Jesus said, "*That isn't necessary, you feed them.*"[(2)] Even I could understand that! But what exactly was Jesus planning to feed them?

I looked at the crowd, and then I looked at Shimon and said, "That's a lot of people to feed!" I may not know all of my words, but I knew my numbers, and it would take a lot of food to feed them.

Jesus turned to one of the men and asked, "*Where can we buy bread to feed all these people?*"[(3)] The man replied, "*We'd have to work for months to earn enough money to buy food for all of them!*"[(4)] The man seemed to be a bit put off when Jesus immediately responded, "Don't look at what you don't have. Look to see what the Father has already given you. *How much bread do you have? Go and find out.*"[(5)]

While Jesus and the man were talking, I tugged on Shimon's sleeve and showed him the food my mother had placed in my sack. Though I couldn't understand everything that was being said, I had a pretty good idea, and I wanted to help any way I could.

Shimon turned to another one of Jesus's followers and showed him that I was offering to give all I had. The man called out to Jesus and said, "*There's a young boy here with five barley loaves and two fish. But what good is that with this huge crowd?*"[(6)]

· · ·

I didn't wait to hear Jesus's answer. I stood up and walked over to give Him my small sack of food. I wasn't thinking about how little I had. I wasn't thinking about how little it was compared to the great need. I just knew that I owed Him everything I had. As I handed the sack to Jesus, I looked into His eyes. He looked back at me with an expression that was both tender and welcoming. I knew He would know what to do with the food in my sack. He smiled and thanked me as He took the sack from me.

After Jesus received my food, He looked at His followers and said, "*Truly, I say to you, unless you turn and become like children, you will never enter the Kingdom of heaven. Whoever humbles himself like this child is the greatest in the Kingdom of heaven.*"[7]

As I stood there at His side, Jesus said to His followers, "*Tell everyone to sit down.*"[8] Once they had been seated, Jesus lifted the sack toward heaven and gave thanks to the Father for the food ... and for my faith. He then began to break the loaves into pieces, giving the pieces to each one of His followers to distribute to the people. They continued to carry the bread from Jesus to the people until everyone had received enough.

Then Jesus did the same with the fish. After everyone had eaten until they were full, He said, "*Now gather the leftovers, so that nothing is wasted.*"[9]

They filled twelve baskets to the brim with the leftover pieces of bread and fish. As the twelve baskets were set side by side, I looked up at Jesus and smiled. Yes, He had known exactly what to do! And I knew from that moment that I always would trust Him! Jesus wrapped His arm around me and told me He was proud of me. He told me that I had shown everyone there what it meant to have faith. And He told me to continue to trust Him by faith.

Just before He directed me to return to Shimon's side, He said, "Tell your parents that Samuel and David are fine. The Father is watching over them, just like He is watching over you. You will see your brothers one day, and they will see you and your parents. It will be a great day of celebration! And I will be there as well. Until then, Jonathan, follow Me!"

Shimon and Simon walked me back to rejoin my father on the hill with our flock. They carried two of the baskets of bread and fish and gave them to my father for our family. Though my dad had seen what took place from a distance, he was still overwhelmed to see and receive the baskets of food. Shimon told him that Jesus's miracle had all begun with my unselfish act. And he said everyone had learned from me that day. Then he said goodbye and returned to join the rest of the followers of Jesus.

I don't know when I will see Shimon again or when I will next see Jesus. But I know that I will. It may not be in Chorazin; it may be in heaven, with Samuel and David. Because the One who stood before me – the One who gave me the gift of hearing and so much more – also gave me a promise. And I will trust Him with all that I have … and all that I am.

∼

MARTHA – THE DILIGENT HOSTESS

$\mathcal{M}$y name is Martha. Many of you know me as the sister of Simon (whom most of you know as Lazarus), and Miriam, whom some of you call Mary. I am the firstborn child of our father, Jephunneh, and our mother, Mirella.

You may recall that our father built our home here in the heart of Bethany soon after my brother was born. Papa was a successful vintner who expanded the production of his vineyards through the purchase of land, as well as pioneering horticultural techniques that were adopted by other vineyards throughout our region. He was well respected in our community.

My mother often told me that I inherited his intelligence, his industriousness, and his temperament. Though Papa was slow to give compliments, my mother often told me how proud he was of me, and I always strived to live up to that praise.

But I also knew I would never be my father's heir – no matter how capable I might be. I would never be able to direct our family's vineyards. Our customs and our laws would never permit it. So, my father continued to pray for a son – a son who would be his heir and ensure that the family business and our family home would remain in our possession. Jehovah God answered my father's prayers and my brother, Simon, was born when I was ten years old.

Four years later our sister was born. It was a day of great joy overshadowed by great sorrow. We were delighted by the birth of a precious baby but overwrought by the death of our mother during childbirth. I was assisting the midwife in the delivery of my sister, so I was there in the room with my mother. After giving birth, my mother began hemorrhaging and the midwife was unable to stop it. My mother died even before my father was introduced to his baby daughter.

A day that began with the joy of birth ended with the grief of a funeral processional. My father named my sister Miriam, which means "sea of sorrow," because of the circumstances surrounding her birth. From that day forward, Miriam held a special place in my father's heart because she was the last gift his precious Mirella had given him. Even to this day, her birthday is a bittersweet day in our household – we celebrate life and we remember death.

For me, that day signaled a coming of age. I became the matriarch of our family. It became my job to care for my four-year-old brother, my infant sister, and my grieving father. I quickly became grateful for not only the abilities I inherited from my father, but also the strength I inherited from my mother.

As the years passed, my father never gave much thought to arranging a marriage for me. And truth be told, I didn't either. My life was filled with caring for my family and running our household. Ours is one of the more prominent families in Bethany so we are expected to host important social gatherings. My father quickly learned he could entrust the planning and oversight of those events to me. The financial success of our vineyards enables us to employ a few servants to assist me – and I am grateful for their help!

· · ·

Ten years ago this week, Papa died. He was usually the second person to arise each morning; I was the first. But on that particular day the entire household was awake and moving around. I sent one of the servants to check on my father. He appeared to have died peacefully in his sleep. The physician told me that my father's heart had just stopped beating. Though I grieved his loss, I knew he was reunited with my mother. Our family has always believed in the resurrection of the dead – and at times like this that brings us great comfort.

My brother was nineteen years old when he became the patriarch of our family. Our father knew that Simon did not have his ability for business, so Papa had long ago hired an overseer to direct the day-to-day affairs. He is a trustworthy man with a son named Amari, who is the same age as my brother and has grown up as part of our family. My brother's transition into his new responsibilities was easy thanks to my father's wisdom. I was grateful for my father's foresight and careful planning.

Simon modeled our father's example and assumed his role as a prominent man in the village. As time passed, Amari's father said it was time for him to step down as overseer. Amari would now step into the role, but his father would be available to guide him when needed. Each man played his part. Gratefully, Jehovah God enabled us to walk through a difficult time with grace and strength.

That is, until the night Simon announced he had leprosy. Of all of the tragic events we had suffered, this was the most devastating. Simon was twenty-five years old. As he walked away from our home that night, we feared he would never return. In many respects, leprosy is worse than death. It separates you from everyone who loves you. You are an outcast from society. And your days are filled with hopelessness and desperation, as are the days of your loved ones.

Miriam and I knew our lives would never be the same. How could they be? Our brother was destined to suffer and die, and all we could do was make sure he had food, clothing, and a mat to sleep on. We were permitted to visit him from a distance, but we weren't able to touch him or console him. And he even discouraged us from visiting. He wanted to be sure we didn't contract the disease ourselves.

Almost immediately, many in our village began avoiding us. Those we had called friends no longer extended even a common courtesy. Though we knew their actions were driven by fear, we felt unwelcome in our own hometown. We felt like strangers in our synagogue and were avoided in the marketplace. Invitations to our home were refused, and we no longer received invitations to the homes of others. In some ways, we felt as isolated as Simon.

I also realized that when my brother died, the ownership of our home and vineyards would pass to another male relative. Miriam's and my futures would be in question. We had no idea how another relative would treat us. We could lose everything.

For two years, Miriam and I prayed for our brother every day from morning to night. We asked Jehovah God to heal him and to restore him to us. We prayed, believing that God could heal him if He so chose. We asked Him to have mercy on our brother … and on us. But each time we were able to see Simon, his condition had worsened. We feared the end was near.

One afternoon, one of our servants announced that Amari was at the door. He was bringing a message about Simon. I walked slowly to the door because I dreaded what he would say. I did not want to hear that my brother had died. The longer I delayed in hearing the news, the longer he would be alive in my heart.

Miriam and I arrived at the door at the same time. But to our surprise, Amari was excited, not mournful. "Your brother has been healed by Jesus of Nazareth!" he exclaimed. "Simon is here outside of the village! He has instructed me to carry a message to Phinehas the priest that arrangements should be made for Simon to present an offering in eight days in accordance with the law. He will be declared clean on that day! He told me to tell you that you cannot see him until then – but you will see him on that day!

"He also told me to tell you two more things. First, Jesus told him to tell you, 'The Father has heard and answered your prayers!' Second, Jesus has given Simon a new name. He now will be called 'Lazarus' because God has helped him and healed him!"

We could not believe our ears! Our brother was not only alive, he was healed! God truly had answered our prayers. Before the day was done, Miriam and I had already planned a great party we would host to celebrate the return of our brother. It would be unlike any celebration the people of Bethany had ever seen – and the invitation list would include everyone – even those who had shunned us!

A few weeks later, we received word that Jesus had arrived in Bethany. He was coming to see Lazarus. As soon as we heard the news, our brother ran to greet Him, and Miriam and I followed close behind. When we got to Jesus, the two men were embracing. Miriam got there just a few steps ahead of me and immediately fell to her knees before Him. She began to kiss the hem of His garment.

When I arrived, I bowed my head before Him and gave Him thanks. He reached out and lifted my head, turning my eyes toward His. Then He did the same to Miriam. I had never had anyone look at me like that. His gaze put me at peace. I felt like every weight I had ever carried had just been lifted. I felt unconditional acceptance – not because of anything I had done. And for the first time in my life, I wasn't thinking about the next thing I had to do. Time seemed to stand still!

Lazarus broke the silence and introduced Miriam and me to Jesus – though I don't think any of us required an introduction. I knew that He knew me even better than I knew myself! Then Lazarus invited Jesus and all of His followers to come to our home to dine. I quickly assessed the crowd and realized I was about to host fifty people! And for the first time, I wasn't stressed over the thought.

That was the first of many times Jesus came to our home. He would always be welcome, if for no other reason than the fact He healed our brother. But as time passed, we realized there were so many more reasons. He became our Teacher. He became our Lord. He became our Friend.

Most of the time we didn't know when Jesus would arrive. He would show up at our doorstep. Believe it or not, that didn't bother me. Whether He came with a handful of people or a hundred, He was always welcome in our home.

Such was the case last night. Lazarus was in Jerusalem attending to business, so that meant Miriam and I would not only serve Jesus and His followers, we would be their hosts. There were about eighty people with Him this time. I sent one of the servants to slaughter a sheep, another to gather vegetables from the garden, and another to begin baking bread.

As the oldest, the responsibility of host would primarily fall to me. I made sure Jesus and our other guests were all comfortable and their needs were being met. I looked in on the servants to make certain dinner preparations were well underway. There were a lot of details for me to balance!

From the moment Jesus sat down, Miriam was kneeling at His feet. That's what she usually did when Jesus came to visit. It was how she expressed her gratitude, servitude, and affection. But usually Lazarus was there to host Jesus, and I was able to concentrate on serving Him.

This evening, however, I needed Miriam's help. As the evening progressed, I approached Jesus and said, *"Lord, doesn't it seem unfair to You that my sister just sits here while I do all the work? Tell her to come and help me.*"[1]

I thought Jesus would be supportive of my plight, so I was surprised when He replied, "*My dear Martha, you are worried and upset over all these details! There is only one thing worth being concerned about. Mary has discovered it, and it will not be taken away from her.*"[2]

His words felt like a knife to my heart. Was He not appreciative of all my hard work and the love I was expressing for Him through my service? I wanted His experience as our honored guest to be the best it could possibly be.

But as I looked in His eyes, I remembered that first day I had met Him. I remembered how I felt in His presence, and I realized that He wasn't belittling my efforts, rather He was reminding me that my work on His behalf must never become a substitute for spending time with Him. My work must always flow out of my time with Him.

It was an important lesson for me to learn. I can't say that I have fully mastered it. But the Master is always gracious to remind me. Whenever I am struggling, I think back to the day when the One who stood before me showed me that He loves me not because of what I have done, but because I am His.

∼

REUBEN – THE RICH YOUNG RULER

$\mathcal{I}$ am Reuben, the oldest of my father's six sons, and I grew up in Jerusalem. My father is a member of the Great Sanhedrin – a position he has held since I was a mere boy. He serves that grand body as its treasurer, overseeing the finances of the temple. His position has not only provided him with great influence among our people, it has also brought him great wealth.

He is a contemporary and confidant of our former high priest, Annas, and together they crafted many ways to increase the temple treasury – which also brought them personal gain. Their relationship dates back to their early years in rabbinical school and blossomed into a strong, lifelong alliance.

I was educated by the finest scholars among the most elite and brightest minds our people had to offer. I never knew "want," as I always had whatever I desired. One of those desires was my wife, Rebekah. She is the eldest child of another one of the leaders of our Great Sanhedrin. Our fathers determined while Rebekah and I were young that we would wed. The marriage of their two eldest children would create a powerful alliance of two leading families!

. . .

When Rebekah grew up to become the most beautiful young woman in Jerusalem, there was no denying that Jehovah God had richly blessed me! Our families arranged for us to own one of the grandest homes in our city – located next door to the palace of the high priest. God had not yet blessed us with children, but we were still young and looked forward to those days. Truly, we were counted among those who were the most blessed by God!

Ever since I was a young boy, I studied the law and was considered to be one of the leading experts. Over the years, I was frequently called upon by the high priest Caiaphas to provide counsel to the Great Sanhedrin as they deliberated the weighty issues brought before them.

My desire, though, was not just to be an authority on the law but also to honor God through my obedience of His law. Rebekah and I always strived to be models of godly living before our friends and neighbors. I presented my gifts regularly into the treasury of the temple – not only because my father is the treasurer, but also because I knew it honors God and displays righteous living. I took great care to make certain others were watching me as I presented my gifts so they could be challenged by my example.

And I was equally attentive to the needs of the poor. As a matter of fact, there was a beggar who took up residence at the gate to my home. He suffered from open sores that covered his body. He was the most pathetic man I had ever seen. I instructed my servants to provide him with scraps from our table three times each week so he would not starve. After all, I knew that God would have me do no less. King Solomon himself wrote, *"He that is gracious to the poor honors God."*[1] Rebekah told me not long ago that she had instructed our servants to give the man one of my cast-off robes to cover his body. Truly, we were seeking to live uprightly before the law.

Recently, I heard of a Teacher from Nazareth who is traveling throughout the hills of Galilee performing miracles and teaching from the Scriptures. I was told He teaches in a way that seems not only to be astounding the masses but also some of my more learned brethren. He has taught in the courtyard of the temple during some of the feast days, but each time I was prevented from hearing Him due to more pressing affairs.

A while back, two of the members of the Sanhedrin – Nicodemus of Capernaum and Joseph of Arimathea – were espousing some of this Teacher's sayings to their brethren in the council. Though their words were not well received by the other members, I was intrigued. I felt this Man, whose name is Jesus, may have something worthy of consideration.

One of my favorite pastimes when I was together with other scholars and scribes was to debate questions such as, "Which is the greatest commandment?" or "What must we do to be certain that we have eternal life?" I had been debating questions like those since I was in school, but I had never heard a definitive or authoritative answer. As I listened to Nicodemus, it sounded like Jesus may have the answers I was seeking.

I knew Jesus would soon be returning to Jerusalem for the upcoming feast. Ironically, some of the priests were discussing ways they might entrap Him the next time He appeared in the temple. They were crafting questions in such a way that no matter how He answered them, He would either lose favor with the crowds or incriminate Himself before the Roman authority. Either way, they felt they would win. But I did not want to collaborate with that group. I also didn't want to wait until the Teacher came to Jerusalem. If this Jesus had the answers I was seeking, I would go and find Him!

Rebekah did not want me to make the journey to see Jesus. She told me I should wait until He returned to Jerusalem. But she also knew my mind was made up. I told her I would only be gone for a few days. As I passed through the gate to leave my home, I noticed my dogs were licking the place where the beggar usually sat. They were known to lick his open sores each day. I asked one of my servants where the man had gone. He told me that he had died. I wasn't truly saddened by the news, rather I received it matter-of-factly. I found myself thinking that upon my return home, I would instruct my servants to find another beggar to assist, so I could continue to honor my obligation to help the poor.

I learned that Jesus was currently teaching outside of Bethabara on the east side of the Jordan, so I set off in that direction to see Him. When I arrived, He was surrounded by children. Apparently, their parents had brought them to Him asking that He bless them. I heard Him say, *"The Kingdom of God belongs to those who are like these children. I tell you the truth, anyone who doesn't receive the Kingdom of God like a child will never enter it."*[(2)]

That was exactly what I had come to talk to Him about! As I approached Jesus, I knelt down. I was aware some of the other religious leaders had already come to see Jesus before me. Their purpose was to entrap Him. But mine was to sincerely seek out this Teacher with the hope He would give me some answers.

"Good Teacher, what must I do to inherit eternal life?"[(3)] I said.

It took me by surprise when Jesus responded by saying, *"Why do you call Me good?"* Then He went on to say, *"Only God is truly good."*[(4)]

In addressing Jesus as "Good Teacher," I was using a title of respect. It was the same title I had always used to address other mentors and teachers whom I greatly admired. But this was the first time anyone questioned my motives!

Without waiting for a reply, Jesus went on to say, *"You know the commandments: 'You must not murder. You must not commit adultery. You must not steal. You must not testify falsely. You must not cheat anyone. Honor your father and mother.'"*[(5)]

.   .   .

I will confess that I was relieved after hearing His answer. I was expecting something much greater. I confidently replied, *"I've obeyed all these commandments since I was young."*[6]

But it was Jesus's follow-up statement that radically altered the rest of our conversation. *"Go and sell all your possessions,"* He said, *"and give the money to the poor, and you will have treasure in heaven. Then come, follow Me."*[7]

"What!?!" I thought. "Sell all of my possessions!?!"

I quickly thought back through all of the law – starting with the Ten Commandments. Jesus had just asked me about each of the last six commandments – and I could honestly say I had honored those! And the first four commandments had nothing to do with selling all of my possessions, they simply had to do with loving and honoring God with our whole heart, soul, and mind. What does that have to do with selling all of my possessions?

Surely, Jesus didn't understand how much I possessed! It's one thing to say that to a poor man who has very little, but I possessed great wealth. And I was using that wealth to help others – like my offerings at the temple and my gifts to the man at my gate!

God had blessed me with great wealth. Apparently, I deserved it. Surely, He would not have me squander it by selling it all! And what would Rebekah say if I went home and told her I was going to sell our beautiful home? Or what would our parents say about this preposterous idea? They would certainly declare that I had lost all reason!

I came seeking a good answer from this Teacher, and He told me to do something that was impossible! He was asking too much! I was willing to do whatever was necessary – within reason. But how could Jesus possibly ask me to sell all that I possessed? Surely, a good and loving God would never ask that of me. I desired to honor God – but that was a price greater than I was willing to pay!

No one ever considered me to be a sinner. I was always considered to be a good man. I was confident my good works would be sufficient to merit favor with God. Sadly, I turned and walked away. I had come to Jesus for an answer, but He had given me one I could not accept. Perhaps He was not as good of a teacher as I had been led to believe. As I turned, I caught one last glimpse of Him. I saw sadness in His eyes as He looked at me. But He didn't plead with me or say anything further. He had given me His answer and was leaving the response to me.

As I walked away, I decided I would return home through Jericho. At this time of year, the city was always a pleasant respite from the worries of life. Undoubtedly, I would encounter friends who were also there on holiday. It would give me time to recover from the emptiness I felt as a result of my conversation with Jesus.

But as I approached the city, I was stopped by bandits. The ringleader, who the others referred to as Barabbas, demanded all of my possessions. I couldn't help but think that his request was somewhat ironic in light of what Jesus had just said. Everyone was telling me to surrender all I had!

But in this bandit's case, he was threatening me with bodily harm if I did not heed his demand. At least Jesus had made no such threat. I emptied my pockets of all my coins. Then he told me to surrender the ring on my finger. My father had given me that ring – and it was one of my most prized possessions. I refused.

The blade in the bandit's hand did its work quickly and silently. I was dead before my body hit the ground. Instantly, my soul was transported from my body to a place that was unfamiliar. I was surrounded by fire, listening to great wailing and gnashing of teeth. Despair and anguish were palpable. I realized I was not in a place of eternal reward. My greatest fear had been realized. I was in a place of eternal death and suffering, and hopelessness overtook me.

But in the midst of my torment, I looked into the distance and saw a much different place. I was sitting in complete darkness, but that place seemed to be surrounded by light. I squinted my eyes to see more clearly, and I recognized the beggar who had been by my gate. He was resting in the arms of another man. Though I had never seen that man, somehow, I knew he was our father Abraham – the patriarch of us all! Abraham was giving rest to the beggar!

I cried out, *"Father Abraham, have some pity! Send* the beggar *over here to dip the tip of his finger in water and cool my tongue. I am in anguish in these flames."*[8]

But Abraham replied, *"Son, remember that during your lifetime you had everything you wanted, and* this beggar *had nothing. So now he is here being comforted, and you are in anguish. And besides, there is a great chasm separating us. No one can cross over to you from here, and no one can cross over to us from there."*[9]

I called back in desperation. *"Please, Father Abraham, at least send him to my father's home. For I have five brothers, and I want him to warn them, so they don't end up in this place of torment."*[10]

Abraham responded, *"Moses and the prophets have warned them. Your brothers can read what they wrote."*[11]

But I knew my father and my brothers were unconvinced, just as I had been, so I said, *"No, Father Abraham! But if someone is sent to them from the dead, then they will repent of their sins and turn to God."*[12]

. . .

To my great sadness, Abraham replied, *'If they won't listen to Moses and the prophets, they won't be persuaded even if someone rises from the dead.'*[13]

At that moment, the words of Jesus came back to me. He had answered me, and I had refused to accept His answer. My good works would never be good enough. I could never do enough to inherit eternal life because human effort cannot please God. The beggar had entered into eternal life because He had believed in Jesus and trusted Him with *all* of his heart. I, however, had been unwilling to give Him the one possession He required of me – my heart!

I wished I could return to the One who stood before me that day and receive the promise of eternal life He extended. But there was no going back! I had chosen my riches over Jesus … and now the sadness in His eyes would remain with me forever.

~

HEPZIBAH – THE ADULTERESS

$\mathcal{M}$y name is Hepzibah and I grew up as the only child of a shopkeeper here in Jerusalem. My mother was struck with the fever and died when I was four years old. In many respects, my father died at the same time. He blamed God for my mother's death and would no longer speak of Him. We never again observed any of the religious feasts, attended synagogue, or went to the temple.

Love died in our home that day as well. No longer were there any expressions of affection. Don't misunderstand me, my father never treated me badly; he just never again expressed any love for me in any way. He became very cold and distant. The last hug I ever remember receiving was from my mother before she fell ill.

I don't think my father stopped caring about me, but I believe his heart broke so deeply that he lost his capacity to love. Perhaps he was trying to protect his heart from ever again feeling such pain. I attempted to ask him about it a few times, but he would simply look off into the distance and walk away. I eventually stopped asking. When I tried to express my love for him, it was rejected. So, I grew up desiring love and affection, but it was never requited.

. . .

My father never thought about arranging a marriage for me. I don't know why. Maybe it was because his marriage had ended so tragically. As the years passed – and I got older and older – I tried to talk to him about it, but he just shrugged me off. I was still living in a cold, empty house with my father when I was in my early twenties.

Each of my days pretty much looked the same. I kept my father's house, cleaned and mended his clothes, and prepared his meals. The highlight of each day was going to the market to purchase food. For the most part, those were the only conversations I had each day. The food vendors became the family and friends I craved. There was one in particular who always took additional time to speak with me. He was the butcher, and one day I noticed he started quietly adding a little extra meat to my purchase.

His name was Alon and, though he was closer to my father's age, he seemed to be genuinely interested in things that interested me. We would talk about faraway lands and the places I would love to visit. He was originally from northern Galilee. I had never traveled farther than a few miles outside of Jerusalem. So, his stories about the Mediterranean Sea and the Galilean hills captured my imagination. As time went on, he confided to me that he looked forward to my arrival each day.

One day when I showed up at his stand, he invited me to meet him at the pool of Bethesda at the end of the day. It would give us more time to talk without customers interrupting. I welcomed the opportunity. I had never been invited to go on a walk. I had never been invited to go anywhere with someone else. The time passed slowly as I waited to meet him. Then it passed quickly as we walked from the pool to the gardens and back again. The last person who had been this genuinely interested in me was my mother. My heart began to sing again.

That walk was the first of many in the gardens. Though we talked every moment we were together, we never talked about his personal life. I did not know anything about his family, and every time I asked he redirected our conversation. After a while, I stopped giving it a thought. Our time together was now what I lived for. I could endure everything else knowing I was going to spend time with Alon.

Our walks in the evening were now a regular event. My father never asked me why I was gone – and I never told him. As long as there was food on his table when he arrived home, he seemed quite content not to know.

But the absence of my father's love no longer bothered me. There was another man in my life who was more than making up for it. I realized I had fallen in love with Alon. I had never felt this way before. And I was fairly certain he felt the same way about me.

It was now October. The late afternoons and evenings were cooler, and the sun was beginning to set earlier. We had met in the garden on the Mount of Olives. This was becoming our favorite place to walk. But that day, a bad storm blew in out of nowhere and began pelting us with driving rain. The sky turned dark and the wind was fierce.

Alon told me I could not travel home in that kind of weather. He told me he knew of a place nearby that we could shelter from the rain and the wind. The storm raged outside, but the place seemed strangely quiet and comforting. I felt safe with Alon.

I won't go into detail about that night, but suffice it to say that Alon and I lay together as if we were husband and wife. The storm continued throughout the night, so we stayed in that place until the next morning.

It was barely light outside when we heard a loud knock. A voice demanded that we open the door. Alon cracked the door open, and several men pushed their way inside. To our surprise, there stood a woman, two priests, and four temple guards.

. . .

I soon learned that the woman was Alon's wife! She began screaming and hitting him.

"I knew you had been up to no good for some time, but even in my wildest imagination I never believed you would be unfaithful to me!" she shouted. Then as I lay there on the bed, she unleashed her wrath on me.

Eventually, she ran out of strength. Though her anger didn't subside, her screaming and flailing did. She turned to one of the priests who I quickly learned was her brother. "We will take them both to the temple to be condemned and stoned as the law requires!" he said.

But as angry as the woman was with her husband, she apparently didn't want him stoned to death. "I am certain this is all the fault of this harlot and not my husband. Take her, but leave him for me to deal with!" she told her brother.

The law was clear that both the man and the woman caught in the act of adultery were to be stoned to death. But the other priest, who had been silent up until now, turned to the woman's brother and said, "This may be just the opportunity we have been looking for to entrap Jesus. Leave the man for your sister to deal with. All we need is the woman." Then with a smile, he added, "I am certain Caiaphas and Annas will reward us for our efforts!"

The woman's brother seemed pleased with the suggestion. He instructed the guards to take hold of me and bring me to the temple. They at least allowed me to put on my cloak, though the rest of my garments were left there in the room. As we walked out the door, I looked back at Alon as he was facing his wife's wrath. He didn't return my gaze. In fact, he looked relieved.

A jumble of emotions raged inside me. My heart was broken. The only man I had ever loved – and the only man I thought loved me – had been using me and deceiving me. He had never loved me; he only lusted after me. That thought devastated me. My need for love had blinded me to reality.

And now I would be publicly berated and tried as an adulteress, subjected to shame and ridicule. Then I would be pummeled with stones until I died. Alon would suffer no such punishment. I alone would stand before the crowd. My sad and pathetic life was about to come to an end.

When we arrived at the temple, I was taken into a gathering of religious leaders. They all looked away from me with disdain. Obviously, they weren't expecting a woman to be brought into their presence – particularly one in such disarray. The two priests who had arrested me walked over to speak with the one who appeared to be the high priest. They spoke in hushed tones. Soon a smile crossed the lips of the high priest. I couldn't imagine why he was smiling. Nothing about this situation merited a smile. He turned to the council and the guards and instructed them to take me into the courtyard where Jesus was teaching.

This was the second time I had heard the name Jesus mentioned. I did not know who He was, but apparently, He would determine my fate.

The Man teaching in the courtyard was surrounded by a great crowd. As soon as we arrived, the crowd began to stir. The Man stopped speaking. All eyes turned toward me. I noticed that each of my accusers was picking up a stone. Suddenly everything became quiet.

The priest who earlier suggested that I, alone, be brought to the temple turned to the Man and smugly said, *"Teacher, this woman was caught in the act of adultery. The law of Moses says to stone her. What do You say?"*[1]

The Man looked at me. I was now certain He was the One they had referred to as Jesus. I stood there in fear and shame before Him and before them all. Behind me stood my accusers – the religious leaders –

with an air of superiority, haughtiness, smugness, and contempt. Around me was the crowd – leering at me and craning their necks to see what Jesus was going to say or do. The only One who didn't look at me with condemnation was Jesus.

After a few moments, He stooped down and began to write in the sand. He wrote as if He weren't paying any attention to me or what was going on around Him.

I was close enough to see what Jesus was writing. He was writing a list of names, and beside each name He was writing a sin. By one He wrote "adultery." By another He wrote "blasphemy." By still another He wrote "thievery." And on and on. He must have listed twenty names. But none of them was mine!

Though I did not know the names of my accusers, it looked as if Jesus were listing them in a ledger along with a specific sin each had committed. Was Jesus going to accuse them? These were obviously sins that these men would want to keep private. Not only would these sins be a great source of embarrassment, but if made public they could cost these men their positions of influence ... perhaps some of them might even be stoned to death.

The priests continued to demand an answer. But when Jesus looked up, He didn't look at me, He looked at them and said, "*All right, but let the one who has never sinned throw the first stone!*"[2]

No one made a move. They just stared at what Jesus had written in the sand. After a few minutes, the only sound was that of the stones dropping from my accusers' hands. Then they turned and walked away.

Jesus looked at me and said, "*Woman, where are your accusers? Didn't even one of them condemn you?*"[3] "*No, Lord,*"[4] I said. My eyes met His as He said, "*Neither do I. Go and sin no more.*"[5]

. . .

I was stunned. A few moments earlier, I believed I would soon be dead, but now I was being told I could go. Just moments ago, I felt completely alone. There was no one who cared for me. My father had emotionally abandoned me. The man I thought loved me had deceived me. The crowd had leered at me. The religious leaders had condemned me. But now, surprisingly, I no longer felt alone. I knew there was One who truly loved me. I also knew I could no longer remain in Jerusalem. I would leave my father's home. But I knew there was One I would follow. I would join the group of men and women who were followers of Jesus.

He hadn't condemned me; He had forgiven me. And I knew that the One who stood before me would never deceive me. He would never forsake me or abandon me. I had found the true love I had been looking for all of my life … and I would follow Him.

≈

CELIDONIUS – THE BLIND MAN

My name is Celidonius and I grew up as an only child in Siloam, a small village just south of Jerusalem. My mother, Imma, and my father, Matthias, both grew up in our village, so everyone knows us. My father is a hardworking carpenter who has done work for most everyone in Siloam.

My mother is known for her beautiful voice; in fact, some say she sings like a meadowlark. From an early age her melodic sonnets soothed everyone within earshot. My father tells me he first heard her sing when he was a young boy. He says he was so smitten by her voice that he knew right then he would one day marry her.

My earliest memories are my mother's voice and the brightness of her songs. I was born without the ability to see, but through her music I was able to discover the beauty of the world around me. My parents were devastated that I was blind. As a matter of fact, they chose not to have any more children for fear they would be born the same way. But I was never exposed to their sadness or discouragement.

. . .

On the contrary, my mother was always joyful and cheerful whenever she was around me. She was my sunlight – even on those days when I felt sorry for myself. She would not allow me to languish in my melancholy; rather, she would lead me on a lyrical journey to faraway places and describe in great detail the beauty that surrounded me. I never felt as if I were missing out on anything growing up. In many respects, I felt like I was experiencing so much more – and in many ways, I believe I was.

However, I was not oblivious to the gossip in our village about me and the speculation about what sins my parents had committed to cause my blindness. Though I couldn't see their faces, I could hear their every word. I soon realized that the world around me was not quite so kind as the world my parents had created for me.

My father would often allow me to accompany him to the synagogue. I was always in awe of the words of God as the rabbi read from the Scriptures. I worked at memorizing the words so I could recite them to myself later. I found great strength and encouragement in those words. Over time, I became particularly fascinated by the words of the prophets about the coming Messiah. My heart raced when the rabbi read, *"And when He comes, He will open the eyes of the blind and unplug the ears of the deaf."*[(1)] I prayed that the Messiah would come soon and open my eyes!

Another place I enjoyed spending time was the pool inside of our village. The waters in the pool are fed from the Gihon Spring to the north, and it is part of a system of smaller pools that was designed by King Hezekiah to serve as freshwater reservoirs. But the pool of Siloam is the largest of them all, measuring two hundred twenty-five feet in width. It is occasionally used as a mikvah for ritual bathing, but residents primarily use it for swimming. I recall many hot summer days when I accompanied my father to the pool to cool off. During the warmer times of year, it was always a major gathering place in our village.

As I grew older, my parents explained that I needed to learn how to be independent. I would not always have them to rely on; plus, I did not want to be a burden to them. Though I would never be a skilled carpenter like my father, God had gifted me with a soothing voice like my mother's. She and I had been singing together for as long as I could remember, and I had an endless repertoire of songs stored in my heart.

When I became an adult, one of my parents led me each day to a place just outside the gates of our village. We would find a shady spot for me along the heavily traveled trade road to Jerusalem. I would then serenade weary travelers as they passed by me. My hope was that my songs would lighten their hearts as they journeyed, and they would return the gift by sharing a coin or two with me.

Some travelers also gave me food or other trinkets. I became well-known by those who regularly traveled the road, and many started to watch for me. Some would ask me to sing their favorite song. Others would stop to rest and have a conversation with me. Some learned my favorite foods or my preferred trinkets and started carrying them on their journey specifically for me.

One day, I sensed a large group of people approaching me on the road. I began to sing just a little bit louder to attract their attention. I strained my ears to hear what I could. It sounded like a Teacher answering His students' questions. I sensed someone walking over to me, so I stopped singing and looked up in the direction of my approaching visitor.

"May God's peace be on you, brother," he said. Then he handed me a piece of bread. He asked how long I had been blind and why I was sitting here along the road. I explained I had been blind since birth, and I came here each day to sing for travelers as they passed by. I told him they would often share a few coins or a little food with me for my effort.

Suddenly, I heard the man call out to his group, *"Teacher, why was this man born blind? Was it because of his own sins or his parents' sins?"*[2]

. . .

It must have been the Teacher who replied, *"It was not because of his sins or his parents' sins. This happened so the power of God could be seen in him."*[3]

I had heard a lot of reasons over the years as to why I had been born blind. But I had never had anyone say, *"so the power of God could be seen in me!"*[4] Those accompanying this Teacher were silent, obviously puzzled by what He said. How was the power of God being displayed through my life as I sat here beside the road? Though I am grateful to God for the singing voice He gave me, there is nothing powerful or very God-like about me!

The Teacher spoke again saying, *"We must quickly carry out the tasks assigned us by the One who sent us.*[5] The time is quickly coming when we will no longer be able to do any work. But the Father has placed Me here in the world for just such a moment. *I am the light of the world.*[6] And where there is light there can be no darkness."

As I listened to Him speak, I could tell He was walking toward me. I heard Him spit on the ground in front of me. I had no idea what He was doing! I wanted to ask, but I refrained from doing so. The next thing I knew, He was spreading something on my eyes. It felt like mud! Why was this Man spreading mud on my eyes?!

Then He said to me, *"Go wash yourself in the pool."*[7] Immediately, I stood to my feet. I had no idea who this Man was, or what He had just done, but He spoke with such authority I felt compelled to obey.

I stood there trying to figure out how I was going to make my way to the pool. I was grateful when someone walked up to me and placed my hand on his shoulder. Quietly the man said, "Follow me."

When we got to the pool, I knelt down and began to wash my eyes. As the mud disappeared, I began to squint. What was that? Light? It was brighter than I ever imagined! I instinctively raised my hand to shield my eyes. As I did, the light was no longer as bright. I moved my hand away and the brightness returned. The light was changing because of my hand ... and I could see it!

My eyelids began to blink rapidly. As my eyes began to adjust, my senses were bombarded with the new sensations of light and color.

I looked at the man who apparently led me to the pool. I stood and held his face in my hands. I had never seen another person. I had never seen anything! Suddenly, I was overcome with joy.

"Where is the Man who spread the mud on my eyes?" I asked. The man pointed to another Man in the distance and told me His name was Jesus. I wanted to run to Him, but I had never run before. I had never even walked without the aid of another person. As I headed toward the One who had just given me the ability to see, I remembered the promise from Isaiah that I had so often repeated – *"And when He comes, He will open the eyes of the blind and unplug the ears of the deaf."*[8]

When I got to Jesus, I knelt at His feet. I tried to express my thanks – but the words seemed so insufficient. I looked up at Him and He smiled at me. I had never seen anyone smile before. Then He told me to get up and go back into the village and find my parents. I had no idea where they were. I had no idea where my home was! Every step would be a new adventure!

As I made my way to find my family, I kept wondering: Was my sight given when Jesus applied the mud? Or was it given when I walked in obedience to the pool? Something inside me said it was the latter – that Jesus gave me sight in response to my faith. But one thing I now knew for sure – why He had said, *"so the power of God could be seen in him."*[9]

.   .   .

People in my village couldn't believe their eyes when I arrived. Several pointed at me and asked, *"Isn't this* Celidonius, *the man who used to sit and beg?"*[10] The response among them was mixed. I told them, *"Yes, I am* Celidonius! *The man they call Jesus made mud and spread it over my eyes and told me, 'Go to the pool of Siloam and wash yourself.' So, I went and washed, and now I can see!"*[11]

My neighbors said I must go see the Pharisees in the synagogue so they, too, could praise God. But first I wanted to see my parents. "Come with us to see the Pharisees," they said, "and then we will take you to see your parents."

The reaction of the Pharisees shocked me when I shared my news. Instead of rejoicing in the miracle with me, some began to denounce Jesus because He had given me my sight on the Sabbath. They set out to disprove the miracle. They questioned me again to see if there were inconsistencies in my story.

"What's your opinion about this Man who healed you?"[12] they asked.

"My opinion? *"I think He must be a prophet.*[13] Who but a prophet could do these things?"

The Pharisees then sent for my parents so they could question them, as well. That was the first beneficial thing they had done since I arrived. I wanted to see my parents! When they arrived, I could not believe my eyes. My mother was beautiful! I had always known she was – but now I could see her with my own eyes. I ran to them and we embraced, as tears of joy streamed down our cheeks.

The Pharisees were growing impatient with our family reunion and interrupted us with questions. Yes, my parents confirmed – I was their son Celidonius, and yes, I had in fact been born blind. No, they had no idea how I was now able to see, short of a miracle.

. . .

People from the village began to stream into the synagogue to see me for themselves. They had heard about the miracle, but they wanted to see me with their own eyes.

It was obvious the Pharisees were trying to discredit Jesus by discrediting the miracle. It was equally obvious they would seek retribution against anyone who stood in their way. But my parents' testimony left little doubt that a miracle had taken place. So, now the Pharisees acknowledged the miracle but continued in their attempt to dishonor Jesus. *"God should get the glory for this, but we know this man Jesus is a sinner."*[14]

"I don't know whether He is a sinner," I replied. *"But I know this: I was blind, and now I can see!"*[15]

The more they tried to discredit Jesus, the more I was drawn to Him. *"Look!"* I exclaimed. *"I told you once. Didn't you listen? Why do you want to hear it again? Do you want to become His disciples, too?"*[16]

My question unleashed their fury. *"You may be His disciple,"* they said, *"but we are disciples of Moses! We know God spoke to Moses, but we don't even know where this Man comes from."*[17]

"Why, that's very strange!" I replied. *"He healed my eyes, and yet you don't know where He comes from? We know that God doesn't listen to sinners, but He is ready to hear those who worship Him and do His will. Ever since the world began, no one has been able to open the eyes of someone born blind. If this man were not from God, He couldn't have done it."*[18]

"You were born a total sinner!" they raged. *"Are you trying to teach us?"*[19]

. . .

They were so furious they "excommunicated" me from the synagogue. This would be the first and last time I would see the inside of our synagogue. The crowd gasped. The Pharisees had just wielded the only real power they had over me – and my only offense had been that I spoke the truth.

The synagogue was the center of our village life. Being thrown out of the synagogue was tantamount to being ostracized from the village. My parents and my neighbors would no longer be permitted to have anything to do with me. On what should have been the happiest day of my life, I sadly turned and walked out of the synagogue. The Pharisees turned their backs to me. My parents stood there stunned, and the crowd watched in disbelief.

As I walked through the village, Jesus came upon me and asked, *"Do you believe in the Son of Man?"*[20] I answered, *"Who is He, Sir? I want to believe in Him."*[21] *"You have seen Him,"* Jesus said, *"and He is speaking to you!"*[22] *"Yes, Lord, I believe!"*[23] I said. And I fell down at the feet of Jesus and worshiped Him! Ironically, the Pharisees' arguments had convinced me that Jesus truly is the One whose coming was promised.

Since I was no longer welcome in my synagogue or village, I decided right then to follow Jesus as one of His disciples. As we headed out of town, a man and woman came running to catch up with us. It was my parents! They told me that if I could not remain in the village, neither would they. They wanted to be with me and learn more about this One who had given me sight. As our journey continued, Jesus opened their eyes, as well.

My mother began to sing a most glorious tune. Soon I raised my voice with her:

> *Sing to the Lord a new song;*
> *sing to the Lord, all the earth.*
> *Sing to the Lord and praise His name;*
> *every day tell how He saves us.*
> *Tell the nations of His glory;*

> *tell all peoples the miracles He does,*
> *because the Lord is great; He should be praised at all times.* [24]

As we continued to sing, Jesus stopped walking and so did the rest of His followers. Everyone lifted their voice to join with us as we sang to the One who stood before me … and He received the praise and worship He alone is due!

～

MIRIAM – THE ONE AT HIS FEET

*M*y name is Miriam, but most of you know me as Mary. I am certain you remember my brother, Lazarus, and my sister, Martha. Surely you have heard the story of how Jesus of Nazareth healed my brother of his leprosy. It was a miracle of God! And our lives have not been the same since.

Before my brother contracted leprosy, ours was a life of privilege and ease. Our father's industriousness had made our family quite prosperous. We wanted for nothing and we enjoyed the best of everything. We were one of the leading families in our town and enjoyed the privileges of that station.

But I don't want you to think we took all of that for granted. We did not. We knew our prosperity was a gift from God. We knew that He had blessed us abundantly. We tithed as the law required, but we also gave generously over and above that. We gave to help the poor and needy in our community. Our father taught us to be faithful stewards of all that God had entrusted to us.

. . .

Our father also taught us to be kind to our neighbor – whoever they may be. We were raised to lend a hand when needed and to treat everyone equally regardless of their social status. We strived to live at peace with everyone and to honor God in all that we did. As a result, our community was very fond of us – I dare say, they even loved us.

So, when Lazarus came down with leprosy we were taken aback. My family had always believed leprosy was God's punishment for unconfessed sin. But Martha and I knew that could not be the case with our brother. Even our priest and good friend Phinehas agreed that God was surely not punishing Lazarus. I continually asked God why He was allowing this disease to ravage my brother's body. Surely it must be a mistake! He did not deserve to suffer that way!

After Lazarus went away, Martha and I noticed that most of our friends and neighbors began to treat us differently. Many who regularly dined in our home barely spoke to us now. The many invitations we used to receive now became very rare. It was almost as if Martha and I had leprosy, too. I can honestly say that the affront did not weigh heavily upon us because our attention was directed toward our brother. But we were still aware of the slight.

We had been hearing stories about Jesus and the miracles of healing He was performing. Word was spreading about Him throughout the land. But we did not think He would come near enough to a leper to heal him. Our laws forbid us from coming in contact with someone who has leprosy. So, we were certain no man of God would do so – even this Jesus.

You cannot imagine how amazed we were when Amari, the overseer of our vineyard, came to us with the message that Jesus had healed Lazarus. Our hearts soared! It was all we could do to stay away from him for the eight additional days required by our laws. But Phinehas assured us that he had examined Lazarus's body and he had been made clean. Those days passed slowly until we were finally able to reunite with our brother. He, who had been close to death, was now restored to us. Our celebration continued for weeks!

. . .

We invited our friends and neighbors to join us for a grand celebration. Some of them responded cautiously, questioning whether Lazarus had truly been healed. Others were embarrassed for the way they had treated us while Lazarus was suffering from leprosy. But over time, all of our neighbors witnessed our brother's healing and joined us for the festivities. And we decided to set aside our hurt feelings and welcomed them back into our lives.

The day Jesus arrived in Bethany is one I will never forget. The news reached Lazarus that Jesus and His followers were on the outskirts of town. Without hesitation, Lazarus ran to meet Him – and Martha and I quickly followed. Lazarus never stopped running until he ran straight into the arms of Jesus.

Tears were streaming down Lazarus's cheeks and Jesus was smiling broadly. I don't know how long the two men stood there with their arms wrapped around one another, but they were still embracing when Martha and I arrived. I immediately fell at the feet of Jesus and began to kiss the hem of His garment. Martha bowed her head and began to give Him thanks.

Jesus reached down and helped me to my feet. I will never forget the look in His eyes as He gently turned Martha's and my faces toward His. His eyes were kind and tender but also strong and assuring. I was no longer conscious of anything or anyone else around me. It was as if He and I were the only two standing there. I felt a calm and a peace that I would feel every time I was in His presence.

Lazarus interrupted the silence and introduced Martha and me to Jesus. Quickly, he added, "Jesus, You and Your followers must come to our home to dine!" I noticed Martha giving the crowd a quick look as she calculated how much she would need to do to entertain fifty guests for dinner. But she never blinked. Martha would make it happen. If anyone could, she could!

. . .

We all began the short journey to our home. I will confess I wasn't much help to my sister that night. All I wanted to do was sit at the feet of Jesus – focused on His every word with rapt attention.

I had the opportunity to ask Jesus why my brother had contracted leprosy. "Surely, it wasn't God punishing him for his sin, was it?" I asked. "No," Jesus replied. "It had nothing to do with his sin. It was so the works of God could be displayed through him."

God had chosen Lazarus to display His glory through him! That had never crossed my mind. That meant Jesus had not come upon Lazarus by chance. He had sought out Lazarus. Jesus had known of his condition long before He even saw Him!

I used to blame God for my brother's affliction. But the reality was that God had entrusted him with a gift – the gift of being used by God to bring glory to His name. It caused me to look at those events very differently!

From then on, whenever Jesus was near Bethany, he would lodge and dine with us. We knew Jesus to be the Messiah – our Messiah – but in some ways, He also became like a brother to us. He had become part of our family – and we had become part of His.

Our lives were again filled with laughter and hope. Our relationship with Jesus gave us a sense of security that we had never felt before. It was as if nothing terrible could ever happen to us again – because we were friends of Jesus. He had said that those whom He has made clean would never again be unclean. So, it must follow that those whom He healed could never again become sick. At least, that's what we thought.

. . .

Until the day Lazarus fell ill. Early that morning he collapsed in the vineyard. Amari and a few of the workers carried him to our home. Martha placed her hand on his forehead. "He is burning with fever," she said. "Send for the priest and the midwife to come treat him." Martha and I helped the men put him in bed while two of the men ran to get Phinehas.

Soon after they arrived, the midwife applied a poultice to our brother's body to help relieve his fever. Lazarus had not been conscious since his collapse, so he could not tell us anything. Phinehas was perplexed. He did not know what was wrong with Lazarus, but he told us he feared that Lazarus would not survive.

Martha and I looked at each other and exclaimed in unison, "Then we must send for Jesus. He will heal him! He will make our brother well. He has done it before, and He will do it again! Our brother will not die!" With that, Amari sent off one of his swiftest men to carry the message to Jesus.

During His last visit, Jesus had told us that he would be staying in Bethabara during the winter. It would require a day's journey for a swift messenger to reach Him. Then it would take Jesus another day to travel here. Lazarus needed to survive through the night and all the next day so Jesus could arrive and make him well. Martha and I began to pray asking God to keep our brother alive.

We never lost hope. We knew the Father would hear our prayers. He had heard us before! And we knew Jesus would come. He had come to Lazarus before. We knew He would do it again. We were friends of Jesus. Surely our brother couldn't die. That's what we believed … right up to the moment Lazarus took his last breath.

He didn't live through the afternoon. The messenger would not have even arrived in Bethabara to tell Jesus. We were too late! I was so overwhelmed with grief I could not function. I was so certain that my brother would not die. Surely, Jesus wouldn't permit it. Jesus must have known Lazarus was sick. After all, He knew Lazarus had leprosy before He ever saw him. And we had heard reports where Jesus healed people who were not in His physical presence merely by speaking the words. Undoubtedly, He could have healed Lazarus – the one He loved – from a day's journey away. I began to sink into a deep hole of depression and grief.

Martha, true to her nature, took charge. She immediately began giving instructions to everyone in the room to prepare our brother's body for burial. His body would need to lay in the tomb before sunset, so preparations needed to be done quickly. Each person was given a task – except me. I was so distraught I could not move or speak.

Somehow, a few hours later, I found the strength to walk beside Martha in the funeral processional. All I remember is the wailing and crying of the crowd that surrounded us. I was incapable of crying. I was so consumed by grief that I could not feel anything else – until I heard the loud thud of the stone when it was moved into place to cover the opening of the tomb. That sound unleashed a flood of tears that would not stop.

That night and the next day passed slowly – slower than any day I have ever known. How could I face Jesus when He arrived that night? How could I ever trust Him again? Until now, I had always looked forward to Jesus's arrival – but that was no longer the case.

Martha was directing the great crowd of friends who had come to comfort us as we prepared for Jesus's arrival. She kept a watchful eye for Him. But He didn't come! Our messenger returned saying he had given the message to Jesus, but there had been no sign that He and His disciples were preparing to travel here. The only thing the messenger had to report was the statement Jesus made in his presence: *"Lazarus' sickness will not end in death. It has happened for the glory of God so that the Son of God will receive glory from this."*[1]

. . .

But Lazarus's sickness had ended in death! Even Jesus hadn't been able to prevent it! I sank deeper into my pit of depression. And as each day passed, I sank a little deeper.

It was now late afternoon on the fourth day since Lazarus's body had been placed in the tomb. We were at home surrounded by the many friends and neighbors who continued to try to console us. Martha was dealing with her grief by keeping everything – and everyone – organized.

I no longer expected Jesus to arrive. I didn't understand why He hadn't come. But it was too late for Him to do anything. So, I was somewhat surprised when Amari came to tell us that Jesus had arrived. He was waiting at the outskirts of town. I thought back to that first day Jesus had come to Bethany. I had been so excited to see Him. That day, we could not contain our joy as we ran to Him. I thought of the way He had smiled at me and looked into my eyes. But today was very different. And truth be told, I didn't want to see Jesus.

Martha told me she would go speak with Him. In a little while she returned and said, *"The Teacher is here and wants to see you."*[2] As much as I didn't want to go, I knew I must. Martha instructed Amari's son, Asher, to walk with me because I was not yet very steady on my feet. When we arrived and saw Jesus, I let go of Asher's arm and fell at Jesus's feet saying, *"Lord, if only You had been here, my brother would not have died."*[3] As the last word crossed my lips, I began to weep uncontrollably.

Those who had been in the house with me had followed me to this place. I heard them also begin to wail. Then I heard Jesus interrupt them and ask, *"Where have you put him?"*[4]

Someone in the crowd responded, *"Lord, come and see."*[5] At that moment, Jesus began to weep, and He reached down and helped me to my feet so we could walk together to the tomb. At the time I thought Jesus's tears were tears of grief over Lazarus's death. I would soon realize that He had an altogether different reason for weeping.

. . .

When we arrived at the tomb, He instructed someone in the crowd, *"Roll the stone aside."*[6] By then, Martha had also joined us at the tomb. She began protesting, *"Lord, he has been dead for four days. The smell will be terrible."*[7] To which Jesus replied, *"Didn't I tell you that you would see God's glory if you believe?"*[8]

It was then I remembered what Jesus said to me that day I asked why Lazarus had contracted leprosy. His response was, "So that the works of God could be displayed through him." I suddenly realized how small my faith was and how easily I had turned my back on Jesus. I understood now that Jesus had not been weeping over Lazarus's death; He was weeping over my disbelief!

Tears continued to flow down my cheeks, but they were no longer tears of grief over my brother; now they were tears of grief over my sin against my Master!

In that moment, I heard Jesus say in a loud voice, *"Father, thank You for hearing Me. I know that You always hear Me, but I said it out loud for the sake of all these people standing here, so that they will believe You sent Me."*[9]

Then He shouted, *"Lazarus, come out!"*[10]

The crowd around us grew silent. They were amazed that Jesus would say such a thing. But I knew that my brother was going to walk out of that tomb. Lazarus's illness was not unto death. It was so the works of God could be displayed through him! I immediately knew my brother was alive!

All eyes were on the entrance of the tomb. It seemed like time stood still, but suddenly my brother came hopping out! His hands and feet were bound in grave clothes, so he was unable to walk. His face was wrapped in a headcloth, so Jesus told those closest to him, *"Unwrap him and let him go!"*[11]

Amari stepped forward and began to unwrap Lazarus. Soon others joined him. In a matter of minutes, they had freed him – and there standing in front of us was my brother!

Martha ran toward him. I hesitated because I didn't know which to do – fall at the feet of my Lord or run to my brother. I finally chose the latter.

The crowd began shouting, "Hosanna!" Then one by one, everyone in the crowd began to kneel at the feet of Jesus. Every person there knew they were standing on holy ground.

Martha, Lazarus, and I walked together to Jesus and knelt at His feet. I was back in that place of calm and peace that can only be felt in His presence. I knew that from then on, I would always choose to remain at His feet. I would always choose to worship and adore Him. Because the One who stood before me is worthy!

JUDAS ISCARIOT - THE AMBITIOUS ONE

*M*y name is Judas and I grew up in the village of Kerioth, about ten miles south of Hebron in Judea. You have often heard me referred to as Judas Iscariot because the word "Iscariot" means "man of Kerioth."

My father grew up as the eldest son of a poor man who worked in the fields of a wealthy landowner outside of Hebron. My father became a hired hand for that same landowner and worked for him well into adulthood. But he desired more for himself and more for his young son.

When I was still a boy, the Romans announced an opportunity for people to settle in the uninhabited lands of southern Judea. The Romans wanted those areas populated in order to better secure the eastern frontier of their empire. As an inducement, settlers were promised ownership of their own land. My father seized that opportunity and led our family from Hebron to Kerioth to join in the eastern expansion. He could finally own a piece of land where he could raise his own crops.

Life was hard there. There was a reason the land had been uninhabited for so long. It was a desert with minimal rainfall and no rivers or streams nearby. We prayed each year for enough rain to keep our wells from running dry and our crops irrigated. But some years the rain didn't come, and those years we had little to show for our efforts.

Though my father had been "given" the land, the Roman authorities failed to tell him we must pay an annual tax on the land. And that tax was due whether his crop was plentiful or not. My father's dreams of achieving his own success became swallowed up by one hardship after another.

But my father never stopped encouraging me to dream and pursue my ambitions. He told me not to settle for what I had but always reach for more. He had worked in the fields since he was a child, so he had a very limited education. My mother, on the other hand, had always been an avid learner. She passed along her hunger for learning to me, and my father passed along his ambition.

When I was fifteen, my mother died from complete exhaustion. Both she and my father had aged twenty years in the five years we had lived in Kerioth. Five years after my mother passed, I witnessed my father's death as the pressures of paying his unpaid taxes took a toll on his already weak heart. I blamed the Roman occupation for both of my parents' deaths, and I vowed I would do everything in my power to see their oppression brought to an end.

There was nothing left to keep me in Kerioth. The day after I buried my father, I set out to pursue my own ambitions. I eventually made my way to Tiberias. I decided I would join up with the growing movement of zealots seeking to cast off the chains of our Roman oppressors.

Over time, I realized the zealot movement lacked cohesive leadership. They had recently attempted to overtake a group of Roman soldiers who were transporting taxes to Caesarea. Unfortunately, the mission failed miserably and most of the raiding party was killed, including one of the main zealot leaders. When I heard about the disastrous results, I knew the current leadership did not have the foresight or the leadership to oppose the tyranny of the Roman regime. I needed to look elsewhere if I hoped to see Roman oppression brought to an end.

I had heard rumors of a baptizer at the Jordan River who was preaching about the promised Messiah. The prophets had said the Messiah would deliver our people and establish His kingdom. That was a plan and someone I could follow, if the baptizer was correct.

I was told I would find the baptizer, whose name was John, in Aenon, so I purposefully made my way there. It had been several weeks, and I kept hearing the baptizer refer to a Man called Jesus. According to John, this Jesus was the Promised One. I learned that He and His followers were traveling through Galilee, so I decided to head back north and find Him.

I eventually found Jesus on the shore of the Sea of Galilee at Bethsaida. He was in a boat just offshore teaching a large crowd that had gathered. When He was done teaching, Jesus instructed the fishermen to cast their nets. When they did, their nets, and very soon their boats, were filled with fish to overflowing. The crowd around me gasped. I heard them talking about lepers whom Jesus had healed, and the lame who could now walk, the blind who could now see, and the deaf who could hear. This Man was able to perform miracles! I could follow such a Man!

I knew this Jesus was different from anyone I had ever seen or heard. He taught with great authority. Here was a Teacher! When He directed the fishermen to take their boats back out, they had obeyed without question. Here was a leader of men! This Man could lead our people to overthrow the oppression of Rome.

And if He was the Promised One, His closest followers would become the leaders in His kingdom. Then and there, I made the decision to do whatever was needed to become one of His closest followers. As Jesus and His disciples began to walk along the shore, I joined the crowd following Him.

· · ·

I began looking for every opportunity to make myself known to Jesus. I looked for ways to get close to Him and His closest followers. I knew that in order to become a leader, they must first see me as a servant. So, I became a servant to all. I watched for a need to arise, then promptly went about meeting it. I quickly became known as the one to turn to if you needed anything done. Gradually, I began to earn their trust.

Peter, who was becoming the leader of the smaller circle of disciples around Jesus, started drawing me into that inner circle. Jesus began to take notice of me. Soon, He called me by name. As the days continued, I began to notice He was treating me differently from the others. There was something keeping me at a distance, but I didn't know what it was. Perhaps Jesus was waiting to see what I could do for Him as one of His followers ... and one of His future leaders!

Several days later, after Jesus healed a paralytic man who had been lowered through the roof of the synagogue, we departed from the village of Capernaum. On our way out of town, we passed a tax collector sitting in his collection booth on the side of the road. He was collecting taxes from anyone bringing goods to sell into the village, as well as from those who had made a purchase and were taking goods out of the village. I quickly noticed he was having a very profitable day. Jesus stopped directly in front of him, turned and said, "Matthew, *follow Me and be My disciple!*"[1]

Peter and James looked at one another and James said, "Doesn't Jesus know what this man does for a living? There isn't anyone lower than a tax collector! Why would Jesus invite him to become one of us?" But they – and I – were even more surprised when Matthew immediately got up, left everything, and joined us. I was wary of this new addition. I had already set me eye on becoming treasurer of this group, and I did not want that honor to fall to this tax collector!

But I was relieved when soon after that Jesus called all of us together and announced He had chosen twelve of us to be His apostles. I listened intently as He called out the names. It was no surprise that Peter, Andrew,

James the son of Zebedee, and John were the first named. They had a unique relationship with Jesus, and I would have been greatly surprised if those four fishermen were not a part of this group.

He continued to call out the other names – *"Philip, Bartholomew, Thomas, and Matthew."*[2] Matthew? How could Jesus choose that tax collector over me? I began to quietly seethe. Was Jesus not going to choose me?

Jesus continued, *"James the son of Clopas, and Thaddeus."*[3] They, too, were to be expected. After all, they were Jesus's cousins. That was ten; only two names to go!

The next name Jesus called was Simon. The other apostles called him the zealot to distinguish him from Simon Peter. Obviously, Jesus had chosen him because he had been a revolutionary. But why hadn't Jesus chosen me? There was only one name left!

"And Judas Iscariot,"[4] Jesus said to complete His list of apostles. Jesus had chosen me! I could barely contain my excitement. There for a moment, I thought He was going to overlook me. I was afraid that all of my hard work and effort had yielded no results – just like my father. But when Jesus said my name, I felt a rush of relief and accomplishment course through my veins. My work had paid off! I was now in the inner circle! I would continue to show my worth to Jesus as one of His trusted lieutenants. When Jesus had called my name, I had to suppress the big smile that tried to spread across my face. I had to receive this good news with humility. It took all I had to look humble!

My second pleasant surprise was just a few days later when the inner circle chose me as treasurer. Even Matthew had surprisingly voted for me. Again, it was all I could do to react with grace and humility. "Each of you is so much more qualified to assume this responsibility than I am," I said. "But I will bow to your wishes and endeavor to prove worthy of your trust."

. . .

Watching over the treasury would be an important leadership role with this group, but it would become an even greater role when Jesus established His kingdom. Everything was going according to my plan! And I didn't mind having the treasury at my disposal when I needed a coin or two!

As the months continued, I kept watching for Jesus to make His move and declare Himself as the Messiah. I could not imagine why He had not already established His kingdom. There had been many perfect opportunities for Him to do so. He was attracting larger crowds every day.

As a matter of fact, He had recently taken a young boy's sack lunch and fed a crowd I estimated to be fifteen thousand people. When everyone had eaten their fill, the other apostles and I collected twelve full baskets of leftover food! The crowd had begun to clamor for Jesus to be their King. They had witnessed what Jesus could do, and they wanted Him to rule so they would never have to work for food again.

It was clear they were preparing to force Jesus to declare Himself as King. I could not contain my excitement as I watched the reaction of the crowd. Now was the moment when Jesus would be raised to His rightful position as Messiah.

But instead of embracing the will of the people, Jesus told us to get into the fishing boat and cross to the other side of the lake. He would meet us there. He then slipped away quietly into the hills to escape the crowd. Another moment had come ... and gone!

But the ultimate moment occurred just a few weeks ago. Jesus's close friend, Lazarus, had died while we were in Bethabara. When He heard the news, Jesus delayed traveling to Bethany to console Lazarus's sisters, or so we thought. He kept telling us we were going to witness His glory, but we didn't know what that meant. Yes, we had previously witnessed Him raise two people from the dead on the day they died. But the body of Lazarus had already been in the tomb for four days. His body would have begun to decompose. What glory is in that?

After we arrived in Bethany, Jesus told the crowd that was gathered to roll away the stone. Then He had shouted, *"Lazarus, come out!"*[5] Lo and behold, Lazarus came walking out of that tomb! The crowd stood there in awe! Peter, James, and John lifted their outstretched arms in praise and worship as tears streamed down their cheeks. They fell to their knees in adoration before Jesus. Andrew and Phillip removed their sandals as they lay prostrate before Jesus. The rest of the apostles, except me, lifted their voices and began to sing "Holy, Holy, Holy" as they, too, fell to their knees before Him. Martha and Mary ran to their brother to embrace him, then together they all knelt at the feet of Jesus.

I couldn't refrain from smiling as I thought to myself, "Finally Jesus will take His rightful place on the throne. All that I have waited for will now occur. Having performed this miracle, there is nothing to stop Jesus from establishing His kingdom!"

In the days that followed, people throughout the provinces heard what Jesus had done. They were ready to crown Him King. The religious leaders were frightened of Him. They knew their days of power were over. I knew that our Roman and Herodian leaders had only a few thousand soldiers at their disposal. They would easily be overthrown when all of our people rose up behind Jesus. And after what I had just seen, I knew that even Rome with all of its military power and might would be forced to bow before Jesus!

But the weeks continued to pass, and Jesus still hadn't made His move! Seven weeks had gone by without Jesus taking a solitary step toward assuming His rightful throne. Tonight, we had dinner with Lazarus and his family. As we began to eat, Lazarus's sister Miriam slipped into the room carrying a beautiful alabaster jar. Quietly, she knelt beside Jesus's feet and opened the jar. She began to anoint His head and His feet – wasting that expensive perfume! Jesus continued to eat without acknowledging her. The rest of us remained silent as we watched.

. . .

Suddenly, I couldn't take it anymore and had to speak up. *"That perfume was worth a year's wages. It should have been sold and the money given to the poor."*[6] A few of the other disciples nodded in agreement and joined me in scolding Miriam for what she had done.

Then Jesus spoke up and told us to leave her alone. *"Wherever the Good News is preached throughout the world, this woman's deed will be remembered and discussed."*[7]

I was seething. Jesus's rebuke made me look foolish in front of the others. I had faithfully followed Him for almost three years. Sure, I had helped myself to a few coins from the treasury here and there, but that wasn't my problem with what Miriam had done! The money we could have received for this perfume was nothing compared to the big treasure that awaited us when Jesus establishes His government. Why is Jesus wasting His time sitting at this table, when He could be sitting on His rightful throne in Jerusalem? This young woman's expression is nothing compared to what the masses would do if Jesus stepped up and assumed His rightful position as King.

I decided I could no longer rely on Jesus to do what needed to be done. Someone needed to force His hand. Suddenly, the thought crossed my mind that perhaps that was exactly what Jesus was waiting for. Perhaps He was waiting for one of us to step forward and take the initiative. Jesus had specifically selected each one of us to be His apostles. Had He selected me for just this purpose? Had nothing yet occurred because I hadn't taken the initiative? Is that why Jesus had kept me at more of a distance than the other apostles?

At that moment, I knew what I needed to do. I would help Jesus take the steps He needed to take. Jesus would be grateful to me! Perhaps that was why Jesus had rebuked me tonight – not because of what I said, but because Jesus was frustrated that I had not already acted.

. . .

The high priest and the rest of the high council were obviously plotting to kill Jesus. But they seemed to be incapable of executing a plan. They lacked proper leadership – just like the zealots. Jesus had probably frustrated their effort while He waited on me to step forward. That made perfect sense! No one was able to take the next step until I did.

This is my moment! After we arrive in Jerusalem tomorrow, I will find time to slip away and talk to the high priest. Jesus will know what I am doing. He is counting on me to work out the details. I will help the religious leaders arrest Jesus. I will arrange the best time and place so the crowd won't interfere. Then when the religious leaders make their move, Jesus can declare Himself and call out the crowd to follow Him as their promised King. Finally, He will establish His government and I will ascend into my rightful position. Victory is in sight!

I turned from my thoughts and looked at Jesus. He was looking back at me. Our eyes met. I smiled and nodded. He didn't smile in return, but I didn't notice. I would take care of this for Jesus. All was forgiven. Jesus hadn't really meant to rebuke me, He was just getting my attention. It had worked. I was truly sorry I hadn't realized it sooner. After all, it had been seven weeks since He raised Lazarus from the grave!

Finally, the One who stood before me will receive the honor that is due Him ... and I, Judas, the man from insignificant little Kerioth, will make it happen!

EPHRAIM – THE TANNER

$\mathcal{M}$y name is Ephraim, and I grew up in the small village of Bethphage on the eastern slope of the Mount of Olives. The village is a Sabbath day's journey of less than two-thirds of a mile from Jerusalem along the road to Jericho.

The men in my family have been *bursis* – hide and leather tanners – for many generations. My father taught me the craft, just as I am training my twelve-year-old son, Yamin. The hides we prepare are used to make sandals and shoes, as well as straps and harnesses for animals, skin bottles for transporting liquids, and writing materials. A ritually important use of our hides is for Torah scrolls – both the straps to bind them and the pages that contain their written content.

As you can imagine, the curing and tanning of hides is quite foul smelling, so no one wants us located nearby. As a matter of fact, our law requires that our tannery be situated at least seventy-five feet from the outskirts of our village on the east side. But in the words of the Talmud: *"The world can exist neither without a perfume-maker nor without a tanner – happy is he whose craft is that of a perfume-maker, and woe to him who is a tanner by trade."*

. . .

Our trade is profitable, but it does come at a cost. Tanners are exempt from appearing at the temple on pilgrimage festivals because our unpleasant odor prevents us from gathering with other men. From the days of our Babylonian captivity until only recently, we had to have our own synagogues, but that is no longer the case.

My tannery consists of two small rooms and a courtyard. Inside the rooms are vats made of stone masonry, plastered within and without. The hides are smeared on the flesh side with a paste of slaked lime and then folded up and allowed to stand until the hair loosens. After the hair and any remaining flesh are removed, the skins are soaked in a concoction of dog dung and then in a mixture of fermenting bran and leaves. After drying, the leather is blackened on one side by rubbing on a solution made by boiling vinegar with metal, and then the skin is finally given a dressing of olive oil.

Upwind of my tannery is a small stable where I keep the animals I use to transport my finished hides. By keeping my stable upwind, I shelter my animals from the unpleasant odor, so they do not repulse my customers. Right now, I am stabling a donkey and its three-year-old colt.

As a matter of fact, I will never forget the day that colt was born. Over four years earlier, Yamin had become ill with a high fever. My wife and I thought he was going to die. But by the grace of God, he did not. However, the fever left him unable to speak. For four years we prayed that God would heal him.

The day the colt was born was also the day that Jesus of Nazareth passed through our village on His way to Jerusalem for Passover. As He traveled by our tannery, He looked over and saw Yamin watching me as I assisted the donkey in giving birth. He stopped and walked over to join us. There was a delight in His eyes as together we all witnessed the miracle of birth. I saw Him turn His eyes toward the heavens and say, *"Father, You are the giver of life, and Your light lets us enjoy life."*[1]

.   .   .

Then He knelt and looked at Yamin. I had no idea who this Man was, but I saw both a gentleness and a genuine look of concern. Though we did not know Him, He apparently knew of my son's condition. He cupped Yamin's head in His hands and said, "Father, *Your goodness is as high as the mountains. Your justice is as deep as the great oceans. You protect Your people as well as the animals.*[(2)] Glorify Your Son by restoring this young boy's voice."

Suddenly I heard my son say, "Papa, the colt is born! God has given him life!"

I don't know which one of us was more startled – my son, that he could speak, or me that I had just heard his voice! Slowly, I turned in amazement from my son to the Miracle Worker as He began to stand to His feet. "My Lord, how can I ever thank You for restoring the voice of my son? How can I ever repay You? Praise be to Jehovah God! My son who has been mute for four years can now speak!"

Jesus looked at me and said, "Do not tell anyone what has happened, because My time has not yet come. But give glory and honor to the Father who has led Me to you today."

Then He turned and walked away. As He did so, I called out to the handful of men who were traveling with Him, saying, "Please tell me this Man's name!"

One of the men looked back and said, "Our Teacher's name is Jesus of Nazareth." I could tell by the look on his face that he, too, was amazed by what Jesus had just done. I didn't know if the man had ever seen Jesus heal before, but I knew no one could ever tire of seeing the healing power of God. As I knelt there embracing my son, watching Jesus as He walked away, I didn't know if I would ever see Him again, but something told me I would.

. . .

A few days later, I delivered a supply of tanned hides to the stoa of the temple to be used in making Torah scrolls. While I was there, a number of merchants were talking about how a Man named Jesus had driven the merchants and money-changers out of the temple. He had rebuked them saying, "*Stop turning My Father's house into a marketplace!*"[3] I reflected on how Jesus sought glory for the Father – not only through miraculous healing but also through impassioned correction. Oh, how I longed to see Him again!

In the years that followed, Jesus's name became quite notorious. I frequently heard reports – even in our small village. People from all over the land were flocking to hear and see Him. He was able to make the blind to see, the deaf to hear, the lame to walk – and as I well knew, the mute to speak! It had even been said that He had raised the dead to life. I would never forget the day He had stopped at our stable!

To my surprise, Jesus did come to see me again, just a few months ago. I was never so startled, and never so happy, as when He called out my name. "Ephraim," He said, "I need your help."

He was standing there alone without His followers. I ran to Him and knelt at His feet. I was careful not to touch Him and make Him ceremonially unclean. I looked up into His eyes and said, "All that I am and all that I have belongs to You, Master. Just tell me what you need."

"I will be returning to Jerusalem in a few months for the Passover," He said. "On the day I arrive, I will need that little colt that was born on the day you last saw Me. I will send two of My disciples to collect the colt and its mother."

"Oh, Master," I replied. "You ask so little! You have done so much for me, can I not repay You in a far greater way?"

. . .

"You will be helping to fulfill a prophesy of old," Jesus said. "The Father will again be glorified through your obedient act. Your actions will never be measured by the amount you give, rather by the amount of faith with which you give it."

"Then Jesus, it is Yours," I said. "I will watch for Your disciples, and everything will be ready."

That was four months ago. The feast of Passover begins in four days. I had Yamin tie up the donkey and the colt just outside the stable ready for the Master. We kept a careful watch for His disciples. At mid-morning, they appeared. Yamin saw them first as they were untying the animals. He called out to me and the two of us walked over to them.

"Why are you untying the colt?"[(4)] I asked.

"The Lord needs them,"[(5)] they replied, looking a little apprehensive.

"They are ready for the Master's use, just as I promised Him," I said. I could see they were surprised by my reply, so I went on to say, "Jesus asked me to have them ready for Him a few months ago when He was here for the Feast of Dedication. He told me He would send two of His disciples to retrieve them when it was time. He even described the two of you so I would know what you look like."

They still looked a little unsure of what to do when they asked, "Do we owe you anything for the use of your animals?"

"No. Three years ago, Jesus healed my son," I replied as I pointed to Yamin. "We owe Him a debt we can never repay. This is just a small way for us to show Him our gratitude. You can return them when you come back by here later this afternoon."

. . .

The men's concerns seemed to be put to rest by my response, so I went on to ask them, "Have you heard about the crowd that is gathering in Jerusalem?"

"We know that a large crowd of pilgrims comes to Jerusalem each year from all over for Passover," one of the men replied.

"Yes," I said, "but this year there are many more. People have been arriving for days. Many who would not have chosen to come to Jerusalem to observe the Passover have come to see Jesus! They have heard that He raised a man from the dead who had been in the grave for three days. Hundreds of thousands of people have gathered in Jerusalem – and many for the express purpose of seeing Jesus. There has never been such a crowd!

"Jesus must have something very special planned for this crowd," I continued, "and His plan must include this donkey and its colt!" I could tell these two men didn't know what I was talking about.

"Peace be with you," I said as I sent them on their way. I turned to Yamin and said, "Let's close the shop and go see what Jesus has planned."

We followed the men at a distance. When they arrived at the place where Jesus was, He said, "I will ride the colt alongside of its mother from here to the temple."

I was suddenly reminded of the writing by the prophet Zechariah:

Look, your King is coming to you. He is righteous and victorious, yet He is humble, riding on a donkey – riding on a donkey's colt.[6]

Several men placed their garments over the colt to make it more comfortable for Jesus as He rode. He began His journey into the city, and Yamin and I followed. It quickly became apparent that He was going to enter the city through the king's entrance – the Eastern Gate. News quickly spread that Jesus was approaching. The people began to pour out of the city to join the procession. Many began to spread their garments on the road ahead of Him. Others laid down palm branches they had cut in nearby fields.

A multitude soon surrounded Jesus so that He was in the center of the procession. The crowd began to shout over and over, *"Praise God for the Son of David! Blessings on the One who comes in the name of the Lord! Praise God in highest heaven!"*[7] Yamin and I added our voices to theirs.

The shouts grew louder and louder as more people joined the procession. It seemed as if the entire city was in an uproar as Jesus entered. I noticed that some of the Pharisees had even come out to see what all the commotion was about. When they saw Jesus, they indignantly called out to Him, *"Teacher, rebuke Your followers for saying things like that!"*[8]

Jesus answered them saying, *"If they kept quiet, the stones along the road would burst into cheers!"*[9]

I came upon a few people who were unaware of who Jesus was. *"Who is this?"*[10] they asked. I told them, *"It's Jesus, the prophet from Nazareth in Galilee."*[11]

When He arrived at the temple, Jesus dismounted the colt, and the crowd parted so that He could enter. I am not permitted inside the temple because of my trade, so I can't tell you what happened next. Yamin and I made our way back to the tannery.

"Wasn't that glorious, father?" Yamin remarked.

·   ·   ·

"I have never seen anything like it!" I agreed. "I have seen the arrival of King Herod and many Roman generals and leaders, but never have I seen anyone received like Jesus was received today. We welcomed our King today! We welcomed the One whose coming was foretold!

"And Yamin, it was Jesus who enabled you to lift your voice in praise. And it is Jesus who will always be worthy of your praise!"

Jesus apparently did not stay in the temple very long that day, because soon the two disciples returned the donkey and its colt to my stable. "The Master sends His thanks to you," they said. But I couldn't help thinking that we were the ones that needed to give thanks – thanks for a healing three years ago and thanks for allowing us to witness the fulfillment of the promise from long ago.

I didn't know what the days ahead would hold, but I knew the One who had knelt with my son, the One who had stood before me, and now the One who had ridden into Jerusalem on the colt, would always be my King … and He would always be my Lord.

∾

SHIMON – THE SHEPHERD

I am a shepherd named Shimon, and I grew up in the hills surrounding the town of Bethlehem. I am one of the shepherds who stood in awe when the angels announced the birth of Jesus. I ran with my father and the others to the stable where Jesus was born.

I didn't see Him again until the day He was baptized by John the baptizer at the Jordan River. I was one of John's disciples at the time. Jesus and I spoke ever so briefly the day He was baptized, but I marveled when He addressed me by my name. How could a newborn baby have known my name? And how could a grown Man possibly remember something that had happened the night He was born? But I soon came to realize that Jesus knew everything about me – past, present, and future. And I have been following Him ever since.

I am not one of His apostles, but Jesus has permitted me to see and experience much of what they have. I was with Him for most of the experiences you have read about in this volume. He even permitted me to be one of the few who joined Him the day He raised Jairus's daughter from the dead. And I, like everyone else, trembled at His feet the day Lazarus came out of the tomb. There is no denying that Jesus is the Messiah – the Promised One. He is the Son of the Living God!

.   .   .

Though I have accompanied Jesus to Jerusalem to observe the Passover on several occasions, I had a sense before we came that this time would be different. But I had no idea how different!

This past Sunday, Jesus sent Andrew and me to retrieve a donkey and its colt from Ephraim, the tanner. We were surprised when Jesus announced, "Today we will enter the city through the Eastern Gate." Ordinarily we entered the city in a very inconspicuous way through the Sheep Gate. But on this day, Jesus had chosen to enter through the gate used by kings – and His arrival was anything but inconspicuous! We marveled at how the people welcomed Jesus into the city. Shouts of "Hosanna" reverberated from every corner!

I looked at the faces of His close followers – His apostles and the others. They were all smiling. Everyone was grateful that the people were receiving Jesus in the manner He deserved. But when I saw Judas Iscariot nearby, he appeared to be especially happy about all the attention Jesus was receiving.

"The donkey's colt was the animal used by all of our ancient kings as they processed among the people," he commented. "Jesus is presenting Himself as King today. The Messiah has arrived! Today will be the day!" Honestly, I did not know what he meant by that last statement. And truthfully, neither of us knew what Jesus would do next.

When we arrived at the entrance to the temple, Jesus dismounted the colt and the crowd parted so He could enter. As He walked through the Court of the Gentiles, I could tell He was looking to make sure the tables and stalls had not been returned to the courtyard. Jesus had made that same visual check every time He had entered the temple since He cleansed it three years earlier. This time was no exception, but I sensed He had an even greater purpose for doing so that day.

.   .   .

The religious leaders were keeping a close watch on Jesus. We knew they were agitated by the crowd's spontaneous demonstration of praise. But we didn't know that they had come to the conclusion that if they did not destroy Jesus now, they themselves would be destroyed. We didn't realize it, but Jesus was forcing the religious leaders to act in the time and way He and the Father had chosen.

Off in a corner, I saw the former high priest Annas standing with his son-in-law, Caiaphas, the current high priest. They were watching Jesus's every move. Annas was speaking to the younger man in hushed tones, while Caiaphas nodded his head in agreement. I now know that it was the calm before the storm, but I did not realize the extent of the storm that was coming.

Jesus was fully aware of the battle that would rage over the next few days. It wasn't until much later that I realized He was discussing it with *His* Father as He walked through the courtyard. And, though I did not know exactly what the priests were discussing, I knew they were plotting against Jesus. The others gathered in the temple kept watching Him, as well. They were waiting for Him to teach or perform miracles. But they would need to wait until the next day. Eventually, Jesus let us know it was time to return to Bethany for the night.

As we were leaving , my brother Jacob and his helper arrived with a drove of sheep they were delivering to the temple merchants. My brother planned to stay in the city for the night, so after a brief reunion, I arranged to meet up with him when we returned the next morning. We continued on our journey, and Jacob made his way to the merchants' stalls.

That is when I saw Judas again. His smile from earlier had vanished. Now he appeared to be brooding. "Today was an exciting day as the people joyfully welcomed Jesus as the Son of David into Jerusalem!" I said. "Don't you agree, Judas?"

· · ·

"It would have been a much more exciting day if Jesus had allowed them to crown Him King," Judas replied. And I could see there was a storm brewing behind those brooding eyes.

The next day, Jacob told me that when he arrived at the animal pen with his sheep, there had been quite a commotion. Annas had just directed the merchants to set up their stalls in the outer Court of the Gentiles so they would be ready for the morning. He said that the larger attendance of pilgrims this year would require additional stalls – and those stalls needed to be inside the temple's court.

But everyone sensed there was another reason for such a sudden change. They remembered the day Jesus had cleared out the temple and how the priests had backed down from Him. They knew the priests had not attempted to bring the stalls and tables back into the temple since then. Everyone present was aware Jesus had just left the city. How would He react when He returned in the morning? But it was not their right or role to question the high priest. If that is what he wanted done, that is what they would do.

When we arrived the next morning, Jesus immediately saw the tables and stalls. He saw the brisk trade that was taking place at the money-changers' tables, the dove sellers' tables, and the animal stalls.

Then He declared, *"It is written: 'My house will be a house of prayer.' But you have made it 'a den of robbers.'"*[1] He turned over the tables and chairs, and drove the merchants from the temple, just as He had done three years earlier. But this time the merchants were not surprised. They had expected Jesus to act this way. They exited the court quickly and returned to their stalls and tables in the stoa. They knew they were being used as pawns by the priests in their plot against Jesus. Even the crowd seemed to be expecting Jesus's reaction.

I again observed Annas and Caiaphas standing in a corner watching it all. I was somewhat surprised by their expressions. Instead of shock and dismay, they looked smug and victorious, as if everything had gone according to their plan. They acted as if Jesus's actions were exactly what they wanted. The priests were obviously planning something!

People began to flock into the temple to be healed by Jesus and to listen to His teaching. He received them all, one by one. When the afternoon was drawing to an end, He announced that it was time for us to return to Bethany for the night.

When we arrived back at the temple on Tuesday, the priests, teachers, and elders were all waiting for Jesus. The majority of the members of the Sanhedrin had gathered to confront Him. As a part of the orchestrated plot, they were now feigning their shock and offense by His actions. They voiced their objections to what He had done on Monday, saying He had completely undermined their authority. He had demonstrated a flagrant disregard for their position. He had never once come to them seeking their approval for His actions.

As far as they were concerned, they had never delegated Him any authority, and He had ignored their official positions for far too long. They had now become unified by their fear. They considered Him a threat, and their motivation was simply selfish ambition. They feared they would lose their power over the people. So, as they stood before Jesus that morning, they demanded, *"By what authority are You doing all these things? Who gave You the right to do them?"*[2]

But Jesus knew this was all part of their plot. They were not seeking truth. They were looking for evidence they could use to destroy Him. The merchants had been brought back into the temple for the purpose of setting up this charge. There was nothing sincere about what these men were asking. So, Jesus deftly countered their question with another question, exposing their hypocrisy and their hard hearts. He asked, *"Did John's authority to baptize come from heaven, or was it merely human?"*[3]

. . .

The religious leaders now had another dilemma. How should they respond to Jesus's question? I had been there with John the baptizer when the Pharisees disrespected and accused him. As they now stood before Jesus, they weren't considering "what is true?" or "what is right?" but rather, "what is safe?"

They knew whichever way they answered the crowd would turn on them, and their authority, position, and prestige would be lost. So, they refused to answer His question by pleading ignorance. Which then prompted Jesus to respond, *"Then I won't tell you by what authority I do these things."*[4]

Throughout the day, Jesus used parables to confront the religious leaders and to teach the crowds. Eventually, the religious leaders withdrew from the courtyard to escape the light Jesus was shining on them and their sinful motives. They sequestered themselves behind closed doors – and away from piercing eyes – so they could discuss their dark plans away from the light.

Midway through the day, I noticed Judas Iscariot slip away. It was obvious he did not want to be seen. A little later, I saw him return. I soon discovered what Judas had done. He had witnessed the failed attempts of the religious leaders to entrap Jesus. Time and again, he had seen Jesus outsmart them, outmaneuver them, and outwit them. The religious leaders were just the pawns Judas needed to force Jesus to show His hand. The leaders wanted to arrest Jesus, so if he could help them do that, Jesus would have to declare His authority and establish His kingdom.

Off he had gone to find his "unlikely" allies, to convince them to go along with his plan. The religious leaders knew that whatever they did, it had to be done secretly under the cover of darkness. So, they were delighted when one of Jesus's own disciples approached them to discuss the best way for Jesus to be arrested.

These unwitting allies were all reveling in their own craftiness. The religious leaders agreed to pay Judas thirty pieces of silver to bind their agreement. Thirty pieces of silver is not a lot of money. Judas was too ambitious to betray Jesus for such a paltry sum. And the religious leaders were too pompous to stoop to paying any higher bounty for One they disdained so greatly. The money was merely a formality to seal their agreement. Judas had his sights on much more.

As we left the temple at the end of the day, Jesus told us we were going to spend the night on the Mount of Olives. We would not be returning to Bethany. We had no idea at the time, but Jesus knew the religious leaders had not abandoned their notion of arresting and killing Lazarus. Since Jesus had raised him from the grave, Lazarus's very life had become a threat to these leaders. Jesus did not want to put Lazarus in harm's way at his home in Bethany, so He moved to a different location to spend the night – and Judas knew exactly where He would be.

On Wednesday morning, Jesus announced that He would not be going to the temple that day. Tuesday had been a full day and night, and He told us He needed to spend time away from the crowds with His Father before the arrival of the Festival of Unleavened Bread. He found a secluded area there on the Mount of Olives where He could be alone in prayer. None of us had any idea what was coming.

The next day was the fifth day of the week – Thursday. The Passover Festival would begin at dusk with the Passover Seder and continue for seven days. In preparation for the festival, all of the leaven was removed from the Jewish households. Leaven symbolizes corruption, or sin, thus for the seven days of Passover, we are to only eat unleavened bread. Any leaven that remains in the households on the day before the beginning of Passover is burned. This morning the pungent odor of burning leaven permeated the air in and around the city. Every household was busy completing their preparations.

Those preparations were so important to Jesus that He sent Peter and John to make the arrangements. They invited me to join them. Peter wisely asked Jesus for His specific instructions. All of us knew what preparations were required under the law. And all of us had traveled to

Jerusalem many times before for the observance of Passover. It would have been easy for us to go and do what we believed to be right. But we had learned that Jesus was always very specific in what He would have us do. As usual, Jesus had all the details already worked out. I can't help but wonder how much time and energy we would have needlessly wasted if Peter had failed to ask.

It appeared that Jesus had made prior arrangements for the Passover meal, down to the slightest detail. Here were His instructions: *"As soon as you enter Jerusalem, a man carrying a pitcher of water will meet you. Follow him. At the house he enters, say to the owner, 'The Teacher asks: Where is the guest room where I can eat the Passover meal with My disciples?' He will take you upstairs to a large room that is already set up. That is where you should prepare our meal."*[5] When we arrived in Jerusalem we found everything exactly as Jesus told us it would be.

The women traveling with us also came in order to prepare the meal. The group now included Jesus's mother Mary, Mary Magdalene, Salome (the wife of Zebedee), Mary (the wife of Clopas), Joanna (the wife of Chuza), Suzanna (the widow whose son Jesus raised from the dead), and my mother, Ayda. They busily began their work to make everything ready for that evening.

Later in the day, Jesus and the rest of the apostles arrived. He invited me to remain with them for the Seder as well. We were all enjoying the intimacy of fellowship with Him. But suddenly He did something that shocked us. He got up from His place at the table, took a basin, knelt before each one of us, and washed our dirty feet before drying them with a towel He was wearing around His waist. The Son of the Almighty God was washing our feet! We didn't know what to say or do. A hush fell over the room as Jesus knelt before one man and then the next.

Then Jesus came to Peter, who protested saying, *"Lord, are You going to wash my feet?"*[6] Jesus replied, *"You don't understand now what I am doing, but someday you will."*[7] *"No,"* Peter protested, *"You will never ever wash my feet!"*[8] Jesus replied, *"Unless I wash you, you won't belong to Me."*[9]

. . .

Then in typical Peter fashion, he exclaimed, *"Then wash my hands and head as well, Lord, not just my feet!"*[(10)] To which Jesus replied, *"A person who has bathed all over does not need to wash, except for the feet, to be entirely clean. And you disciples are clean, but not all of you."*[(11)] I was curious what Jesus meant by His last statement. But before the sun rose again, I would understand.

When Jesus finished washing our feet, He put His robe back on and returned to His place reclining at the table.

"Do you understand what I was doing?" He asked. *"You call Me 'Teacher' and 'Lord,' and you are right, because that's what I am. And since I, your Lord and Teacher, have washed your feet, you ought to wash each other's feet. I have given you an example to follow. Do as I have done to you."*[(12)]

Shortly thereafter, Jesus announced, *"There is one here at this table, sitting among us as a friend, who will betray Me. For it has been determined that the Son of Man must die. But what sorrow awaits the one who betrays Him."*[(13)]

The apostles looked at each other, questioning who would ever do such a thing. John was sitting next to Jesus at the table. Peter motioned to him to ask, *"Who's He talking about?"*[(14)] Jesus responded, *"It is the one to whom I give the bread I dip in the bowl."*[(15)]

Then Jesus dipped the bread and gave it to Judas. We all observed it. Peter and John exchanged quizzical looks as if to say, "What does Jesus mean? What is Judas going to do?"

Most of the other disciples thought Jesus was honoring Judas by giving him the first portion of the bread He had dipped. In their minds, Jesus was acknowledging the important role that Judas always played in His ministry. A couple of the disciples even thought that through this honor

Jesus was making up to Judas for having publicly rebuked him the other night at the home of Lazarus.

With sadness in His eyes, Jesus told Judas, *"Hurry and do what you're going to do."*[16] With that, Judas got up from the table and walked out of the room. Most of the disciples assumed Jesus had sent him out on business. As I sat there beside John, watching and listening, I realized Judas was preparing to betray Jesus. I didn't know how or why, but somehow Judas had become so blinded to his sin and so twisted in his thinking, that he, too, thought Jesus was sending him out on business. But he wasn't going out on Jesus's business, or the Father's business. He was going out on Satan's business.

Soon afterward, Jesus led us in a song and then we headed to the Mount of Olives. When we arrived, Jesus told us to remain in that spot while He went a little farther with Peter, James, and John. The four of them walked deeper into the garden, then Jesus told them to wait while He walked a short distance farther. We all knew Jesus was drawing away to talk to His Father.

I looked around to see if Judas Iscariot had rejoined us. He had not. Whatever he was up to was going to happen soon. I knew Jesus was troubled, and we all knew we should be praying to the Father on His behalf. But we were exhausted, and soon, one by one, we fell asleep.

I will confess to you there was a heaviness in my heart. For the first time since I had begun to follow Jesus, I was overwhelmed with sadness and paralyzed with fear. I feared for the One who stood before me and the storm I knew was approaching.

MALCHUS – THE SERVANT

*M*y name is Malchus. My father is a servant to the High Priest Ananus ben Seth, whom you know as Annas. He served Rabbi Annas from the days before he became high priest, and from the days before I was born. I was six years old when our family moved with Rabbi Annas and his family into the palace of the high priest. Of course, we lived in the servants' quarters while they lived in the palace.

Though there was never any question that I was the child of a servant – which also made me a servant – children in a palace tend to find one another. The high priest's oldest daughter, Leah, was a year younger than I was. Though she and I were not the only two children in the palace, we were close in age so it was inevitable that we would play together.

We were both very inquisitive. Together, we would often explore the less frequented rooms in the palace, like the underground cells used to hold those who had been arrested and brought before the high priest for questioning. On rare occasions, we would escape and explore the nearby hills.

.   .   .

Though I never lost sight of her station in life – or mine – we developed a childhood friendship. As I reflect back, it would probably be more accurate to say a loyalty instead of a friendship. And truth be told, it was me extending my loyalty toward her in response to the kindness she extended to me. That unique relationship between us would end up setting the direction for much of my life as I grew into adulthood.

After serving as high priest for nine years, Annas was replaced by Ishmael ben Phabi. Since we were servants to the person and not the position, when Annas moved out of the palace into a large home nearby, our family moved with him. I was fifteen at the time.

Given my age, I now had responsibilities as a servant under my father's charge. He was training me with the skills to one day become a household manager like himself. He rotated me through all of the positions of service within the household to give me a proper understanding of each servant's responsibilities.

Though I had long known Leah for her kindness, I had also known her father for his sternness. He was one of the youngest men to ever become high priest. Annas had begun the climb for that position at an early age. He was an ambitious man who let little stand in his way.

It was a well-known fact that Annas resented the Roman prefect Valerius Gratus's decision to remove him as high priest. The prefect feared that Annas's power over the people could lead to insurrection, so he instituted a new law that a high priest could serve for only one year. Annas looked for ways he could continue to retain – and increase – his power, even under this new ruling. One of those ways was to influence the prefect to choose one of his sons to assume the role. But soon, he ran out of sons.

For several years, he had been mentoring Joseph ben Caiaphas for the role. Caiaphas was an ambitious man, just like Annas, and he was a diligent apprentice. Annas knew that his power was at risk if the prefect chose someone who was not under his control. He knew that the annual selection of a new high priest had to be stopped. He eventually convinced all of the members of the high council that the practice was detrimental to their rule.

And he also recommended that they encourage the prefect to choose Caiaphas as the next high priest. Since Caiaphas was not his relative, even those who were cautious of Annas's motives agreed. As a unanimous body, they petitioned the prefect, who in turn acquiesced to their political pressure. Caiaphas was appointed to the role, and there was no longer a limitation as to the length of time which he could serve.

Though Caiaphas was already greatly influenced by Annas, the ever-crafty older man knew he still needed to strengthen their relationship even further. What better way than for Caiaphas to marry Leah? The fact that she was an attractive and desirable woman made the union even more enticing. So, Leah became Caiaphas's wife, and Annas became his father-in-law, maintaining – and perhaps even increasing – his power and influence over the people of Israel.

When Caiaphas's new bride moved into the high priest's palace with him, he found that he needed to staff his household differently. He needed a more capable household manager. Leah quickly recommended me to her husband, and Annas further affirmed the choice. It gave Leah a friendly face in the palace, and it gave Annas another set of watchful eyes in the high priest's home. Annas never questioned that my loyalty to him would be any less than my father's.

It was a great honor for me to again be a servant of the high priest – and this time I wasn't the household manager's son, I was the household manager of the most powerful Jew in Israel, except perhaps his father-in-law. It was with great pride that I stepped into this role. I sought to please my master, his wife, my father, and the one to whom I believed I owed the most – Annas.

· · ·

But another member of the family soon stole all of our hearts. During their fourth year of marriage, Leah gave birth to her baby daughter, Rachel. She soon became the apple of her father's eye, and the only time I ever saw any tenderness in Annas's demeanor was when his granddaughter was nearby.

My rule of the household, under the authority of my master, was without question. And as time went on, I became well-known throughout the city. The people afforded me respect. I eventually lost sight of the fact that their respect was out of fear and not because I had earned it. They knew I was the eyes and ears of the high priest. They also knew if I observed any disloyalty to him I would report it straightaway – and they knew his retaliation would be swift. As the years went by, that fear grew among the enemies of Caiaphas, as well as his friends.

In recent years, a Man from Nazareth named Jesus began to make quite a name for Himself. He came on the scene at the age of thirty. Up until then He lived an obscure life. He was quickly recognized as a gifted Teacher. Jesus had a command of the Scriptures that was said to surpass that of Hillel the Elder, not to mention my master or his father-in-law. But His notoriety went beyond even that. Numerous people said He was a Miracle Worker – able to make the blind to see, the deaf to hear, and the lame to walk.

Three years ago, He came to the temple to observe the Feast of Passover. When He entered the temple, He overturned the money-changers' tables, drove out the merchants, and shouted, *"Get these things out of here! Stop turning my Father's house into a marketplace!"*[1]

That evening, my master and his father-in-law were discussing the Man's actions and their ramifications. Annas was quick to point out that this Man had no authority within the temple. Who did He think He was to take such action? Caiaphas had placed Annas in charge of the merchants' activities in the temple. Those merchants were acting under his authority! Who was this Man to question that?

. . .

What's more, He had cost them quite a bit of money that day – between the damage and the disruption. But even more importantly, the high council had questioned whether Jesus's actions were, in fact, correct. A number of the members had apparently spoken up saying they, too, questioned the practice but had been reluctant to say anything.

They all agreed that the merchants should conduct their trade out in the stoa – which had been built for that purpose – so the decision was made that the merchants would not return. That caused Caiaphas and Annas great chagrin, but both men knew they would look for a future opportunity to set this straight!

The discussion then turned to the Man Himself. Where did He come from? What did they know about Him? What was He planning to do? They decided to investigate Him further.

As I entered the hall where the two men were speaking, my master called to me. "Malchus, I have a job for you. You are more than a servant to me. You are a trusted ally. One on whom I know I can depend. There is a Man who threatens everything that we believe. He places Himself above the authorities that were established by the patriarchs Moses and Aaron themselves. He is a troublemaker.

"I am certain that He will remain in the city for the remainder of the festival. I want you to inconspicuously go to the temple and into the streets and listen to what this Man has to say. Listen for any statement He makes that is contrary to our laws – or to Roman laws. He is a threat to us and our way of life. He will make a mistake, and I will be grateful to you when you help us catch Him!"

I did as my master directed me. I was confident I would hear something that I could report back to him. But as the week continued, I heard no such thing. Everything He spoke appeared to be consistent with the Scriptures – at least from a servant's point of view. I listened as He responded to questions from the scribes and Pharisees. Each question seemed to be designed to surface Jesus's treachery.

But He appeared too smart to step into their traps. He responded to each one in a way that turned the question of who was truly following the Scriptures back on His questioners. However, I remained confident that it was just a matter of time before Jesus made a mistake.

Each day I also saw Him perform miracles. I was certain there were reasonable explanations for each one. I vowed I would discover what tricks He was using. But the week ended with nothing for me to report back to my master. Jesus left the city, and I turned my complete attention back to managing the household.

In the years that followed, whenever Jesus returned to Jerusalem, my master would send me to be his ear, listening for Jesus to make a mistake. The Passover is now upon us again. As usual, I have heard many hushed conversations about Jesus between my master and his father-in-law.

Recently, I heard them agree to bring the merchants back into the courtyard of the temple. They knew Jesus had returned to the city. As a matter of fact, *everyone* knew Jesus had returned. It was quite a spectacle when He rode into the city on the donkey's colt the other day. The crowd seemed prepared to crown Him as king. My master and Annas were quite upset. They said if they didn't do something now it would be too late. They would lose their positions. I feared for my master.

The two men decided that Jesus would unquestionably react to the merchants being back in the courtyard. When He did, they would charge Him with taking action in the temple without proper authority. Apparently, many of the members of the high council who had supported Jesus's actions three years ago no longer felt the same way. A growing number were becoming concerned about their own survival. The high priest now had the votes in the high council to convict Jesus over the question of His authority.

. . .

I was in the temple on Monday morning. Jesus did not disappoint. He chased the merchants out of the temple. To be honest, He didn't need to exert much force – they were all expecting Him to act this way! I saw my master and his father-in-law in a corner of the courtyard. They appeared quite pleased that their plan had succeeded. I was somewhat surprised that they chose not to confront Jesus there and then.

It was Tuesday morning before they did so. But Jesus again slyly evaded their question by asking them, *"Did John's authority to baptize come from heaven, or was it merely human?"*[2]

When the Pharisees refused to answer His question, He refused to answer theirs. They had been unsuccessful in closing the trap around their prey again! I saw my master's look of disgust as he and his father-in-law turned and walked away.

I stayed and listened to Jesus for a while. But this time wasn't any different. He didn't say anything that would give my master what he needed to discredit Jesus. I left while He was still speaking to attend to other matters at the palace.

Later that night when my master returned home, I expected him to be in a foul mood. But surprisingly, he seemed quite beside himself. While the servants were serving him and Leah their dinner, I heard him explain to her that one of Jesus's disciples had come to them that afternoon offering to deliver Jesus into their hands. They still weren't sure how they would present charges against Him, but they were confident that once He was arrested some of His followers would turn against Him and testify against His treachery. My master seemed very pleased with himself – and I was pleased for him.

Tonight is the eve of Passover. My master came to me earlier tonight and said, "Malchus, gather the other male servants. Take torches, swords, and clubs. Gather in the courtyard outside the palace and accompany the temple guards and Roman soldiers. Tonight, you all will arrest Jesus and bring Him to me! Our long wait is over. Just like always, you are my ear tonight. Go and report back to me all that happens!"

As we assembled in the courtyard, I approached the captain of the temple guard. There was another man standing with him. I did not know him, but I knew I had seen him before. "Malchus, "the captain said, "this is Judas. He will lead us to the place where we will arrest Jesus!" Yes, that's where I had seen him. He is one of the followers of Jesus! I was surprised that he was willing to help us. Judas, the captain, and I led the soldiers and the servants as we set out on our mission.

We marched across the Kidron Valley toward the Mount of Olives. As we drew closer, it appeared we were headed to the Garden of Gethsemane. With each step, I grew conflicted. I was proud that my master had entrusted me with this responsibility. Tonight, I would finally defend my master and put an end to this interloper's treachery against him. But somehow, Jesus had never seemed that treacherous to me!

Our torches were casting eerie shadows as we got near the garden. Suddenly, men who apparently were sleeping began to stir as they heard us approach. These were some of Jesus's followers. Judas didn't seem to be very interested in them. He had another prize in his sights. The captain told some of the guards to stay there and watch those men while the rest of us continued on.

My heart was pounding. I could feel the adrenaline coursing through my veins. I had my club ready to swing at anyone who made a move. We had no idea how His followers would react. Obviously, we had caught them by surprise, but now they were fully aware of our presence.

Then I saw Him! He was right there in front of us. As Judas walked up to Jesus, I heard him loudly say, "Rabbi!" and then he greeted Him with a kiss. Jesus responded by saying, "*Judas, would you betray the Son of Man with a kiss?"*[3] Immediately the captain of the guard told the soldiers and the temple guards to take hold of Jesus and arrest Him.

Suddenly, one of the men with Jesus – a little older, a little bigger, and a little burlier than the rest – drew his sword. He was standing in front of me, just a little to my right. I raised my club to knock his sword out of his hand. But the man was quicker than I was. I felt his blade slice off my ear.

I dropped my club and clutched the right side of my head. My ear was no longer there. As blood poured down my neck, my knees buckled, and I dropped to the ground. I looked down and saw my cloak was already covered in blood. My severed ear was there on the ground. My head started to spin, and I knew at any moment I was going to black out.

I heard someone shout, *"No more of this! Put away your sword. Don't you realize that I could ask My Father for thousands of angels to protect us, and He would send them instantly?"*[4]

Then I sensed someone kneeling in front of me. It was Jesus! He reached down and picked up my ear, then placed His hand on the side of my face. Instantly the pain stopped! What was Jesus doing? He took His hand away, and I immediately raised mine. My ear was back in place – right where it was supposed to be! I was no longer bleeding! Had I imagined my ear being cut off? I looked down again at my cloak soaked in blood. No, I had not imagined it.

Jesus was still there kneeling before me. I looked into His eyes. Here I was on a mission to arrest Him. But He wasn't looking at me with hatred or contempt – all I saw in His eyes were gentleness and kindness. This Man I despised because of what I thought was His betrayal of my master was anything but treacherous. He had shown me mercy. He had shown me compassion. He had healed my pain. I mouthed the words, "Thank You." But they were so inadequate. I began to tremble before Him.

· · ·

It all lasted only seconds, but it left an indelible print on my heart and in my mind. As I looked at the faces of those around me, they, too, were looking on in disbelief. But then I saw the captain of the guard reach down, take Jesus by the hand, and jerk Him to His feet. As I knelt there, they tied ropes around Jesus's wrists. The man who had cut off my ear, and all the rest of Jesus's followers, had run away. The guards looked conflicted over whether or not they should chase after them.

I heard Jesus say, *"Am I some dangerous revolutionary that you come with swords and clubs to arrest Me? Why didn't you arrest Me in the Temple? I was there every day. But this is your moment, the time when the power of darkness reigns. And since I am the One you want, let these others go."*[5]

Either the captain agreed with Him, or he didn't have orders to arrest the others – so he commanded the soldiers and servants to take Jesus and go. In a few minutes I was left kneeling there all by myself. The chaos had vanished, and I was left alone in silence.

I was torn about what to do. My master had ordered me to return and report to him about the arrest of the treacherous One. But I now knew Jesus was not the one who was treacherous, my master was! And I now had a new Master. The wrong one had just been arrested. I wasn't sure what to do next, but I knew I could not continue living my life as I had before. It was time to say goodbye to a childhood friend. It was time to say goodbye to my father. He would never understand what I was about to do. And, of course, it was time to say goodbye to my former master.

I am no longer the ear of Caiaphas; I now listen to the One who stood before me.

∾

ANNAS – THE HIGH PRIEST

y name is Annas and I am a Sadducee by birth – and by choice. My father was a Sadducee and a member of the Great Sanhedrin. Though I excelled in my studies under some of the most renowned minds of our day, my greatest teacher was my father. He taught me how to build relationships with people of influence and leverage those connections into positions of influence and power for myself. From an early age, I aspired to become the youngest person to ever become high priest. At twenty-nine years of age, I achieved that goal!

A significant step along the way was the opportunity to serve as a scribe to Herod the Great when I was nineteen. Many of you know that he received a visit from wise men from the east who were seeking a baby they said was the newborn King of the Jews. I was the one who counseled Herod to direct them to Bethlehem with instructions to report back the location of the baby. Neither Herod nor I had any interest in going to worship the baby. Herod saw the baby as a threat to his rule. Garnering the baby's location would enable him to eliminate that threat.

It would have been a brilliant plan if the wise men had not chosen to return home without reporting to Herod. However, not one to be stymied by those who fail to do my bidding, I suggested a new plan to Herod. I advised him to dispatch some of his most trusted soldiers to Bethlehem, and the villages immediately surrounding it, to kill all of the baby boys aged two years and under. When the soldiers returned to Jerusalem having completed their mission, I thought the potential threat had been eliminated. Herod rewarded me greatly for my counsel.

For the next thirty years, not another word was said about the child. I had not given Him another thought until one day I heard about a Man who was captivating the people with His words and His miracles. People were beginning to suggest that this Man named Jesus was the promised Messiah. I was one of the few who knew that His age coincided with the birth of the baby the men from the east had sought. Were this Man and that baby the same person? Had the baby somehow survived?

Three years ago, at the time of our annual Passover celebration, this Jesus arrived at the temple. He saw the merchants and money-changers at their tables inside the court of the Gentiles within the temple walls. I had implemented that practice nineteen years earlier near the beginning of my tenure as high priest. I had done so in order to increase the amount of funds flowing into the temple treasury. And since it was my idea, I made certain that a portion of the profits made it into my pocket, as well.

Though I was no longer the high priest when Jesus came to the temple, my son-in-law, Caiaphas, was. He had designated me to oversee the operation of the merchants and money-changers. It had proven to be a profitable enterprise for all of us. That is, until Jesus arrived. He chased the merchants and the money-changers out of the temple! I was enraged that a Man with absolutely no authority would attempt such a thing – and challenge the power and control of those of us in leadership. I was prepared to bring charges against Him before the High Council of the Sanhedrin until I realized that a majority of our group was now questioning whether the practice was wrong. They were saying that this Teacher from Nazareth was correct, and we should discontinue the custom.

. . .

Over the years, I have learned to be patient and fight my battles when I know I can win. I chose to view this as a temporary setback and not press the issue against Jesus at the time. I would wait until I knew I had the support of the high council firmly in my grasp before proceeding further. My son-in-law agreed to help me build a case against Jesus.

In the years since, we routinely sent scribes and priests to question and discredit Him. We contested His healing powers and attempted to credit them to demons. Ironically, that argument has continued to fall on deaf ears. It is difficult to deny that the blind can now see, the deaf can hear, the lame can walk, and the dead have been restored to life. These are not acts of demons; these are miracles of God!

The most dramatic example took place less than two months ago when a man who had died in Bethany walked out of his tomb four days later in response to Jesus's command. People throughout our nation are ready to declare Him as the Messiah! I have considered having the man named Lazarus arrested and killed for collaborating with Jesus to orchestrate an elaborate hoax. But I am finding that there are too many witnesses to the fact that he truly was dead and buried.

On multiple occasions our people have confronted Jesus with questions we were certain would result in His downfall. Several of our priests brought a woman caught in the act of adultery before Him, forcing Him to choose between condemning her or contradicting the law of Moses. But somehow, He had quietly and deftly reminded each of the accusers of his own personal sins – those they thought were hidden – and one by one, each of the men had retreated. No one had remained to accuse the woman.

On another day we sent a group of Herodians to ask Him if it was lawful to pay taxes to Caesar. If He said "yes," the crowd would rise up against Him. If He said "no," He would be inciting sedition against Rome. I was certain there would be no escape for Him this time. But He skillfully asked our scribes if they had any Roman coinage on their person. When one presented a denarius, Jesus asked, *"Whose picture and title are stamped on it?"*[1]

"Caesar's,"[2] they replied.

"Well, then," He said, *"give to Caesar what belongs to Caesar, and give to God what belongs to God."*[3]

Our people were so astounded by His answer that they immediately retreated.

Each time, Jesus eluded our grasp. But now more members of our high council have become convinced that Jesus is a threat to our way of life – not only as a people, but specifically to each of us who enjoy our positions of authority. If Jesus establishes His kingdom, we will no longer have those positions. We will no longer enjoy the livelihoods to which we have become accustomed.

Some of the high council members were part of the group that had accused the adulterous woman. But they realized they couldn't risk Jesus divulging their secret sin to anyone else. Others had been a part of the group that had posed the question about taxes to Him, and they resented being made to look foolish in front of the people. The time had come. The high council was finally ready to act!

All we needed was a catalytic event – and that would be easy to orchestrate. Caiaphas and I did just that a few days ago. I instructed the merchants and money-changers at the temple to return to the Court of the Gentiles on Monday morning. We knew that when Jesus arrived, He would clear them out just as He had done three years earlier. This time we were prepared to challenge Him on the question of His authority. I had patiently waited for this opportunity for three years, and now my time had come!

. . .

One of His disciples, a zealot by the name of Judas, unexpectedly came to us Tuesday to tell us he would help us arrest Jesus. He would help us find the right time and place so we wouldn't incite a crowd to come to His defense. I couldn't imagine why this man was willing to help us – and for only thirty pieces of silver. But if he delivered on his promise, I didn't care what his motives were! As they say, my enemy's enemy is a friend. Everything was working together in our favor!

During the three years I waited for my plan to come to fruition, I did my best to stay in the background. I wanted the arrest and downfall of Jesus to be attributed to others. Since I, in fact, had the most to gain, I did not want our efforts to be undermined by a charge of avarice against me. I wanted the charges to clearly point to Jesus's violations of the laws of Moses and His disloyal acts against Roman authority. We would need the latter in order to convince Pontius Pilate to have Him crucified. And anything short of crucifixion would be insufficient!

The plan was finally coming together. Last night I received word from Caiaphas that Judas was prepared to deliver Jesus that very night. Caiaphas arranged to send a mob of temple guards, Roman soldiers, priests, and servants to arrest Jesus. They were heading to the Garden of Gethsemane. I told Caiaphas that I wanted Jesus brought to me first. I wanted to be certain we had our witnesses and accusations prepared before we brought charges against Him before the high council. I also wanted the personal satisfaction of looking Him in the eye so He would know I had defeated Him once and for all! That which Herod's soldiers had bungled so many years earlier, I was finally completing!

I dressed in my priestly robes, though I no longer held the position of high priest. I wanted to make sure Jesus knew I still held power. I had a great chair set in my formal meeting chamber, placed on an elevated platform, so I would be looking down on Him as we spoke. There would be no doubt about the extent of my authority over Him!

Jesus's hands were bound as I had instructed. I had seen Him on a few occasions from a distance. I had intentionally delayed a face-to-face meeting until the time was right. As I looked at Him now, He did not look as formidable as I expected. I sat above Him as a judge. He stood beneath me as a prisoner!

I asked Him what He had been teaching. I did not ask Him about His miracles. I did not want to hear about His miracles. They were of no consequence to the charges I was going to bring against Him. I wanted our conversation to avoid any reference to the miraculous.

I knew what He had been teaching, but I wanted Him to tell me personally. Unfortunately, the scribes and Pharisees I had previously sent had failed to bring back solid reasons that could be used to accuse Him. But I am much craftier than they are. I will succeed where others have failed. I always do!

Jesus told me, *"Everyone knows what I teach. I have preached regularly in the synagogues and the Temple, where the people gather. I have not spoken in secret. Why are you asking Me this question? Ask those who heard Me. They know what I said."*[4]

His answer did not catch me by surprise. As a matter of fact, I had fully expected it. One of the temple guards standing nearby slapped Jesus across the face – just as I had instructed him to do before I entered the room. *"Is that the way to answer the high priest?"*[5] he demanded.

But rather than catching Jesus off guard and putting Him on the defensive, He replied, *"If I said anything wrong, you must prove it. But if I'm speaking the truth, why are you beating Me?"*[6]

Jesus had a very clear understanding of our laws, just as I did. I was aware that I needed to walk carefully now that I had stepped into the light. I was no longer orchestrating this from the shadows. My ego had temporarily gotten the better of me, and I had placed myself in a vulnerable position.

Everything that was now being done to Jesus was illegal under Mosaic law. Obviously, Jesus knew that as well as I did.

Since I am no longer the high priest, I do not have the legal authority to detain or question Him. The law requires that there be witnesses *before* an arrest takes place. But we were still trying to find someone who could accuse Jesus of having said or done anything that violated the law. Our law forbids a trial from beginning at night; and yet, here we are. A few moments ago, when the guard slapped Jesus, he had violated the law. No prisoner was ever to be struck in any way who had not first been proven guilty.

I recognized I wasn't making any progress here. All I was doing was putting myself in jeopardy, so I instructed the guards to deliver Jesus to Caiaphas. I would continue my work there – but for now I would return to the shadows.

The entire high council had assembled in the home of Caiaphas. I reported what had occurred in my home. I told them I believed the best course of action was to demand that Jesus admit to being the Son of God. That would be blasphemy! And we would have what we needed before many witnesses.

After we spoke briefly about our course of attack, we instructed the guards to bring Jesus into the room. This was the first time Caiaphas had seen Jesus up close. I could tell he was silently sizing up the Man.

After a few moments, Caiaphas asked Jesus, *"Tell us, are You the Messiah?"*[7]

Jesus replied, *"If I tell you, you won't believe Me. And if I ask you a question, you won't answer. But from now on the Son of Man will be seated in the place of power at God's right hand."*[8]

.   .   .

Several council members shouted, *"So, are You claiming to be the Son of God?"*[(9)]

Jesus replied, *"You say that I am."*[(10)]

We would take that as His admission! I nodded my head at the other members of the high council. In unison they declared, *"Why do we need other witnesses? We ourselves just heard Him say it. He is guilty! He deserves to die!"*[(11)]

Caiaphas directed the guards to take Jesus away. Then he told everyone who was not part of the high council to leave the room. The guards locked Jesus in a cell in the lower foundation of the palace while we deliberated. We had all heard Jesus admit that He was the Son of God. And earlier this week, we had heard the crowds refer to Him as King. Jesus had made no attempt to deny those claims. As a matter of fact, He had said, *"I tell you, if these were silent, the very stones would cry out."*[(12)]

We had enough to convict Him of blasphemy and bring a charge of sedition before Pontius Pilate. Now, we just needed to make sure Pilate did what we needed him to do!

I saw someone move at the back of the room. It was that man Judas – the one who had betrayed Jesus. He had stayed in the room when everyone else left. *"I have sinned,"* he shouted, *"for I have betrayed an innocent man."*[(13)]

"What do we care?" I retorted. *"That's your problem."*[(14)] What did this man think we were going to do? Was he really that naïve? He had played his part, and now we had no further need of him. Caiaphas motioned to the temple guards to remove him.

. . .

Suddenly Judas threw the thirty pieces of silver on the floor and stormed from the room. I didn't know what he was going to do next, but frankly I didn't care. He was a betrayer. No one would ever listen to him again!

Caiaphas directed one of the servants to pick up the coins. Earlier this week, the Sanhedrin had been debating what to do with foreigners who die in Jerusalem. Judas's parting action had just given us the answer. He had no idea how much he had helped us this week!

"It wouldn't be right to put this money in the temple treasury,"[(15)] Caiaphas said. "Use it to buy a field that can be used as a cemetery for the burial of foreigners. Call it the "Field of Blood.""

Caiaphas instructed the guards to make ready the prisoner. We were going to deliver Him to Pilate. Victory was now within our grasp. We set out on a victory march! The One who had stood before me was now a convicted Man!

～

PILATE – THE PREFECT

My name is Pontius Pilatus, but most of you know me as Pilate. I am the fifth Roman prefect to govern this contentious province of Judea. Initially I was grateful to Emperor Tiberius for honoring me with this appointment. But that was before I spent time among the Jewish people – and specifically their religious leaders.

Not only do they believe in only one God, they believe their God is the only true God. They look down on us – their conquerors and rulers – for our more enlightened belief in many gods. Every day they bring petitions to me complaining about something our soldiers have done that has offended their religious sensibilities. And whenever I demand anything of them, they counter that they cannot comply because they are observing a religious feast. It seems like they are always observing a religious feast!

To add insult to injury, they refuse to enter my palace to have an audience with me. They say it would make them ceremonially unclean – so whenever they come to complain, I have to go outside to speak to them. I now understand why the first three prefects were so grateful their assignments were brief. Regrettably, I have already been in this role for more than three years.

. . .

But I digress. Allow me to tell you a little about myself. I come from a distinguished family. My grandfather was Pontius Aquila. He faithfully served as a member of the tribunal under Julius Caesar until their falling out. Caesar underhandedly confiscated some of our family's land in Naples to honor the request of his mistress, Servilia. She had long coveted our land and Caesar appropriated it in order to earn her affection.

From that point forward, my grandfather became one of the leaders of the opposition. After their falling out, Caesar often said whenever he was making a promise to someone, "That is, if Pontius Aquila will allow me." Ironically, my grandfather eventually formed an alliance with Servilia's son, Brutus, and her son-in-law, Cassius, that led to Julius Caesar's assassination at the hands of sixty men. My grandfather was one of those men. It was Caesar's death that led our empire to transition from being under the rule of a monarch to being ruled as a republic. My grandfather was one of the leaders of that effort.

My father, Pontius Cominus, served with distinction as an officer of the legionary cavalry. He then became a leader during the early years as our empire was learning how to function as a republic. He served honorably as a member of the Roman senate under Emperor Augustus.

I grew up in the magnificent city of Rome during those years. All roads lead to Rome – and it is unquestionably the center of civilization as we know it! I enjoyed a privileged education under the tutelage of some of the greatest minds the world has ever known. My family enjoyed a measure of wealth, and we were well connected politically and socially.

My wife, Claudia, had a very similar upbringing and our wedding was considered one of the premier social events of the year. Soon after marrying, I embarked on what would prove to be a distinguished career as an officer in the cavalry. I quickly demonstrated a great prowess with the javelin and became celebrated as a champion. My notoriety continued to rise. That was what subsequently led Emperor Tiberius to appoint me to my current position. Unless I fail here, I will eventually be reassigned to an important role in Rome. That day cannot come soon enough for me!

In the early days of Rome's occupation of this land, a client king was put in place to govern the people. The first was Herod the Great. He accomplished many great things on behalf of Rome, on behalf of the Jewish people – and without a doubt, on behalf of his own self-interest. One of those accomplishments was the city of Caesarea Maritima along the Mediterranean Sea overlooking a beautifully designed port. The city includes event arenas that are second only to those in Rome and a beautiful palace Herod had built for himself. The one consolation of this assignment is that Claudia, my son, Aquila (named for his great grandfather), and I call that beautiful palace home.

Rome has declared Caesarea Maritima to be the capital city over Judea, Samaria, and Idumea – for which I am grateful. But it has proven to be another point of contention with the Jews. They will only recognize Jerusalem as their capital. So, I am forced to maintain a praetorium (the palatial residence of a Roman governor) in Jerusalem inside the Antonio fortress. I reside there a few weeks each year – removed from the beauty of the Mediterranean Sea – typically during the major feast celebrations of the Jews.

Rome has assigned me a half legion of soldiers (approximately three thousand men) to maintain order throughout the three provinces. Most of the soldiers have been recruited from within the provinces, with the officers having been dispatched from Rome. My role as prefect is to maintain order among the people, to make certain tribute taxes are appropriately collected and transmitted by the tax collectors to Rome, and ensure that any spark of insurrection is immediately extinguished.

I am not required to insert myself into the day-to-day politics and administration of the provinces. That is left to their Sanhedrin. Since their rules of law center around their religious beliefs, I leave them to interpret those laws as they see fit, unless they violate Roman law or require capital punishment. Those matters are all referred to me to decide.

Those distinctions should be simple enough to make – and probably elsewhere in the world they are. But the Jews are a unique people, and they exhaust me with their continual arguments and disputes. Today is one of those days!

Early this morning, a mob appeared at my gate – not a delegation, as would have been much more appropriate. It was a mob led by the high priest and the other members of their high council. As usual, they were demanding – not requesting – an audience with me which, of course, meant I needed to go outside to meet with them.

I am well aware of the Teacher called Jesus. He has been making quite a stir throughout the region for the past three years. I've been told He is a Miracle Worker and a well-spoken Teacher. He has been growing in popularity with each passing month. Even some of the soldiers in my charge have been drawn to His teaching.

Several times over the past three years, I have sent a few trusted spies to listen to His teaching and observe His actions to make sure He was not attempting to lead an insurrection against Rome. I have heard some people refer to Him as the King of the Jews, but I believe that it is strictly a religious designation.

There has been nothing about this Man that caused me – or would cause Rome – any reason for concern. As a matter of fact, I have found His teachings to be very enlightening. He encourages love for your neighbor, respect for authority, and a challenge to do good to others. As far as I am concerned, I prefer His teachings far above those of the legalistic Jewish priests with whom I am in regular contact!

. . .

But I also know that the religious leaders are afraid of Him. They are concerned His teachings and His miracles are loosening the yoke they have placed on their own people. They fear their authority is being undermined by One who is not under their control. And they are worried about their positions, their power, their prestige, and, most importantly, their wealth.

Last Sunday, the streets were overrun by a crowd as they welcomed Jesus into the city. I watched the processional closely. There was nothing this Man did that pointed to a revolt. He had entered peacefully. And if He were truly a religious king, He had entered with great humility. Believe me, I have seen political and military leaders make their grand entrances, and none of them came riding in on a donkey's colt!

My spies informed me that Jesus had overturned the tables inside the temple the next day. But those same spies told me those tables were erected to provoke a reaction from Jesus. These were the religious leaders I had to contend with each day, and I was enjoying watching them get the comeuppance they so rightly deserved.

The entire high council now stood before me declaring, *"This man has been leading our people astray by telling them not to pay their taxes to the Roman government and by claiming He is the Messiah, a king."*[1]

I knew these men. I knew that every one of them was more than willing to lie to me to get his way. I knew there was nothing trustworthy about their report. The only One I truly respected was the Man they were accusing. So I asked Him, "Are you the King of the Jews?"[2]

Jesus replied, *"You have said it."*[3]

He was correct! The religious leaders had said it. I had said it when I asked Him the question ... but Jesus had never said it. I turned to Annas and Caiaphas – who I was pretty certain were the ones behind all of this – as well as the other members of the high council and said, *"I find nothing wrong with this Man!"*[(4)]

Rather than respectfully submit to my ruling, they insisted, *"But He is causing riots by His teaching wherever He goes – all over Judea, from Galilee to Jerusalem!"*[(5)] I knew that wasn't true! Did these religious leaders really think I was that oblivious to what was going on?

But I was also mindful that my primary charge as prefect was to maintain peace between Rome and these people. A riot under my watch would not bode well for a future assignment in Rome. And the people were greatly influenced by their religious leaders who were now standing before me.

Suddenly, I had an idea. When the religious leaders said, "… from Galilee to Jerusalem …." I remembered that Jesus was from Nazareth. He is a Galilean. If He has done anything wrong, it is for Herod Antipas to decide. He is the governor over Galilee!

"Oh, is He a Galilean?"[(6)] I asked. "Then He must be brought before Herod Antipas, since Galilee is under his jurisdiction!" The religious leaders began to debate with me, but when they saw I was resolute about my decision they departed for Herod's palace. Like me, he resided elsewhere but often came to stay in Jerusalem during the feasting days. So, gratefully he was here, and I could defer the matter to him.

However, it wasn't long before the mob returned to my gate. Herod Antipas had sent them back to me. He had apparently joined in this mockery of justice!

Try as I might, I could not avoid making a decision. I was not prepared to sacrifice my own well-being for this Jew, even though He was innocent of every charge being made against Him.

.   .   .

Then I remembered I had one more option at my disposal. A prevailing custom called for the prefect to commute one prisoner's death sentence at the time of Passover. The criminal Barabbas was scheduled to be crucified this day. If there was one thing the Jews and I could agree on, it was that Barabbas deserved to be crucified.

I sat down on the judgment seat as I prepared to announce my decision. But I was interrupted by a messenger who had been sent by my wife, Claudia. The message read: *"Leave that innocent Man alone. I suffered through a terrible nightmare about Him last night."*[7]

Over the years, Claudia had become one of my most reliable counselors. Her discernment had become even more invaluable to me in my dealings with the Jewish priests. She shared my angst.

In light of her counsel, I decided to place the question before the people. Who would they choose to have me release – the criminal Barabbas or the Teacher Jesus? I was pretty confident which man they would choose. Setting Jesus free would then be according to the will of the people, and the religious leaders would not be able to blame me for the decision.

But I underestimated the ability of the chief priests and elders to persuade the crowd that now stood before me. They cried out for the release of Barabbas! The Pharisees had craftily made sure that the crowd assembled before me would blindly follow their lead. So, when the religious leaders cried out, "Barabbas!" so did the crowd.

I called for the prisoner Barabbas to be brought before me. After he arrived, I posed my question to the crowd one more time. This time their response was even more deafening – "Barabbas!"

"Then what should I do with Jesus who is called the Messiah?"[8] I asked.

.   .   .

"Crucify Him!"[9] the mob roared back even louder.

I turned to the centurion and directed him to remove the chains and ropes binding Barabbas. I couldn't believe my ears as I told him he was set free. Barabbas knew better than to stand there. He immediately began to make his way out into the crowd. As he did, the ropes removed from him were now being placed on Jesus.

I made one final attempt to save Jesus by ordering the centurion to have Him scourged. Though I knew that Jesus was without guilt, I still permitted Him to go through the brutality of a Roman scourging. I was hopeful that would satisfy the blood thirst of the religious leaders and the crowd.

Over the years, our Roman soldiers have perfected scourging into a macabre art. The scourge is a short whip made of two or three leather thongs or ropes connected to a handle. The thongs are knotted with pieces of metal or bones at various intervals with a hook at the end. The scourge is intended to quickly remove flesh from the body stopping just short of death.

But even that did not satisfy the crowd's lust for His blood. The religious leaders and the crowd continued to cry out for Him to be crucified. Such was His state when I acquiesced to the religious leaders and turned Jesus over to the soldiers.

I sent for a bowl of water to wash my hands before the crowd as I said, *"I am innocent of this man's blood. The responsibility is yours!"*[10]

The people yelled back, *"We will take responsibility for His death – we and our children!"*[11]

. . .

But no matter what they said, and no matter how hard I scrubbed, I could not wash the innocent blood from my hands of the One who stood before me.

~

ANTIPAS – THE ETHNARCH

I am Herod Antipas, one of King Herod the Great's favored sons. The fact that I was a favored son is an important distinction. I was sixth in the line of succession for his throne. I am the second son of King Herod's fourth wife, Malthace. I had one older brother, four older half-brothers by my father's three previous wives, and one younger half-brother, Philip, by his fifth wife.

Being a favored son was so important because my father had three of my older half-brothers executed for what he deemed as insurrection. Since my father followed Jewish law and their dietary restrictions, the emperor of Rome, Caesar Augustus, was once heard to remark, "It is better to be Herod's pig than his son!" The pig would never die at my father's hand. So, we all knew to watch our father carefully!

As a result of those executions, my remaining older half-brother, Herod II, and his beguiling wife, Herodias, had become the intended heirs to my father's throne. But my older brother, Archelaus, and I successfully convinced our father right before his death to change his will so that we would each reign over portions of the kingdom – and Herod II would be left with nothing.

. . .

When I was seventeen, my father arranged for me to marry the lovely Phasaelis, a princess of Nabataea. The Nabateans are a tribal kingdom situated to our east, centered around the city of Petra, south of the Parthian empire. It was a marriage of political expedience arranged to solidify a treaty between our lands. Regrettably, she and I never held much affection for one another – particularly because I had my eye on my sister-in-law, Herodias.

Though my father had many faults, including being a terrible father, he was a masterful ruler. From an early age, I knew I needed to watch him and learn. He deftly navigated through the political upheaval in Rome as the empire was evolving from a monarchy to a republic. He chose the right candidate for emperor, which enabled him to assume his position as tetrarch over the Judean provinces with the strong backing of Rome.

The Romans had conquered our land twenty-seven years before they named my father as client king. During those years, their rule was chaotic, and our lands were suffering while the regions around us were prospering. In the years following my father's ascent to his position, he led us into a time of aggressive rebuilding and prosperity. He developed strong alliances with the religious leaders, providing them with greater autonomy in their religious affairs and practices.

My father was always watchful for anyone or anything that threatened his rule. For example, thirty-three years ago some wise men from the east visited my father to seek out a baby they said would be the King above all other kings. They were following a star that had only recently appeared, and they believed it would lead them to the baby.

The scribes and priests attending to my father told him the prophets said the Promised One would be born in the town of Bethlehem. My father relayed that information to the wise men and told them to seek the baby there. He told them to return to him after they found the child so he could go and worship Him, as well. Actually, it was the high priest Annas, a scribe in my father's court at the time, and I who suggested this plan.

· · ·

When the wise men did not return to my father, it was Annas and I who convinced him to send his soldiers to kill all the male children two years and younger near Bethlehem. It was only days later that my father contracted a disease that caused his body to begin deteriorating.

No one knew what kind of illness it was. But I always wondered whether God was bringing His judgment on my father for the massacre of the children. When Annas and I once spoke of it, all he said was, "Perhaps."

My father traveled to the city of Jericho with its Roman baths and springs to convalesce. But his condition continued to worsen. He subsequently attempted suicide to escape his excruciating pain. Honestly, I'm not sure which caused his death – his illness or a successful suicide attempt. What I do know is that Caesar Augustus honored his final wishes. The rule over his kingdom was divided between Archelaus, Philip, and me.

Archelaus ruled over Judea, Samaria, and Idumea for a short while until Augustus removed him for incompetence. Governance for that region was then turned over to a series of Roman prefects. Philip rules over the regions of Trachonitis, Gaulanitis, and Batanea on the eastern side of the Jordan River. I am the ethnarch (governor) over Galilee and Perea. But, obviously, all of us serve at the pleasure of Rome and must bow to her authority.

Once my rule was established, I did something that had worked very successfully for my father. He had built the port city of Caesarea Maritima – named in honor of Caesar Augustus – on the coast of the Mediterranean Sea. Since that city lay within the provinces ruled by Archelaus, I set out to build my own capital city along the shore of the Sea of Galilee.

I named it Tiberias in honor of the current emperor of Rome. I was certain that the decision to name the city in his honor would garner me favor with Rome – just like it had for my father – and I was correct. I chose the location because of the natural mineral hot springs that are situated within and immediately around the city.

My one miscalculation was that since the city has no connection with Jewish history, the orthodox Jews consider it a pagan city and will not step foot inside its gates. Accordingly, I ended up resettling many non-Jews from rural Galilee and other parts of my domain in order to populate my new capital.

In addition to my new city, the second possession I sought was a new bride! I was bored with my Nabataean wife. After my father died, there was no one to tell me I had to maintain my marriage for political reasons – and I had my eye on the beguiling Herodias. She was actually my father's granddaughter through one of my now dead half-brothers. But my grandfather favored her, so he had arranged for her to marry Herod II, whom, at the time, he had intended to ascend to his throne as tetrarch upon his death.

But thanks to Archelaus and me, Herod II and Herodias did not ascend to the throne. Rather, they were destined to live out their lives as private citizens living in Rome. It was a very comfortable life – but Herodias considered her life unfulfilled because it did not come with the power and influence she desired to have.

So, Herodias was seduced by my power, and I was seduced by her wiles and charms. We decided to escape our current marriages so we could marry one another and fulfill our personal desires. Normally such a divorce and remarriage wouldn't have made much of a ripple among the Galilean and Perean populace. However, there was one person – John the baptizer – who took great offense with our plan, and he was not going to be silent about it.

John's condemnation of our union as adultery was quite the talk of the region – particularly among the orthodox Jews. Though we didn't need popular support to divorce and remarry, we were offended by the accusations being directed at us by that wild man crying out in the wilderness. In fact, it was Herodias who took the greater offense. I could have easily ignored the homeless prophet's accusations, but Herodias was not so dismissive. She talked me into arresting the baptizer.

Ultimately, my decision to imprison John was actually to protect him from my vindictive wife! I knew that as long as John was imprisoned under my decree, she was powerless to do anything to him. I feared John because I knew he was a good and holy man. On more than one occasion, I had summoned him to come speak with me. I was often perplexed by what he said, but I knew he was speaking truth, and I had a hunger to understand. But all the while, my wife continued to watch for an opportunity to exact her revenge.

Finally, her opportunity arrived. It was my forty-eighth birthday and Herodias encouraged me to host a party for the high officials in my government, the officers of my army, and the leading citizens of the land. She instructed our household manager, Chuza, to spare no expense in making this a most memorable celebration – with the finest food, the finest drink, and the finest music.

When the night arrived, the celebration was intoxicating. My every lustful desire was being satisfied. Herodias had also made arrangements for her daughter, Salome, from her previous marriage to Herod II, to come in and perform a dance for me and my guests. At the instructions of her mother, the girl seduced me in my drunken stupor through her alluring dancing. When it was complete, I foolishly told her, *"Ask me for anything you like, and I will give it to you. I will give you whatever you ask, up to half my kingdom!"*[1] The girl obviously did not know what her mother had planned, because she went out to ask my wife what she should ask for. At the direction of Herodias, the girl returned to me and said, *"I want the head of John the baptizer, right now, on a tray!"*[2]

I immediately regretted what I had said. But because I had made the vow in front of my guests, I could not refuse her. I dispatched a message to the executioner at the fortress to cut off John's head and have it brought to me. That decision has haunted me every day since!

As a matter of fact, I told Herodias that Salome had to leave the palace. Just the sight of her brought back visions of John's severed head on the tray. The matter was soon resolved. Not unexpectedly, her beauty and charms had also caught the eye of my half-brother, Philip, the night of my birthday celebration. He decided to make her his wife. I warned him not to make her any promises that he might later regret!

I was familiar with the ministry of Jesus and was well aware of His growing popularity among the people. I received numerous reports about the miracles Jesus was performing throughout Galilee and the crowds that were flocking to Him. But I never considered Him a threat to my rule. He was a religious leader and did not appear to have any aspirations to be a political leader. If I had thought otherwise, I would have arrested Him long ago.

However, I knew that Annas and the other religious leaders viewed Him as a threat to their own power – and honestly, that was fine with me. I liked having them anxious about the security of their positions. It kept them off balance.

After the baptizer was beheaded, I did wonder whether Jesus was really John returned from the dead to torment me. But I quickly remembered He had already been performing His miracles long before John died. My concern had more to do with my guilty conscience over John's death than over anything Jesus had done.

My household manager, Chuza, had told me how this Man healed his young son. He even tried to convince me to become one of His followers. But he quickly stopped proposing the idea when I showed absolutely no interest.

. . .

I once thought about traveling to see Jesus perform His miracles for myself. I could then determine once and for all who He was, and what, if anything, I needed to do about Him. But I did not want to give Him – or anyone else – the idea that I was concerned by traveling into the countryside to seek Him out. So, I didn't pursue the idea any further.

Today, I am in Jerusalem. Since most of the people I govern come to Jerusalem to observe the religious feasts, I leave my palace in Tiberias and travel here to the city. Though I do not strictly adhere to Judaism, my pilgrimage here seems to placate my Jewish subjects. This is one of those lessons I learned by example from my father. He taught me to always be near my people, prepared to govern, should an issue arise.

This morning I was informed that Jesus was being brought before me. Apparently, the religious leaders had finally been able to arrest Him on some fabricated charge. They had delivered Him to Pilate with the intention of having Him put to death. I knew Pilate had no more concerns about this Man than I do. He was not going to be bullied by Annas and Caiaphas into crucifying an innocent man. But, Pilate had redirected them to me since Jesus is a Galilean. I smiled to myself as I thought about how masterfully Pilate had avoided being coerced by the religious leaders. But I was not going to allow them to manipulate me, either!

I was, however, delighted to finally have an opportunity to see Jesus perform a miracle with my own eyes. I asked Him a series of questions intended to elicit a miraculous act from Him. I was expecting Jesus to perform for my enjoyment. But to my consternation, He never spoke a word. Apparently, He did not realize I had the power to influence Annas and the others to stop this madness. I had never intended John any harm, and I certainly didn't intend to harm this Man. But He needed to help me help Him. He needed to answer my questions and satisfy my curiosity.

In the meantime, Annas, Caiaphas, and the others continued to shout accusations. Between their shouts and His silence, I decided not to expend any of my influence to save Him. If He was determined to not seek my assistance in avoiding His death, then who was I to stand in His way! So, I decided to support the priests in order to glean some political capital for myself.

I began to ridicule the Man and scorn Him as the King of the Jews. In an attempt to gain even more approval from the religious leaders, I called for one of my old robes to be placed on Him to add to the mockery.

But, having once been manipulated into executing the baptizer, I refused to be manipulated again. I would send this matter back to Pilate. Since the religious leaders of Judea were seeking the death of Jesus in Judea, it must be decided by the prefect of Judea. Pilate had attempted to avoid making a decision by sending Jesus to me. But, out of respect for Pilate's position, I must now defer back to his authority.

One day I will remind Pilate how magnanimous I was to him today. I commanded the entire entourage to go back to Pilate. As I watched Jesus being led away like a lamb headed to the slaughter, I found myself wondering if He was the same King whom Annas and I had plotted to kill so many years ago. Was Annas still plotting? And was I just as complicit today as I had been then?

Soon after the crowd left my palace, I began to feel the same sinking feeling in my stomach that I felt the day I had the baptizer executed. I had Herodias to blame for John's fate, and I blamed Jesus Himself for His own fate. But still, I couldn't shake the feeling that I had blood on my hands. The spies I sent to follow the mob soon returned to inform me that Pilate had authorized the crucifixion of Jesus. They told me he publicly washed his hands in front of the people declaring, *"I am innocent of this Man's blood!"*[3] But I knew He would never be able to wash that blood away.

At noon today, darkness fell across the entire city. It was as dark as night. My spies reported that Jesus was hanging on the cross. It remained dark until He took His last breath. I wasn't at Golgotha to witness His crucifixion personally. I wasn't there to witness His last breath ... but I knew when it happened.

The One I conspired to have killed as an innocent baby has now been killed as a spotless lamb. His blood has been shed and now it is on the hands of everyone who had a part in His death. I can pretend to be innocent, but I know better. The darkness that settled over our city has now settled over my heart – and I fear it will never go away. The One who stood before me is now dead, and I will forever be remembered as one of those responsible for shedding innocent blood.

BARABBAS – THE CRIMINAL

*M*y parents gave me the name Jesus Barabbas when I was born. But over the years it was shortened to just Barabbas – which is probably the name by which you know me. I am the eldest son of a rabbi. I spent my early years in our synagogue in Jericho learning and debating the teachings from the Torah.

My father became a member of our local Sanhedrin when I was a little boy. He taught me that the Sanhedrin was made up of rabbis from two different schools of thought. One was known as the Pharisees. They held to the unbending legal tenets of the Mosaic law contained in the Torah, as well as the oral teachings known as the Talmud.

The other school of thought was that of the Sadducees. Their philosophy was also rooted in the Mosaic law, but they did not adhere to the oral rabbinical teachings, neither did they hold to the belief of resurrection. They firmly believed that death was the end – a belief that was greatly influenced by Greek philosophy during the years of captivity.

The Pharisees had little regard for those who did not believe or practice the Jewish faith. They abhorred our pagan Roman leaders. But the

Sadducees were more compromising in their beliefs – particularly when it worked to their personal advantage. They tended to be more open to pursuing political alliances that furthered their agenda, including alliances with the Romans. My father was a Sadducee and gained greater prestige among their ranks as time went on. By my early teen years, he had become a member of the Great Sanhedrin in Jerusalem.

As I grew into adulthood, my father and I grew more at odds with one another over Roman rule. My father was convinced that the only path was compromise. He believed there was no way we would ever overcome them militarily, so we had to be willing to make concessions to receive "a few crumbs from the table" of our Roman rulers. I, on the other hand, was not willing to make any concessions to simply settle for crumbs. We had not sought Roman rule; they had robbed us of our freedom. We needed to do whatever was necessary to regain that freedom – personally, and as a nation.

My thinking was becoming more aligned with the growing zealot movement of freedom at any cost. One day I met a man by the name of Judah the Galilean, who was rising as a leader within that movement. He was bitterly opposed to the heavy-handed oppression of Roman rule that amounted to the equivalent of enslavement, as well as the tyrannical actions of the Herodian leaders. Some of the rebels who were following him were doing so for religious reasons. But others, like me, were motivated more by the desire for greater personal freedoms – and truth be told, the allure of unbridled power and financial gain.

Judah selected several men, including me, to make up a raiding party. We were to detain travelers along the road between Jericho and Jerusalem. We targeted tax collectors and wealthy Jews who were known collaborators with the Romans. Having grown up in that region, I knew the area surrounding that road very well. I knew the best places to surprise unsuspecting travelers.

Initially, no one was harmed. Our mere show of force intimidated our victims. They gave us all the treasure they had so they would come to no harm. A portion of the proceeds went into our own pockets, and the balance went to the zealot treasury to support the movement. As time went on, our victims became more resistant, which in turn prompted us to become more violent. But Judah was always very clear that we were never to take anyone's life.

One day he came to us with a plan to seize control of the armory in Herod's palace. We met significant resistance from a contingent of Herod's soldiers. Some of our men lost their lives, as did some of the soldiers. Several of us, including Judah and me, were able to escape with a small quantity of weapons – but more importantly, with our lives.

As time went on, stories about me began to circulate in the cities and villages around Jerusalem and Jericho. I often found people looking at me warily. I was earning the reputation as someone with whom you didn't want to trifle. Whenever my father and I saw one another, our conversation would quickly deteriorate into heated words. Eventually, we ceased to have any contact whatsoever. My father told me that as far as he was concerned, I was dead to him.

A number of years ago I met two men who, though I didn't know it at the time, would change the course of my life. They told me they wanted to join the zealot movement. They shared a hatred for the Romans and the Herodians. Though I didn't think either one of them would have the stomach for the violence, I still was drawn to them. I knew they would be trustworthy – perhaps too trustworthy. On occasion we would meet in Jerusalem. One of the men, Shimon, was a shepherd. The other, Simon, was a Galilean farmer. They both made the decision to travel to Tiberias to join the zealot leaders Zadok and Judah.

Months later, Judah sent word that he needed my help again. He was putting together another raid. Taxes collected from all of the nearby provinces are ultimately brought to the port city of Caesarea Maritima for transport by ship to Rome. There is no naval force that compares to that of Rome, so the cargo would be safe once it was on the sea.

· · ·

However, the taxes would be at risk as they traveled across the land. Since all roads that "lead to Rome" from this part of the world pass through Caesarea, the road to Caesarea was the most vulnerable. Judah and Zadok agreed that if they wanted to disrupt the affairs of their Roman despots – and gather needed resources to fund a rebellion – Caesarea Maritima was where they needed to send a rebel group.

The raid would be led by Judah, but he wanted me to help lead this group because of my experience. When I arrived in Tiberias, I was surprised to learn that Shimon and Simon were a part of the raiding party.

The treasure would be transported to Caesarea by a Roman centuria of eighty soldiers. I found out which centuria and went about enlisting six of their number to assist us. The large reward I offered quickly won them over.

There were fourteen men in our raiding party, including Judah and myself. We, together with our six new allies, would overpower the remaining seventy-four soldiers and escape with the tax collection. Though the numerical odds were against us, the element of surprise gave us an advantage. That is, until somehow the Roman centurion discovered that six of his men planned to betray him.

While they were en route, the centurion had his remaining soldiers arrest them and interrogate them. Once they extracted the truth, they quickly executed the six men. So, when the remaining Roman guard entered the pass where we intended to surprise them, they knew exactly what was waiting for them.

Judah had divided our raiding party into three groups. Two of the groups would attack from each side of the pass and the third would come from the rear. Judah directed me to lead the group that would attack from the rear. I selected Shimon and Simon to join me because I wanted to keep a watchful eye over them.

. . .

As the soldiers walked into the pass, I immediately realized there were too few of them to be a Roman centuria; the soldiers I had recruited to help us had assured me it would be a full centuria. But only half that number had entered the pass – and I didn't see my six recruits. I knew something was wrong.

I signaled Shimon and Simon to stay where they were. I spotted movement up over the ridge to our right, then quickly saw movement on the opposite ridge, as well. Those soldiers were flanking our other two groups from the rear. And though I had not seen movement to our rear, I knew some of the soldiers would be coming from that direction, too. Obviously, the Romans knew of our planned raid. We would be caught in between the soldiers, just like we had been that day at the armory.

I also knew these Romans would not take any prisoners. Our men would be slaughtered. I was too far away from the other two groups of our men to warn them. I motioned to Shimon and Simon to quickly and quietly move toward me, and the three of us took cover inside a nearby cave.

Just then, Judah gave the signal for the rebels to attack. But as they did, the Roman soldiers advanced on them from all sides. Very little fighting actually took place. Our men were out flanked, outmanned, and outmaneuvered within moments. Thankfully, none of the soldiers had seen us retreat into the cave.

Judah and two others were killed in the brief skirmish. It looked like two or three other zealots had also been able to escape. As the soldiers surrounded the remaining men, the three of us watched helplessly as the centurion gave the order to execute them. The whole affair was over as quickly as it had begun – without any Roman casualties. We had suffered an overwhelming defeat.

We remained in the cave until the soldiers moved on. It was best that the three of us split up. I went in one direction and Shimon and Simon went in another. I decided right there and then that I was done assisting the rebels. From now on, I would make my own plans and watch out for myself.

I headed back toward the Jericho road. It had always proven to be profitable for me – the merchants, tax collectors, and priests never seemed to run out of treasure for me to take, and they never were prepared for an attack. I never once faced large numbers of soldiers. From time to time, I would enlist someone to help me. One who stayed with me the longest was a young man from Gerasa by the name of Enos. He was very gifted at being a thief, and our time together was very profitable – for us.

I was becoming somewhat notorious in that part of Judea. After the repeated pleas of victimized tax collectors to the Roman prefect, soldiers were dispatched to keep a more watchful eye. I decided it was time to lay low for a while. So, I went north to the obscure village of Chorazin in Galilee and Enos returned to Gerasa in the Decapolis.

One day in Chorazin, I saw Shimon and Simon. It had been six years since we parted ways. They told me they had gone searching for the Messiah and had found Him. "His name is Jesus," they said. They told me about the miracles they had seen Him perform and the truths He taught. They told me about the change He had made in both of their lives, and that they had become His followers. I could see the change, and I could see they were happy.

I told them I had heard about this Man and about His miracles. But when they asked if I would like to travel back with them to meet Jesus for myself, I declined. I told them I was glad that they had found who and what they were looking for. But I also made it clear that I, too, had found what I was looking for and it wasn't following anyone else. "But who knows," I said, "perhaps our paths will cross again one day, and I will meet Him then!" I wished them well and they continued on their way. Though I trusted them, I decided to move to another village where no one would know I was there.

. . .

When summer returned, I decided the soldiers would have given up by now, so I headed back to the Jericho road. More bounty awaited from unsuspecting travelers. I knew I wouldn't have a lot of time before the soldiers would again be sent to capture me. So, I assembled a team of four other men in order to target a few larger prizes.

We were just outside of Jericho, planning our next raid, when a solitary man approached from the direction of Bethabara. Initially I planned to ignore him, but as he approached, I could see from his clothing that he was very wealthy. I was convinced that even the jewelry he was wearing would be more than worth the effort. So, we detained him and told him to give us all of his possessions. Surprisingly, he made a joke and said that someone else by the name of Jesus had just told him to do the same thing! I had no idea what he meant.

He emptied his pockets of all his coins. But I noticed he was wearing an expensive ring on his finger. He refused to give it to me, saying his father had given him that ring – and it was one of his most prized possessions. I noticed it was monogrammed with the letter "R." I asked him what it stood for. He said, "My name – Reuben." I told him if his father could afford to give him that ring, he could afford to give him another one. I would change the "R" to a "B" and now it would stand for Barabbas!

The blade in my hand did its work quickly and silently. He was dead before his body hit the ground. That ring fit perfectly on my finger. Too bad he hadn't been willing to just give it to me! The ring soon became one of my most prized possessions.

I always knew that one day my luck would run out. Eventually, I would be in the wrong place at the wrong time. It proved to be true one week ago. It is springtime and the roads are full of travelers. It appears that everyone is coming to Jerusalem for Passover this year. And, as usual, many of the pilgrims are wearing their finery!

.   .   .

I was sitting by the road, leaning against a large boulder and dressed like a beggar. My hand was upraised to receive whatever modest coins a passerby might give me. As I looked up at this particular traveler, I saw the large weight of gold he wore around his neck, the golden bracelets encircling his wrists, and the bejeweled rings on his fingers. He reached into his pocket and withdrew a mite to place in my hand.

"Surely, kind traveler," I said, "you have something more you can give a needy man begging alongside the road." To which the traveler replied, "No, I do not. This is all I have for you!"

The man didn't realize how quickly I could stand and have my knife pressed against his throat. And he definitely did not expect my two companions when they appeared from behind the boulders with swords in hand. Or so I thought.

He immediately raised his hands and shouted, "Please don't hurt me. I will give you everything I have!"

"Do you have more for me than that single mite you offered a moment ago?"

He smiled at me and said, "Yes, you can have all that I have and all that my friends have."

Suddenly, eight soldiers emerged from the brush on both sides of the road. Two of them had arrows trained toward us, and the other six had their swords drawn. The traveler revealed the sword he was wearing beneath his cloak. "Barabbas," he said, "if you and these two men want to live another day, you will drop your knife and swords, and give me back my mite!"

.   .   .

They bound our hands and put chains on our legs – and then they beat us. They were careful to make sure we could still walk. They had no intention of carrying us back to Jerusalem. I heard one of the soldiers say to the man who had been disguised as a traveler, "Centurion, the prisoners are ready for the journey."

"Good," the centurion said, pointing to me. "Pilate is expecting them – particularly this one! Soldiers, you will each enjoy your reward tonight!"

As we entered the city of Jerusalem, we stopped for a flock of sheep being herded in front of us. As we began to move, one of the soldiers shouted at me, "Pick up your feet, Barabbas! Your cross is waiting for you!"

We were taken to the prison inside the Antonio fortress. It is used as a holding place only for those who are condemned to die by crucifixion. I knew I wouldn't be kept here long. The centurion told me that my two compatriots and I would be crucified on Friday. In the meantime, we waited in that dark, dank, filthy prison with three other men who were to be crucified on Thursday.

The prison is basically a dungeon below ground. The only light comes from a small opening that is used to climb down into the antechamber at the entry to our cell. The ceilings are so low I could not stand upright. For three days we had no interaction with anyone, except the soldier who brought us a bucket of slop to eat once each day. I wondered if the food would kill us before the cross did.

Two days ago, I heard someone climbing down the ladder. It wasn't time for the soldier to bring our food. I wondered what was about to happen. We weren't supposed to be crucified yet. Perhaps they had something else in store for us. After a few moments, I heard a voice haltingly call out, "Barabbas, it's Shimon!"

.   .   .

Slowly, I made my way toward the gate. As I peered out, I saw him – but I was puzzled why he was there. There were no soldiers with him, so I doubted he was being placed in our cell. I asked why he had come. Shimon answered, "I have come for two reasons. First to thank you for saving my life that day outside of Caesarea Maritima. If you had not stopped us, both Simon and I would have been cut down by the Roman soldiers. I know that in the years since then you may have taken the lives of others, but on that day, you saved ours. So, I thank you."

Second, he told me that though I had saved his physical life, it was Jesus who had truly saved him. He had set him free from the bondage of sin and his past. Jesus had taken away his pain and brokenness and replaced it with healing and purpose. He reminded me that when we had last seen one another, I had said, "Perhaps our paths will again cross one day, and I will meet Jesus then."

Shimon continued, "This may be the closest that your path ever crosses with His before you are placed on a cross in two days. But Barabbas, I want you to know that you can believe in Him today. Whatever you have done, He can and will forgive you, if you will only believe in Him. Turn to Him before it's too late!"

I can't describe how I felt. My heart had become hardened over the years. I didn't think there was anyone on the face of this earth who cared about me. I had turned my back on my family. I had no friends. And yet, this man had risked a lot to come to me with this message. I knew that he genuinely cared – and he was telling me that Jesus genuinely cared, too. A solitary tear made its way out of my heart and began to form in my eye.

"You're welcome," I said. "Saving your life was probably one of the best choices I ever made." And with that, I turned and walked back into my corner of the cell. I did not want him to see the tear as it trickled down my cheek. I heard a soldier call out to him, and then he climbed up the ladder and left. I knew that I would soon be doing that, but I would be headed to a very different place. After Shimon was gone, I continued to think about what he said. But I knew it was too late for me.

· · ·

I had been found guilty by a legal tribunal that had condemned me to death. I deserved my sentence. There would be no appeal. There would be no mercy. My sentence had been issued, and my fate was sealed.

Two days later I awoke to the reality that this was the day I would die. I listened for the soldiers to come for us. As the hours went by, I heard the crowd shouting my name in the distance. It began as a dull roar, but the shouts quickly became louder – *"Crucify him!"*[1] The crowd was obviously calling for my blood. The time of my execution had arrived. The soldiers came to my cell and led me out with my hands bound and my legs chained.

But to my surprise, instead of being led to Golgotha under the weight of a cross, I was led to the courtyard outside of the praetorium to stand before Pilate. There was another Man, also bound, standing there as well. Then the unimaginable happened.

I was being set free – and this Man standing before me was going to die in my place! I heard Pilate say the Man's name was Jesus. This was the One about whom Shimon had told me. Here I was, clothed in my unrighteousness deserving to die for my transgressions, and I was being set free! But the Man who stood before me clothed in innocence – the One who had no sin – was undeservedly being condemned by Pilate to be crucified. He would endure my cross. Jesus was paying the price for my release.

Pilate directed the centurion to remove my chains and ropes. As the last one fell off, I saw Shimon's face in the crowd. Pilate told me to go. I made my way through the crowd to Shimon. I stopped and stood in front of him for a moment. I told him I was headed out of Jerusalem to Emmaus, and I asked him to come see me. There was a conversation we needed to have.

· · ·

I turned back for one last look at the One who had stood before me … the One who was now undeservedly taking my place.

YITZHAK – THE TRADESMAN

 y name is Yitzhak and I grew up here in Jerusalem. My ancestors were counted among the remnant that returned here over five hundred years ago with Zerubbabel from Babylon. Those early generations led the effort in rebuilding Jerusalem from the debris left by the Babylonian destruction of the city. My ancestor Pedaiah, son of Parosh, was charged by Nehemiah with the responsibility of rebuilding the section of the wall leading to the Water Gate.

Once the rebuilding was completed, the men returned to their original trade or special craft to meet the demands of a growing city. My ancestors were fullers and weavers. Fullers clean the sheep's wool and pound it with sticks to clean and prepare it to become cloth. They also clean and retexture old cloth so it can be reused. Weavers, of course, use the wool, as well as flax, to create beautiful woven fabrics of all colors, textures, and styles.

Those early ancestors abutted the building that housed their shops to the area of the wall rebuilt by Pedaiah. As the business grew over the years, other family members added more rooms. Eventually business grew to the point that the family residence was moved to rooms above the shops. Those rooms now serve as my family's home. With the growing number of pilgrims traveling to Jerusalem for the special feasts, I decided to add a large room on the upper level about three years ago to help accommodate the demand. The rent I charge for that room helps provide additional income for my family.

Jehovah God has continued to bless our business through many generations, and I am now one of the leading tradesmen in Jerusalem. One day my oldest son, Uriah, who is fifteen, will take over the business from me, just as I did from my father. Uriah is a special gift to my wife and me from God – as a matter of fact, He has given him to us twice!

Three years ago, my son was helping me finish the construction of the upper room. We were setting the final roof tiles when my son lost his footing and fell to the street below. I scurried down as fast as I could. Several of my neighbors were already there by his side. My son was not moving, and I could not tell if he was breathing. Gratefully, a neighbor had already run to get the physician.

I felt so helpless as I stared at my son. All I could do was cry out to Jehovah God to help me. Just as I did, a Man knelt beside me. He appeared to be one of the pilgrims who had traveled to Jerusalem for Passover. He had been passing by when Uriah fell and came over to see if He could help.

The next thing I knew He took my son by the hand and said, "Young man, I say to you, rise!" Immediately, Uriah sat up. He looked at me, then he looked at the stranger. The stranger returned my son's look and said, "Young man, behold your father." Then He looked at me and said, "Father, behold your son!"

The Man then rose to His feet and reached down to help Uriah stand. My son said he felt fine and that nothing hurt; it was as if he had never fallen. I looked at him in disbelief. Just a moment before he had been lying there crumpled on the street! The neighbors gathered around us stood there with their mouths agape as if to say, "How can this be?"

. . .

I was still on my knees looking up at the Man when I said, "Who are You? And what did You do?"

"Yitzhak," He said, "you cried out to the Father for help. He heard your prayer and your son has been made whole. All so that the Father might be glorified."

"Sir," I replied, "how is it You know my name, but I don't know Yours? Even so, I know I have You to thank for restoring my son!"

"Thank the Father for hearing and answering your prayer," the Man said as He reached down and helped me stand to my feet. Smiling broadly He added, "Thank Him for giving you your son once again! And now go, give the boy something to eat."

Then He turned and began to make His way toward the temple. My neighbor came to my side and said, "His name is Jesus. He is from Nazareth. And He created quite an uproar in the temple yesterday. He drove out all of the merchants and money-changers. He cleansed the temple just like Ezra the priest had done so many years ago in the presence of our ancestors.

"The religious leaders were irate and demanded, 'What are You doing? If God gave You authority to do this, show us a miraculous sign to prove it.'[1]

"'All right,' Jesus had replied. 'Destroy this temple, and in three days I will raise it up.'[2]

"'What!' they exclaimed. 'It has taken forty-six years to build this Temple, and You can rebuild it in three days?"[3]

. . .

"I thought it was a strange thing for Jesus to say to the religious leaders," my neighbor continued. "But now that I have seen Him awaken your son, I believe He can do anything He says He can do!"

"So do I!" I exclaimed, before I ran to catch Him and thank Him one more time.

Jesus returned to Jerusalem several times after that. Each time He created quite a stir in the temple. The religious leaders continued in their attempts to discredit Him, but each time the city was filled with witnesses who had observed how Jesus rebuffed, rebuked, and corrected the religious leaders. The reports continued of countless people who were healed by that very same touch that made my son whole.

Jesus stopped by to see me personally when He was here for the Feast of Dedication a few months ago. He asked me if my upper room was available for Him and His followers to celebrate the Passover. I told Him it was His to use whenever He needed it and for as long as He liked. He explained He would need it off and on from Passover through the Day of Pentecost. It was such an insignificant way for me to thank Him for all He had done – but I was glad I could repay Him in some small way.

He told me He would send some of His followers on the morning before the Passover to make preparations. He asked me to have one of my servants meet them at the Sheep Gate and then lead them to the room. I told Him I would have my servant carry a pitcher of water so they would know to follow him.

Yesterday morning a few of His disciples arrived to make their preparations. They said, *"The Teacher asks, 'Where is the guest room where I can eat the Passover meal with My disciples?'"*[(4)]

Though Jesus had said His followers would prepare the meal, I had asked that He allow me to provide the meat and grains they would need. He had graciously permitted me to do so. When they arrived at the room, everything was in place, and they busily began their preparations to make things ready.

Later in the day, Jesus and the rest of His disciples arrived. Before He made His way to the upper room, He stopped to greet Uriah and me. He thanked me for providing a place for Him to spend this special time with His followers. He asked Uriah to bring a basin of water and a towel to the upper room and set it by His place at the table. He said He would need them for something He planned to do that evening.

As we were talking, I could tell something was wrong. Jesus's demeanor was different, and the disarming smile I had become accustomed to was absent. His eyes had the appearance of flint, as if He were solely focused on what was before Him. Uriah and I had been in the street the other day when He entered the city riding on the colt of a donkey. We had joined our voices with the others in shouting, "Hosanna!" But I knew much had happened in the four days since then. The whole city knew about how He had again driven the merchants and money-changers out of the temple.

It was clear that the religious leaders were plotting something against Jesus. No one knew what it was, but there was a sense of foreboding among the people. If the rest of Jerusalem and I were aware of it, I knew Jesus was even more aware of it. That had to be weighing heavily on Him.

I told Jesus to let me know if He needed us to do anything else for the remainder of His time. I assured Him we would have the room ready for His arrival each evening. I asked if He would be able to join our family for a meal before He left Jerusalem. He smiled and thanked me for the invitation, but He never gave me an answer. Then He continued upstairs to gather with His followers.

They remained in the upper room until very late in the evening. Most of the men left with Him as they headed toward the Mount of Olives. After cleaning up from the meal, I saw the remainder of His party leave, heading in a different direction. Apparently, they would be lodging somewhere else.

All was calm when I finally retired to bed for the night, but when I awoke this morning it was anything but calm! I heard shouting in the street: "Jesus has been arrested! The religious leaders have bound Him, and their temple guards are delivering Him as a prisoner to Pontius Pilate! They say they plan to crucify Him!"

I could not believe my ears! This was madness! What were the religious leaders thinking? What were their accusations against Jesus? If there was ever anyone who didn't deserve to be crucified, it was Him!

A frenzy ignited as the news spread throughout the city. There were many like me who were weeping and unable to comprehend what was happening. Others were shouting, "He claims to be the Son of God! Crucify Him!" And there were still others who were just curious to see what all the excitement was about.

It wasn't long before I heard that He was being led through the streets like a common criminal to be crucified. Uriah and I pushed our way through the crowd assembled to gawk at Him. We gasped when we saw Him. He was unrecognizable. His face was broken and bruised. The robe on His back was covered in blood. Someone had placed a crown of thorns on His head and pushed it into His skull. It was such a contrast to a few days ago when we witnessed Him riding on the donkey's colt through these very streets!

The sight of Him made me nauseous. I could not stand to see what they had done to my Lord! My grief was greater than anything I had ever experienced. Uriah and I retreated from the crowd and wept in each other's arms. I wanted to help Jesus, but I didn't know how. I hadn't felt that helpless since the day Uriah fell from the roof. Jesus had been there to lift Him up that day. But now, who was going to lift up Jesus?

. . .

When we finally made it back home, I headed to the upper room. That was one of the last places Jesus had been, and I hoped I would feel closer to Him there. As I entered the room, I discovered one of His disciples – the one called Peter. He, too, was weeping uncontrollably. Neither of us could speak. I did not want to interrupt His time of sorrow, so I made my way back downstairs to find my own quiet place.

"Father," I cried out, "three years ago I called out to You to save my son, and You did! Father, now would You please save Your Son?"

Soon, the sky turned dark – as black as night. And it remained that way for several hours. I began to realize that the pain I felt paled in comparison to the pain God was feeling. I knew there was nothing greater than a father's agony when his child is suffering. God had chosen to relieve my pain ... but He was now choosing to endure His own.

I then remembered what Jesus had told the religious leaders: If the temple was destroyed, He would raise it up in three days. Could it be?

The One who had stood before me said the Father had chosen to restore my son to bring glory to His name. I knew He was choosing to not save His Son for the same reason ... to bring glory to His name!

~

MARY – THE MOTHER OF JESUS

I am Mary, and by now all of you know my story. I was born in the village of Nazareth. My mother died when I was nine years old, leaving my father, Eli, and me to walk through our sorrow together. When I was fifteen, my father arranged for me to marry his friend Joseph, the carpenter. He was a good man and a good husband. He walked through an experience with me that no man had ever walked through before … and never will again.

As you know, soon after our betrothal was announced, an angel told me that the Spirit of God would come upon me and I would bear the Son of Almighty God. That was a lot for me to comprehend – and a lot for a fifteen-year-old to bear. I was going to be the mother of the Son of God.

But imagine how Joseph felt. We had not yet become husband and wife. And yet, I was expecting a child – and it wasn't *his* child. He would be the father to a child who was not his flesh and blood. He would be the father to the Son of the Living God. That was a lot for him to take in! But when the angel confirmed it to him in a dream, Joseph never questioned it. He never backed away from what God had called him to do. My husband walked by faith, and he was a good father to Jesus and to the other children we later conceived together.

. . .

We endured many trials. Those who had been friends and neighbors – and even family members – cast aspersions on us. They refused to accept the truth of who Jesus was and accused us of sinful behavior. Even now, there are those who look upon me as a sinful woman. It is an accusation I have had to endure for over three decades.

But the blessings of being the mother of Jesus have been so much greater! Throughout His life, I have seen how His Heavenly Father has cared for Him. It started with the shepherds who came to the stable the night Jesus was born. We had been refused entry into a warm, comfortable room. Instead, I had given birth to Jesus on a stable floor surrounded by a few animals and my precious husband. Then the shepherds appeared and told us how a multitude of angels had announced the birth of Jesus!

A few weeks later, Jesus and I were visited by a group of wise men who had followed a star to find Him. They had brought royal gifts to honor Him. Yes, there were those who had refused to admit who Jesus was, but there were a very special few who knew all too well!

The Heavenly Father protected us from the evil intentions of Herod the Great, and He provided us with a safe place to live for a couple of years in Egypt. He brought us back to Nazareth and blessed us with six more children – four boys and two girls. Jesus was a good big brother to all of them. He was a good son. He honored His parents – both His Heavenly Father and His earthly parents.

There was only one time Jesus caused us concern. He was twelve, and He had remained behind in the temple in Jerusalem after we left to return home. But He wasn't being disobedient to us, He was being obedient to His Heavenly Father.

A few years later, my husband died. I can't imagine what it would have been like to walk through that sorrow without Jesus beside me! He was my comfort and my strength. He kept assuring me that we would all be together again, in a place where there would be no more pain and no more suffering. We would be together in His Heavenly Father's house.

For eight years, Jesus was the patriarch of our family. He led His half-brothers to provide for us through their carpentry work. Joseph had always been proud of Jesus's carpentry skill. Jesus encouraged His half-sisters to stay close to me and help me. He took over the role that Joseph had always filled as the spiritual leader of our home. He taught us to pray to His Father in a way that was more intimate than I had ever heard.

One day He told me it was time for Him to leave and be about His Heavenly Father's business. I was really sad because I knew our times together would never be the same. I now would share Him with a world the Father had sent Him to serve and to save. I knew that my son James, as well as my other sons and daughters, would care for me – but it would be different. There's just something about knowing the Son of God is sleeping in His bed over there in the corner of the room. Yet, I knew this was why He had come. This was why the Father had sent Him – and now I had to transition from being His mother to becoming His follower.

If I were to pick one day when that transition occurred, it was the day of the wedding feast in Cana. My dear friend Salome and her husband were hosting their daughter's wedding feast and had run out of wine. I did not want them to be embarrassed so I turned to my son for help. I went to Jesus as His mother, but as I watched Him turn the water into wine, I became His follower. Just a few of us witnessed the miracle that day, but it was only the first of many that would follow.

As Jesus went about His ministry throughout Galilee, I stayed in our home with my younger children. My older sons were already married, and we had all moved from Nazareth to Capernaum. Jesus came to see me many times, but I began to long to travel with Him. There were already other women who had become part of His growing number of followers.

. . .

After all of my children were married, I did begin traveling with Jesus. In fact, I was in the crowd following Him when He made His entry into Jerusalem this past Sunday. It was a magnificent sight to watch the people acknowledge Him as they shouted, *"Blessings on the One who comes in the name of the Lord!"*[1]

But I became frightened for Him when He drove the merchants and money-changers out of the temple the next day. I knew the priests were plotting against Him, and I worried their retribution would happen soon.

I stayed in Bethany on Tuesday and Wednesday in the home of Lazarus, Martha, and Miriam. They had become like family to Jesus ever since He cleansed Lazarus of his leprosy. I was so glad for this time to get to know them better. On Tuesday morning, Jesus told me He would not be returning to Bethany to lodge that night, but I should remain there and join the other women on Thursday when they traveled to Jerusalem. I would help prepare the Passover meal. I savored my time over the next two days with this special family, but I couldn't get rid of my sense of foreboding.

On Thursday, I joined Mary Magdalene, Salome (the wife of Zebedee), Joanna (the wife of Chuza), Suzanna (the widow whose son Zohar had been raised from the dead), and Ayda (the mother of Shimon the shepherd) at the upper room in Jerusalem. I never ceased marveling at the stories these women shared of how Jesus had transformed their lives. Though I had only met some of them recently, we had become like family. In some respects, I felt like they had welcomed me into Jesus's extended family.

This Passover meal was different from any we had ever experienced. It began with Jesus washing the feet of His disciples, but it continued with Him saying that the bread He was breaking represented His body that would be broken. He went on to say that the cup of wine He passed represented His blood that would be poured out as a sacrifice. My sense that something horrible was going to happen returned.

. . .

Like everyone else, I was surprised when He said one of His disciples was going to betray Him. Then it appeared that Jesus sent Judas away. Was Jesus sending Judas to foil the betrayal – or was he a part of the betrayal? I found myself with more questions than answers.

Jesus announced that He was going to take the rest of His disciples to the Mount of Olives for the night. The rest of us would return to Bethany. The other women and I cleaned up after the meal. Then, together with my brother-in-law Clopas and a few of the other men, we went back to Lazarus's home. I had a fitful night's sleep. I could not shake the feeling that something diabolically evil was at work.

Early this morning, we were awakened by a loud commotion and shouting. Most of the disciples had just arrived from the Garden of Gethsemane where, they reported, Jesus had been arrested! A large mob of priests, temple guards, and soldiers led by Judas had come upon them as they slept. The disciples had all scattered in fear. When the other women and I asked what had happened to Jesus, they bowed their heads in shame and told us they did not know.

I quickly scanned the group looking for Peter and John, but they were missing. I turned to Andrew and James and asked where their brothers were. Apparently, they had run off in a different direction, but no one knew where they had gone. Ayda asked about her son, Shimon, and was told he had followed Peter and John. Salome and Ayda were now concerned for their sons, as well.

Lazarus had friends in Jerusalem who could help us get answers, so he decided he and a group of us should leave right away. But Martha disagreed. "Lazarus, you know the religious leaders have been plotting to arrest you. Jesus told you to remain here in Bethany so that no harm would come to you. You can't go into the city. Jesus would not want you to do so."

.   .   .

Clopas spoke up. "Some of the other men and I will go find out what is happening. I agree that it is too dangerous for Lazarus and the apostles to show their faces in Jerusalem right now. We do not need anyone else arrested. That would not do Jesus, or any of us, any good!"

"I'm going with you!" I said. "Surely they will not refuse a mother trying to find her son."

Clopas and Lazarus were hesitant, but they quickly realized I was not going to take "no" for an answer. The other women said they were coming with me. I quietly told Martha and Miriam it was best for them to stay in Bethany to make sure their brother didn't do anything foolish. They agreed. The rest of us immediately set out.

When we arrived in Jerusalem, we learned that Jesus had been taken before Pilate by the high council. They had demanded His crucifixion. Pilate had repeatedly said He did not find Jesus guilty of anything. But the priests had been unrelenting. They had stirred up the crowd to demand that Jesus be crucified. Pilate finally gave in, and now Jesus was being held in the fortress. I could not believe my ears! My son – the Son of God – was to be crucified! Surely, His Heavenly Father would not permit it!

We found John and Shimon at the entrance of the fortress. Salome and Ayda were relieved to see their sons were unharmed. John told us he had spoken with friends on the Sanhedrin, but they said there was nothing they could do to help Jesus.

Shimon mentioned that he had been to the fortress two days earlier and had met the centurion in charge. He sent a message to him to see if I could at least see and speak with my son. While we waited for an answer, John and Shimon told us about the events since the arrest of Jesus in the garden. They described the appearances before Annas and Caiaphas, and the political maneuvers between Pilate and Herod Antipas. Then they told me about the brutal beating Jesus had received at the hands of the Roman soldiers.

· · ·

I was overcome with anguish. I had experienced the grief and sorrow of death, but I had never experienced such evil and brutality. I turned my eyes toward heaven and silently asked the Father, "Why won't You save Your Son?"

The soldier to whom Shimon had spoken returned with an answer from the centurion: "The city is in an uproar over Jesus. No one is permitted to see Him. His mother will need to speak with Him as He hangs on the cross!" I could not believe my ears!

Soon, a cohort of soldiers exited the fortress. In their midst were three men – each carrying his own cross. The last of the three was my son! He was barely recognizable. His face had been pummeled. A crown of thorns had been pressed into His scalp. The remaining clothing He wore was covered in His own blood. I gasped as I took in the inhumanity my son was being forced to endure.

The soldier told Shimon that we could follow behind Jesus ... at a distance. I saw my son struggle to even stay on His feet, let alone carry the heavy weight of His cross. The soldiers soon stopped and pulled someone from the crowd to carry it for Him. Even in the midst of all that was going on, my mother's heart was grateful to this man for carrying my son's cross.

As we continued on the road, the other women and I began to wail. But even louder than our cries were the shouts from the crowd ridiculing my son. I thought of the voices that had praised Him on this very road only five days earlier.

When Jesus saw me, He said, *"Daughters of Jerusalem, don't weep for Me, but weep for yourselves, and for your children."*[2] I couldn't help but think, "Jesus, I am weeping for my child."

· · ·

When we arrived at the hill of execution, the soldiers nailed my son to the cross and then stood it upright. They had stripped Him of every piece of clothing. He hung on that cross naked, His body covered with lacerations from the scourging He received. In mockery, the soldiers placed a sign on the cross above Him that read, "The King of the Jews." The wreath of thorns remained pressed into His head.

I heard the priests ridiculing Him. I heard the crowd directing their vile words toward Him. I saw the Romans casting lots for the seamless tunic Jesus had been wearing. It had been a gift from the prophetess Anna that day in the temple soon after He was born. I had preserved it all of those years as a reminder of the Father's faithfulness. Now these soldiers were gambling for it.

Tears streamed down my cheeks as I stood there looking up at my son for hours. It seemed that time had stopped, and brutality had been given free reign. Again, I called out to the Heavenly Father, "Father, why won't You stop this?"

Then suddenly in the midst of the madness and evil, I heard the voice of Gabriel speaking the words he had told me long ago:

"Don't be afraid, Mary, for you have found favor with God! You will conceive and give birth to a Son, and you will name Him Jesus. He will be very great and will be called the Son of the Most High. The Lord God will give Him the throne of His ancestor David. And He will reign over Israel forever; His Kingdom will never end!"[3]

As I stood there looking up at my son – the One who stood before me – I held onto that promise: He is the Son of the Most High! And His Kingdom will NEVER end! It was as if the Father were saying to me, "I can't save My Son from this. I sent Him for this. I can't save Him, because He's come to suffer this so that through Him the world can be saved!"

~

GAIUS MARIUS – THE CENTURION

My name is Gaius Marius, and I am a Roman citizen by birth. I grew up in the beautiful city of Tarentum in Italy. If you look at a map of Italy, you will see it is shaped like a boot. My birthplace is situated at the top of the heel of the "boot" on the Mediterranean shore. My father was a decurion (cavalry officer) who commanded a distinguished Roman cavalry unit.

From the moment I was born, he began grooming me to become a decorated career soldier. As a matter of fact, my namesake was a highly decorated general and statesman who is credited with the strategic reforms that now distinguish our army as the greatest military force in the world.

My father instilled in me that there was no greater service to our emperor than as a soldier in his army. And there was no greater role in his army than as a member of his cavalry. I learned how to ride a horse when I was four years old. My father taught me how to wield the gladius (a short sword) while riding a horse by the time I was seven. He made sure that I received a sufficient education so I could rise in the ranks once I began to serve.

. . .

I enlisted in the army on my eighteenth birthday. My father told me it was one of the proudest days of his life. I rapidly rose through the ranks as I distinguished myself with my weaponry skills. My leadership abilities were rewarded when I became the commanding officer over a unit of eight men (a contubernium), followed two years later as a cavalry officer (decurion) leading a one-hundred-twenty-man alae. An alae is the cavalry unit within a legion. Three years later I was given the command of a four-hundred-eighty-man cohort.

Nine years ago, I came under the command of Pontius Pilate. He was a tribune over the forces stationed in Thessalonica in the Macedonian province. I enjoyed my life and service for all of my years in the army, but I must confess Thessalonica stands out above the rest.

The city is situated on the northern coast of the Mediterranean Sea. The weather is moderate, the landscape and the seascape are beautiful, and the people are friendly. It is a senatorial province versus an imperial province, which means there is less risk of rebellion. Day-to-day life closely resembles that of Rome itself, and a soldier's role is primarily to defend against the threat of outside forces.

Pilate promoted me to the rank of centurion, reporting directly to him and leading the half legion under his command. He assured me that he would be rising through the ranks of Roman leadership and he would bring me along with him. When he told me a little over three years ago that he had been named the prefect over the Judean province, I knew I had a move in my immediate future.

The Judean province is an imperial province, which means there is much greater threat of rebellion from within. I quickly learned that a source of potential rebellion was the Jewish religious leaders themselves. They resent our presence, our religion, and our way of life. They deem their beliefs to be far superior to ours, and they believe their only true leader is their God.

. . .

The emperor has chosen to keep their local governing body, called the Sanhedrin, in place to administrate local customs and disputes. But the individual members of the Sanhedrin are a contentious group of men who debate among themselves in ways that far surpass the disagreements within our own Roman senate. In Thessalonica, I was admired and respected by the people of the city. In Jerusalem, I am looked down upon and treated with disdain.

Though most of my officers followed me from Thessalonica and Italy, our foot soldiers have been recruited from within these provinces. They do not have the professionalism and character of the soldiers I am used to leading. Because we are continually on the brink of rebellion, our soldiers are the brute force used to maintain law and order. Even though these men are locals, the Jewish people view them as instruments of Roman oppression. So, they are despised by the Jews. But because they are not Roman citizens, they are also looked down on by our Roman officers and leaders.

Truth be told, these rank and file soldiers are not selected for their good character; they are selected for their sadistic brutality and fighting ability. Most of the time, they are forced to control their growing hatred for the Jewish people, which leaves them frustrated that they can't physically express that hostility. So, when they are unleashed to mete out punishment, their response is most often cruel and sadistic.

Much of my time here has been squelching numerous attempts by local zealots to break into our armories or overtake convoys transporting Roman tax receipts. And then there are the religious leaders who needlessly call on me to send soldiers to settle their disputes. Suffice it to say, I am counting the days until I can leave this forsaken region of the world.

Usually, I am barracked at the armory in Caesarea Maritima. At least it permits me a view of the Mediterranean Sea, as I remember my more idyllic days on its other shores. But several times each year, I am forced to relocate my command to Jerusalem. Though Caesarea Maritima is the official capital of the province, Jerusalem is the traditional capital. The city holds no attraction for me.

Our prefect has rightly determined that our presence needs to be clearly seen in the city during their religious festivals. Their Passover, for example, celebrates their escape from their Egyptian captivity, so it is a time when rebellion can easily flourish. Additionally, a large percentage of the Jewish population from throughout the provinces converge on Jerusalem for the observance of the festival. The sheer numbers here cause it to become a potential tinderbox.

We have been keeping an eye on a Jewish Teacher and Miracle Worker from Galilee by the name of Jesus. He has been traveling throughout the provinces preaching His message of repentance, salvation, and good works. He has performed unparalleled miracles, including bringing the dead back to life. More people than ever have flocked to Jerusalem this year – in order to see and hear Him.

Pilate has ordered me to make sure His motive is not rebellion – and I have continually confirmed that His purpose is religious, not political. He is not a threat to Rome, but He is a threat to the religious leaders. The people are turning away from them in increasing numbers and choosing to follow Jesus. A dangerous situation is developing, but Jesus will not be the initiator – it will be the religious leaders.

This past Sunday I saw Him ride into the city on a donkey's colt. It was a magnificent entry with the people shouting His praises and placing their garments and palm branches in His path. I have never seen anyone welcomed into a city with such zeal – and I have seen our emperor make an entry many times. But again, this Man's entry was not as a conquering hero or a boisterous rebel, it was more as a humble Teacher. He won their hearts not with threats and might, but with truth and humility. I was in awe of Him as He passed by me. I found myself admiring Him as a true leader.

.   .   .

Another memorable event occurred two days prior to Jesus's grand entry. A dangerous criminal by the name of Barabbas had eluded our grasp for three years. He is a zealot who became a common murderer and thief, leaving death and destruction in his path. In addition to his other crimes, he was stealing Roman tax receipts – a crime that Pilate would not ignore.

After many failed attempts, I decided to personally lead a small group of my most trusted men to capture this criminal once and for all. I set my trap for him on the road to Jericho, and he did not disappoint me. He stepped right into it, and I was able to arrest him, as well as two of his accomplices, bringing Pilate his prize.

I didn't realize it at the time, but the arrival of Jesus and the arrest of Barabbas were two events that would greatly impact my life.

Two days ago, a man by the name of Shimon came asking permission to speak with Barabbas. I don't normally permit a man condemned to death to have a visitor, but something inside me told me I needed to hear this man's request. When the soldiers brought Shimon to me, I immediately recognized him. He had been one of the followers with Jesus when He entered the city the other day. What could he possibly have to do with Barabbas?

Shimon told me he was a shepherd from Bethlehem who was now a disciple of Jesus. He also said that when he was a younger man, Barabbas had saved his life. This shepherd believed his God would have him thank Barabbas before he died. He then asked if he could speak with the criminal. I asked Shimon a few questions about his family and then about Jesus. I couldn't understand why he would care about expressing gratitude to such a despicable man before he died.

My soldiers were shocked when I gave Shimon permission to speak with Barabbas for a few minutes through the gate. As he left my presence, I called out to him, "Tell your Teacher that the religious leaders are plotting against Him. He needs to be careful. I would not want to see any harm come to this Miracle Worker."

Unfortunately, that is exactly what happened today. The religious leaders demanded the arrest and crucifixion of Jesus. The prefect knew that Jesus was innocent, but he was unable to dissuade the religious leaders or the crowd. As events continued to unfold, it became apparent that if Pilate did not agree to put Him to death the people would riot. He and I both knew the consequences he would face from Rome if that happened.

There is a custom that the prefect releases one prisoner at Passover each year. Pilate posed the choice of releasing Jesus or Barabbas to the crowd. He and I were both certain the crowd would choose Barabbas. If there was one thing that we and the Jewish leaders had ever agreed on, it was that Barabbas needed to be executed for his crimes.

But we underestimated the hatred of the religious leaders toward Jesus. Pilate directed me to remove the chains and ropes that were binding Barabbas. I expected Barabbas to smirk at me like he had won. But he didn't. He was as surprised as I was. He knew he didn't deserve to be set free, and I could tell by His expression he knew Jesus *did* deserve to be set free.

Pilate told me to take Barabbas's ropes and place them on Jesus. He then made one final attempt to keep Jesus from being crucified by ordering me to have Jesus flogged. He hoped it would satisfy the blood thirst of the religious leaders and the crowd.

The least noble command I have ever given my soldiers was that order from Pilate. However, I am a man under authority, so I followed orders. Even so, I was revolted by the pain and torture this innocent Man suffered. But even after putting Jesus through all of that, the religious leaders and the crowd continued to cry out for Him to be crucified. Pilate finally gave in to the religious leaders and turned Jesus over to my soldiers.

. . .

As I said earlier, these soldiers were particularly cruel and sadistic. They poured out all their pent-up frustrations and hatred on Jesus. And I knew I could not constrain them except to make sure they delivered Him alive to Golgotha.

I cannot begin to describe the unbridled brutality, torture, and humiliation those men unleashed on Jesus as they pummeled Him with their fists. Even the mockery of the robe placed on His shredded flesh and the crown of thorns pressed into His brow were intended to subject Him to more pain and torture. I refused to watch.

While that was taking place, I received a message from the shepherd who had visited Barabbas. He was seeking permission for the mother of Jesus to see and speak with her son. I knew I could not subject anyone's mother to the pain of seeing her child in this condition. I told the soldier to return and tell them that I could not permit her to do so. My message read, "The city is in an uproar over Jesus. No one is permitted to see Him. His mother will need to speak to Him as he hangs on the cross."

I could not allow the soldiers' brutality to continue any longer, so I sent word for them to prepare the prisoners to leave the fortress. I led the cohort of soldiers and the three men to be executed through the crowd assembled in the streets. Each man carried his own cross. The first two men were Barabbas's accomplices. The third was Jesus. But He was barely recognizable. All three men had been beaten, but it was obvious that Jesus's beating had been much more severe.

Jesus was struggling under the weight of the cross. I directed two soldiers to pull a man from the crowd to carry it for Him. Once he was in place shouldering the cross, we continued to Golgotha. In all of my years in Thessalonica, I had never had to oversee a crucifixion. But in this forsaken place, it had become a regular occurrence.

. . .

The place of crucifixion was located just outside the city wall along the trade road leading into Jerusalem. Part of the death penalty was the victim must die in the most conspicuous and humiliating way possible. It also reinforced the ironclad rule of Roman law and served as a further deterrent to those who may be considering breaking the law.

Once we arrived at our destination, we nailed the three men to their crosses and set them in place. Even that action was designed to cause them the greatest possible injury. The two criminals cried out in pain. I directed the soldiers to offer them a drink of the pain-deadening wine that would give them temporary relief.

The two criminals accepted the wine, but Jesus refused. We had not offered the narcotic out of compassion. It was intended to extend the time that a victim would suffer the humiliation and brutality of the cross. Excruciating pain accelerates the onset of death; deadening the pain slows it down.

At noon, a veil of darkness fell across the land and with it an eerie silence. The priests and the crowd suddenly stopped shouting. Fear began to overtake everyone assembled on the hill, including the soldiers. At first the crowd asked, "What is causing the sky to turn dark?" But soon their question was, "Who is causing the sky to turn dark?" Was it because of Jesus? Was Jesus Himself doing this? Everyone there had heard of the miracles He performed, and many had witnessed them personally. They began to murmur, "Is Jesus truly the Son of God? Is God preparing to punish us for what we have done to His Son?" I watched as many in the crowd began to scatter.

Jesus was now physically depleted. He had suffered more pain in the past eight hours than anyone I had ever seen. His physical body was dehydrated. His lips were so parched He could barely whisper the words, "*I am thirsty.*"[1] As I looked at Him, I thought to myself, "This is not why I enlisted. There is nothing distinguished or honorable in crucifying this innocent Man." For the first time in my career, I was ashamed to be a soldier of Rome.

. . .

One of my soldiers moistened Jesus's lips with cheap sour wine by putting a soaked sponge on the end of a branch and holding it to His mouth. Haltingly, He uttered His last words – *"It is finished!"*[2]

As He bowed His head and released His Spirit, the earth quaked. The crowd that had remained now ran away in fear, except for Jesus's mother and His followers gathered with her. I realized even the man my soldiers had made carry Jesus's cross had remained. It appeared that he and I had come to the same conclusion.

As I looked up at the One who had stood before me, I said aloud, *"This Man truly was the Son of God!"*[3]

JOSEPH – THE PHARISEE

$\mathcal{M}$y name is Joseph. I am from Arimathea, also called Ramah, located in northern Judea, approximately ten miles east of Joppa. It is the birth and burial place of the prophet Samuel, the last judge of Israel. At the time, it was considered to be in the hill country of the tribe of Ephraim. Our family is able to trace our ancestry back to the generation that was Samuel's neighbors.

Those early generations were farmers. The soil in Arimathea is fertile, and our ancestors primarily planted grains and vegetables. Jehovah God blessed our family with bountiful harvests over the majority of those years, and they lived so far up in the hills that the Babylonians did not take them into captivity.

In the millennium since the days of Samuel, our family amassed a large amount of farming land. My grandfather eventually stopped farming and began renting the land to tenant farmers who then worked it. This provided him with a steady income, regardless of the conditions of the crop.

. . .

By the time my father, Matthias, became the landowner, he was considered one of the wealthiest men in the region. Wealth brought him status and influence, as well as a significant voice in local and regional governance. At an early age, he became a member of the local Sanhedrin – but it wasn't long before he was selected as a member of the Great Sanhedrin in Jerusalem. He was known as a just man and enjoyed a respected position on the high council.

I am my father's eldest son, and together with my brother, Jonathan, we enjoyed a privileged upbringing with the best education. God has blessed me with a good memory and quick comprehension. I was able to excel in the sciences as well as the Torah and the Talmud. By the time I was fifteen, I was being recognized by my teachers, my peers, and others for my knowledge and understanding in those subjects.

My teacher, Hillel the elder, praised me for my progress and permitted me to assist him in teaching a few students who were just a few years younger than I am. The group included Nicodemus (who would become one of my closest friends), Gamaliel (who would become a respected teacher in his own right), and Annas (an ambitious student who would become one of our youngest high priests). God permitted me to not only assist in their learning but also the development of their character, with one regrettable exception – Annas.

By the time I was seventeen, I decided to make a break from my father in one important regard. My father was a Sadducee. Over the years, I had seen him make subtle accommodations for the sake of political compromise. I was under the conviction that we need to live our lives as the children of Jehovah God in accordance with His law to bring honor to Him. There can be no compromise for political advantage or personal gain – which is a behavior I have come to see regularly among my Sadducee brothers.

But I have also seen a propensity among my Pharisee brethren to put their piety on public display in order to impress and receive praise from others. Those insincere efforts are merely intended to elevate their own importance. I am committed to walking uprightly and humbly before God. I know I will never be a perfect man, but I am committed to strive to be a good man before God and not a prominent Pharisee before the people.

During my mid-twenties, I was selected to become a member of our local Sanhedrin, filling the position my father once held. I knew I was selected because of our family's wealth and my father's reputation, but I prayed that God would grant me the wisdom and discernment to serve the people faithfully. In the years that followed, I earned a reputation for being fair and wise in my deliberations among my fellow members and our community.

My father died when I was in my thirties. As his oldest son, I was his heir. All of our family's holdings passed to me. I was now the wealthy landowner with two young sons of my own and responsibilities to our tenant farmers. My brother helped me manage our properties, just as he had helped our father. His partnership enabled me to continue my duties on the local council.

When I was forty, I was selected to become a member of the Great Sanhedrin. By that time, my former pupil, Annas, had been high priest for five years. He was a constant reminder why I had chosen not to become a Sadducee. But I was grateful to again be following in my father's footsteps into a role that many great men had held, and some of my friends – Nicodemus and Gamaliel – were also now holding.

In keeping with my responsibilities, I moved my family to Jerusalem. Life here is much different from the quiet town of Arimathea, but we gradually learned how to live in this large city. We also were unaccustomed to such a large Roman presence. We had rarely seen a Roman in Arimathea, but here they were everywhere. The politics also were much greater. I realized I had much to learn in my dealings with the Romans, the Herodians, and the high council leadership. There were days my wife and I longed to return to Arimathea, but we knew Jehovah God had brought us here for His purpose.

. . .

We were well settled in Jerusalem by the time I first heard of Jesus of Nazareth. Annas's son-in-law, Caiaphas, was now the high priest. There were many similarities between the two men!

I'll not forget what happened about three years ago. There was great debate taking place within the Sanhedrin. We were in the midst of the Passover celebration. The day before, Jesus had overturned the money-changers' tables and driven the merchants and their animals out of the temple. He had declared, *"Get these things out of here. Stop turning My Father's house into a marketplace!"*[1] Annas and Caiaphas had confronted Him over who had given Him the authority to make such demands. But we were all so surprised by His actions that no one knew what to do.

Our debate that day was about how we should respond. We all knew Annas was responsible for situating the merchants inside the courtyard so he could better control the trade in a way that profited the temple – and himself. When King Solomon originally built the temple, he had made arrangements for the animals to be housed and sold outside of the temple in the stoa. That prevented business from taking place within the temple grounds where it would distract from worship and prayer. The Torah was silent about the practice, but rabbinical tradition seemed very clear.

The Sanhedrin was divided on the issue along the lines of the Pharisees versus the Sadducees. Though Caiaphas wanted us to talk about Jesus's actions, it quickly became a debate over the practice itself. The Pharisees believed the trade should not be conducted within the temple walls; the Sadducees supported continuation of the practice. A number of us felt it was wrong from the beginning. But no one challenged them for fear Annas and his allies would retaliate. This was an opportunity to set the matter right.

The debate continued for three days, but finally several of the Sadducees agreed with our point of view, and the decision was made to keep the merchants outside the temple. It was obvious Annas and Caiaphas were not pleased, but they did not press it further. I knew, however, that it wouldn't be the last time the matter was discussed.

With that settled, there wasn't much point in discussing whether Jesus had authority to do what He did. So, no further discussion took place – at least in the main chamber.

Later that week, Nicodemus told me he had requested a private conversation with Jesus. He believed that Jesus is the Promised One – the Light sent by God to deliver us from our sins. Nicodemus said he had considered leaving the Sanhedrin to follow Jesus like other men were doing. But he believed that God wanted him to stay, at least for now. I, too, wanted to know more about Jesus!

A couple of weeks later, Caiaphas asked me if I knew a rabbi by the name of Ashriel who lived in Arimathea. I told him I did. I had known his father and grandfather, as well. Caiaphas told me that Ashriel's great-grandfather, Simeon, had been a priest in the temple for many years. When he was very old, he supposedly had seen a baby he believed was the promised Messiah. Ashriel was with him that day. Caiaphas and Annas had decided to travel to Arimathea to interview him and wanted several from the council to join them. I agreed to go. I wanted to witness the conversation firsthand – and it would provide me with the opportunity to visit my home and briefly spend time with my oldest son, Matthias, and my granddaughter, Naomi. Gamaliel and Nicodemus agreed to join us, too.

When we arrived at Ashriel's home, Caiaphas told us that Annas would lead the conversation. Ashriel looked at the group gathered at his doorway warily until he spotted me in the midst. "Joseph, it is good to see you!" he said. "We miss seeing you and your family at the synagogue!"

"And we miss all of you, as well!" I replied. "We look forward to the day we can return." To the consternation of Annas, I then explained why we were there. Ashriel clearly trusted me, so I hoped to set his mind at ease. It appeared to work, so I relinquished the conversation to Annas.

"Why did Simeon believe the baby he saw was the Messiah?" Annas asked.

"He never doubted that the day would come," Ashriel said. "Even though it had been almost one hundred years since God had given him the promise that he would see the Messiah before he died, his faith was as strong that day as it had been on the day God first spoke to him.

"That morning, when he saw the baby and His parents, he just knew! He told me to help him walk over to the baby. His step grew quicker and steadier and he told me his heart was pounding in his chest. When we arrived at the family, Papa asked if he could see the baby. I'm sure his actions seemed strange to them, but they kindly turned their young son so Papa could look into His eyes.

"Tears began to stream down his cheeks! I'll never forget his words when he turned to the baby's mother and said, 'This Child of yours will cause many people in Israel to fall and others to stand. The Child will be like a warning sign. Many people will reject Him, and you, young mother, will suffer as though you had been stabbed by a dagger. But all this will show what is really in the hearts of people.'[2]

"She didn't speak a word but simply nodded at my great-grandpa. I was struck by her tenderness. I could see why Jehovah God had chosen her to be the mother of His Son. When Papa reached to pick up the baby, she willingly handed the tiny bundle to him.

"The baby didn't stir or make a sound as Papa held Him. Rather the baby seemed to be looking intently into my great-grandpa's eyes. It was as if the baby knew him. And I became convinced the baby *did* know him.

· · ·

"As Papa held Him in his arms, he looked up toward heaven and said, *'Lord, I am Your servant, and now I can die in peace, because You have kept Your promise to me. With my own eyes I have seen what You have done to save Your people.'*[(3)]

"Papa returned the baby to His mother's arms and blessed her and the father. We watched as the mother and father walked away. Papa turned to me and said, 'These people have no idea that they have been in the presence of the Son of God,' as he pointed at the other people moving about the temple.

"Papa died not long after that. But he did so knowing his lifelong mission was complete."

"Did they tell you the baby's name or where they were from?" Annas asked.

"No, they did not," Ashriel replied, "and we never asked."

As Annas continued to ask questions, I found myself wondering if Jesus was indeed that baby. I believe the other men did, too, but no one said it out loud. I thought about what Simeon had said to the baby's mother, "He will show what is really in the hearts of people." And I knew that was true!

In the years that followed, Caiaphas and Annas frequently brought up the subject of Jesus before the Sanhedrin. They would repeatedly raise false accusations. "He is Beelzebub!" "He is a demon." "He is a false witness." "He is a fraud." Occasionally they would say things that were closer to what they really believed. "He is leading the people away from us. He is usurping our authority. We are in danger of losing our power."

Both of these men became obsessed with defeating Jesus. This went far beyond the way He had embarrassed them the day He cleansed the temple. These men feared Him, and they knew if they didn't discredit Him soon, it would be too late. But they didn't want to just discredit Him, they wanted to destroy Him.

For months they sent messengers with their feeble attempts to entrap Jesus into saying something they could use against Him. But every time, Jesus responded in a way that revealed their treachery.

I began to sense that more members of the Sanhedrin were starting to fear Jesus. Not long ago, a group of them brought a woman before Jesus who had been caught in adultery. Based upon hushed conversations I had overheard in the hallway, I knew it had been another attempt to entrap Him. But apparently Jesus had revealed a secret sin that each of the planned accusers had committed. They had scattered in fear. But now they were siding with Annas. They feared what would happen if Jesus ever revealed what He knew about them. They wanted Him silenced. Annas and Caiaphas were now gaining a majority among the council.

By now, I also had become a secret follower of Jesus. Like Nicodemus, I believed in Him, but I believed God would also have me remain a member of the Sanhedrin. I knew that if I ever announced I was His follower, I would be removed from the council.

But this week, everything began to happen quickly! The people had welcomed Jesus into the city on Sunday with an overwhelming reception. I had never seen anything like it! The people kept shouting their praises of Hosanna! More of our council became afraid that the crowd was prepared to crown Jesus as King, and the Sanhedrin would be disbanded.

Sometime between Sunday night and Monday morning the high council met and gave Caiaphas permission to bring the merchants back into the temple. It was obvious when Jesus arrived that morning that it had been done for the sole purpose of creating an offense against Him.

. . .

On Tuesday, I heard rumors that one of Jesus's disciples was prepared to betray Him and help Caiaphas and Annas arrest Him. Nicodemus and I both raised questions before the Sanhedrin, but Caiaphas dismissed any discussion of the matter. I was beginning to fear for Jesus's safety. I attempted to get a message to Him about what was taking place, but my attempts were unsuccessful.

This morning, I awoke to the news that Jesus had been arrested. He had been taken before the high council and found guilty of blasphemy against God and sedition against Rome. He was now being taken before Pilate to be put to death. I could not believe my ears!

Before I knew it, Pilate had declared Him guilty and He had been delivered to the fortress to be executed. I received a message from John, one of the disciples of Jesus, asking if there was anything Nicodemus or I could do to stop this madness. I responded that a few of us had already attempted to dissuade the religious leaders, but we had failed. And now that the death order had been granted by Pilate, there was nothing that could be done to reverse it, short of an edict from Caesar himself.

Jesus was going to be crucified today. My mind couldn't comprehend it! Many of the religious leaders were now headed to Golgotha to witness His crucifixion. I could not bring myself to go. I returned home and began to weep. I wept for Jesus. I wept for His mother and His disciples. But then I began to weep for our people. God had sent His Son and we had rejected Him! His blood would forever be on all of our hands!

At the noon hour, the sky turned black. Day had become night. It was a sign of the judgment that awaited us for what our people were doing to God's Son. Then a thought came to mind. The law precluded an honorable burial for one who was executed for violating the law. Jesus's body would be left hanging on the cross overnight in disgrace. There was no way I could permit that to happen to the body of my Lord.

. . .

I was sure His family and His disciples had not given this any thought. I knew they were overwhelmed by everything else that was happening. Whatever was to be done would need to happen quickly before sunset and the beginning of Sabbath.

I decided to go to Pilate and request Jesus's body. I was hoping Annas and Caiaphas had not done anything to block His body from being buried. I knew I would no longer be a secret follower of Jesus. My actions would be a clear expression of my opposition to what they had done to Him. My Sanhedrin brothers would consider it an outright betrayal. I would be jeopardizing my position on the Sanhedrin, my influence in the community, and even my personal wealth. But that was of no consequence – it had to be done!

Straightaway I went to the praetorium to seek Pilate's permission. Because of my position, he received me and came outside to speak with me. He seemed surprised that a religious leader was now offering to bury the body of the One whose death we had demanded. He told me that He did not believe Jesus was guilty of anything. He said Jesus was only being crucified because of the pressure from the other religious leaders.

It almost seemed like he was telling me that he had no choice in the matter and was not responsible for Jesus's death. But that wasn't true. He, too, was guilty of what was being done. After a few more minutes, he gave me a document granting me permission to receive Jesus's body once He was declared dead.

It was mid-afternoon, and I was certain the hour was close. I had already decided to bury His body in the tomb I recently had made for myself. I stopped at one of the shops in the city and purchased a linen shroud for His burial.

When I arrived at the foot of the cross, I was horrified at what they had done to Jesus. I saw the evidence of the torture and pain they had inflicted. Just then, I heard Him say, *"It is finished!"*[4]

· · ·

I could not move. I fell to my knees and wept. John walked over to console me, but he was weeping as well. Nicodemus soon joined us. He asked me if any preparations had been made for the burial of Jesus's body. I told him my plan. He said he had embalming ointment to prepare the body. I reminded him that his assistance would be seen as betrayal by the Sanhedrin. His only response was, "I can no longer be a secret follower!" I got up and approached the Roman centurion with the document Pilate gave me.

There was another man there at the foot of the cross. I had seen him standing by himself when I arrived, weeping and worshiping. Now as Nicodemus and I prepared to take Jesus's body to the tomb, he came to me and said, "I carried His cross to Golgotha, and now I will carry His body to the tomb."

Soon after we had placed Jesus's body in the tomb and sealed it with a great stone, a group of Roman soldiers appeared. Evidently, when Caiaphas and Annas learned of my arrangements for Jesus's body, they petitioned Pilate to post guards so no one could remove His body and declare that He had risen from the grave.

As I looked at the soldiers, I pictured the One who had stood before us and about whom it had once been said, "This Child of yours will cause many people in Israel to fall and others to stand. The Child will be like a warning sign. Many people will reject Him, and you, young mother, will suffer as though you had been stabbed by a dagger. But all this will show what is really in the hearts of people."[5]

∽

SIMON - THE CYRENE

My name is Simon. My wife, our sons, and I live in the small Roman province of Cyrene situated on the northern coast of Africa. Our city was first settled by the Greeks over six hundred years ago, so our people have been most heavily influenced by Grecian arts, sciences, and culture. Prior to our being conquered by Rome, the rule of the Ptolemaic Kingdom and the Seleucid Empire fostered a significant migration of Greek-speaking Jews to Cyrene. My great-grandparents were a part of that diaspora, so our family is a part of that ever-growing population of Hellenistic Jews in Cyrene.

Every year since my twelfth birthday, I have made the journey to Jerusalem for the celebration of Passover. Next year, my oldest son, Alexander, will be twelve and he will join me. But this year he and his brother remained at home with my wife. It is a difficult journey for children. The trip involves between three and four weeks of travel each way from Cyrene to Jerusalem, allowing for the fact that as Jews we do not travel on the Sabbath.

Because of the distance, Cyrenian Jews have established our own synagogue in Jerusalem, which not only enables us to study the Scripture together in our own language but also provides us with a place to stay.

Each year I remain in Jerusalem for the full week of the feast, which means I am away from my family for about two months. I look forward to the day my family will be able to make the journey with me.

Normally I make the pilgrimage with my friends. We typically depart early, so we have two to three days in Jerusalem to rest from our journey before Passover begins. But this year I was delayed. My youngest son, Rufus, had fallen ill with a high fever. I was not going to leave on a two-month journey with him in that condition. By the grace of Jehovah, his fever broke after two days, and my wife and I knew he was on the road to recovery. With her blessing, I departed, knowing that I would no longer be arriving in Jerusalem early.

Jehovah blessed me with good weather and safe travel, so I was able to arrive as planned on the first day of Passover. From the moment I reached the city, I was overwhelmed by the number of people. There were many more gathered this year than I had ever seen before. My journey always takes me through the city of Alexandria, which is said to be the largest city in the world with a population of over five hundred thousand. But as I arrived in Jerusalem, I heard people saying there were many more than that number gathered here for the celebration of Passover this year.

As I walked through the streets, people were standing shoulder to shoulder. There seemed to be an unusual tension in the air. Passing through the crowd, I kept hearing people speak of the Man called Jesus. I had heard about Him on my last two trips to Jerusalem. Some had called Him Teacher. Many had spoken of His miracles. Some had even told me how three years ago He had driven the merchants out of the temple.

Last year I personally heard Him speak as He was teaching in the outer courtyard of the temple. He spoke with a knowledge of the Scriptures and an authority that surpassed any rabbi or priest I had ever heard. But today as I pressed through the crowd, the people weren't talking about His teaching or His miracles. They were saying, "Jesus is being crucified!" I couldn't imagine what He might have done to earn that punishment. But some spoke as if they believed He deserved it.

. . .

My progress to the Cyrenian synagogue suddenly came to a halt. A group of Roman soldiers was making a pathway through the crowd. They were escorting three men, each carrying a cross. Obviously, these men were being led to the hill I had passed on my way into the city – the hill they call "the place of the skull."

Suddenly, one of the men stumbled and fell under the weight of His cross. As I looked closer, I saw that He was bleeding from deep wounds all over His body. His face was bruised and cut beyond recognition. Someone had pressed a crown of thorns deep into His skull. He had been brutalized in the most inhumane way I had ever witnessed. As I looked at this poor broken Man, I felt a wave of nausea and thought I was going to be ill.

But just then a Roman soldier reached out and pulled me into the pathway. He brought his face right up to mine and shouted at me, "You! Carry His cross!" I was tired from my long journey. I was overwhelmed by the crowd pressing in around me. I felt sick from the revolting sight of this bloodied and beaten man before me. Whoever He was and whatever He had done, no one deserved to be treated like that! And now I had been startled and manhandled by this soldier. My instinct was to let my fist fly across this soldier's chin. But wisdom prevailed and I stayed my hand.

The soldier must have realized what I was thinking, because he raised the handle of his whip and struck me across my face. Some of his fellow soldiers were now beginning to make their way toward me, as well. I knew that anything short of compliance would be fruitless, so I raised my hand to yield to the soldier. He again shouted at me, "Pick up His cross!"

I reached down and lifted the weight off of the Man lying before me and placed it across my shoulders. It was a heavy burden to carry. I could not imagine how this battered Man had been able to carry it to this point. The Man looked up at me through His disfigured face. At that moment, I realized who He was.

. . .

He didn't look anything like I remembered ... except for His eyes. And they told me so many things. First, He was thanking me for taking up His cross. Second, He was showing me the full weight of the burden He was carrying. And third, He was telling me that He still was the One with authority, even in the midst of this chaos and evil. At that moment, I was no longer carrying the cross because of the soldier's threats. I was carrying the cross to ease the burden of this Man.

The soldier shouted in my ear, "Move or you will be put on a cross beside Him!" I was now part of this procession of death. I sensed that Jehovah God had ordered my every step from the moment I first left my home until now in order to time my arrival. I had unknowingly arrived in the city, at the exact moment, to carry the cross for Jesus. As we continued along the path, I began to hear shouts from the crowd. Some were shouting, "Crucify Him!" Some sneered, "If You are the Son of God, where are Your angels to help You!" But most were crying out brokenhearted, "Jesus!"

There were a few women in the procession following Him. I heard their grief-stricken cries. After a short distance, Jesus turned to them and said, *"Daughters of Jerusalem, don't weep for Me, but weep for yourselves and for your children."*[1] He went on to explain what would happen in the days to come. Even as these soldiers were leading Him to His death, He was speaking as One in authority!

The soldiers continued to yell at us to keep moving. On more than one occasion, I felt the sting of a Roman whip across my back. When we arrived at the place of execution, the soldiers shouted at me to put down the cross. Then the soldier who had pulled me from the crowd told me I was free to go.

As I staggered a few feet, no longer under the weight of the cross, I knew I may have completed my task – but I was by no means free to go! My heart compelled me to remain right there at the foot of the cross. The women who had been following Jesus stood there crying as His hands and feet were nailed to the cross.

. . .

I learned that one of the women was Jesus's mother. She and the others were joined by two men who told me they were followers of Jesus. One was named John, and the other's name was Shimon. I knew Jesus had many followers, so I asked John and Shimon where the rest of them were. They told me that many were fearful and had gone into hiding. Some had abandoned Him. Some had denied Him. And one ... had betrayed Him.

I looked at this handful of men and women, and something inside urged me to say, "I will not abandon Him. I will remain here with Him until the end."

I had so many questions. But right then, they didn't seem important. Because I knew the One they were affixing to that cross was so much more than a mere Miracle Worker.

The earth shook as the cross with Jesus on it was dropped into the hole in the ground. Jesus's cross was in the center, and the other two men who had carried their crosses in the procession were now hanging on each side of Him. One of the men called out to Jesus, "So You're the Messiah, are You? Prove it by saving Yourself – and us, too, while You're at it!"[2] But the other criminal said, "Don't you fear God even when you have been sentenced to die? We deserve to die for our crimes, but this Man hasn't done anything wrong."[3] Then he said, "Jesus, remember me when You come into your Kingdom."[4] And Jesus replied, "I assure you, today you will be with Me in paradise."[5]

Even on the cross, Jesus was extending mercy and grace. Who but the Son of God could do that? My heart was so heavy I could not process everything I was seeing. I was witnessing a brutal murder – an injustice. But I would come to learn that the cross was the only way we could be redeemed from our sin and reconciled to a Holy God. God the Father was allowing His only Son to be brutalized so He could be the sacrifice for my sins. His blood was pouring out of His body for me!

. . .

His suffering on the cross came to an end when He declared, "*It is finished!*"[7]

My heart broke as I saw His body slump. The sky had turned dark earlier, and now it fittingly seemed even darker. I fell to my knees and began to weep uncontrollably. I sensed this was part of God's plan, but I could not comprehend what it might be. All I knew was I could not move from this place. It had become holy ground. And the One there on the cross before me was the one true Passover Lamb whose blood had been shed so I could escape death – the death of sin! Today, I had witnessed the everlasting Passover!

A little later, I saw two men who appeared to be members of the Sanhedrin. I was told their names were Joseph and Nicodemus. They were claiming Jesus's body from the soldiers in order to bury Him. As His body was taken down from the cross, I approached the two men and asked if I could carry Jesus.

"The soldiers compelled me to carry His cross," I told them. "But now I believe God is compelling me to carry His broken body to His tomb." With that, I picked up Jesus and carried Him to the place they had prepared for Him.

I knew that my journey with Jesus hadn't ended at the cross, and somehow, I knew it wouldn't end at the tomb. I knew that the One who had stood before me on His cross would still call upon me to take up my cross and follow Him.

~

ABRAHAM – THE PATRIARCH

*M*y name is Abraham. I am the father of Isaac and the grandfather of Jacob, whom God renamed Israel. I am the patriarch of God's chosen people. It is important for you to remember that I died 1,850 years before the death, burial, and resurrection of Jesus. But you need to know that Jesus's death today on the cross has had a great impact on my life, as well.

When I was seventy-five years old, Jehovah God gave me a promise. He said, *"I will make of you a great nation, and I will bless you and make your name great, so that you will be a blessing. I will bless those who bless you, and him who dishonors you I will curse, and in you all the families of the earth shall be blessed."*[(1)]

There is only one person who has ever been born on this earth through whom all the families of this earth have been blessed. When God gave me that promise, He was referring to that One who would enter into this world through my descendants. He was referring to Jesus. Approximately forty-three generations have followed me as my descendants, leading up to the birth of Jesus through His mother Mary. I am His earthly great-grandfather forty-three generations past. The promise Jehovah God gave me was fulfilled through the birth of Jesus.

. . .

I am a descendant of Adam and Eve, just like you. That means their sin nature coursed through my veins just like it has through every generation before me and every generation after me. I sought to walk uprightly before God – but I often failed. Still, by His grace and not my merit, He chose to bless me and use me as His servant. However, I am still a sinner in need of a Savior. Even the patriarch of God's chosen people cannot enter into heaven apart from the sacrificial shed blood of Jesus.

My son Isaac was in his teens when God came to me and said, *"Take your son Isaac, whom you love, and go to the land of Moriah, and offer him there as a burnt offering on one of the mountains of which I shall tell you."*[2] So Isaac and I, together with two servants, arose early the next morning and made our way south toward the city of Jerusalem to the mount of Moriah. On the third day of our travels, I looked up and saw the place that God was directing us to go.

At the base of the mountain, I instructed the servants to wait. Isaac and I would go alone for the rest of the journey. I laid the wood for the burnt offering on Isaac's shoulders to carry, and I brought the fire and the knife. As we climbed the mount, Isaac turned and asked me, *"My father, behold, the fire and the wood, but where is the lamb for a burnt offering?"*[3]

I will confess that I didn't quite know what to say to my son. I was walking in obedience to Jehovah God, my Father, and I would trust Him. So I said the only thing I knew to say, *"God will provide for Himself the lamb for a burnt offering, my son."*[4] My son was satisfied with my answer – because he trusted me. When we reached the place that God had shown me, I built the altar and prepared the wood for the fire. Even as I bound my son, he trusted me. He never struggled – and he could have very easily overpowered me. He didn't even question me when I laid him on the altar.

My heart was in my throat as I raised my knife above my son. This was my son – the son through whom God had promised that all nations would be blessed. Did God intend to bless the nations through his death as a sin offering on this altar? My heart ached – but I had learned that I must trust God.

Just as I raised my hand to plunge the knife into my son's heart, an angel of the Lord called out to me from heaven saying, *"Abraham, Abraham! Do not lay your hand on the boy or do anything to him, for now I know that you fear God, seeing you have not withheld your son."*[5] As I looked up, I saw a ram caught in a thicket by his horns. The ram hadn't been there a moment ago. I reached down and embraced my son. I removed his bindings and together we bound the ram and offered the sacrifice to Jehovah God.

The angel of the Lord again called out and said, *"Because you have done this and have not withheld your son, your offspring will possess the gate of his enemies and in your offspring shall all the nations of the earth be blessed."*[6]

It was then I realized God would truly provide the lamb as a sacrifice for our sin. But not just any lamb. It would be His Lamb – the only Lamb truly worthy to be slain. And He would present His Lamb at just the right moment at just the right place – perhaps this very place in the land of Moriah. He had asked me if I was willing to sacrifice my only son of promise.

Was God preparing to sacrifice His only Son of promise? Even now I feared His hand would not be stilled. His sacrifice would be given. His sacrifice would bless all the nations. And His sacrifice would be given through my offspring. I had climbed the mount that morning with a heavy heart, and now I descended the mount with a heart that was still heavy. My son had not been sacrificed on that day, but one day a Son would be sacrificed on that mount. He would be a Son who also would be born somewhat unexpectedly in an unusual way. He would be born of a promise. And He, too, would one day willingly climb that mount.

. . .

I died believing that promise of a coming sacrifice. I died knowing that my sins could be covered only by the shedding of His blood. And I knew that the God who promised to send His sacrifice would be faithful.

Though my body was buried in a tomb when I died, my soul and spirit lived on. But my soul and spirit could not immediately go to heaven. The sacrifice for my sins had not yet taken place. The price of my redemption had not yet been paid. So, my soul and spirit went to a place called Hades, meaning "the place of the dead."

There were two parts to Hades. One was paradise. It was the place that my soul came to rest, together with the souls of those who also died believing God's promise. You know many of their names. There are those who were already here when I arrived, like Abel, Methuselah, Noah, and Job. There are also many who have come since, like my son Isaac, David, Daniel, Nehemiah, and a beggar by the name of Lazarus.

The other part of Hades is often called Sheol. It is a dark place filled with great sadness and grief. It is inhabited by demons and the many souls who have died without believing in the promise of the coming sacrifice. There was a great chasm that separated Sheol from paradise.

You may recall that Jesus Himself spoke of this place. He even talked about me, as well as a beggar named Lazarus and a rich man you know as Reuben. There are many of us who have been awaiting the sacrifice for our sin – and now the day has come!

The perfect Lamb of God – the One who had no sin – took on our sin, paying the price with His shed blood. The Father led His Son to the top of a hill called Golgotha. As Jesus hung on that cross, He could see the very place – Moriah – where I had led my son to offer him as a sacrifice. But Jehovah God did not stay His own hand as He did mine. My son was kept from being sacrificed, but His Son had come for the express purpose of being sacrificed.

. . .

His blood was shed. He suffered the pain and the agony – all for you and me. He gave His life as the ransom for many. Then He breathed His last … and died.

But let's back up to the moment when Jesus declared, *"It is finished!"*[7] At that moment, He also said, *"Father, I entrust My spirit into Your hands."*[8] Remember, Jesus was as much man as if He were not God at all. That means that at the moment of Jesus's death, His soul and spirit departed from His body – which is the exact same thing that happened to me and will happen to you at the moment of your death. Joseph and Nicodemus did not lay Jesus in the tomb. He had already departed. They were just laying His dead body in that tomb.

But Jesus's spirit came to Hades and gathered all of us who had been justified by faith in His coming and led us to heaven. He went before us and set us free! Our faith had now become sight. Our promised Savior had paid the ransom. We were no longer awaiting His arrival – His victorious work had now been completed. It truly was finished!

I cannot adequately tell you the rejoicing and praise that poured from our mouths, when Jesus in all of His glory arrived in Hades to lead us into heaven. We cried:

> *"Salvation comes from our God who sits on the throne*
> *and from the Lamb!"*[9]

The rejoicing and praise continue to this day. And many voices continue to be added to ours. You see, Jesus emptied paradise that day and brought us all to our eternal home. Paradise no longer exists in Hades. It is no longer necessary. Those who have died in Christ since His death on the cross now come directly to their eternal home here in heaven.

Throughout my time in paradise, I heard accounts from those who were a part of the generations who came after me. Those who spoke of God's glorious deliverance. Joseph, the son of Jacob, told me of his deliverance from slavery and prison. Jacob, the son of Isaac, told of deliverance from famine. Esther told of deliverance from death and destruction. A recent arrival, John the baptizer, told of Jesus's miracles – the blind who could see and the lame who could walk. Each one lifted his or her voice to declare, "Holy, holy, holy! Worthy is the Lamb!"

After Jesus led us to our eternal home, He returned to Hades and entered into Sheol. There He proclaimed His victory over Satan and over sin to the fallen angels who are held in captivity there. As glorious as that news had been for us, it was devastating to those in Sheol. Satan is a defeated foe. There will be no second chance for them. Those who rejected the promise of His coming have sealed their own fate. The "good news" is "bad news" for them. One day Jesus will return – not as their Savior, but as their Judge – and cast them all into the eternal flames of hell. Until that day, Sheol will continue to be their place of torment.

I knew there was only one more enemy that remained for Jesus to defeat. It was the enemy of death. And to do that He would need to arise from the dead. It had been a busy three days while His body laid in that tomb, but now it was time for Him to defeat that last foe. And I knew the One who stood before me would be victorious over all. Because He who has promised is faithful!

Note from the author:

i feel compelled to include a brief word of explanation, because i may have introduced you to a truth in this story you had not heard before. The apostle Peter tells us that Jesus was very busy while His body was laying in the tomb. In 1 Peter 3:19, we read that Jesus's spirit entered into Hades and proclaimed His victory over sin and death to the fallen angels that Jesus's half-brother, Jude, describes in Jude 1:6. The apostle Paul writes in Ephesians 4:8, that in fulfillment of the prophecy recorded in Psalm 68:18 – *"You ascended on high, leading a host of captives in Your train ..."* (ESV) – that Jesus gathered all the redeemed who had been awaiting His redemption and took them from paradise to their permanent dwelling in heaven. That train into heaven would have included Abraham, David,

Joshua, Daniel, the beggar Lazarus, and all those who had been previously justified by their faith in the coming Savior. Those were some great, "gettin' up" days in the spirit world for those whose faith had now become sight (2 Corinthians 5:7)! Excerpted from my book *Taking Up The Cross, Ch. 54.*

~

MARY – THE MAGDALENE

I am Mary, the oldest child of a successful merchant named Jacob, who made his fortune from the sea. I grew up in the fishing city of Magdala along the western shore of the Sea of Galilee. But my father was not a fisherman; he was an astute merchant. He saw the opportunity to take the enormous supply of fish that the fishermen of our village were catching each day and supply them to cities throughout the Roman world.

He acquired a plot of land right along the shore and built a large warehouse where the fish could be salted and dried. Magdala is situated along the trade route between Damascus and Caesarea Maritima. Soon, Magdala fish were becoming a popular food on tables from Alexandria to Damascus. My father built a stone wharf at the water's edge to make the off-loading of the daily catches more efficient for the fishermen. As a result, more fishermen regularly sold their daily catches to my father and his profitable business thrived even more.

My younger brother, Lemuel, and I enjoyed a privileged upbringing commensurate with my father's wealth. He was one of the leading citizens of our city, and we lived in a palatial home just south of the synagogue. My father spared no expense in building our home, including the colorful mosaic floors that ran throughout.

In many ways, I took after my father. He affectionately called me his little rose. He would often say that I was not only beautiful like a rose, I was also resilient like one. He took great care to teach and train me in his business affairs. He told me that even when I was quite young he could see I had his business acumen and entrepreneurial spirit. I was able to look at changes that were taking place around us and anticipate the business opportunities those changes created.

By the time I was twenty, I was my father's right hand, assisting him in most of his ventures. As a matter of fact, I am the one who convinced my father to seize the tremendous business opportunities that would come from the construction of our new provincial capital, Tiberias, just a few kilometers to our south. I persuaded him to utilize the skilled carpenters and stone carvers he had assembled for our building projects in Magdala and build some of the most majestic buildings in the new city.

My brother, Lemuel, on the other hand, was content to follow my father's – and my – direction. He had no desire to lead, but he was a hard worker who could see things through. We all made an excellent team! But suddenly one day, just as work was commencing on our projects in Tiberias, my father died.

After the initial shock passed, my mother, brother, and I discussed how we would proceed with the family's business. My father often spoke about putting a plan in place for how we should continue after he was gone, but we had all believed those days were still a long way off. Now they were here, and we needed to make our own plan.

My brother was the first to admit that I was better suited to lead the enterprise. But the harsh reality in first-century Galilee is that women do not run businesses. Their role is to keep the house and quietly support their husbands. Our craftsmen had seen me as a support to my father. They would not respond well to taking their direction from a woman.

Fortunately, my father had a son who could take over the business – at least publicly. So, we all agreed that Lemuel needed to be the public face of our business, but he would take his direction from me. We also agreed that Lemuel needed to take on the Greek name of Adrianus in order for us to be better positioned for our future business dealings with foreigners.

Our plan worked and our enterprise continued to prosper. Though I knew my name would never be publicly associated with anything we did, one day I got an idea. As my father's "rose," I was going to put my "personal" signature on every building we built and every venture we started. Through Adrianus, I instructed our craftsmen to carve a unique rosette into the cornerstone of every building we constructed. The rosette consists of six petals that project from the center of the circle, surrounded by six identical petals that form the perimeter.

My father and I had often talked about the fact that Jehovah God is the greatest builder of all. He created everything from nothing in a matter of six days. I designed the rosette as a picture of God's creative work. The six inner petals represent the six days of creation. The six outer petals represent the six major elements of His creation: light, water, land, plants, animals, and humans – created in His image. In my mind, by affixing this "personal" signature, I was also giving glory to God.

As the years passed, I came to the decision that I would not marry. I did not need a husband to provide for me, and I knew marriage would only complicate our family's business arrangement. I was enjoying my success in life … until everything changed.

One day while I was visiting several of our building projects in Tiberias to evaluate our progress, a woman approached me. She was obviously below my station in life. She had a distant look in her eyes and her speech was erratic. But she was telling me things about myself that no one else knew, such as I was secretly leading our family's business. She knew my ambitions. She knew my continuing sorrow over the death of my father. She knew of the resentment I harbored toward a society that marginalized the contributions of women. She knew about the public approval for which I longed. She told me she could help me with all of those concerns.

I know I should have just kept walking and not paid her any attention. But something inside me wanted to see how she could help me. So, I accompanied her to her hovel in a part of Tiberias I had never visited before. I was a strong woman, but on that day, she caught me when I was weak. It was as if she knew just what to say to convince me to do something that, on a different day in a different place, I never would have agreed to do. She led me down the path toward dark powers, assuring me they would enable me to achieve all I desired. She assured me that every one of my selfish ambitions would be satisfied and I would get what I truly deserved.

In my weakness, I opened myself up to the demons she assured me would bring fulfillment and joy. But once they resided within me, they took control of me. There was no joy, only agony. There was no satisfaction, only desperation.

When I returned home to Magdala, my brother and mother immediately saw the change in me. They feared the worst – and they were right. I was tormented by voices inside me that would give me no peace. I had opened myself up to a power and a presence I did not understand, and of which I could not rid myself. My mother and brother tried to help me, but they, too, were powerless. Eventually they had to banish me from my own home due to my violent and abusive behavior. Once one of the most respected women in our community, I was now one of the most despised. Friends and neighbors feared me and avoided me.

I lost all control of myself. I sought shelter in the caves outside of the city. My body became battered and bruised by injuries I inflicted upon myself.

I was in complete agony. I lost all dignity. My beauty and wealth had been insufficient to spare me from the evil I brought upon myself. I even tried to overcome it through immoral behavior. But nothing helped! The demons inside attacked me every moment of every day. I had become an outcast and my disheveled appearance now masked the beauty I once possessed.

One day, I saw a group of people walking along the shore from the north. They appeared to be going to Magdala. As they grew closer, I could see that one Man appeared to be the Teacher of the group, and the others were His followers. Even from a distance, I could see that the Man was looking at me. But he wasn't staring at me like other men. It wasn't a look of curiosity or fear. To my astonishment, it was a look of compassion!

He walked straight toward me. Part of me wanted to flee. Part of me wanted to attack Him. But part of me was curious. When He was standing six feet away, He stopped and looked into my eyes. I began to convulse and fell on my knees in front of Him. My demons cried out, "What do you want with us, Jesus, Son of the Most High God?"

I heard the Man reply, "Come out of this woman, you unclean spirits! I cast you into Sheol to await the day of your judgment! Leave this woman and be gone!"

No sooner had He spoken than I collapsed at His feet. He then gently reached down and took me by the hand and said, "Mary, arise, for you have been set free!"

As I stood to my feet, I looked into the eyes of the One who had just set me free. I saw His compassion, but I also saw His authority. He was my Savior and my Lord. He had set me free from my prison. He had done what I could not do – what no one could do! I did not deserve to be saved. I had imprisoned myself due to my own foolish decisions. But despite all of that, He had saved me. I knew immediately I would follow Him wherever He led!

. . .

He told me His name was Jesus. He gently told me to return to my home and tell my mother, brother, and everyone I encountered that God had shown His mercy on me today. He assured me that those who have been set free are free indeed!

When I arrived home, my mother and brother immediately noticed the change in me. After a moment, they ran to me and embraced me. I told them that a Man named Jesus had set me free! He had done what no one else could. I told them that I needed to find out more about Him. He had saved my life. I needed to return to Him to thank Him.

My mother told me before I did anything else, I needed to bathe and change my clothes. Afterward, I barely recognized my own reflection. I hadn't seen myself in many years! I wanted to just sit and talk with my family, but I knew I needed to go and thank Jesus. However, I had no idea where to look for Him.

Right then a messenger delivered a note to my brother from Simon, the Pharisee. The message read, "Jesus of Nazareth is joining me as my guest for dinner this evening. You are invited to join me as well." Even though I had become an outcast, I was grateful that my brother had been able to maintain his position of importance. I was also grateful to know where I would find Jesus. Lemuel and I decided it would be wise for the two of us to go to Simon's home separately. I was not an invited guest. He arrived first and joined the rest of the guests around the table with Jesus.

While they were eating, I entered the room carrying an alabaster jar filled with perfume. Without stopping to acknowledge anyone, let alone the host of the gathering, I walked over to where Jesus was reclining with His feet outstretched behind Him. I knelt and began to weep. As I did, my tears fell on His feet, and I wiped them off with my hair. I began to kiss His feet and anoint them with perfume. I had come to express my love and gratitude to Jesus for all He had done for me. I paid no attention to anyone else in the room.

. . .

Suddenly I heard Jesus speak to His host, *"Simon, I have something to say to you. A man loaned money to two people – five hundred pieces of silver to one and fifty pieces to the other. But neither of them could repay him, so he kindly forgave them both, canceling their debts. Who do you suppose loved him more after that?"*[(1)] Simon replied, *"I suppose the one for whom he canceled the larger debt."*[(2)]

Jesus said, "You have answered rightly." Then He turned toward me and said to Simon, *"Look at this woman kneeling here. When I entered your home, you didn't offer Me water to wash the dust off My feet, but she has washed them with her tears and wiped them with her hair. You didn't greet Me with a kiss, but from the time I first came in, she has not stopped kissing My feet. You neglected the courtesy of olive oil to anoint My head, but she has anointed My feet with rare perfume. I tell you that her sins – and they are many – have been forgiven, so she has shown Me much love. But a person who is forgiven little shows only little love."*[(3)] Then looking at me, Jesus said, *"Mary, your sins are forgiven. Your faith has saved you. Go in peace."*[(4)]

The next morning as Jesus left Magdala to continue His journey, I was counted among His number. I joined the other women in the group. I realized my brother had stepped in and directed our business affairs well during my absence, and he could continue to do so. He was God's provision so that I could leave my home and travel with Jesus. Gratefully, I was also able to use a portion of my income from our business to help support Jesus and His apostles in their ministry.

I traveled with Jesus for over two years. Each day, I witnessed Him perform miraculous things. I saw him deliver others who were demon possessed. I rejoiced with them as they experienced their release from bondage. I knew what that felt like! I saw Him enable the blind to see, the deaf to hear, and the lame to walk. He spoke with an authority unlike any other, and He opened my heart and my mind to truth. I had come to know that He is the Son of the Living God.

. . .

Three nights ago, I assisted the other women in our group in preparing the Passover meal, as was our custom. Before the dinner began, I watched in amazement as Jesus washed the feet of each of His apostles. It reminded me of the night I had washed and anointed His feet. But He was worthy of having His feet washed. Here He was humbling Himself and washing His disciples' feet. They were not worthy – any more than I was. And yet He humbled Himself to the point of being their servant.

After dinner, Jesus led His apostles to the Garden of Gethsemane. The rest of us returned to Bethany for the night, never expecting the news the next morning would bring. Like everyone else, I could not believe my ears when we received word that Jesus had been arrested. I accompanied His mother and several of the other women as we hastily made our way to Jerusalem. Surely this would all be settled without Jesus coming to any harm! Surely the religious leaders would come to their senses – or the Heavenly Father would intercede on His Son's behalf!

This was more than His mother Mary could bear, but I knew I needed to be the strong one to help support her through this difficult time. When we arrived in Jerusalem, we were horrified to learn that Jesus was to be crucified! Our hearts broke when we saw the way the soldiers had brutally beaten and scourged Him. We followed Him through the streets of Jerusalem as the crowd ridiculed Him. We watched in agony as He was nailed to that rugged cross.

As I looked up at Jesus, my mind raced back to days past. I pictured Him on the day He freed me from my bondage. I thought of the day He broke the loaves and the fishes and fed the multitude. I remembered His delight as He spoke of the faith of that little boy. I reflected on how patiently He had always answered all of our questions. I recalled the many times I heard Him laugh, as well as the times I saw Him weep over the destructive power of sin. I pictured Him – just the night before – as He had knelt before His apostles and washed their feet.

Suddenly my mind went in a different direction. This time it was unbelief. How could the Father permit this to happen to His Son? Jesus is the Messiah – why hasn't the Father sent a host of angels to deliver His Son and overpower these Roman soldiers? Why is this One who has delivered so many from pain and suffering being forced to endure it Himself?

I was consumed by so many feelings at once – heartbreak, anger, helplessness, hopelessness, and even faithlessness. Jesus had become my life and my hope. What were we all to do? What was I to do? I could no longer see past the death and agony that was right there before my eyes. Then suddenly, Jesus cried out, *"It is finished!"*[5]

I stood by Mary's side as the horror continued to unfold. A soldier thrust his spear into Jesus's side to make sure He was dead. Blood and water flowed from His body. Even after death, they were subjecting my Savior to barbaric cruelty. I embraced Mary as we stood there and wept uncontrollably. Mercifully, the centurion called out to His soldiers that Jesus's body was not to be subjected to any more brutality.

We stood there for quite a while, not knowing what to do or where to go. Many of us had been following Jesus for years, and now that had abruptly come to an end. I was grateful that Joseph of Arimathea and Nicodemus of Galilee had the presence of mind to make arrangements for the burial of His body. And the man who had been pulled from the crowd to carry Jesus's cross now followed the other two men carrying the limp body of my Savior.

I realized we needed to prepare Jesus's body for burial – an act I never imagined doing. I had believed Jesus would establish His kingdom and reign forever. But now, Mary (the wife of Clopas), Salome, Joanna, and Ayda were volunteering to help me do just that. But we would have to delay going to the tomb until after the Sabbath.

We would need sunlight to do what we needed to do, so we waited until just before sunrise on Sunday to leave Bethany and travel to where Jesus had been laid. As we walked, we realized the large stone covering the entrance to the tomb would be too heavy for us to roll away. We hadn't thought through all of the details. But fortunately, the Father had been planning the details for eternity, and He had not forgotten anything!

When we arrived, we noticed the stone had already been rolled away. We immediately presumed someone had taken Jesus's body. Without even walking into the tomb, I left the other women and ran to alert Peter, John, and Shimon. I knew they were staying in the upper room in Jerusalem. I told them the religious leaders had taken Jesus's body. They ran back to the tomb with me to see for themselves.

The men ran much faster than I did, so Peter and John had already been to the tomb and were headed back toward Jerusalem when they met me. They confirmed that His body was not in the tomb, but John said, "He has risen!" Peter, however, did not seem to be so sure.

I decided to continue on to the tomb. At first, I couldn't bring myself to look inside. But when I did, I saw two angels who asked me why I was weeping. "The religious leaders *have taken away my Lord, and I do not know where they have laid Him*,"[6] I said.

I turned to see a Man standing outside the tomb. Thinking He was the gardener, I asked Him, "*Sir, if You have taken Him away, tell me where You have put Him, and I will go and get Him*."[7]

But when He spoke my name, I knew the One who stood before me was my Lord and Master! I instinctively reached out to touch Him. "*Don't cling to Me*," He said, "*for I haven't yet ascended to the Father. But go find My brothers and tell them, 'I am ascending to My Father and your Father, to My God and your God.'*"[8]

Then off I ran to tell the disciples I had seen Jesus … He was alive … and He had stood before me!

CLOPAS – THE UNCLE

I am Clopas, the uncle of the Son of God. That probably sounds as strange to your ears as the realization did to mine. So, let me back up and explain.

I am the son of Jacob the carpenter, and the younger brother of Joseph, the earthly father to Jesus. I was born in Cana of Galilee and lived there much of my life. When I was sixteen, work in Cana became harder to find. Joseph moved to Nazareth while I stayed in Cana with our father. Gratefully, Jehovah God continued to provide my father and me with enough work to keep food on our table.

When I was twenty-eight, I married a beautiful young woman by the name of Mary. Apparently, my brother and I had similar tastes in women since both of us married women named Mary!

God blessed my wife and me with two sons whom we named James and Thaddeus. My eldest, James, even as a boy was shorter than others his age. That continued into adulthood, which earned him the nickname, "James the Less." But don't underestimate him! What he lacks in height, he has always made up for in brawn. Even as a young boy, he was a great helper to me in my work.

As you know, my brother Joseph's first wife, Rebekah, died at a young age. I grieved for him, and I could see how lonely he was. So, no one was more overjoyed than I was when he became engaged to be married. My wife and I had met his fiancée, Mary, and her father, Eli, on our occasional visits to Nazareth, but we never imagined Joseph and Mary would marry because of their significant age difference. Still, we were excited to hear that the wedding feast was planned for December of that year. Joseph was again filled with joy – something that had been conspicuously absent since Rebekah's death.

My wife and I were surprised in early May of that year when Joseph and his fiancée paid us a visit in Cana. I am not as observant as my wife, so nothing appeared out of the ordinary to me when they arrived. Joseph explained that he and Mary had news to tell us. I looked over at my wife and she appeared to already have some idea of what was coming.

"Soon after we announced our betrothal," Joseph began, "an angel of the Lord came to Mary and told her that Jehovah God had chosen her, and the Spirit of God would come over her and she would conceive a child." He went on to explain that the child would be the Son of the Most High God. The prophet Isaiah had written that the Messiah would be born of a virgin – and now God had apparently chosen Mary to be that virgin!

"The messenger of God confirmed the message through Mary's cousins, Zechariah and Elizabeth, and he has confirmed it to me through a dream," Joseph continued. "We know that she is the most blessed of women – but we also know how this appears to our neighbors. The angel confirmed that I should bring Mary into my home as my wife. And I have done so. However, we will not consummate our marriage until after the child is born.

. . .

"You are my closest family, so we wanted you to know and understand as soon as possible. We know how shocking this all sounds. We both have experienced that shock ourselves."

Joseph silently waited for our response. I knew my brother to be an upright man of integrity. I knew he loved God and always strived to stand righteous before Him. His word was all I would ever need to know that what he said was the truth. So I looked at my brother and his wife and said, "We join together with you in praising Jehovah God for His faithfulness in sending His Messiah, for His mercy in allowing us to now sit here in the baby's presence, and for His grace in the way He is enabling you to walk through this with Him. Mary, you truly are blessed by God above all other women. And Joseph, our God has chosen well to choose you to be the earthly father to His Son."

Joseph and Mary stayed with us for two days before they returned to Nazareth. My wife and I talked about how our lives would be different in light of this news. We were to be an "uncle and aunt" to the Messiah. Our son James, and later our son, Thaddeus, would be His "cousins." Never would we have imagined such a thought when we heard the prophecies about the Messiah. How could we have ever supposed that God would allow an unknown family from Cana to bear witness to His Son in such a way? He is indeed a merciful and gracious God!

My wife and I are both of the tribe of Judah and the line of David. So, when Caesar decreed that every person needed to return to their ancestral home for the census, we traveled with Joseph and Mary to Bethlehem. My wife's sister and her husband live in Bethlehem, so my Mary and I had made plans to stay with them in their small home, while Joseph and his wife would be staying with our cousin Achim.

It was while we were in Bethlehem that God's Son was born. The morning following Jesus's birth, Joseph came to my sister-in-law's home to seek me out. He told me the baby had been born the night before and how a group of angels announced the birth to shepherds in the hills. He described how they had come to worship the child. He was in awe of all that had occurred.

But he also told me that Achim had not received the announcement about Mary's pregnancy well. He did not believe the child was the Son of God. He was convinced that either Mary or both of them had broken their vows. Joseph and Mary had been forced to spend the night in Achim's stable, but that morning he had agreed to allow Mary and the baby to stay in the house until her time of purification was completed. "However," Joseph told me, "I am not welcome in their home. This morning I went to the synagogue and registered for the census. Now I am headed to Jerusalem to find work for the next few weeks until Mary's time is completed."

"Brother, I am so sorry that you have been received in that way," I replied. "I would see if you could stay here in this home, but I know they have no room."

"I know that Jehovah God has a divine plan in all of this," Joseph responded, "so we will trust Him to use even this to further His purpose in everyone's lives."

My family and I returned home two days later. None of us knew it would be several years before we would see Joseph and Mary again or meet their special child. But as you know, the Heavenly Father directed them to Egypt to keep Jesus from harm. By the time they returned to Nazareth, we were living there, as well. We had moved to Nazareth to help care for Mary's ailing father. We remained there after he died in order to watch over Joseph's home and maintain the carpentry trade he and his father-in-law had started.

Our second son, Thaddeus, was born soon after Joseph and Mary returned from Egypt. For the next several years, we enjoyed our shared life together in Nazareth. God blessed us all bountifully! Joseph fathered four sons – James, young Joseph, Jude, and Simon – and two daughters –

Mary and Salome. Jesus was the model oldest son and an attentive big brother. He grew, not only in height but also in wisdom and maturity.

One time in particular, when Jesus was twelve, we all traveled to Jerusalem together for the observance of Passover. Several other families from town joined us. Over the years, the neighbors' ill treatment of Joseph and Mary had diminished and had even been forgotten by some. So, trips to Jerusalem were a break for everyone from their daily routine and great cause for camaraderie and fun. The men and women would travel in their separate groups and the older children would do the same. It was possible to go for days without seeing an older child because they were off with the others.

We had begun our journey back home from Jerusalem when Joseph and Mary discovered that Jesus was missing. Knowing how distraught they were, I decided to join them in their search. My wife agreed to take the rest of their children, together with ours, and continue on home accompanied by our neighbors.

For three days we scoured the city for Jesus. Finally, on the fourth day, we found Him in the temple sitting among the rabbis. He was seated with his back toward us, so He did not see us when we arrived. But we noticed how the people sitting around Him marveled at what He was saying. He spoke in a way that astounded them – not only because He was so young – but also because His understanding surpassed that of most of the teachers.

I'll never forget Jesus's response when Joseph and Mary told Him about their frantic search. *"Why did you need to search?"* He asked. *"You should have known that I would be in My Father's house."*[1]

I don't believe His parents or I fully grasped the implications of His answer, but it did make us reflect on His words. That would not be the last time we would ponder the things He said. We became more and more mindful that Jesus was not just any young man, He is the Son of the Most

High God.

Joseph and I, together with all of our sons, worked as carpenters for another eight years – until Joseph died. Jesus then assumed the responsibility as the patriarch of His family for eight years. He honored His father Joseph's memory and lovingly cared for His mother and His family. As the years went by, I realized I was no longer viewing Him as my nephew – I had come to view Him as my Master. Until one day, He announced to all of us that His time had come.

Soon we began hearing reports of the miracles He was performing and the crowds that were gathering to hear His teaching. A group of men began to follow Him as His disciples. One day when He returned to Nazareth to see His mother and His family, both of my sons announced that they believed they were supposed to follow Him as His disciples.

It was interesting to me that my sons – His cousins – believed they should follow Him, but His own brothers did not. There appeared to be a hesitancy on their part to fully accept Him as the Son of God. There was no such hesitancy in the hearts of my sons. But, part of me was grateful that Jesus's four half-brothers remained in Nazareth to help me carry on with our carpentry trade.

There were a few women who were also now traveling with Jesus. His mother Mary would do so on occasion, but the other women were doing so full time. I was somewhat surprised when my Mary announced that she, too, believed she was supposed to follow Him. While she and my sons did what the Heavenly Father had called them to do, I remained in Galilee to work and help provide financial support for their travels.

I saw them often, though. Jesus spent most of His time traveling throughout Galilee. His fame and reputation were far-reaching. Ironically, every town and village throughout Galilee welcomed Him with open arms ... except His hometown of Nazareth.

.   .   .

Jesus had always been liked and respected by the townspeople, first as a boy and later as a carpenter earning a living in our town. But, regrettably, their familiarity with Him, and the lingering memory of what some still believed to be questionable circumstances surrounding His birth, caused the town to never recognize Him for who He is.

So, for the past two years, I have traveled to nearby towns to see Him and my family – because Jesus has never returned to Nazareth. Mary and her family have now moved to Capernaum. I will probably soon move to another town, as well. Perhaps, back to Cana, my birthplace.

This past week, I joined my family as we all followed Jesus to Jerusalem to celebrate Passover. It has been an emotional week, beginning with the celebratory entry into the city. As the uncle of the Messiah, I was overjoyed by the recognition finally being given to Jesus. But the last vestige of that joy disappeared Friday morning with the news of His arrest. My joy quickly turned to horror as I witnessed the cruelty inflicted on Him, followed by my inconsolable sorrow after He declared, *"It is finished!"*[2]

After Jesus's body was taken to the tomb for burial, I remained with His mother, my wife, and the other women who had been gathered at the foot of the cross. I would accompany them to the home of Lazarus in Bethany, where we would all remain for the Sabbath. I asked John and Shimon if there was anything else I could do.

Shimon told me he had promised to go to Emmaus to speak with Barabbas. I knew they had a history together, and I knew Shimon had visited him in prison earlier in the week. Shimon said he didn't have the strength to have a conversation with him now after what had just occurred. But he knew he was supposed to go speak with him. I agreed to accompany him, and we arranged to meet in Bethphage early Sunday morning after the Sabbath.

· · ·

Today is Sunday. This morning, my wife and several of the other women departed for the tomb with spices and ointments to anoint Jesus's body for burial. The Sabbath sunset had prevented them from doing so the day He died. I left for Bethphage to meet Shimon. While I was waiting for him, my wife and the other women came running to tell me Jesus's tomb was empty! They gave me an amazing account about seeing angels who said Jesus was alive. But since they were somewhat hysterical, it was difficult to discern what they had really seen and heard.

When Shimon arrived, he told me that he, Peter, and John had also been to the tomb, and that Jesus's body really was gone. But the question still remained – where was the body of Jesus?

Shimon and I discussed all that had happened as we made our way to Emmaus. It is a small village seven miles northwest of Jerusalem. As we walked, Shimon told me what had happened when Jesus was arrested, then about the stops at the homes of Annas and Caiaphas. He told me about the trials before Herod and Pilate. And in light of the surprising release of Barabbas, he told me about his brief visit with him in prison on Wednesday.

We didn't know what to make of it all. Shimon had been one of the shepherds who heard the angels' announcement of Jesus's birth. I was Jesus's uncle. I, too, knew about all of the angelic pronouncements. There was no question in either of our minds that Jesus was the Son of God who did powerful miracles. And, without question, He was the mightiest Teacher either of us had ever heard. We believed He was the Messiah who had come to rescue Israel.

But the leading priests and religious leaders had been successful in their scheme. They had manipulated Pilate to condemn Him to death, and He had been crucified. Now all of our hopes that He was the Messiah had been dashed. His death made no sense! Had we been wrong?

. . .

As we continued on our way, Jesus joined us – though we did not know it was Him. My own nephew, and Master, was a stranger to me! In our defense, we weren't looking for Him, let alone expecting Him to join us on this journey. We thought He was dead and gone. We were blinded by our grief – and our doubts.

Our fellow traveler began to explain the prophecies regarding the Messiah, one by one, with great clarity. When we arrived in Emmaus, we asked Him to join us for a meal. We would look for Barabbas after we ate. Then as Jesus took the bread and broke it – just as He had during our many meals together – our eyes were opened! I looked into His eyes … and I saw my Lord and my Savior! At that very moment, He disappeared. We could not contain our joy! We knew we must rush back to Jerusalem to tell everyone the good news!

As we walked outside, Barabbas approached us. Shimon quickly explained to him that we had just seen Jesus. Surprisingly, he was less shocked than we had been. He told us that on Friday morning when he had been set free, he knew Jesus was to be crucified in his place. He knew he owed his life to Jesus. And he knew he must do whatever he had to do to follow Him.

Barabbas said when he looked into the eyes of Jesus that morning, he knew beyond any shadow of doubt that He truly was the Son of God. "I knew the grave would never be able to hold Him," he added. "The Son of God could never be conquered by death. I was surrendering my life to a living Lord who was taking my place and paying my debt!"

Shimon and I looked at each other. Through that one encounter with Jesus, Barabbas had demonstrated more faith than any of us. We were looking into the eyes of a man whose life had been transformed! Within the hour, the three of us were on our way back to Jerusalem to tell the others what we had seen and heard.

. . .

That night, we all gathered back in the upper room. Everyone looked at Shimon and me suspiciously when Barabbas followed us into the room. We quickly helped him tell his testimony. Simon the Cyrene had accompanied Joseph of Arimathea and Nicodemus. Simon told how he, too, had come to know beyond any question that Jesus is the Son of God. After hearing their stories, the others were more at ease and welcomed Barabbas and Simon into the room.

We had gathered in secret. Yitzhak, the proprietor, was making sure no one would disturb us. The door to the room was locked. The room was abuzz as people took turns sharing. Mary Magdalene told about how Jesus had spoken to her as she stood outside the tomb. John shared how he and Peter had witnessed the empty tomb and his belief that Jesus truly is the Son of the Living God. My wife Mary, together with Joanna, Salome, and Ayda relayed their encounter with the angels in the tomb, and then how Jesus appeared to them on their way to report to the disciples. Peter told everyone that Jesus was alive and had appeared to him earlier in the day. Finally, Shimon and I shared how Jesus appeared to us as we were walking along the road.

The rest of the disciples looked bewildered. They kept hearing these reports from brothers and sisters whom they respected, but this was all still hard to believe. Jesus had been subjected to unspeakable brutality and had died on the cross. They had witnessed it, albeit from a distance after they scattered. Could this be a part of the religious leaders' plot to not only murder Jesus but to defame His teachings and His miracles? Was this all part of the plan to draw out His close followers and arrest us, as well? At that moment, there was still more fear than faith present in the room.

Then, suddenly, Jesus appeared! The grave couldn't hold Him! Death couldn't defeat Him! The locked door could not keep Him out! If there had been any windows in the room, some of the men might have jumped out! They thought they were seeing a ghost. So, it is no wonder that the first words out of the mouth of the One who stood before me were, *"Peace be with you!"*[3]

SIMON PETER – THE ROCK

*M*y name is Simon – at least it was until Jesus changed it. I grew up in Bethsaida on the north shore of the Sea of Galilee. I was a fisherman who later became a fisher of men. My father, Jonah, was teaching me how to swim and fish before I learned to walk. I once would have told you that my father taught me everything I needed to know about being a good fisherman. That is, until I met Jesus! But I'm getting ahead of myself.

My father died ten years ago. So, as his oldest son, I became the head of our family and our part of a fishing business. My father was in a partnership with his friend, Zebedee, for many years. The two men learned they could be more successful working together than apart. As their respective sons grew, we all became a part of the business – Zebedee's sons James and John, and my younger brother Andrew and myself.

Jehovah God continued to bless our efforts with bountiful harvests from the sea. Herod Antipas's decision to construct his new capital city, Tiberias, brought even more hungry mouths to our nearby communities. As I am sure you know, no self-respecting Jew will set foot in the city, but we began trading with the Tiberian food merchants who came to us.

Demand was high, business was good, and our enterprise continued to prosper.

The greatest of God's blessings in my life is my wife, Gabriella. She is a wise, strong, and understanding woman. Those who know me will tell you I am an impulsive man with the tendency to act first and think later. Many times, I have come home discouraged by the events of the day, often the result of my own missteps. But my dear Gabriella would lovingly and patiently reason with me, caution me to go slowly, and encourage me to rise above my trials and disappointments. In sickness, she has been my comfort; and whenever I have followed my heart, she has been right there to cheer me on.

In His sovereignty, God did not grace us with a son, but He has blessed us with two beautiful daughters – Sarah and Iscah – who thankfully take after their mother. They will *be known for their beauty that comes from within; the unfading beauty of a gentle and quiet spirit.*[1] My future sons-in-law will be blessed men – just as I have been!

Our increased trade enabled Zebedee and me to hire additional men to work with us on our boats, including my brother-in-law, Thomas, and my brother's friends, Philip and Bartholomew. Hiring those additional fishermen proved to be especially helpful when several years ago, Andrew and John came to us and asked to be released from their work responsibilities so they could seek out the prophet, John the baptizer. He was creating quite a stir as a prophetic voice crying out in the wilderness with a message of repentance. Andrew and John felt God leading them to become his disciples. Zebedee and I released them without hesitation to follow their God-given pursuit. Our fishing enterprise would enable us to provide them with the means to provide for themselves.

A little more than three years ago, Andrew and John returned home. They excitedly shared with us that they had met the One whom the baptizer had declared to be the Messiah. They told us that His name was Jesus and He was from Nazareth. He had spoken to them out of the writings of the prophets with an authority like they had never heard.

. . .

A few days later, when Jesus arrived in Bethsaida, Andrew took me to meet Him. Jesus looked at me very intently, as if He were looking into my very soul and knew everything I had ever done and everything I would ever do. Then He spoke. *"You are Simon, son of Jonah, but I will no longer call you Simon, for you will be called Peter, which means 'a rock'".*[(2)] He saw me in a way that I could not see myself. And for the first time in my life, I was struck silent. All I could do was marvel at this Man!

When Jesus set out for Capernaum, Andrew and John accompanied Him, as did Philip and Bartholomew. I remained in Bethsaida to attend to our business. But my every thought was about Jesus. I knew that my life would never again be the same, and my heart was being drawn to follow Him. But what would I do regarding my responsibilities – to my wife, my family, and my business partner?

That night, I told Gabriella about meeting Jesus. I told her what He had said to me. "Gabriella, I believe He is the Promised One," I said. "Though we only just met, I believe He knows me better than I know myself. I believe my life will be different because of Him. I believe all of our lives will be different because of Him!"

My wife looked at me and said, "Have you considered the possibility that you may be meant to travel with Him and become one of His disciples?" I couldn't believe she was asking me that question! I had been struggling with that very idea ever since I met Jesus.

"I can't just leave and follow Him," I replied. "I can't abandon you and the girls, or Zebedee and the business. God has called me to be your husband, a father to Sarah and Iscah, and a partner to Zebedee. I cannot turn my back on you or what God has called me to do."

"You are a man of honor, Simon," Gabriella said. "That's one of the many reasons I love you. And I know you will never abandon me or your family. But I also know that if God calls you to follow the Messiah, you must do so. And we must all trust God to take care of us. His call on one of us is a call on all of us. If God so leads, the girls and I will go to Capernaum to live with my mother. We will be fine. I will trust God – and you must, also! Let us watch and see how God leads!"

Shortly thereafter, Andrew and the other men returned. They told us about how Jesus had turned water into wine at a wedding celebration in Cana. They had seen Him cast out an evil spirit from a man in Capernaum. They had heard Him teach in the synagogue in a way that astounded even the rabbis. There was no question that Jesus was unlike any man they had ever known.

A few days later, we had been fishing all through the night but hadn't caught any fish. We were washing and mending our nets the next morning when Jesus arrived onshore and began to preach to a crowd gathering around Him. Our fishing boats were there at the water's edge.

As the crowd pressed in, Jesus asked me if He could step into one of the boats and be pushed offshore a little ways so He could more easily speak to the crowd. I didn't hesitate and did exactly what Jesus asked. When He was done teaching, He turned to me and said, *"Now go out where it is deeper, and let down your nets to catch some fish."*[3]

"Master, we worked hard all night and didn't catch a thing," I replied. *"But at Your word, I'll let the nets down again."*[4] As soon as the nets were in the water, they began to fill with fish. I called out to Zebedee and the others to come out in the other boat and help Thomas and me bring in the catch. Soon both boats were so full of fish that we feared they would sink. I had never experienced anything like that!

Realizing what had just happened, I cried out to Jesus saying, *"Oh, Lord, please leave me, for I am a sinful man."*[5] Jesus looked at me and said, *"Do not fear! From now on you will be fishing for people!"*[6]

. . .

I looked up and saw Gabriella and our daughters in the crowd. She was smiling at me and nodding her head. We both knew what I must do. To Zebedee's credit, he knew, too. James, John, Andrew, Thomas, Philip, Bartholomew, and I were all now preparing to leave and follow Jesus. Zebedee never once asked us to reconsider our decision. He knew Jesus's call on our lives to follow Him was also a call on his life to stay and maintain the business so he could provide for us financially.

I said farewell to my wife and daughters. Zebedee bade farewell to his sons – and to his wife, too, since she had decided to come with us. Immediately we all departed with Jesus. We had no idea what the journey would entail. We watched in amazement as Jesus stilled the winds and the seas. We witnessed Him heal the lame and the blind. Lepers were made whole. Those possessed by demons were set free. Multitudes were fed with a mere pittance of food.

One night, Jesus even summoned me in the midst of a storm to step out onto the waves and walk toward Him. Miraculously, I walked on the water … until I took my eyes off of Him. My impulsiveness often caused me to speak out, sometimes correctly, but often requiring correction from my Master. But even when Jesus rebuked me, I knew He loved me. It became apparent to all of us that Jesus was preparing me to become a shepherd to our band of disciples – in spite of my many imperfections.

The months and years passed quickly. Just a few weeks ago we were back in Jerusalem to celebrate Passover. I will never forget our entry into the city on the first day of that week. Jesus rode into the city on the back of a colt. The people poured out of the city to cheer Him along with shouts of "Hosanna!" They laid garments and palm branches in His path. It appeared that the entire city was prepared to welcome Him as our Messiah.

But soon the week took a very unexpected turn. On the eve of the Passover, we all gathered in an upper room to share in our traditional Passover Seder, just as we had on previous occasions. But it quickly became clear that this occasion would be different.

. . .

Soon after we arrived, Jesus got up from the table and kneeled before each one of us to wash our dirty feet. The Son of the Almighty God was washing our feet! We sat there in shock not knowing what to do or say. This was our Lord and our Master serving us in such a menial way.

When Jesus came to me, I protested. But He said, *"Unless I wash you, you won't belong to Me."*[7] Then in my impetuous way, I exclaimed, *"Then wash my hands and head as well, Lord, not just my feet!"*[8] Jesus patiently responded, *"A person who has bathed all over does not need to wash, except for the feet, to be entirely clean."*[9]

When Jesus returned to His place at the table, He asked, *"Do you understand what I was doing? Since I, your Lord and Teacher, have washed your feet, you ought to wash each other's feet. Do as I have done to you."*[10]

As we ate our Passover meal, I thought about what Jesus said and His message became clear. If He served, we are to serve. If He humbled Himself for the sake of the kingdom, we are to humble ourselves for the sake of the kingdom. If He gave all for us, we are to give all for Him.

My thoughts were interrupted when Jesus said, *"Here at this table, sitting among us as a friend, is the man who will betray Me."*[11] I couldn't believe my ears! How could that be?

Later as we were walking together to the Garden of Gethsemane, I said to Him, *"Lord, I am ready to go to prison with You, and even to die with You."*[12] But I was shocked when He responded that I would deny Him three times that very night.

As most of you know, that is exactly what I did. After Jesus was arrested that night, I denied that I even knew Him. My denial wasn't even to those in authority who were making accusations against me, it was to household servants who were more curious than they were accusatory. Then, at the very moment of my third denial, my eyes met with His. To my even greater sorrow, His gaze was not accusatory or condemning, rather it was one of love and forgiveness.

Jesus had known what I would do. He had known that day when He first called me "Peter." He had chosen me to walk with Him as a trusted follower, knowing I would deny Him. A flood of shame and sorrow cascaded over me. With tears streaming down my face, I ran to get as far away from Jesus as possible!

I didn't know where I was headed. I was drowning in remorse and I couldn't bear to see His unmerited compassion one more time. This sensation of drowning was far worse than the day I had sunk in the storm-tossed sea – because this time I couldn't call out to Jesus to rescue me. My shame wouldn't permit me!

My feet eventually led me back to the upper room. No one else was there. Most of the others had apparently fled to Lazarus's home in Bethany after the arrest, except the few who had stayed with Jesus. I didn't know what was happening to Jesus, but I had a pretty good idea.

Late that night, John arrived at the upper room. He told me that Jesus was dead. He recounted all that had happened. Then he explained that he had been looking for me. The writer of Proverbs talks about a *"friend who sticks closer than a brother."*[13] That night, all throughout the next day, and into the following, John was that kind of friend when I so desperately needed one. I sometimes wonder what I might have done if he had not been there with me. But in retrospect, I know Jesus was ministering His grace to me through John.

Imagine John's and my dismay when Mary Magdalene showed up at the room early Sunday morning to tell us that someone had taken Jesus's body. We immediately ran to the tomb. John was the faster runner, so he arrived before I did. But John stopped at the doorway and looked in. I charged past him and ran right into the tomb.

There we saw the linen wrappings neatly rolled up. It was at that moment that John would later tell me that *"he saw and believed."*[4] He couldn't yet prove that Jesus was risen, but He believed it with all his heart. I had not yet come to that place. I didn't know what to think. John decided he would go see Jesus's mother who was with the others in Bethany. I decided to return to the upper room. I still couldn't face the others, knowing what I had done.

Throughout the hours that followed, I was in turmoil. Had Jesus's body been taken, or had He risen from the grave like He had said He would? I had seen Him raise people from the dead on three occasions. I knew He had power over the death of others. But did He have power over His own death? And if He had risen from the dead, how could I ever face Him? I wanted to see Him. I wanted to tell Him I was sorry. I wanted His forgiveness ... but my shame left me in doubt as to whether I could accept it.

As the hours passed, I continued to wrestle with my guilty conscience. Suddenly, Jesus appeared right before me! He didn't walk into the room, He just appeared. "Peace be with you, Peter," He said. Hearing His voice, I began to weep uncontrollably. Jesus stepped toward me and embraced me – and He didn't let go. I have no idea how long we stood there with His arms wrapped around me. I kept saying, "Jesus, I am so sorry!" And He lovingly responded, "I know you are, Peter. I forgive you!"

Jesus knew that He needed to correct me. And He would do so several days later – on the same shoreline where He had first called me to follow Him. But for now, He knew that my broken heart and spirit needed to be healed. And that healing needed to occur before He and I were together in that same room with the other disciples later that night.

. . .

At that moment, I knew my journey with Jesus would never be over. I *would* follow Him to my death. He had extended His grace, His mercy, His love, and His forgiveness to me a sinner, even when I denied Him. And I knew – by His grace – I would never again deny the One who stood before me.

~

THOMAS – THE BELIEVER

 $\mathcal{M}$ y name is Thomas and I have a twin sister, Gabriella. She and I grew up in the town of Capernaum, along the shore of the Sea of Galilee. Our father was a fisherman, so it will not surprise you to learn that I also grew up to become one, and my sister became the wife of a fisherman. As a matter of fact, you are well acquainted with my brother-in-law – Simon Peter, another apostle of Jesus.

After my father died, I went to work with my brother-in-law and his partner Zebedee. Gratefully, my wages enabled me to provide for my widowed mother, as well as my own meager needs. I was one of the fishermen who remained with Simon and Zebedee while Andrew and John left to follow the baptizer. And I continued to remain with them when Philip and Bartholomew also left to join Andrew and John in following Jesus.

But I will never forget the day that Jesus told Simon to take his boat back out from the shore and cast his nets. I had been working alongside him on the boat throughout the night. We had nothing to show for our labor. We had called it a night and had finished mending and cleaning our nets when Jesus gave Simon those instructions. I was in the boat with him when suddenly the nets became weighed down with fish. We both thought the catch was going to sink the boat. I've heard it said that seeing is believing, and I truly believed that day!

When Simon Peter and James announced that they, too, were leaving to follow Jesus, my heart was already compelling me to do the same. Gabriella had decided that she and her daughters would be moving to Capernaum to live with our mother. Simon and Zebedee assured me my mother would be well cared for. There was nothing to prevent me from being obedient to what my heart was telling me to do. I got out of the boat and followed Jesus that day – not so much by faith, but with a confidence that the details had already been worked out.

In the weeks and months that followed, I saw Jesus perform one miracle after another. I saw people who had never before seen receive their sight, and people who had never before heard receive their hearing. But there was one night in particular that stands out for me above the rest.

We were in a boat crossing the sea when a storm came up. Peter called out to me, "Go wake up Jesus, and tell Him that we're about to sink in this storm. We need Him to help bail water!" I made my way to where Jesus was sleeping soundly despite the storm. I reached down and shook Him awake saying, *"Teacher, don't You care that we're going to drown?"*[1]

As Jesus opened His eyes, He looked at me and saw the fear on my face. He looked at the waves crashing over the sides of the boat as He stood up. I reached to hand Him a bucket so He could help bail water, when suddenly He said with a booming voice, *"Silence! Be still!"*[2]

At first, I thought He was speaking to me! But suddenly the wind stopped, and the waves calmed. We all stood there with our mouths open in awe and disbelief. Jesus looked at us and said, *"Why are you afraid? Have you been with Me all of this time, but still have no faith?"*[3]

. . .

I heard my friend Bartholomew softly say what all of us were thinking: *"Who is this Man that even the wind and waves obey Him!"*[(4)]

Jesus lay back down and slept the rest of our journey. I don't think any of us spoke another word until we arrived at the shore. I know I didn't. I continued to marvel at what I had just seen!

But even that paled to what we witnessed a few months ago. We were wintering in Bethabara when we received news that Jesus's friend Lazarus was sick. We had been avoiding travel to Judea because we knew the religious leaders were plotting against Jesus. So, we were glad to hear that He did not intend to travel to Bethany. Or so it appeared, until two days later when He announced that Lazarus was dead, and now He intended to travel there.

That did not make sense to any of us. And why had He said, *"For your sakes, I'm glad I wasn't there?"*[(5)] He was going to go to Bethany. Lazarus was already dead, so He wouldn't be able to help him. And He would be walking into the lair of those who were plotting to do Him harm. There was nothing good about this plan.

In case you haven't realized it yet, I am the pragmatist in this group. A situation has to make sense to me before I will act. And this didn't make sense! But, I am also a follower of Jesus. I truly love Him with all of my heart. When I chose to follow Him that day on the shore, it was with all of my being. If the storm comes up and the boat sinks, I am prepared to die with Jesus. If the religious leaders send their guards to arrest Him, I will go to prison with Him. If He places Himself in harm's way, I will be there with Him, right by His side. So, that day, I said to the rest of the disciples, *"Let's go, too – and die with Jesus."*[(6)]

You've heard about the miracle. You know what happened. In obedience to Jesus's command, Lazarus walked out of the tomb that day. No one died as I had feared. Rather, the dead came to life! I don't know if I would have believed it if I hadn't seen it. But I saw it with my own eyes!

. . .

A few weeks ago, the night before Jesus was arrested, we could tell He was trying to prepare us for something. We had no idea what it was, but we all felt uneasy. He kept saying that He was going away. Our minds were preoccupied with the thought that Jesus was about to establish His kingdom. With His triumphal entry into Jerusalem four days earlier and His cleansing of the temple the next day, we were certain the time had come. He was going to take the Messiah's rightful place on His throne, and we – His trusted companions – would join Him as leaders in His kingdom. But now He was talking about going away! Why would He do that? It didn't make sense to any of us!

As usual, Jesus knew exactly what we were thinking. He said, *"Don't let your hearts be troubled. Trust in God, and trust also in Me. There is more than enough room in My Father's home. If this were not so, would I have told you that I am going to prepare a place for you? When everything is ready, I will come and get you, so that you will always be with Me where I am. And you know the way to where I am going."*[7]

I looked around the room and everyone seemed befuddled. Jesus wasn't making any sense, so I spoke up. *"No, we don't know, Lord. We have no idea where You are going, so how can we know the way?"*[8]

Jesus answered me, saying, *"I am the way, the truth, and the life. No one can come to the Father except through Me."*[9]

I'd like to tell you that Jesus's response made everything clear for us – but at the time, it did not! It made us even more confused. He was talking about going when we thought He was going to stay. At that moment, we had all become somewhat pragmatic, and we wanted to know what practical steps He was going to take to establish His government. But instead, He was telling us spiritual truths that we could not comprehend. Only later, would we realize He was preparing us for the events that would begin to unfold that very night.

. . .

By the time we arrived at the Garden of Gethsemane, we were mentally and emotionally exhausted. Even though Jesus asked us to stay awake and pray, we all immediately fell asleep ... until our greatest fear came to fruition. They came to arrest Jesus! One by one we awoke as the mob came upon us – soldiers with their spears, servants with their clubs, and Judas leading them all.

I saw the other disciples begin to scatter, and soon I was following them. I was almost paralyzed with fear, just like that night in the storm. We were all going to die! And now they had arrested Jesus, so He couldn't help us. I was the one who had said, *"Let's go – and die with Jesus."*(10) And now when I was faced with that possibility, I was running away. I thought I loved Him with my whole heart, but I was abandoning Him! Peter and John took off in one direction, the rest of us headed for Bethany.

When we got to Lazarus's home, I stayed by myself. I could not face anyone. As the day continued, the news kept getting worse. By nightfall, we learned that Jesus was dead. His body had been laid in a tomb. Jesus had always turned defeat into victory, but now He had been defeated – or so it seemed.

Was this what He was trying to prepare us for the other night in the upper room? Somehow, the words I remembered Him saying were not comforting my troubled heart. Jesus was dead. I had abandoned Him. And all of my hopes had been dashed.

For the next two days, I hid out in an isolated place in one of Lazarus's vineyards. I needed to think about what to do. Where would I go? What would I do? I had never believed this could happen. I was drowning in my own self-pity, and it was driving me away from everyone else.

On Sunday, I heard excited voices. Some of the women were saying Jesus had risen from the grave. He had spoken to them – or so they said. We were all to meet at sunset in the upper room. I could not bring myself to go. I could not face the others. I knew they, too, had scattered, but my shame had become all consuming. I did not truly believe Jesus had risen from the grave; but if He had, I could not face Him. My shame crippled me, and I stayed hidden in the vineyard.

The next day, my brother-in-law Peter came looking for me. He told me that Jesus had appeared to them all in the upper room. He was alive! Peter went on to explain how Jesus had appeared to just him earlier in the day. He said Jesus had forgiven him. Peter had run away like the rest of us on the night of His arrest, but he had been so afraid he also denied even knowing Jesus. And yet Jesus had embraced him and forgiven him. "He's forgiven you, as well," Peter added. "He's forgiven us all!"

Part of me wanted to believe Peter. I wanted to believe Jesus was alive. I wanted to be forgiven. I'm not sure if it was shame or denial that refused to accept his word that Jesus was alive. But I said, *"I won't believe it unless I see the nail wounds in His hands, put my fingers into them, and place my hand into the wound in His side."*[11]

Sadly, my shame and skepticism robbed me from experiencing the joy of seeing Jesus for eight more days. It wasn't until the following week, when this time I was present with my fellow disciples, when Jesus stood before us.

Jesus declared, *"Peace be with you,"*[12] followed by a rebuke directed at me. It was a truth I needed to hear – and one I would finally embrace from that day forward. He said, "Don't believe simply because you see; believe because of Who I am and what I have said!"[13]

Later that evening Jesus told us to make our way to Capernaum and wait for Him there. It would give many of us an opportunity to see our families. After we had been there for a day, Peter decided we needed to go fishing. He enlisted the other fishermen in our group to join him – Andrew, Philip, Nathanael, the brothers James and John, and me. We had all grown up on the sea and fishing was "in our blood," so we were easily persuaded. We would fish all night, then rest throughout the day. The rest of our group slept each night and found other ways to pass the time in the village each day.

One morning, we had been out on the sea all night with no success. Suddenly, a Man on the shore called to us and told us to throw out our net on the righthand side of the boat one more time. Even though we didn't have any idea who He was, something told us to obey. As we did, the fish struck the net, just like they had that day in Bethsaida when Jesus told Peter to do the same thing. Suddenly, we all realized who the Man was, prompting John to exclaim, *"It's the Lord!"*[(14)]

Peter jumped into the water and made his way to Jesus. The rest of us brought in the fish then sailed for shore. When we reached Jesus, He was already cooking some bread and fish over a charcoal fire. He told us to bring some of the fish we had caught and add it to the rest. He was preparing breakfast for us. Soon, all of us were gathered there with Him around the fire.

Jesus was getting us ready to go out into the world and share His Gospel message, making disciples who would in turn make other disciples. He even used breakfast that morning to illustrate the point. We were like the fish He had already prepared on the fire. He had called us and taught us, but now there would be others who would be added through the work He would do through us – just like the fish we now added to the fire. He would show us where to cast the net; we would pull it in.

After breakfast, Jesus turned to Peter and asked him, "Peter, *do you love Me more than these?*[(15)] Do you love Me above all others? Do you love Me in a way that causes your love for everyone else to pale in comparison?"

I could tell Jesus's question caught Peter off guard. He hastily replied, "Of course, I love You, Jesus. How could You think otherwise?"

·   ·   ·

But then Jesus asked him a second time. This time his response was in greater earnest, wanting to leave no doubt of his love for Jesus. When Jesus asked him a third time, it was obvious Peter was deeply wounded by the question.

"Lord, You know everything. You know that I love You,"[(16)] Peter replied.

Peter wanted to assure Jesus he loved Him with all of his heart, soul, and mind. But why did Jesus keep asking the same question? And then it dawned on me – we all knew Peter had denied Jesus three times on the night of His arrest. Though Jesus had already forgiven Peter, He was now restoring him to his position of leadership among us.

In many ways, this conversation was for our benefit. Peter was confessing His love, and Jesus was confirming Peter's responsibility as "the rock." Jesus was asking Peter to confirm his love once for each time he had denied Him. Jesus knew we all needed to hear Peter confess his love that way.

In response to each of Peter's answers, Jesus replied: *"Feed My lambs,"* *"Take care of My sheep,"* and *"Feed My sheep."*[(17)] Jesus was not only publicly restoring Peter to his apostleship and leadership, He was reminding each of us to be not only fishers of men, but also shepherds of His sheep – caring for them, protecting them, and nurturing them.

Then He turned His attention to all of us, telling us we each have a path He has laid out for us to follow. We are to keep *"our eyes on Jesus, on whom our faith depends from start to finish."*[(18)] He cautioned us not to be distracted by the people who surround us or the events unfolding around us. We are to persevere to the finish.

Jesus lingered that day and spent time with each one of us personally, just as He had done with Peter. It was afternoon when He invited me to walk with Him along the shore. "Thomas," He said, "the Father gave each of you to Me. Each of you – except Judas – has repented of your sin and each of you belongs to Me, and all who are Mine belong to the Father.

"I am now preparing to go, but I will send My Spirit to empower you, guide you, and direct you in all truth. For a time, I will not be with you physically, but I will never leave you nor forsake you. Use the practical mind the Father has given you to nurture My sheep in the way they should go as they follow Me and obey My commands. But never forget to hold onto My truth even when you can't yet see it. Trust me and follow Me in all that I have shown you."

Later that evening, Jesus departed. A short while later we were gathered in Bethany, just as He had instructed us. It had been forty days since He had risen from the grave. One hundred twenty of us were gathered on the hill that day. As the One who stood before me began to rise into the clouds, I knew I would see Him again ... because believing is seeing!

～

JUDE – THE BROTHER

$\mathcal{M}$y name is Jude. I am my mother Mary's fourth son, the third by her husband Joseph. I am six years younger than my half-brother Jesus, three years younger than my brother James and one year younger than my brother Joseph. I have one younger brother, Simon, and two younger sisters, Mary and Salome. My youngest sister was named in honor of a woman who befriended my mother as a young girl when she was pregnant with Jesus; she continues to be a life-long friend.

As you might guess, I am a carpenter, just like the rest of my father's sons. I was fifteen when my father died, but I am grateful to Jehovah God for the years He gave me with him. My father was a righteous man, a loving husband, and a caring father. He and my mother stood strong when most everyone else doubted them, and he obeyed his God without hesitation, even in difficult moments. My father will always be my hero. I was allowed to see firsthand why Jehovah God chose him to be the earthly father to His Son. Of all the men who ever lived, God chose him for that honor, and my father wore the honor well!

I was six years old before I learned that Jesus was my half-brother. Until then, neither my brothers and sisters nor I knew any different. He was our big brother. We looked up to Him. He helped our father teach us to be godly men and hardworking carpenters. When our father died, He became the leader of our home for eight years until He said it was time for Him to be about His Heavenly Father's business.

Two years ago, I saw the men in our village of Nazareth reject Jesus as the Son of God. Despite the wisdom He demonstrated and the miracles He had performed, they rejected Him. They scoffed, *"He's just a carpenter,* the illegitimate son of Mary and Joseph. We know His brothers, *and His sisters live right here among us."*[1] I overheard Jesus say, *"A prophet is honored everywhere except in his hometown and among his relatives and his own family."*[2]

I regret to this day that it wasn't only the village that had rejected Him, my brothers and I rejected Him, as well. It's difficult for me to explain what was going through our heads. From the time we learned of Jesus's true parentage, a degree of separation entered into our relationship with Him.

First, it's hard to live with and live up to an older brother who never does anything wrong. Don't misunderstand me, Jesus never lorded over us as our older brother, let alone as the Son of God. We knew He loved us. He was always humble and gracious. He treated us with compassion, concern, and camaraderie.

We all worked hard together, but we also played hard together. We had good times together. He taught me how to swim, how to carve like a craftsman, and how to play ball. He taught us all how to honor our parents, how to study the Scriptures, and how to treat one another with love and respect. But Jesus never sinned – not once! Our parents were always careful not to say, "Why can't you be more like Jesus?" But we still placed that pressure on ourselves.

Second, He had a special relationship with our parents that we would never have. I'm not complaining, because we knew our parents loved each one of us equally. We knew they viewed us all as gifts from God. But we also came to know the stories surrounding Jesus's birth. It's hard to compete when you know that angels announced your brother's birth and wise men brought Him gifts from the east. As I said, our parents loved all of us ... but they *marveled* at Jesus.

Third, He knew all things. Again, please don't misunderstand me – He never acted like a "know-it-all." But the fact was, He did know it all. I will never forget going to the synagogue with Him and seeing how the rabbis were in awe of His ability to teach from the Scriptures. My brothers and I knew no one would ever be in awe of our ability to teach.

You might say it was jealousy on our part, but I don't think it truly was. I think it was more a feeling of inadequacy. We would never measure up – not that Jesus or our parents ever expected it.

I think there were times even our parents didn't completely know what to do or think. One of those times was when Jesus had remained at the temple in Jerusalem after the rest of us had begun our journey back home to Nazareth. When they finally found Him four days later, He told them, *"You should have known that I would be in My Father's house."*(3) He was doing what His Heavenly Father had called Him to do. How were my parents supposed to react to that?

More recently, Jesus was in Capernaum teaching in the synagogue. My mother, my brothers, and I had just arrived in the city. We were helping our mother get settled in her new home. She was concerned that Jesus was not getting enough rest, and He was wearing Himself out with His teaching and the many miracles He was performing. She wanted Him to come to her home and rest.

The crowd was so large we could not get into the synagogue – so, my mother sent word to Jesus that she and His brothers were waiting outside to speak with Him. He responded with the question, *"Who is My mother?*

Who are My brothers? Anyone who does the will of My Father in heaven is my brother and sister and mother."(4) What were we supposed to say to that?

Now, let me be clear – my brothers and I never once doubted that Jesus was the Messiah. We knew the stories. We had the proof. Our confusion was not over whether He was the Messiah; our confusion was over what it meant for Him to be the Messiah. Even in the midst of our sense of inadequacy and insecurity, we believed He had come to establish His kingdom. We believed He had come to rule over the world, but we did not understand that He had come to save the world.

Last fall, my brothers and I looked for Jesus in Galilee before we traveled to Jerusalem to observe the Festival of Tabernacles. We asked Him to come with us. We wanted Him to put His miracles on display for everyone to see. Jerusalem would be filled with pilgrims. We knew a large number of His followers had recently abandoned Him after He called them to a life of surrender rather than the life of prosperity they were seeking from Him. We told Him the festival would be an opportunity to attract many more followers.

We knew the religious leaders were plotting against Him, and we did not want any harm to come to Him. We reasoned that the more the crowd honored Him, the safer He would be. And soon, the crowd would have to rise up and crown Him as their rightful King. We wanted that for Jesus – but we also knew it wouldn't do us any harm, either. Surely, the brothers of the Messiah would hold positions of importance within His kingdom!

A number of Jesus's disciples encouraged Him to follow our advice and join us. They, too, thought it was time for Him to declare Himself – particularly His disciple Judas Iscariot. But Jesus told us He would not be joining us. We were offended that He did not heed our advice. Jesus no longer seemed to care what we thought. Our feelings of inadequacy and uncertainty were now turning into bitterness.

. . .

Later we learned that Jesus did arrive at the festival halfway through the week, contrary to what we thought He was going to do. There was quite a stir when the priests attempted to entrap Him by bringing an adulterous woman before Him. Apparently, their plan had again failed, but we accused Him among ourselves of having misled us. We decided we would no longer try to help Him since He didn't seem to want our help!

Our mother kept telling us to trust Him, that He knew exactly what He was doing. He was following His Heavenly Father's plan. She was now traveling with Him as a part of His ever-growing number of followers. Truth be told, we probably resented that, as well. In our minds, our mother was showing Him partiality by following her favored son.

A few weeks ago, my brothers and I again traveled to Jerusalem to celebrate the Passover. We were amazed as we watched the entry of Jesus and His disciples into Jerusalem. We had never seen anything like it. The crowd was overwhelmingly welcoming Him. It was quite a procession. We didn't know what to make of it. Was Jesus finally going to follow our advice? But the next day, He created quite a disturbance in the temple, and it appeared that He was not going to do anything to declare Himself or establish His kingdom.

That Friday morning, we received word that Jesus had been arrested! Our fears for Him had come to pass. He had failed to do what needed to be done – and now, without the crowd behind Him, the religious leaders were going to destroy Him. We sincerely were afraid for Him. We took no pleasure in what was happening. But we also feared for ourselves. What would His arrest mean for us? The religious leaders would know we were His brothers. Would they now come for us, as well? Herod the Great had sought to kill all the boys born around His age when He was a baby. What would prevent the religious leaders from gathering up and murdering His brothers?

Though we decided to remain out of sight in the city, we still heard the passersby as they updated one another on the latest news about Jesus. He had been taken before Pilate. He had been taken before Herod Antipas.

He had been brought back to Pilate. And now ... He was carrying His cross to Golgotha. Our fear soon melted into sorrow over how we had abandoned our own brother. The darkness we felt inside prevented us from noticing the darkening skies outside.

A few hours later, we heard the news that we knew was coming. Jesus was dead! The religious leaders had won. They had defeated the Messiah. They had overcome the Promised One. Woe to them! Woe to our people! Woe to us – His brothers who had refused to stand with Him!

I cannot begin to describe our shame and our guilt. We thought of the grief our mother was experiencing. We should have gone to comfort her. But we were ashamed. When we, as a family, should have been consoling her, we abandoned her, as well.

Night fell and Sabbath began. We went through the motions, but we knew God was not answering our prayers. We had abandoned our brother. We had abandoned His Son!

The next night after Sabbath had concluded, there was a knock at our door. It was our uncle Clopas. Our mother had sent him to seek us out. She was staying in Bethany with Jesus's other disciples. Clopas told us what had happened the day before while Jesus hung on the cross. He told us how in the midst of His own agony and pain, Jesus had consoled our mother. I don't think he realized how his words added to the shame we were already feeling. Then he told us how Jesus had charged His disciple John with taking care of our mother as John stood there beside her at the foot of the cross.

He couldn't have cut us any deeper if he had plunged a knife into our hearts. We had failed to come alongside our brother and our mother, so Jesus had given the one who stood there with her the responsibility to care for her. It should have passed to my older brother James, but neither he nor any of us had been there. Like I said, I don't believe our uncle's intention was to heap guilt on our heads, but his words had that effect, and we mourned even more after he left.

Late in the afternoon the next day, we received a message from our mother. It simply read, "Your brother is alive! Come quickly!" The messenger directed us to an upper room in the heart of the city. Though we could not believe that Jesus was truly alive, we were grateful that our mother wanted to see us, so we hurried to the meeting place.

When we arrived, dozens of His followers were gathered in the room. In the midst of them was our mother, surrounded by the other women who had traveled with Jesus. A number of them were speaking excitedly about how Jesus had appeared before them earlier in the day. Several of the men also told us how they had seen Him, including our uncle Clopas.

Could it be true? Or were all of these people delirious? We knew that Jesus had reportedly raised others from the dead, but surely a dead man could not bring Himself back to life. We embraced our mother. She had not yet seen her son, but tears of joy were streaming down her face. As we gathered around her, suddenly her face brightened. She was looking at something behind us. We turned and followed her gaze. There, standing before us in the middle of the room, was Jesus! *"Peace be with you!"* He said.[5]

Suddenly our eyes, which had refused to see Jesus for who He truly is, were opened to the truth. The shell enveloping our hearts shattered. Our hearts of stone became flesh, and we believed. As I looked at my brother, tears began to stream down my cheeks. I fell to my knees and cried out, "Brother ... Jesus ... Master, forgive me."

I soon realized that James, Joseph, and Simon were all kneeling beside me saying the same thing. Oh, the years we had wasted by refusing to believe. But no more! Jesus is risen and we will follow Him forevermore!

. . .

For the next forty days, my brothers and I saw Jesus on several occasions. One of those times it was only the five of us. It had been a long time since we had been together as brothers, and it would be the last time on this side of eternity. Jesus told us He would soon be leaving to sit at the right hand of His Heavenly Father.

But He also told us that while His body had lain in the tomb, His spirit had entered into Hades and led all of the righteous to heaven. He told us that our father Joseph had been in that procession, walking right behind Him. Jesus would soon be with not only His Heavenly Father, but also His earthly father. And He told us that both of them were proud of us – the men we had become and the faith we now held tightly in our hearts.

Then He said, "Brothers, follow Me!"

I saw Him one last time. We all did. It was there on the hill outside of Bethany. Just before He ascended into the clouds, He told us He was going to send His Spirit to empower us. He said that through His Spirit, He would be with us always. He told us to go in His Spirit and make disciples from every language, people, tribe, and nation.

I looked at the One who stood before me – yes, my big brother – but forevermore my Master and my Savior! And I would forever be His servant. I knew I had been *called to live in the love of God the Father and the care of Jesus Christ*, for I truly am a recipient of *His mercy ... His peace ... and His love*.[6]

~

PLEASE HELP ME BY LEAVING A REVIEW!

~

i would be very grateful if you would leave a review of this book. Your feedback will be helpful to me in my future writing endeavors and will also assist others as they consider picking up a copy of the book.

To leave a review, go to:

amazon.com/dp/B08W293KF6

Thanks for your help!

~

THE COMPLETE EYEWITNESSES COLLECTION

For the entire family

BOOK #1

Little Did We Know

... Eyewitnesses to the Advent

This book is a collection of twenty-five short stories for the advent season from some familiar and some not-so-familiar people. These stories have been written with teens and adults in mind. Experience the truth of the glorious arrival of the baby in the manger through the lens of these fictional, first-person accounts of the prophecies and events heralding the birth of Jesus.

BOOK #2

Not Too Little To Know

... Children who witnessed the Advent

Experience the Advent through the eyes of ten children who witnessed the glorious arrival of the Promised One. Join Isaac, Salome, Sarah, Yanzu and others in their journeys as they share their own fictional eyewitness accounts of the prophecies and events surrounding the birth of Jesus. Some of the characters may be fictional, but the truth they tell is very real!

This illustrated chapter book has been written for **ages 8 and up**. It is a companion to *Little Did We Know*, a collection of short stories written for teens and adults. Though both books stand alone, their stories intertwine into **a delightful Advent journey for the entire family.**

Book #3

The One Who Stood Before Us

... Eyewitnesses to the Resurrection

A collection of **forty short stories** for the **Lent and Easter** season from some familiar and some not-so-familiar people. These stories have been written with teens and adults in mind. Walk with those who walked with Jesus — some as followers, some as friends and some as foes. Join them on the three year journey that led to the cross ... but didn't stop there. Experience the miracles they witnessed, the truth they learned, and the One they came to know. Some of the characters in these fictional first-person accounts may be unreal, but the truth they all tell is very real!

Book #4

The Little Ones Who Came

... Children who witnessed the Resurrection

Jesus said, *"Let the little children come to Me. The kingdom of God belongs to people who are like these little children. I tell you the truth. You must accept the kingdom of God as a little child accepts things, or you will never enter it."*

It's not really about our age. We must all come to Jesus with faith like little ones. We're never too old ... and we're never too young.

Experience the ministry, crucifixion and resurrection of Jesus through the eyes of ten children who share their own fictional eyewitness accounts. Some of the characters may be fictional, but the truth they tell is very real!

This illustrated chapter book is a collection of ten short stories written for **ages 8 and up**. It is a companion to *The One Who Stood Before Us*, a collection of short stories written for teens and adults. Though both books stand alone, their stories intertwine into **a delightful Lent and Easter journey for the entire family.**

BE ON THE LOOKOUT FOR

~

COMING SEPTEMBER 10, 2021

BOOK #3 OF THE

THROUGH THE EYES SERIES

Through the Eyes of a Prisoner

A Novel — **Paul was an unlikely candidate to become the apostle to the Gentiles** ... until the day he unexpectedly encountered Jesus. You are probably familiar with that part of his story, and perhaps much of what transpired in his life after that. **But two-thirds of his life story is not recorded in detail, though Paul gives us some hints in his letters.**

God is always at work in our lives; often before we realize it. The same can be said of Paul. **Through this fictional novel**, we'll explore how God may have used even those unrecorded portions of his life to prepare him for the mission that was being set before him. We'll follow him from his early years in Tarsus through his final days in Rome.

Throughout those years, Paul spent more time in a prison cell than we are ever told. It was a place where God continued to work in and through him. The mission never stopped because he was in prison; it simply took on a different form. Allow yourself to be challenged as you experience **a story of God's mission – through the eyes of a prisoner who ran the race that was put before him – and the faithfulness of God through it all.**

Pre-order your copy today!

~

For more information, go to

wildernesslessons.com or kenwinter.org

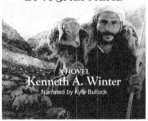

SCRIPTURE BIBLIOGRAPHY

~

Much of the story line of this book is taken from the Gospels according to Matthew, Mark, Luke, and John. Certain fictional events or depictions of those events have been added.

Specific references and quotations:

Preface

[1] John 1:1, 14

[2] Hebrews 2:17

[3] John 1:29

[4] Hebrews 4:15

[5] 2 Corinthians 5:21

[6] Colossians 2:15

[7] Colossians 2:9

[8] John 8:31-32

[9] 2 Timothy 3:16-17

1. John - the beloved

(1) Luke 1:17

(2) John 1:36, 29

(3) John 1:38a

(4) John 1:38b

(5) John 1:39

(6) John 2:4

(7) John 2:10

(8) John 20:31

2. John - the baptizer

(1) Matthew 3:7-9, 11-12

(2) Luke 3:10-14

(3) Luke 3:16

(4) Matthew 3:10

(5) Matthew 3:14-15

(6) Luke 3:21-22

(7) John 1:29-31

(8) John 1:36

3. Andrew - the introducer

(1) Matthew 3:3, 11

(2) John 1:36

(3) John 1:38

(4) John 1:39

(5) John 5:39, 46

(6) Deuteronomy 18:15-18

(7) John 1:42

(8) John 1:43

(9) John 1:45-46

(10) John 1:47-50

4. Salome - the mother of the bride

(1) John 2:10

5. Zebedee - the fisherman

(1) Luke 5:4

(2) Luke 5:5

(3) Luke 5:8

(4) Luke 5:10

(5) Luke 18:29-30 (ESV)

(6) Deuteronomy 31:6 (ESV)

6. Nicodemus - the inquirer

(1) John 2:16

(2) John 2:18

(3) John 2:19

(4) John 2:20

(5) John 3:2

(6) John 3:3

(7) John 3:4

(8) John 3:5-6

(9) John 3:9

(10) John 3:10-21

7. Endora - the woman at the well

(1) John 4:7

(2) John 4:9

(3)John 4:10

(4)John 4:11-12

(5)John 4:13-14

(6)John 4:15

(7)John 4:16

(8)John 4:17-18

(9)John 4:19

(10)John 4:20

(11)John 4:21-24

(12)John 4:25

(13)John 4:26

(14)John 4:29

(15)John 4:42

8. Chuza - the steward

(1) John 4:48

(2) John 4:49

(3) John 4:50

(4) John 4:52

(5) John 4:53

9. Lazarus - the friend

(1) Luke 5:12

(2) Luke 5:13

(3) Luke 5:14

10. Yanis - the paralytic

(1) Luke 5:20

(2) Luke 5:21

(3) Luke 5:22

11. Susanna - the grieving mother

(1) Luke 7:13

(2) Luke 7:14

(3) Luke 7:16

12. James - the son of thunder

(1) Mark 4:35

(2) Mark 4:38

(3) Mark 4:39

(4) Mark 4:40

(5) Mark 4:41

(6) Luke 7:19

(7) Luke 7:22

(8) Luke 7:23

(9) Isaiah 35:5-6,10

(10) Luke 7:23

13. Enos - the demoniac

(1) Mark 5:8

(2) Mark 5:7

(3) Mark 5:9

(4) Mark 5:9

(5) Mark 5:12

(6) Matthew 8:32

(7) Mark 5:19

14. Deborah - the suffering woman

(1) Mark 5:30

(2) Mark 5:31

(3) Mark 5:34

15. Jairus - the faith-filled father

(1) Luke 4:18-19 (referring to Isaiah 61:1-2)

(2) Luke 4:21

(3) Luke 4:34

(4) Luke 4:35

(5) Luke 4:36

(6) Luke 4:38

(7) John 4:50

(8) Luke 5:22

(9) Mark 5:23

(10) Mark 5:30

(11) Mark 5:31

(12) Mark 5:35

(13) Mark 5:36

(14) Mark 5:39

(15) Mark 5:41

16. Jonathan - the boy who gave what he had

(1) Luke 9:12

(2) Matthew 14:16

(3) John 6:5

(4) Mark 6:37

(5) Mark 6:38

(6) John 6:9

(7) Matthew 18:3-4

[8] John 6:10

[9] John 6:12

17. Martha - the diligent hostess

[1] Luke 10:40

[2] Luke 10:41-42

18. Reuben - the rich young ruler

[1] Proverbs 14:31

[2] Luke 18:16-17

[3] Luke 18:18

[4] Luke 18:19

[5] Luke 18:20

[6] Luke 18:21

[7] Luke 18:22

[8] Luke 16:24

[9] Luke 16:25-26

[10] Luke 16:27-28

[11] Luke 16:29

[12] Luke 16:30

[13] Luke 16:31

19. Hepzibah - the adulteress

[1] John 8:4

[2] John 8:7

[3] John 8:10

[4] John 8:11

[5] John 8:11

20. Celidonius - the blind man

(1) Isaiah 35:5

(2) John 9:2

(3) John 9:3

(4) John 9:3

(5) John 9:4

(6) John 9:5

(7) John 9:7

(8) Isaiah 35:5

(9) John 9:3

(10) John 9:8

(11) John 9:11

(12) John 9:17

(13) John 9:17

(14) John 9:24

(15) John 9:25

(16) John 9:27

(17) John 9:28

(18) John 9:30-33

(19) John 9:34

(20) John 9:35

(21) John 9:36

(22) John 9:37

(23) John 9:38

(24) Psalm 96:1-4 (NCV)

21. Miriam - the one at His feet

(1) John 11:4

(2) John 11:28

(3) John 11:32

(4) John 11:34

(5) John 11:34

(6) John 11:39

(7) John 11:39

(8) John 11:40

(9) John 11:41-42

(10)John 11:43

(11)John 11:44

22. Judas Iscariot - the ambitious one

(1) Luke 5:27

(2) Matthew 10:3

(3) Matthew 10:3

(4) Matthew 10:4

(5) John 11:43

(6) John 12:5

(7) Mark 14:9

23. Ephraim - the tanner

(1) Psalm 36:9 (NCV)

(2) Psalm 36:6 (NCV)

(3) John 2:16

(4) Luke 19:33 (ESV)

(5) Luke 19:34 (ESV)

(6) Zechariah 9:9

(7) Matthew 21:9

(8) Luke 19:39

(9) Luke 19:40

(10) Matthew 21:10

(11) Matthew 21:11

24. Shimon - the shepherd

(1) Luke 19:46 (ESV)

(2) Mark 11:28

(3) Mark 11:30

(4) Mark 11:33

(5) Luke 22:10-13

(6) John 13:6

(7) John 13:7

(8) John 13:8

(9) John 13:8

(10) John 13:9

(11) John 13:10

(12) John 13:12-15

(13) Luke 22:21

(14) John 13:24

(15) John 13:26

(16) John 13:27

25. Malchus - the servant

(1) John 2:16

(2) Mark 11:30

(3) Luke 22:48

(4) Matthew 26:52-53

(5) Matthew 26:55-56

26. Annas - the high priest

(1) Matthew 22:20

(2) Matthew 22:21

(3) Matthew 22:21

(4) John 18:20-21

(5) John 18:22

(6) John 18:23

(7) Luke 22:67

(8) Luke 22:67-69

(9) Luke 22:70

(10) Luke 22:70

(11) Luke 22:71

(12) Luke 19:40

(13) Matthew 27:4

(14) Matthew 27:4

(15) Matthew 27:6

27. Pilate - the prefect

(1) Luke 23:2

(2) Luke 23:3

(3) Luke 23:3

(4) Luke 23:4

(5) Luke 23:5

(6) Luke 23:6

(7) Matthew 27:19

(8) Matthew 27:22

(9) Matthew 27:22

(10) Matthew 27:24

[11] Matthew 27:25

28. Antipas - the ethnarch

[1] Mark 6:22-23

[2] Mark 6:25

[3] Matthew 27:24

29. Barabbas - the criminal

[1] Mark 15:14

30. Yitzhak - the tradesman

[1] John 2:18

[2] John 2:19

[3] John 2:20

[4] Luke 22:11

31. Mary - the mother of Jesus

[1] John 12:13

[2] Luke 23:28

[3] Luke 1:30-33

32. Gaius Marius - the centurion

[1] John 19:28

[2] John 19:30

[3] Matthew 27:54

33. Joseph - the pharisee

[1] John 2:16

[2] Luke 2:34-35 (CEV – paraphrase)

[3] Luke 2:29-30 (CEV)

[4] John 19:30

[5] Luke 2:34-35 (CEV – paraphrase)

34. Simon - the Cyrene

[1] Luke 23:28

[2] Luke 23:39

[3] Luke 23:40-41

[4] Luke 23:42

[5] Luke 23:43

[6] John 19:30

35. Abraham - the patriarch

[1] Genesis 12:1-3 (ESV)

[2] Genesis 22:2 (ESV)

[3] Genesis 22:7 (ESV)

[4] Genesis 22:8 (ESV)

[5] Genesis 22:11-12 (ESV)

[6] Genesis 22:16-18 (ESV)

[7] John 19:30

[8] Luke 23:46

[9] Revelation 7:10

36. Mary - the Magdalene

[1] Luke 7:40-42

[2] Luke 7:43

[3] Luke 7:44-47

[4] Luke 7:48, 50

[5] John 19:30

[6] John 20:13

[7] John 20:15

(8) John 20:17

37. Clopas - the uncle

(1) Luke 2:49

(2) John 19:30

(3) John 20:19

38. Simon Peter - the rock

(1) 1 Peter 3:4

(2) John 1:42 (HCSB)

(3) Luke 5:4

(4) Luke 5:5

(5) Luke 5:8

(6) Luke 5:10

(7) John 13:8b

(8) John 13:9

(9) John 13:10

(10) John 13:12-15

(11) Luke 22:21

(12) Luke 22:33

(13) Proverbs 18:24

39. Thomas - the believer

(1) Mark 4:38

(2) Mark 4:39

(3) Mark 4:40

(4) Mark 4:41

(5) John 11:14

(6) John 11:16

[7] John 14:1-4

[8] John 14:5

[9] John 14:6

[10] John 11:16

[11] John 20:25

[12] John 20:26

[13] John 20:29 (paraphrase)

[14] John 21:7

[15] John 21:15

[16] John 21:17

[17] John 21:15-17

[18] Hebrews 13:20-21 (ESV)

40. Jude - the brother

[1] Mark 6:3

[2] Mark 6:4

[3] Luke 2:49

[4] Matthew 12:48, 50

[5] Luke 24:36

[6] Jude 1-2

~

～

LISTING OF CHARACTERS

~

Many of the characters in this book are real people pulled directly from the pages of Scripture — most notably Jesus! i have not changed any details about a number of those individuals —again, most notably Jesus — except the addition of their interactions with the fictional characters. They are noted below as "UN" (unchanged).

In other instances, fictional details have been added to real people to provide backgrounds about their lives where Scripture is silent. The intent is that you understand these were real people, whose lives were full of all of the many details that fill our own lives. They had a history before they met Jesus ... and they had a future after they met Him. They are noted as "FB" (fictional background).

In some instances, we are never told the names of certain individuals in the Bible. In those instances, where i have given them a name as well as a fictional background, they are noted as "FN" (fictional name).

Lastly, a number of the characters are purely fictional, added to convey the fictional elements of these stories . They are noted as "FC" (fictional character).

~

Jesus - the Son of God (UN)

The angels:

Gabriel - a messenger from God (UN)

Michael - the archangel (UN)

Jesus's earthly family:

Joseph - husband of Mary - earthly father of Jesus (FB)

Rebekah - first wife of Joseph (FC)

Mary - wife of Joseph - mother of Jesus (FB)

Eli - father of Mary (FB)

James - half-brother of Jesus (FB)

Joseph - half-brother of Jesus (UN)

Jude - half-brother of Jesus (FB)

Simon - half-brother of Jesus (UN)

Mary - half-sister of Jesus (FN)

Salome - half-sister of Jesus (FN)

Clopas - brother of Joseph - uncle of Jesus (FB)

Mary - wife of Clopas - aunt of Jesus (FB)

Jacob - father of Joseph and Clopas (FB)

The baptizer and his family:

John the baptizer - son of Zechariah and Elizabeth (FB)

Zechariah - father of John the baptizer (UN)

Elizabeth - mother of John the baptizer (UN)

Adriel – nephew of Elizabeth - guardian of John (FC)

Joanna – wife of Adriel (FC)

The apostles and their family members:

Simon Peter - apostle of Jesus (FB)

Jonah - father of Simon and Andrew (FB)

Unnamed mother of Simon and Andrew (FB)

Gabriella - wife of Peter (FN)

Milcah – mother of Gabriella and Thomas (FN)

Sarah – oldest daughter of Peter and Gabriella (FC)

Iscah – youngest daughter of Peter and Gabriella (FC)

Andrew - brother of Simon Peter - apostle of Jesus (FB)

James - son of Zebedee - brother of John - apostle of Jesus (FB)

John - son of Zebedee - brother of James - apostle of Jesus (FB)

Zebedee - father of James and John (FB)

Salome - wife of Zebedee (FB)

Philip - apostle of Jesus (UN)

Bartholomew (Nathanael) - apostle of Jesus (UN)

Thomas - brother of Gabriella - apostle of Jesus (FB)

Matthew - apostle of Jesus (UN)

James (the Less) - son of Clopas - cousin of Jesus - apostle of Jesus (FB)

Thaddeus - son of Clopas - cousin of Jesus - apostle of Jesus (FB)

Simon the zealot - apostle of Jesus (FB)

Judas Iscariot - the betrayer (FB)

Unnamed father of Judas Iscariot (FC)

Unnamed mother of Judas Iscariot (FC)

Those who became followers of Jesus, and their family members:

Shimon - the shepherd (FC)

Ayda - mother of Shimon - one of the women who traveled with Jesus (FC)

Jacob - brother of Shimon (FC)

Salome - childhood friend of Mary - mother of bride at Cana (FC)

Joachim - husband of Salome (FC)

Mary - daughter of Salome - bride at Cana (FC)

Ruth – youngest daughter of Salome - sister of bride at Cana (FC)

Jacob - husband of Mary - groom at Cana (FC)

Samuel - master of ceremonies at Cana wedding (FN)

Chuza – royal chamberlain to Herod Antipas (FB)

Joanna - wife of Chuza (FB)

Samuel - son of Chuza and Joanna (FN)

Shachna - father of Chuza - royal chamberlain to Herod the Great (FC)

Yanis - the paralytic (FN)

Unnamed four friends of Yanis (FB)

Susanna - grieving mother (FN)

Kadan - husband of Susanna (FC)

Zohar - Susanna's son who Jesus restores to life (FN)

Zahara - Zohar's betrothed (FC)

Enos - the demoniac (FN)

Barabbas - the criminal (FB)

Unnamed father of Barabbas - member of Sanhedrin (FC)

Deborah - the woman with the issue of blood (FN)

Matthias -- Deborah's fiancé (FC)

Jairus - rabbi in Capernaum (FB)

Ilana - daughter of Jairus (FN)

Unnamed wife of Jairus and mother of Ilana (UN)

Jonathan - the boy who gave all he had (FN)

Jesse – the shepherd – father of Jonathan (FC)

Maacah – mother of Jonathan (FC)

Martha - sister of Lazarus (FB)

Lazarus (Simon) – the man Jesus raised from the dead (FB)

Miriam (Mary) - sister of Lazarus (FB)

Jephunneh - father of Martha, Lazarus and Miriam (FC)

Mirella - mother of Martha, Lazarus and Miriam (FC)

Amari – vineyard overseer for Lazarus (FC)

Unnamed father of Amari – vineyard overseer for Jephunneh (FC)

Asher – son of Amari (FC)

Celidonius - the blind man (FN)

Imma - mother of Celidonius (FC)

Matthias - father of Celidonius (FC)

Ephraim - the tanner who lends his donkey and colt (FN)

Yamin - son of Ephraim (FC)

Yitzhak - the tradesman who owns the upper room (FC)

Uriah - son of Yitzhak (FC)

Ashriel – rabbi and great grandson of Simeon (FC)

Simeon – the priest God promised would see the Messiah (UN)

Adina – daughter of Ashriel (FC)

Simon - the Cyrene (FB)

Unnamed wife of Simon the Cyrene (FC)

Alexander - son of Simon the Cyrene (FB)

Rufus - son of Simon the Cyrene (FB)

Mary Magdalene (FB)

Jacob - father of Mary Magdalene (FC)

Lemuel (Adrianus) - brother of Mary Magdalene (FC)

The religious leaders and teachers, and their family members:

Hillel - the elder (FB)

Shimon - son of Hillel (FC)

Gamaliel - grandson of Hillel - member of Sanhedrin (FB)

Shebna - younger brother of Hillel (FB)

Ishmael - son of Shebna - father of Salome (wife of Zebedee) (FB)

Camydus - youngest brother of Hillel (FN)

Seth - son of Camydus - father of Annas (FB)

Annas - scribe to Herod the Great, high priest (AD 6 - 15) (FB)

Leah - daughter of Annas, wife of Caiaphas (FN)

Caiaphas - high priest (AD 18 - 36) (FB)

Rachel – daughter of Caiaphas and Leah (FC)

Malchus - servant to Caiaphas (FB)

Ishmael ben Phabi - high priest (AD15-16) (UN)

Nicodemus - rabbi in Capernaum - Pharisee (FB)

Joseph of Arimathea - Pharisee (FB)

Matthias - father of Joseph of Arimathea - Sadducee (FC)

Unnamed wife of Joseph of Arimathea (FC)

Matthias (named after his grandfather) – oldest son of Joseph of Arimathea (FC)

Naomi – granddaughter of Joseph of Arimathea - daughter in Matthias (FC)

Jonathan - brother of Joseph of Arimathea (FC)

Reuben - rich young ruler (FN)

Rebekah - wife of Reuben (FC)

Lazarus - the beggar at the gate (FB)

The Samaritans:

Endora - the Samaritan woman at the well (FN)

Unnamed husband #1 of Endora (FC)

Unnamed husband #2 of Endora (FC)

Ibrahim - husband #3 of Endora (FN)

Unnamed husband #4 of Endora (FC)

Unnamed husband #5 of Endora (FC)

Murjan - living companion of Endora (FN)

The woman caught in adultery and those who are a part of her story:

Hepzibah - the adulteress (FN)

Unnamed mother of Hepzibah (FC)

Unnamed father of Hepzibah (FC)

Alon - the adulterer (FC)

Unnamed adulterer's wife (FC)

Unnamed priest - adulterer's wife's brother (FC)

Unnamed priest - adulteress's accuser (FC)

The Herodian rulers and their family members:

Herod the Great - the tetrarch (UN)

Malthace - 4th wife of Herod, mother of Antipas (UN)

Herod Antipas - 6th son of Herod the Great - ethnarch over Galilee and Perea (2 BC - 39 AD) (FB)

Phasaelis - princess of Nabataea - first wife of Herod Antipas (UN)

Herodias - granddaughter of Herod the Great - divorced first husband Herod II, wife of Antipas (UN)

Salome - daughter of Herodias and Herod II (UN)

Herod Archelaus - 5th son of Herod the Great - older brother of Antipas - ruler over Judea, Samaria and Idumea (2 BC - 6 AD) (UN)

Herod II - 4th son of Herod the Great - did not rule - first husband of Herodias (UN)

Herod Philip II - 7th son of Herod the Great - ruled Trachontis, Gaulantis and Batanea (2 BC - 34 AD) (UN)

The Romans and their family members:

Valerius Gratus - 4th prefect of Judea, Samaria and Idumea (15AD - 26AD) (UN)

Pontius Pilate - 5th prefect of Judea, Samaria and Idumea (26AD - 36AD) (FB)

Pontius Aquila - grandfather of Pilate (UN)

Pontius Cominus - father of Pilate (FC)

Claudia - wife of Pilate (FB)

Aquila – son of Pilate and Claudia (FC)

Gaius Marius - the centurion (FN)

Julius Caesar - emperor of Rome (BC 49 - 44) (UN)

Caesar Augustus - emperor of Rome (BC 27 - AD 14) (UN)

Emperor Tiberius - emperor of Rome (AD 14 - 37) (UN)

The patriarchs:

Abraham - the patriarch (FB)

Isaac - son of Abraham (UN)

∼

ACKNOWLEDGMENTS

I do not cease to give thanks for you ....
Ephesians 1:16 (ESV)

❧

to my wife, life partner, best friend
… and beloved, LaVonne,
for choosing to trust God as we follow Him in this faith adventure
together;

to my family,
for your love, support and encouragement;

to Sheryl,
for helping me tell the stories of the ministry and passion of Jesus in a
much better way;

to Dennis,
for your humble spirit and your creative eye;

and most importantly,
to the One who one day will stand before us all
– our Lord and Savior Jesus Christ!

OTHER BOOKS WRITTEN BY
KENNETH A. WINTER

◞

THROUGH THE EYES SERIES

BOOK #1

Though the Eyes of a Shepherd

A Novel — **Shimon was a shepherd boy when he first saw the newborn King in a Bethlehem stable.** Join him in his journey as he re-encounters the Lamb of God at the Jordan, and follows the Miracle Worker through the wilderness, the Messiah to the cross, and the Risen Savior from the upper room. Though Shimon is a fictional character, we'll see the pages of the Gospels unfold through his eyes, and **experience a story of redemption – the** redemption of a shepherd – and the redemption of each one who chooses to follow the Good Shepherd.

.

BOOK #2

Though the Eyes of a Spy

A Novel — **Caleb was one of God's chosen people** – a people to whom He had given a promise. Caleb never forgot that promise — as a slave in Egypt, a spy in the Promised Land, a wanderer in the wilderness, or a conqueror in the hill country. We'll see the promise of Jehovah God unfold through his eyes, and **experience a story of God's faithfulness – to a spy who trusted Him – and to each one of us who will do the same.**

BOOK #3

COMING SEPTEMBER 10, 2021

Though the Eyes of a Prisoner

A Novel — **Paul was an unlikely candidate to become the apostle to the Gentiles** ... until the day he unexpectedly encountered Jesus. You are probably familiar with that part of his story, and perhaps much of what transpired in his life after that. **But two-thirds of his life story is not recorded in detail, though Paul gives us some hints in his letters.**

God is always at work in our lives; often before we realize it. The same can be said of Paul. **Through this fictional novel**, we'll explore how God may have used even those unrecorded portions of his life to prepare him for the mission that was being set before him. We'll follow him from his early years in Tarsus through his final days in Rome.

Throughout those years, Paul spent more time in a prison cell than we are ever told. It was a place where God continued to work in and through him. The mission never stopped because he was in prison; it simply took on a different form. Allow yourself to be challenged as you experience **a story of God's mission – through the eyes of a prisoner who ran the** race that was put before him – and the faithfulness of God through it all.

THE LESSONS LEARNED IN THE WILDERNESS SERIES

There are lessons that can only be learned in the wilderness experiences of our lives. As we see throughout the Bible, God is right there leading us each and every step of the way, if we will follow Him. Wherever we are, whatever we are experiencing, He will use it to enable us to experience His Person, witness His power and join Him in His mission.

*Each of the six books in the series contains 61 chapters, which means that the entire series is comprised of 366 chapters — **one chapter for each day of the year**. The chapters have been formatted in a way that you can read one chapter each day or read each book straight through. Whichever way you choose, allow the Master to use the series to encourage and challenge you in the journey that He has designed uniquely for you so that His purpose is fulfilled, and His glory is made known.*

Book #1

The Journey Begins

God's plan for our lives is not static; He is continuously calling us to draw closer, to climb higher and to move further. In that process, He is moving us out of our comfort zone to His land of promise for our lives. That process includes time in the wilderness. Many times it is easier to see the truth that God is teaching us through the lives of others than it is through our own lives.

"The Journey Begins" is the first book in the *"Lessons Learned In The Wilderness"* series. It chronicles those stories, those examples and those truths as revealed through the lives and experiences of the Israelites, as recorded in the Book of Exodus in sixty-one bite-sized chapters.

As you read one chapter per day for sixty-one days, we will look at the circumstances, the surroundings and the people in such a way that highlights the similarities to our lives, as we then apply those same truths to our own life journey as the Lord God Jehovah leads us through our own wilderness journey.

BOOK #2

The Wandering Years

Why did a journey that God ordained to take slightly longer than one year, end up taking forty years? Why, instead of enjoying the fruits of the land of milk and honey, did the Israelites end up wandering in the desert wilderness for forty years? Why did one generation follow God out of Egypt only to die there, leaving the next generation to follow Him into the Promised Land?

In the journeys through the wildernesses of my life, i can look back and see where God has turned me back from that land of promise to wander a while longer in the wilderness. God has given us the wilderness to prepare us for His land of promise, but if when we reach the border we are not ready, He will turn us back to wander.

If God is allowing you to continue to wander in the wilderness, it is because He has more to teach you about Himself – His Person, His purpose and His power. "**The Wandering Years**" chronicles through sixty-one "bite-sized" chapters those lessons He would teach us through the Israelites' time in the wilderness as recorded in the books of Numbers and Deuteronomy.

The book has been formatted for one chapter to be read each day for sixty-one days. Explore this second book in the "**Lessons Learned In The**

Wilderness" series and allow God to use it to apply those same lessons to your daily journey with Him.

Book #3

Possessing the Promise

The day had finally arrived for the Israelites to possess the land that God had promised. But just like He had taught them lessons throughout their journey in the wilderness, He had more to teach them, as they possessed the promise.

And so it is for us. Possessing the promise doesn't mean the faith adventure has come to a conclusion; rather, in many ways, it has only just begun. Possessing the promise will involve in some respects an even greater dependence upon God and the promise He has given you.

"**Possessing the Promise**" chronicles the stories, experiences and lessons we see recorded in the books of Joshua and Judges in sixty-one "bite-sized" chapters. The book has been formatted for one chapter to be read each day for sixty-one days.

Explore this third book in the "**Lessons Learned In The Wilderness**" series and allow God to use it to teach you how to possess the promise as He leads you in the journey with Him each day.

Book #4

Walking With The Master

Our daily walk with the Master is never static – it entails moving and growing. Jesus was constantly on the move, carrying out the Father's work and His will. He was continuously surrendered and submitted to the will of the Father. And if we would walk with Him, we too must walk surrendered and submitted to the Father in our day-to-day lives.

Jesus extended His invitation to us to deny ourselves, take up our cross and follow Him. **"Walking With The Master"** chronicles, through "sixty-one" bite-sized chapters, those lessons the Master would teach us as we walk with Him each day, just as He taught the men and women who walked with Him throughout Galilee, Samaria and Judea as recorded in the Gospel accounts.

The book has been formatted for one chapter to be read each day for sixty-one days. Explore this fourth book in the **"Lessons Learned In The Wilderness"** series and allow the Master to use it to draw you closer to Himself as you walk with Him each day in the journey.

Book #5

Taking Up The Cross

What does it mean to take up the cross? In this fifth book of the **Lessons Learned In The Wilderness** series, we will look at the cross our Lord has set before us as we follow Him. The backdrop for our time is the last forty-seven days of the earthly ministry of Jesus, picking up at His triumphal entry into Jerusalem and continuing to the day He ascended into heaven to sit at the right-hand of the Father.

We will look through the lens of the Gospels at what taking up the cross looked like in His life, and what He has determined it will look like in ours. He doesn't promise that there won't be a cost – there will be! And He doesn't promise that it will be easy – it won't be! But it is the journey He has set before us – a journey that will further His purpose in and through our lives – and a journey that will lead to His glory.

Like the other books in this series, this book has been formatted in a way that you can read one chapter each day, or read it straight through.

Whichever way you choose, allow the Master to use it to draw you closer to Him as you walk with Him each day in your journey.

BOOK #6

Until He Returns

Moments after Jesus ascended into heaven, two angels delivered this promise: "Someday He will return!" In this sixth and final book of the *Lessons Learned In The Wilderness* series, we will look at what that journey will look like *Until He Returns*. No matter where we are in our journey with Him – in the wilderness, in the promised land, or somewhere in between – He has a purpose and a plan for us.

In this book, we will look through the lens of the Book of Acts at what that journey looked like for those first century followers of Christ. Like us, they weren't perfect. There were times they took their eyes off of Jesus. But despite their imperfections, He used them to turn the world upside down. And His desire is to do the same thing through us. Our journeys will all look different, but He will be with us every step of the way.

Like the first five books in this series, this book has been formatted in a way that you can read one chapter each day or read it straight through. Whichever way you choose, allow the Master to use it to encourage and challenge you in the journey that He has designed uniquely for you so that His purpose is fulfilled, and His glory is made known.

Lessons Learned In The Wilderness Series: Books 1-3: The Lessons Learned In The Wilderness Collection - Volume 1

The first three books in the *Lessons Learned In The Wilderness* series are also available in a three-book collection as an **e-book** boxset or as a single **soft-cover print** volume. We will walk with the Israelites as God enabled them to overcome the challenges of their exodus from Egypt, their wanderings in the wilderness, and finally, the

giants they faced in possessing the Promised Land. Throughout each step from Exodus through Judges, we will seek to learn the lessons God would teach us through their journey. The collection includes: *The Journey Begins*, *The Wandering Years* and *Possessing The Promise*

Lessons Learned In The Wilderness Series: Books 4-6: The Lessons Learned In The Wilderness Collection - Volume 2

The final three books in the *Lessons Learned In The Wilderness* series are also available in a three-book collection as an **e-book** boxset or as a single **soft-cover print** volume. We will walk with Jesus through the Gospels, as He and His disciples journey throughout Judea, Samaria and Galilee, and then through the Book of Acts as the journey leads to the ends of the earth. Through it all, we will seek to learn the lessons our Lord would teach us as we continue in our journey with Him. The collection includes: *Walking With The Master*, *Taking Up The Cross* and *Until He Returns*

For more information, go to
wildernesslessons.com or kenwinter.org
or my author page on Amazon

WildernessLessons

ABOUT THE AUTHOR

 Ken Winter is a follower of Jesus, an extremely blessed husband, and a proud father and grandfather – all by the grace of God. His journey with Jesus has led him to serve on the pastoral staffs of two local churches – one in West Palm Beach, Florida and the other in Richmond, Virginia – and as the vice president of mobilization of the IMB, an international missions organization. You can read Ken's weekly blog posts at kenwinter.blog.

And we proclaim Him, admonishing every man and teaching every man with all wisdom, that we may present every man complete in Christ. And for this purpose also I labor, striving according to His power, which mightily works within me.
(Colossians 1:28-29 NASB)

PLEASE JOIN MY READERS' GROUP

Please join my Readers' Group in order to receive updates and information about future releases, etc.

Also, i will send you a free copy of ***The Journey Begins*** e-book — the first book in the ***Lessons Learned In The Wilderness*** series. It is yours to keep or share with a friend or family member that you think might benefit from it.

It's completely free to sign up. i value your privacy and will not spam you. Also, you can unsubscribe at any time.

Go to kenwinter.org to subscribe.

∽

Made in the USA
Coppell, TX
02 February 2022

72813601R00225